RETURN
RUMORED WOMAN SERIES
BOOK TWO
MORGAN MAGAURAN

DEMETER MATRIX

Copyright© 2025 by Morgan Magauran

Publisher's note: This is a work of fiction. Names, characters, places, and incidents are either the product of the author's imagination or are used fictitiously. Any resemblance to actual events, locales, or persons, living or dead, is entirely coincidental. However, there is a blend of nonfiction for which references to authors, poets, musicians, thought leaders, and nonprofits are true and links have been provided. Scan the QR code below for a downloadable pdf of these resources. Ultimately, it's up to the readers to discern what is real and what to believe in.

Purchase the series at RumoredWoman.com, discounts available. Free subscribers to MorganMagauran.substack.com receive the first six chapters in your inbox upon release.

Published 2025, Editors: Christina Boyd, and Dana Lee

Cover design by The Book Designers

Cover illustration by Connor Ryan

IDENTIFIERS: Library of Congress Control Number: 2025900185 Paperback ISBN 979-8-9866903-3-9 eBook ISBN 979-8-9866903-4-6.

1. Women Inner Life—Fiction 2. Psychological—Fiction 3. Visionary & Metaphysical—Fiction

Published 2025 Demeter Matrix

RETURN

BOOK TWO

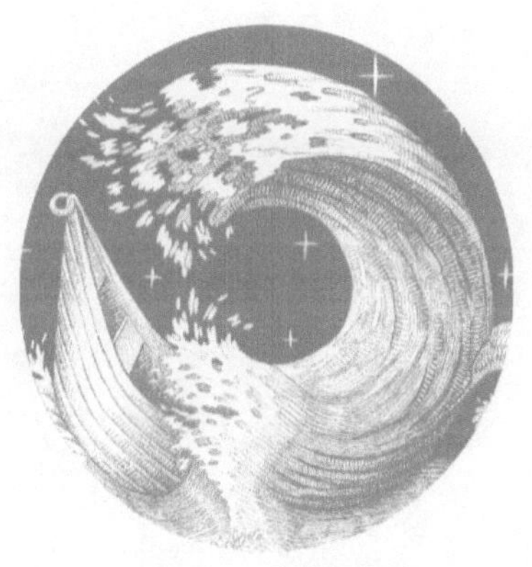

MORGAN MAGAURAN

DEDICATION

To my readers,
May the power of the Great Mystery
have a place in your conversation with life
such that you know Grace.

CONTENTS

DRAFT BLESSING

May the tempo of my life,
allow my heart, mind, body, and spirit to move at the same pace,
the pace of embodied presence.
May my breathing and pausing be a reminder to surrender and
receive guidance throughout my day, to soften, and melt with breath.
May each day unfold with a priority on creative expression,
sensing the deeper currents and stalking the sacred.
May I become patient with uncertainty,
welcoming mystery into my life as my beloved dance partner,
letting go of expectations, even with disappointment,
to honor what is authentic in the moment.
May my connection with the elements re-source my days,
cultivating courage, faith, and my sense of belonging, be-longing.
May a sense of humor be a source of laughter in my days
for enjoying life more fully.
May I be willing to be lost, to venture into terra incógnita,
letting go of my need to know, my need to figure it out to be safe—
trusting life and experiencing the wonder of renewal.
May I live in the inquiry of what if, maybe.
May I tend to myself, others, and our environment
from a connection with myself,
offering kindness, compassion, and spacious witnessing.
May my listening be an invitation and integration.
May I dwell in the place of infinite capacity, my heart, offering LOVE.
May my experience be one of reciprocity with all my relations.
May my presence be enough.

DRAFT VOW

To grow wild by the sea,
to slow down and listen to what I am sensing and feeling,
and to act on it with authenticity and integrity.

to know if I am purring or growling inside
and to let myself be known,

to give voice to my longings and
follow them to a place of belonging, be-longing,

to be in reciprocity with all my relations.

CHAPTER 1

ARRIVAL

THE LULLING SOUND OF waves and a gentle rocking motion held me in a drowsy slumber. Eventually, my eyes focused on wooden slats, as if I'd slept in a giant cradle. I lay curled in the fetal position, on top of a green and blue plaid blanket. A long-sleeved cream linen shift dress, a replica of the one I'd worn with Faith before becoming a mermaid, was bunched at my knees. *At least I'm not naked.*

As I peered over the rail, the skiff tipped precariously to one side until I centered my weight. I was drifting toward an island with a small harbor bordered by houses. In my underworld odyssey, I'd never seen a neighborhood or other humans that weren't an aspect of myself. Meeting the embodiment of my Judgements, Impatience, and Rage, as women with their own voices and mannerisms, had been no holiday. Never seeing them again would suit me. However, I hoped my guides—Faith, Compassion, and Forgiveness—didn't make themselves scarce, along with my Peaceful Warrior who had promised to guard the holy grail of my attention.

Chilled by more than the morning air, I lay back down, knees bent toward the sky. Even though I floated on calm waters, my insides roiled.

When I rubbed my face, crusts of sleep loosened from around my lashes, confirming this wasn't a dream.

Why didn't I wake up in my bedroom? Where in God's name am I? I'd expected to return home, through the mirror, the way I'd left. A few biblical rays of sunlight escaped through the slate clouds.

I called upon Faith but didn't sense her presence. My last memories with Faith were as a mermaid near the shipwreck, where she'd instructed me to compose a vow that reflected my commitment to myself. The opening line, "to grow wild *by* the sea," was decidedly different from being adrift on it. If this was her idea of humor, it was lost on me.

When I'd swum back to where I'd left her with my Peaceful Warrior, eager to share my vow, Faith was alone. She didn't need the spoken word to perceive my thoughts or feelings. After all, Faith was a part of me, even if I'd ignored her for years. She sensed my disappointment at not saying goodbye to my Peaceful Warrior and assured me that she and all the other women I'd met remained my inner companions, available if called upon. Faith had told me it was time to start my journey home as she fastened her pendant around my neck.

My right hand flew to my chest to check if it was there. It was, but this was hardly home, and I felt alone.

I sat up too quickly, and the boat wobbled again. *Slow down, be still.* My dry mouth caused me to search the skiff for drinking water, but the absence of any water or oars made my stomach churn. The skiff had three simple wooden seats: one in the middle and two more toward the bow. I couldn't help but admire its craftsman design—a blend of wood and something that resembled hide. The visible latticework of its frame ran lengthwise from bow to stern and crosswise from port to starboard. If it was a fisherman's boat, it thankfully didn't smell of dead fish.

I inched forward gingerly and hoisted myself onto the middle seat. Gusts of wind nudged against my back while tendrils of hair tickled the sides of my cheeks. A shiver sent my elbows pressing to my sides. Pulling the linen hem over my bare knees didn't help. I wrapped the wool blanket around me, arms crossed, fingers clutching its edges, shielding me from the elements. *It could become a sail if I stretched out my arms, but why bother hastening my arrival? Soon enough, I'll be blown there. Then what?* The sun cast my elongated shadow before me; it would reach shore first.

The quiet harbor consisted of a simple pier without any moored boats. An abandoned row of similar-sized skiffs lined the beach. A half dozen homes sat back from the shore, their spacing widened to the north. A stone bell tower announced itself midway up the island, and clusters of black and white sheep were scattered on the pastures. I hoped its inhabitants spoke English so some aspects of my return would be easier.

My stomach growled. *Eating with no money will be a trick, and where will I sleep? I'm at the mercy of strangers. Homeless.*

No. I have resources—at a distance. I needed a phone to call Ian and a bank so he could wire me money.

A church bell rang—one, two, three, four, five, six, seven, then silence. *7:00 a.m. is barely a civilized hour—no wonder no one is milling about.*

I leaned over to drag my fingers across the sea's clear surface. The frigid temperature was a far cry from the tropical waters I'd swum in with Faith—*not for the faint of heart.*

Nothing about my return resembled what I'd envisioned. I'd expected to go home, mistakenly thinking the only variables in the equation were daytime or evening or if Ian would welcome me back. Faith had said, "*Start* your journey home." Being cast off in a boat with no oars, no money, no shoes, and a shift of a dress felt more like a final test.

Well, it could be worse. It could be raining or snowing with no civilization in sight. I enlisted Patience and Faith to accompany me, recalling my blessing: *May I become patient with uncertainty, welcoming mystery into my life as my beloved dance partner, letting go of expectations, even with disappointment, to honor what is authentic in the moment.*

However, invoking these qualities didn't mean I could live by them. I lifted the blanket over my shoulders and held it out with my hands as a makeshift sail. After a few minutes, my shoulder muscles burned, and my hair hung undisturbed by any breeze. Only the current carried me, so I wrapped myself back up. *Patience, Faith, and Surrender.*

The church bell chimed once. 7:30. I knew the time, but not the day or the month. *What if it's not the same year? What if time moved differently in the underworld and more than a few months have passed? How long can I expect Ian to wait for me without a word?*

As the shore neared, the sea floor became visible and white barnacles covered the rocks. *Crap.* Not a welcome sight for bare feet.

Soon the hull scraped against stones. When I stood, my lower back complained of stiffness, and the boat tilted, but I quickly recovered my balance. The skiff had halted in ankle-deep water. At least I wasn't worried about getting my nonexistent shoes wet.

I shed the blanket in a heap in the bottom of the skiff to keep it dry, hoping this wasn't my only bedding for tonight. My feet found round stones, and though it wasn't sharp underfoot, it was shockingly cold. I hauled the boat onto the shore with both hands, walking backwards, leaving it above the remnant seaweed that indicated the high tide line, and a bit farther in case of a storm.

After crossing the cool, damp sand toward town, the smell of bacon from a café tormented me. My stomach grumbled again, while my mouth watered in futile anticipation. In front of the grocery store, I spied a metal box with a glass window. A newspaper would have told me the date and allowed me to avoid attracting attention to my predicament by asking. Except, when I reached it—it was empty.

Wandering the town, I discovered an oval red sign with gold lettering that read POST OFFICE – ISLE OF IONA. *So that's where I am. Scotland.* Ironically, I'd considered visiting Iona before but negated it because it was too onerous to travel here. The post office's hours were

9:00 a.m. to 5:00 p.m. each day of the week, with an hour break for lunch. How civilized. It was only open on Saturday from 9:00 a.m. to noon and closed on Sunday.

The deserted streets felt odd, not just because of the absence of people, but the absence of any parked cars. Only private homes stretched ahead. Somehow, I'd missed seeing the bank near the storefronts.

When the church bell chimed eight times, I turned around and retraced my steps. The different perspective revealed a red telephone booth near the dock. *Oh, thank god this relic still exists.* Eager to call Ian, I pushed at the folding door until it creaked open and prayed change wasn't required to access the operator. Holding the receiver to my ear, I rejoiced at the sound of a dial tone, and pressed the little white square labeled zero. When it buzzed twice in rapid succession I exhaled.

"Guid mornin'. Operator speaking. How kin ah help ye?"

I had a list of things I needed help with, but I knew she wasn't offering that kind of assistance. "I'd like to place a collect call, please, from Sarah O'Sullivan to the United States."

She replied, "Yer batch, please. It must be a landline. Ye cannae place a collect call to a mobile unless ye have a callin' card."

Thankfully, our rented house still had a landline and I recited our number.

"Hold the line." I gripped the receiver like it was a personal flotation device. It rang and rang and rang until I heard the recorded message in my voice. The irony of listening to myself wasn't lost on me. "Nae answer."

Ian slept with earplugs. "Could you please try one more time?"

She did, with the same results, and I hung up. *Crap.* Even if my friends had a landline, I didn't know their numbers. I didn't even know their cell numbers because they were programmed as favorites on my phone—no memory required. So, plan B: find a bank. Except, I had no identification and was clueless as to my account numbers. Undoubtedly, their security protocols wouldn't look kindly on a barefoot woman. *How can I prove I'm me?*

I aimed for the café, doubtful I'd be welcomed penniless and shoe-less. Asking the day's date might raise suspicion about my state of mind, so I only planned to ask for directions to the nearest bank. The aromas of coffee and baking bread tortured me. A young, red-haired woman wearing an olive T-shirt and white apron over her jeans was setting the outdoor tables with a metal holder for salt, pepper, and jam. I was so hungry even the tiny jam packets tempted me.

"Good morning. Excuse me, which way is it to the bank?"

"Guid mornin'. Ye'll nae be findin' a bank till ye take a ferry to Mull. The next ferry 'tis nae till midday. There are nae mornin' runs on Sunday."

I managed to calmly say, "Thanks so much," before I turned and walked back toward the beach. *No Ian, no newspaper, no bank, no post office today, and barely a common language. Crap. Crap. Crap. My life abhors a plan.* I retreated to the boat to regroup and grabbed my only other possession, draping what had become my security blanket over my shoulder, afraid it was my only bed for tonight. I didn't even have underwear on. Talk about bare necessities.

The shoreline beckoned. I needed to create some distance between me and the scents of breakfast. I wasn't ready to beg for it but couldn't think about anything else if I smelled it. Washed-up seaweed, the color of mustard greens and ripe apples, formed the tideline. It oscillated like the sine curves on a heart monitor. My heart raced. *Now what?* I steadied myself by examining the beach. The seaweed in shades of cranberry was unfamiliar to me. I couldn't help but wonder if it was edible as I followed its trail, even when it meant scrambling over the jetty of rocks to reach the other side. Startled black crabs, too tiny to have any decent meat in them, scurried into crevices.

Am I on my own now? Faith said I had the power to conjure her if I chose. I'd grown accustomed to seeing her. Now, I needed to find a way to feel her. I'd love to ask her why she made my return home so complicated. *Hey, haven't I journeyed enough?* Silence. *Well, if this is a test of my resourcefulness, it's not in my nature to give up.*

My pulse settled as I walked. Up ahead, a woman with a towel over her shoulders traipsed down the grassy hillside toward the beach. When she reached the corner of the fence that had steps beside it, she climbed the two stairs, crossed over the top rail, and then down the other side. *How convenient.* She wore a dark sweater and khaki shorts. I hoped I didn't look as out of place as I felt. We could both be heading for a picnic of sorts. If only one of us had a food basket.

She entered the beach on the far side of another jetty of black rocks and disappeared. I kept walking, and my pulse quickened again. My new plan was to nod good morning and calmly carry on.

When I clambered over the next jetty, her towel and clothes greeted me. As she scampered out of the water straight toward me, I stalled. Her waist had the thickening of mid-life, but her upper body and thighs exuded strength.

"'Tis such a bonnie mornin' ah could nae resist a quick dip. Are ye headin' in yerself?"

I lied. "I'm tempted. It does look inviting." She bee-lined for her clothes, which I stood frozen beside. Her slicked-back gray hair indicated she'd bravely swum underwater. I kept my eyes to her eyes, not wanting to stare at her unabashed naked body. *What is it with me and naked women appearing out of nowhere?* I grabbed the towel beside me and offered it to her, fumbling for a question. "Do you swim each morning?"

She swiftly wrapped herself in it. "Nae, only when the spirit moves me. Today, the light on the water was beckonin'. Ah put the kettle on. Would ye like to join me for a cuppa if ye'r nae goin' for a swim? Ah'd welcome the company."

I didn't hesitate. "Sure. I've not had my morning tea yet. I'm Sarah, by the way."

"Ah'm Katrine. Pleased to meet ye." She toweled off her legs before slipping back into her shorts and pulled on her navy cashmere V-neck sweater, not bothering to turn it right-side in. Apparently, underwear was optional in her world. Katrine bent over and deftly wrapped the towel around her head, twisting it into a turban.

Starting toward the fence line, she said, "Mah home's up the way. How long have ye been on the island?"

I followed. "Oh, not long. I arrived last night." To avoid lying again, I went on the offensive with questions. "How about you? How long have you lived here?"

"All mah life. Ah left for university but had nae fondness for city life. Ah wanted to raise mah bairns here and be close to mah family. Mah husband, God rest his soul, was willin' to oblige and moved here. He grew up in Fife."

"I'm sorry to hear you're a widow. How long ago did he die?"

"It'll be fifteen years this December. A winter gale came up, and he never returned from fishin'. We lost three good men in that storm, all fathers. Makes me grateful ah never had sons. The sea cannae snatch another one of mah men. Ah'v already made mah sacrifice."

"How old are your daughters?"

Katrine used the mini staircase to cross over the fence. I kept pace and came up alongside her as we walked the incline of her pasture. The morning's dew rinsed sand from my feet.

"Mah youngest is about to turn twenty, then twenty-six, and twenty-eight. Mah eldest married last year, and ah'll become a nana any day now. Ah suppose ah could have a grandson. We dinnae ken yet if she'll be havin' a lassie or a laddie. She embraced the mystery on that count."

"That's exciting. Does she live on the island, too?" A barn stood beyond us as we approached her house to the right.

"Nae, all mah bairns left for schoolin' and have yet to return. Luckily, two of them are in Scotland. Mah youngest transferred to Boston

College. Do ye ken it?"

"Yes, I know it well. I'm from the Boston area. The Jesuits are rigorous scholars of the mind while still tending to the spirit. She's fortunate her inner life isn't left out of their education."

Katrine turned toward me and smiled as if I'd struck a chord. "Indeed" was her only response.

When we arrived at her wide-open door, she scuffed her feet on the mat and proceeded in. I did the same. After discarding her towel on the floor, she tousled her chin-length gray hair into a side part.

"Right. Now, let's have ourselves a cuppa."

The entryway bench sat below hooks mounded with flannel shirts and jackets. Clogs, boots, and shoes spilled out from beneath it. Across from the door were four stairs and a landing to the second floor. I followed her around a corner into an open living space.

Immediately, the expansive bay windows facing the shore caught my attention, with two high-backed chairs inviting a respite. "Your home is lovely. What a magnificent view of the sea." The opposite wall had a stone fireplace with seating for a family: a couch flanked by two comfy-looking leather chairs. The kitchen extended beyond it with an outside wall of cabinets that parted to include a wide window above the sink. Anyone washing dishes enjoyed a pastoral scene. Their rectangular wooden kitchen table seated four.

Katrine took an electric kettle, poured less than a cup of steaming water into the silver teapot, then returned it to its base, pushing the button.

"Would ye like a scone with it? Ah baked them yesterday."

"I'd love a scone. How can I help?"

"Ye can fetch us those plates from the strainer and set the table." The table rested against a wall with an angled view of the water. "There's some jam and butter on the counter over here. Ah'll bring the tea when 'tis ready. Have yerself a seat."

Her cell phone sat on the table before me. Standing with my back to her, I quickly tapped it and read, 8:47 Sunday, October 31. No year. Most people knew that bit.

I took the seat that offered me a view of her tea ritual. She placed two cups on a tray, pouring a splash of milk in each. The kettle rumbled and clicked off. Katrine swirled the silver teapot, emptied it into the sink, and placed the pot on the tray. She spooned loose black tea in before pouring freshly boiled water over it. On went the lid to the teapot, and on went the tea cozy. A small metal strainer that rested on a saucer occupied the remaining corner of the tray. Everything fit perfectly.

She brought the tray to the table first and then returned with a warm plate of scones from the toaster oven. I counted six of them. I was already planning to eat two.

"This looks lovely. Thanks so much for inviting me in."

Katrine sat at the end of the table and tucked her hair behind her ears. "Ah assume ye take a spot of milk?"

I nodded. "Yes, thanks."

She placed the porcelain cup on a saucer before me and poured the amber liquid, which mingled with the milk, turning a golden-brown shade, then poured her own, and replaced the tea cozy. "Do ye take sugar?"

"No, I'm good without it. I'll save my sweet tooth for the jam. What flavor is it?"

"That'd be strawberry. Ah put it up mahself this summer from mah garden. 'Tis always a battle between the snails and me, who can harvest more. They may nae be fast, but they're effective at ruinin' a crop."

I wanted to deflect the attention from me and tend to the scones. "What's your daughter studying?"

She sipped what had to be scalding tea. "Maeve's in communications of some kind. Last semester, she made a podcast for a school project. Ah'v yet to sort out how to listen to it. She has a fondness for the old stories. 'Twas her nana's doin', fillin' her head with Celtic fairy tales since she was a wee bairn. Ah dinnae ken how she'll weave it into modern-day interests. Ah'v nae doubt she'll sort it out, though—Maeve's a bard at heart. It runs in her blood."

I reached for a scone, sliced it in half, slathered it with butter, and took my first bite before even adding the jam. "This is divine. I've never mastered the art of baking. Cutting butter in for scones has always escaped me." Katrine passed me the jam. I spread it, admiring the lumps of strawberries. My second bite was even better than the first. *Don't inhale these. Pace yourself.* "How do your other two daughters occupy themselves?"

Katrine was still buttering her scone. "Fiona's a harpist, a music-thanatologist, to be precise."

My brows furrowed. "I'm afraid I don't know what that means."

She softly chuckled. "Very few do. 'Tis more of an ancient tradition that uses music for healin'. It means she plays her harp for people who are dyin' to help ease them on their journey. Fiona says it helps the family of the loved one as well." Katrine held her teacup with both hands. "She adjusts her music to the mood of the room. At times, she also sings. There's nae an instrument she cannae play. She inherited that talent from her dah."

The fleeting look of pride slipped from her face. "She was only eleven when Kieran died. He'd been teachin' her to play his harp since she turned ten. Fiona has Kieran's height and was the tallest in her class, towerin' over the boys at that age." Her description reminded me of Sam, my friend Jocelyn's daughter, and a twinge of homesickness came over me. Katrine continued, "We jested that with her wingspan, she could have been an Olympic volleyball player. However, a harpist was more likely. After he died, she poured all her grief into teachin' herself to play."

She sipped her tea again, looking past me. "Fiona brings a deep current of sorrow into her work and helps people to find their peace. Ah often wonder what she'd have chosen as a career if her father had returned from sea."

A tender silence fell between us that melted me. We lingered in it as we ate the scones.

"Mah eldest, Brìghde has a mind for numbers." Katrine said her name tenderly, BREE-dah, but as she continued, I heard pride in her voice too. "She's in finance, aspirin' to be a fund manager. Honestly, ah cannae explain what she does. It baffles me. Edinburgh is her home now, but given half a chance, she'd relocate to Wall Street. She's approachin' her Saturn Return year. Ah pray becomin' a mum is enough of a change without relocatin' to a different continent. Ah'm nae a fan of planes. They fall out of the sky."

Saturn had wreaked havoc in my life at twenty-nine. I divorced, moved, and changed jobs. While I didn't understand how the planets exercised their influence on us, I had no doubt they did. I tried to discreetly reach for my second scone. She had only finished half of hers. My plan to keep her talking was working—I kept my mouth full.

"Ah'm glad ye like them, ah dinnae ken what possessed me to bake a dozen scones for mahself yesterday. Ah was goin' to bring them to mah neighbor, Angus, but never got round to it. Ah started weedin' mah back garden, and before ah ken it, the sun was settin'." She held the teapot. "Shall ah heat it up a wee bit?"

I nodded and moved my cup closer. "Yes, please. Are you fond of gardening?"

She topped off my cup and refilled her own. "Nae. Ah cannae say ah pay much attention to it. It keeps mah hands busy as mah mind wanders. Ah do like lookin' at it when 'tis done and especially love eatin' food from it. The island grocer offers what it can, but 'tis nae as fresh. We're nearin' the last of the harvest now. Soon, the rains and cold weather will be settin' in.

"Ah'v been jabberin' and nae mindin' the time. Ah'v got horses to feed. They'll be wonderin' what's become of me. Normally, ah'm like clockwork. Ah must apologize for talkin' yer ear off. 'Tis nae like me."

I watched her eyes land on my pendant for the second time. My hand instinctively reached for it. "Oh no, please don't apologize. It's been an unexpectedly enjoyable morning. Can I at least help you tend to the horses? I grew up with them and know my way around a barn. I love everything about them. Even their shit smells good to me."

She had the same soft-throated chuckle as my friend, Veena. "Spoken like a true horsewoman—ah knew ah liked ye." She stood from the table. "Ah'll nae refuse the help, but we'll need to find ye somethin' different to wear. Ah'm guessin' ye'll fit into Fiona's clothes. She took after mah love of horses." Katrine walked away, presumably toward Fiona's bedroom.

I stood while finishing my last bite and had started to clear the table when Katrine interrupted me. "Leave it be. The horses have waited long enough. Follow me."

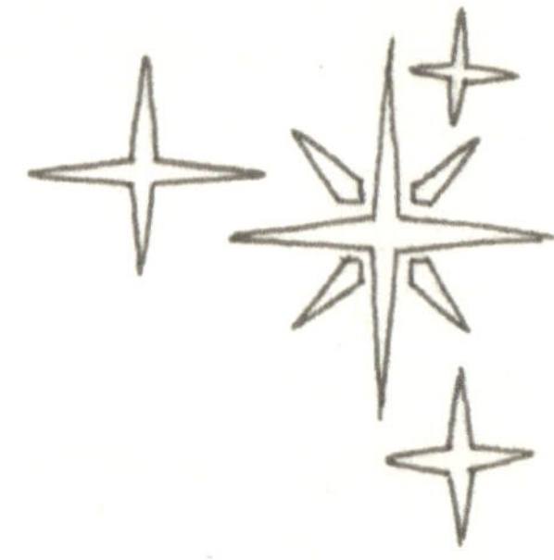

CHAPTER 2
FREEDOM & SANCTUARY

I STOOD BESIDE FIONA's four-poster bed adorned with first-place blue ribbons. Katrine opened the closet door, and an array of blue and black jeans hung inside. A mix of button-down cotton shirts and dresses sparsely populated the rod. The shelf above held a stack of sweaters and shoe boxes.

"What kind of horses do you have?"

She handed me jeans. "Two Friesians, a mare and her son."

"Ohh, I've always admired that breed but never had a chance to ride one."

"Ah fretted over geldin' him, maybe even waited too long. Ah confess some days ah wish ah hadn't. As a stud, he'd have become the family's breadwinner, but finances weren't on mah mind back then. Ah had mah bairns' safety to consider."

She pilfered through the dresser drawers. "Ye'd be doin' me a favor if ye wanted to go for a ride. With two horses and only one of me, they dinnae get the exercise they deserve."

I've landed in heaven. "I'd love to ride with you. Sadly, I've not been on a horse for years, but I grew up riding English and show jumping an

Arabian. I'm fond of spirited breeds."

"Saorsa's nae shy of spirit." She tossed a T-shirt, socks, and a sports bra on the bed. "We'll see how he takes to ye—he's nae fond of strangers, but he behaves better with his mum around. Ye can always ride her. She's agin' well with a strong back." When Katrine opened the trunk at the foot of the bed, the scent of cedar wafted into the room. She pulled out a pair of black leather riding boots stuffed with newspaper. Handing them to me, she asked, "Are ye a size forty?"

European sizes confused me. Holding them beside my feet, I said, "They look like they'll fit."

"After Saorsa's fed and lunged, we'll assess his mood. Am ah keepin' ye from someone?"

"No, I'm traveling alone. No one's expecting me."

She nodded. Her lips rolled over her teeth for a moment and pressed together. "The lavvy is across the hall. See ye downstairs shortly."

When she left, I searched the top drawer for some underwear. Fiona wore bikinis. I borrowed those, too, and prayed that her boots and clothes fit so nothing spoiled my chance at riding the Friesian. I wiggled into her spandex jeans, zipping and yanking to button them; their elasticity was my saving grace. Looking down, I heard my mother's criticism: "You can't wear those. It's as if you spray-painted them on your legs. It's less than flattering." She had a point. My stocky calves were typically hidden. I squatted down to see if I'd risk busting a seam, but they held. Off went the linen shift, and on went the bra and T-shirt that hung long over my hips and remained untucked.

My image in the bathroom mirror held my attention. I'd not seen this kind of reflection for months, only myself embodied in other women. *Have they all taken up residence within me now, including Faith?* My brown eyes looked upon me kindly, the way I'd welcome a friend. The asymmetry of my face was unchanged, but the creases in my forehead had lessened. Everyone always asked if I dyed my hair because the red highlights amidst my dark auburn locks loudly announced themselves. I didn't. I did need to brush it, so I finger-combed the wavy tangles that now hung below my breasts. After splashing water on my face, I cleaned the rim of the glass on the counter, then filled it twice to quench my thirst. Sitting on the toilet for the first time in months felt very civilized. Modern plumbing was a luxury I'd taken for granted and wondered how long it would be until its convenience became invisible again.

I carried Fiona's boots downstairs and sat on the bottom step. Removing the bunched-up newspapers, I noticed the date was from five years ago—unless I'd gone back in time.

Jesus, Mary, and Joseph. Can I do that? If I did, then Ian and I haven't moved in together yet... Which means he didn't see me leave through the mirror with Faith... Maybe we aren't even together? If he didn't see me leave, he'll probably never believe me. What had I said to myself after we argued about dinner? If I had a do-over, what would I do? My head reeled.

The clatter of dishes from the kitchen brought my focus back to my task as I sat on the stairs. I mechanically removed the other wadded-up newspaper.

Would I make different choices if I could go back in time? That's ridiculous. I can't go back in time. Get a grip, Sarah.

I clutched the top of the boot and tried to slide my foot in, but it stuck on the diagonal. Nothing budged until I lifted my butt and put my whole weight into it. Finally, my heel slid into place, and my toes could still wiggle. The upper boot was snug around my calf; getting it off again would be a struggle. Practiced in the technique, I swiftly jammed my other foot in just as Katrine appeared, already changed and wearing ankle-height tack boots.

She eyed the fit of everything and nodded. "Right then, let's be off."

I stood. "Great. Lead the way."

Get your head in the game, Sarah. You're about to meet horses who can sense fear. Horses you want to ride. Breathe.

Katrine strode out the front door toward her barn, and I shook my whole body rigorously to rid myself of the panic that had crept in while sitting on the stairs. I crossed the threshold and followed her past another small, studio-like structure on the right. Katrine slipped between the fence rails instead of using the gate at the corner of the paddock.

The barn door opened directly into the pasture. As Katrine slid it partially open, we were greeted by a chorus of nickering and the mingled odors of hay and manure. A jet-black horse stood in the first stall. His wavy, ebony mane nearly covered his entire neck. He was gorgeous enough to star in his own fairy tale. Katrine unlatched the stall door and opened it for a more intimate greeting. She set her palm flat on his forehead, and he lowered and raised his head, rubbing against her, then snorted at her hip pocket.

"Ah'm without treats, fella." She turned toward me, dropping her hand. "This is Saorsa, Gaelic for freedom."

I stood still before him and waited for Saorsa to make the first move. His chest was massive, and his ears tilted forward, checking me out. When he stretched his nose toward my face, I exhaled. His nostrils flared just below my eyes. I stayed close, breathing with him, feeling his majesty. Then he snorted and rubbed his head against my thigh. I staggered my feet apart for balance and braced myself as I let him convert my hip into a rubbing post, leaving a trail of black hairs on Fiona's clothes. Since horses can't scratch their faces, it's the one thing they know we're suitable for, and it offered me a route to his good graces.

Katrine laughed. "He's already adopted ye." She pointed to a chestnut-colored Friesian watching us from the opening in the adjoining wall. The stall design allowed their heads to connect while still keeping their bodies separated. Katrine affectionately tousled her forelock and I glimpsed a small white diamond mark like a third eye. Her long mane hung with an uneven edge, nearly blending in with the color of her coat, except for a few blonde highlights.

"This is Caim. The meanin' of her name 'tis a wee bit complicated. Roughly, it translates to sanctuary." Katrine walked out, leaving Saorsa's stall door open. I supposed escape wasn't the first thing on his mind. Breakfast was a worthier lure. Hay bales filled the third stall. Down the aisle awaited a wheelbarrow with a pitchfork that I grabbed to muck their stalls. The patter of grain cascading into their buckets filled the air with a waft of molasses.

"Ye'll find the compost pile out the other barn door through the gate on the left. Ye can leave the door open but be sure to close the gate."

I discovered a level, fenced-in pasture that abutted the driveway with a circular path worn amidst the grasses. After pitching the manure and closing the gate behind me, I parked the wheelbarrow where I had found it.

The promise of riding distracted me from the necessities, like where I'd sleep tonight or even what year it was. The barn's familiar scents temporarily anesthetized my anxiety about being so far from home.

An assortment of brushes cluttered a bench outside the tack room. Katrine was in with Caim, currying her sides, causing little clouds of dust to filter through the sunlight.

My old habit of talking to horses, as if they could understand, returned as I groomed Saorsa. "Aren't you a beauty? You're the highlight of my day." I wasn't alone in my conversation. I overheard Katrine chatting with Caim. My left hand moved in circles while my right hand brushed the loosened hair and mud from his coat till he shined. There were no girth marks where sweat and dirt lines often formed from previous rides, another sign these horses were well loved. I heard Katrine using a spray bottle and saw her detangling Caim's tail.

I grabbed the hoof pick. "Anything I should know before I clean his hooves?"

"Dinnae let him get away with makin' ye hold it up for him. Lean into him and make like ye'r goin' to let it go. He can carry his own weight. 'Tis a game he likes to play."

I patted his hindquarters, then ran my hand down along the inside of his leg as I bent over, tugging on his fetlock feathers, asking for his hoof. He lifted it. But as soon as I cupped his fetlock, he dropped it like a dead weight, straining my lower back. I said, "Hey!" and followed Katrine's counsel. He relented. I respected a clever horse.

His hoof was in great shape. "Was he recently shod?"

"Aye. Last week ah took care of it."

Saorsa didn't try his trick for the remaining hooves. I swapped the pick for the hairbrush and spray bottle and brought them both to his nose for approval. He snorted. "It's time to work out a few tangles, fella." The spray had a hint of sandalwood and lavender. The bottle had no label on it, likely a homemade concoction. He stood still as I brushed out his tail but stepped away as I sprayed his mane. "Hey, easy now. Stay here. I'll spray the brush instead."

I stole a moment for more intimacy with a one-arm hug underneath his neck and laid my cheek against his silky coat. He brought his head down, tapping my butt with his chin. A rush of warmth suffused my whole core as I inhaled him. My last task was the finer hairs of his forelock and given his height, he needed to cooperate. "Hey, fella. You want to come down to my size?"

After I rubbed behind his ears, he lowered his head to eye level. I skipped the spray, concerned it might ruin our rapport, and gently combed his hairs. They reached beyond his eyes to midway down his nose, proportional to his graceful mane. His looks were undeniably stunning.

"Thanks, Saorsa. You made that easy." I turned to leave and noticed Katrine watching me from the stall door. Had she seen me hug her horse? She offered an approving smile, and I felt our connection deepen. It's exceedingly rare for people to share their horses with a total stranger. It's like a mum handing over her newborn in the grocery line while she leaves to fetch a forgotten item. It doesn't happen.

Katrine turned without saying anything. I followed her into the tack room that smelled of leather and saddle soap. Two saddles faced me, and two bridles hung from a metal hook to my left. I assumed the black saddle was Saorsa's. As I lifted it onto my forearm, I admired the cast iron and wooden saddle rack.

"This is beautiful craftsmanship."

"'Twas a winter project ah did a few years back when ah was bored."

"You made these?"

"Och aye. Ah'm a blacksmith. Ah shoe mah own horses and enjoy the challenge of takin' on an odd project. Mostly, ah make silverware and jewelry. We walked past mah studio on the way to the barn—ah can offer ye a tour after our ride." She handed me the cavesson and lunge line as she walked with Caim's tack to her stall.

"Yes, please. After dreaming about it, I tried to learn how to make silverware, but the process was so loud, it deterred me."

"The hammerin' can be deafenin' at times. Ah also work in lost wax. 'Tis easier on the arms and ears. That may suit ye better."

Saorsa remained still as I saddled him and loosely fastened the girth. Most horses hate having it tightened immediately. I put on the cavesson that had a noseband with a middle ring for clipping the lunge line, offering the horse a clear signal without interfering with his tongue. He held his head still while I buckled the straps under his jaw. "You really are a dream, Saorsa. Will you be this cooperative when I'm on your back?"

Katrine asked, "Did ye leave his girth loose?"

"Yes." I took the stirrups down to gauge their length using my outstretched arm and shortened both straps by a hole before securing them again. The clop of Caim's hooves on the concrete caused me to turn my head. Katrine waited by the stall door with a tall lunge whip. She left Caim standing in the aisle.

"Ah'll trade ye." She came alongside Saorsa and said, "He prefers to be in front." Katrine walked him out first. I couldn't help but admire his muscular back end as I slipped his bridle off the stall hook and over my shoulder.

"Does he kick?"

"Nae, he'd nae dream of kickin' his mum. Ah'v nae had him around other horses much so ah cannae say if he's truly well mannered." She led us out the opposite barn door from where we'd entered. Caim and I hung back to leave enough space for her to lunge him in the circle. Katrine watched for stiffness as she exercised him, whereas I found his movements simply spellbinding. When she finished, my stomach fluttered at the thought of riding him. Knowing Saorsa would sense my emotional state, I exhaled to calm myself and focused on taking deeper breaths. Our ride would be infinitely more enjoyable if we were both relaxed.

He whinnied and snorted like a dragon, stamping the ground with his front hoof. "Okay, okay, patience. Easy now. Are ye goin' to behave yerself for Sarah?" As Katrine approached with Saorsa, Caim was all ears.

Katrine watched as I removed the cavesson and took it from me. I bridled him and noticed the absence of a nose band. He accepted the bit without delay and began chewing it while I fastened the chin strap, tightened his girth, and released the stirrups. I brought him alongside the mounting block and stroked his neck. "Hey, handsome. Let's have ourselves a lovely ride."

Katrine said, "Let me stand in front of him as ye mount. Ah dinnae want him thinkin' he can walk off on ye. Nae bad habits allowed."

"Sounds good."

I gathered the reins and some of his mane as a security measure as I stepped on the mounting block. In one smooth motion, I placed my left foot into the stirrup and swung my right leg over to ease my weight onto his back. He stood still like a gentleman. Katrine had kept an eye on me, not him.

She rubbed his nose—"Guid man"—and looked at me. "He has a gentle mouth and will respond to yer seat. Ye dinnae need a tight rein, nor much leg." She handed me a riding crop. "Ye likely will nae need it, but 'tis best to let him ken ye have it."

I took it and checked that my reins were free of twists and lying flat against his neck. The butterflies in my stomach had taken flight. "Please feel free to give me any tips."

"Let's walk them out to start. Ah want to warm up Caim. 'Tis been awhile since ah'v ridden her. Ah tend to favor Saorsa with mah time."

After Katrine mounted Caim, she came alongside me. "Ridin' is the second-best way to get to know Iona. We can test if the bogs are dry enough to safely cut across."

Saorsa stretched his neck, asking for more rein, so I loosened them further and followed the rhythm of his head as we walked. I resisted the temptation to grip with my knees, knowing that lousy habit offered no security and only made Saorsa uncomfortable. Instead, I focused on the position of my sit bones in the saddle, and centered my weight. We walked side by side, the sound of hooves clopping on gravel marking our leisurely pace.

"How did you come to own a Friesian horse on Iona?"

Katrine's chin tilted slightly up as a subtle smile graced her lips. "Mah husband won Caim in a poker game. Fishermen play a fair amount of cards to pass the night together. There was a new man on the boat whose family bred horses. He was in debt to Kieran but wanted to keep playin'. He asked Kieran if he'd take a filly as payment. The rest is, as they say, history. We'd half-joked that we'd filled the house with bairns, but our barn was empty. Kieran ken ah was anxious each time he left me." She tenderly patted Caim's neck.

"He'd say, 'Dinna fash yerself, mah love, ah'll always come back to ye.' Ah'd a premonition the sea would take him from me. Ah just dinnae ken it'd be so soon, with our bairns so young. Kieran warned me when we met that the sea was his first love. He'd come from a family of fishermen and told me he could nae give her up because she was in his blood. He even foretold she was the jealous type, but he'd teach her to share. He failed at that. The sea, she always wins. Ah was nae match for her."

I wondered if living on an island with the sea as an enduring neighbor, or making a living upon its waters as a fisherman, imbued the ocean with a life and personality of her own.

"Ah ken how somethin's in yer blood. Ah come from a family of smiths. Ah learned the trade from mah dah, who learned it from mah grandpa and all the way back in time. Ah hold tools that generations of mah kin have held. Generations ah'v never met, but ah swear sometimes they talk to me and guide mah hands. The fire called to me. It drew me in even as a wee lassie, watchin' the flames lick and flicker until ah could safely partake. Maeve will carry on the tradition from me. She's already better than ah was at her age. She made the teapot we drank from today." I heard pride in Katrine's voice.

"Impressive. I assumed it was an heirloom. For sure, it'll become one."

We'd reached another fence line secured by a mint-green rope. "Ah'll get the gate." Katrine clucked Caim next to the post, easily flipped the frayed loop over the top, and then walked the gate open. Saorsa and I followed and waited since neither his gentlemanly behavior nor my skills extended to closing gates.

When he stamped his front hoof impatiently, I instinctively gathered my reins. "Let me guess. This terrain is safe for higher speeds."

"Indeed. Ah often ride out along this pasture. Take the pace yer comfortable with. He's more sensitive than most. He'll pay close attention to where yer lookin' and yer shift in weight."

"Do you mind if I circle him a bit to get a feel for him?"

Katrine nodded. "That'd be wise. Remind him who's the rider and who's the horse before he gets another idea."

Katrine watched as I put him through the paces. I wanted to know if I had Saorsa's attention and how he responded to the use of my seat when I asked for a stop. We circled and created figure eights, alternating between a walk and trot. I felt rusty, but the lines of communication were open between us, and I lightly patted his neck in praise. My fear that I'd forgotten how to ride was unfounded. My body remembered. Saorsa showed signs of ease, licking and chewing on the bit. I breathed easier, too.

As we rejoined Katrine, she offered another approving smile. "Saorsa's very relaxed. It seems ye two are havin' a love fest. While ye'r visitin', please feel free to come by for a ride any time. He needs the exercise. Ah can hear Fiona yellin' at me, 'Mum, ye let him get fat!'"

"Really? Thanks, I'd love that." The irony of having daily rides arranged but nowhere to sleep wasn't lost on me. I shoved my homeless status into the background, knowing it would await me when I dismounted this breathtaking beast. For now, riding invited me to re-inhabit the home of my body, the centered place from which everything else flowed.

Katrine said, "Let's head for the beach."

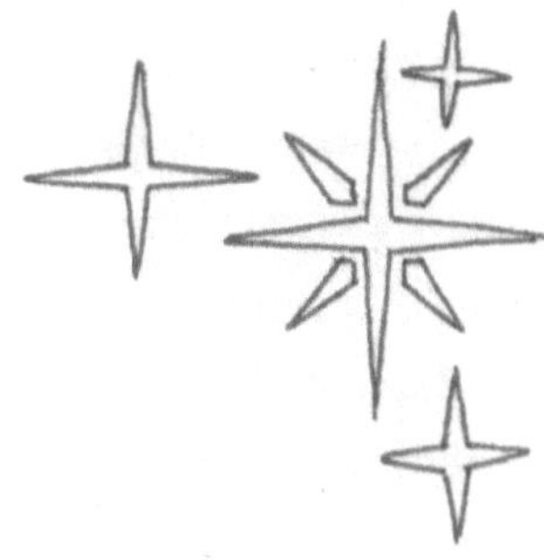

CHAPTER 3
A SPELL

*H*ERE *I AM RIDING a Friesian along a beach in Scotland. How is this even possible?*

Disbelief swept me up again. When Faith guided me in the underworld, I'd become accustomed to having my beliefs challenged. Today, even though Saorsa and I were in the lead, Katrine became my guide. She taught me that the reeds topped with tiny tufts of white cotton balls were indicative of marsh, and we avoided them like warning flags to keep the horses on safe footing as we crossed the bogs.

Thankfully, Katrine didn't attempt to converse while trotting or cantering. For me, riding meant engaging in a conversation beyond words. It reminded me that when I'm supple and centered, even the subtlest squeeze of my hands conveys meaning—this sense of communion with such a powerful being humbled me. My body felt soft and reverent, no longer braced against the world. My pelvis had become more pliant and welcoming, moving with Saorsa in a fluid, rhythmic dance. I felt at home in my skin, as if Faith accompanied me again.

When Katrine suggested we walk back to cool them down, my homeless status leapt the distance from where I'd left it at the barn and muscled its way back into my thoughts. Our return to words felt imminent, so I reengaged my offensive strategy by asking questions. "It must have been difficult being a single mother. How'd you cope?"

"Nae well." She sighed. "After Kieran died, ah was a wreck. His memory was everywhere—mah grief was relentless. Mah world had become a dull chore. Even gettin' up from bed required more of me than ah had to give. Oddly, it was Caim who coaxed me back to life. When Brìghde and Fiona were at school, mah mum often watched Maeve while ah rode every inch of the island. Ah religiously scoured the shore lookin' for any fragments of his boat, but she swallowed every last trace of him. The cliffs to the west became mah widow's walk." Katrine looked as if she was back there again, as if the years had never happened. "Ah could nae imagine mah life without him, so for a time—ah gave up on livin' mahself."

I waited for her memories to release her.

She patted Caim's neck. "Caim was green when we got her. Ah gave mahself over to trainin' her—more than ah raised mah own daughters. Thank God mah mum and friends stepped in. Brìghde mothered Maeve, and Fiona had to fend for herself. Ah'm nae proud of those years, but ah survived. 'Tis only a dull pain now and then. Ah miss Kieran most in the big transitions ah'd expected to share with him. It was tough when Brìghde married, and he was nae there to walk her down the aisle. Now that ache has returned—we cannae be grandparents together."

She choked on the words 'grandparents together,' and her eyes teared up with mine. The back of my throat tightened as I held back my rising emotions, and focused on the sounds of hooves clopping on the ground.

"Trainin' Caim took mah full attention, like the fire demands while smithin'. She offered me a much-needed respite from mah grief. Caim means an invisible circle of protection, and she is indeed—she kept me sane. Eventually, ah recovered mah strength to care for our bairns." She stroked Caim's neck in praise again. "If Fiona wasn't at school, she accompanied me in the barn—groomin' her, neglectin' her studies. Caim was a sanctuary for the two of us. Ah dinnae want to be around folks, so ah spent mah days between mah studio and the barn. Ah needed her calmin' presence. Caim obliged by rollin' in any patch of mud she could find, but her bad habits were nae match for Fiona and mah groomin' obsession. Her coat glistened with an otherworldly sheen."

The sunlight highlighted the red in Caim's coat. "She's still a beauty. What about Maeve? When did she start learning your craft?"

Katrine laughed. "She became mah shadow whenever ah went to my studio. Ah'd done the same with mah dah. Ah'm grateful she has a trade to fall back on if communications dinnae work out for her." Katrine had been looking ahead as she spoke. When she reached the gate, she said, "Listen to me, tellin' ye mah whole life story. 'Tis like ye cast a spell on me. Ah dinnae ken a thing about ye other than ye'r keen on scones, but cannae bake, and ye ride like ye were born on a horse."

A spell. "We can save my story for another time." Katrine had swung the gate open for us, and we walked to the center of the pasture before I dismounted to curb any chance of conversation. My stomach had started announcing itself on the latter part of our ride, and by the time we were back in the stable, rubbing the horses down, its rumblings sounded like another animal in the stall.

Katrine laughed when she heard how persistent it had become. "Ah hear ye clammerin' for another of mah scones."

"I am making a racket. Think of it as me singing your praises. Seriously though, Katrine, thanks so much for this morning. I can't imagine a better welcome and introduction to Iona than sharing tea and scones with you and riding Saorsa. I feel blessed and refreshed."

She appeared on the threshold with her saddle over her arm and bridle in hand. "'Tis been a lovely start to the day. Ah'v appreciated yer companionship. Ye remind me of mah own lasses—as they travel far from home, ah'd want strangers to show them a kindness."

My hand rested on Saorsa's neck. I didn't want to leave the safety of his stall. *Maybe I can sneak back and sleep here.* "You've been more than kind with your generous hospitality."

Katrine simply smiled and tipped her head in acknowledgment.

I noted she hadn't put a halter on Caim. "Will you turn them out to pasture now?"

"Och aye, ah leave their stall's doors open along with one barn door during the day. They can come in if they want some shade from the heat or shelter from the rain." She walked into the tack room.

I stroked Saorsa's neck. "You, my friend, are a dream come true. I hope to be seeing you again soon. Try not to miss me as much as I'll miss you." Reluctantly, I gathered his bridle and saddle as Caim clopped down the aisle and nickered. Saorsa followed her out to the pasture. It was time for me to reckon with real-world matters.

I joined Katrine in the tack room, returning Saorsa's saddle to its rack and resting his damp pad upside down on top of it. Our shared silence was comfortable as I imitated her routine. I dipped Saorsa's stainless steel bit in a small bucket of water and rubbed the grime until it shined before hanging it on the hook.

What can I say if she asks me where I'm staying? How will I dodge it? My chest tightened. I wanted to be honest with Katrine, to be worthy of the radical hospitality she'd shown me. Seeing the saddle rack reminded me she had offered to show me her studio. *Maybe just one more diversion.*

She asked, "Shall ah warm ye a scone or two?"

My stomach answered before I could say yes, and we both laughed.

"Ah'll take that as an affirmative." The phone rang while we walked toward the house. Katrine dashed through the door to answer it. Upon entering, I heard her saying, "Grand. Ah'll be on mah way shortly." She hung up, giddy. "'Tis time. Mah grandchild's on the way. Brìghde's gone into labor and she's headin' to the hospital. Ah'v got to pack up and make a call."

"I'll be out of your way as soon as I change my clothes." Reality rushed back in. I'd hoped to keep it at bay until my stomach was fed again.

Coming back downstairs, I overheard Katrine saying, "Dinna fash yerself, Mary, 'tis okay. Take good care of yerself. Angus can tend them, and ah'll let ye ken when the wee one arrives. Bye for now." Katrine hung up and said, "Feck."

"What's wrong?"

"'Tis Mary. She was meant to care for the horses. But she fell and broke her hip yesterday. She said she called earlier. Ah must have missed the message. Ah'm the worst at checkin' mah machine. Despite Saorsa takin' to ye today, he typically dinnae behave so well with others. Ah'll have to ask…"

I blurted, "I can do it. Take me back out to the barn and walk me through their routine. Let me grab a pen and paper, and I'll write it all down. I can call you if I have questions." I tripped over my words in eagerness to stay.

"Ah cannae ask this of ye—'tis yer holiday. Besides, Mary was to stay overnight here for the week."

"Honestly, I can't imagine a place I'd rather be. It's no problem at all—you'd be doing me a favor. I can ride every day. It'd be heavenly." I hoped she didn't hear the desperation in my voice.

"Ah am in a pickle." She hesitated. "If ye'r sure, it'd be grand. Ye'r a godsend. Who ken when ah decided to swim today ah'd find mahself an angel in disguise." My stomach growled on cue. "Ye'r a hungry angel, nonetheless."

"Ignore my stomach," I said. "Walk me through their routine."

"Ye have to let me pay ye. Mary's cash is already on mah dresser in an envelope with her name on it. We've plenty of feed for the horses, and since they rode out well today, their shoes should be fine."

I pulled Fiona's boots back on. With my shift dress, it was a fashion statement I wouldn't ordinarily make, but I didn't care about my appearance. My stomach grumbled its way to the barn. It may have been launching a protest at the change of plans, but the rest of me was silently proclaiming hallelujah. Faith was still watching out for me. I searched around to locate her but felt her inside as a rush of warmth in my core.

Saorsa and Caim stood head-to-tail beside one another in the field, grooming each other with their lips, itching those impossible-to-reach places. In a way, Katrine and I were doing the same.

Katrine swiftly told me how much hay and grain she fed them and reminded me to close the stall door where the hay was stored to avert a feast. Her barn design was unusual. Typically, a horse's stall had a back door that opened to a paddock, giving them the freedom to be outside or under cover. She'd worked within the constraints of her narrow property to provide them with access via the aisle door.

At the threshold of the tack room, she pointed to the upper shelves. "These blankets are for warmth and rain protection." Walking outside, she showed me the faucet. "Be sure they have fresh water. Ah generally feed them before ah eat dinner and often before breakfast, typically earlier than today. Always lunge Saorsa before ridin' him. He might act up without his mum or me around. Ah alternate their turnout each day by closin' off one of the barn doors. It gives the grass a chance to rebound. After dinner, ah close them in at night. Another shipment of hay comes next week, but ah should be back before then."

We were nearly at the front door when a black cat, with one white front paw, sauntered up and rubbed against her legs.

"Och aye, Sarah meet Demeter. Are ye allergic?"

Demeter came alongside Fiona's boots. "Actually, I am, and cats seem to know that about me."

"Dinna fash. She's an outdoor cat. Ah never let her in the house—despite her yowlin', dinnae relent. She ken mah home is off limits, even when ah leave the door open like today. Occasionally, ah offer her a saucer of milk for her huntin' skills. Her dried food is on the bench above the grain bucket. Her dish is in the tack room. I keep it half full. She keeps mah barn free of mice, and the horses love her."

Demeter had foregone finding any affection from me and wandered back between Katrine's legs. "Does she need to be in or out of the barn at night before I close up?"

"Pay her nae mind. She jumps in and out the window at will." We walked past her car. "The ferry waits for no one. Do ye ken how to drive a manual?"

"Yes, I own one."

"That's rare for an American. Ah thought t'was all big, automatic motors on yer roads."

I grinned at her accurate stereotype. "You're right, but I'm a fan of standards. Downshifting offers more control driving in the snow, and it's all around more fun."

Katrine scampered straight up the stairs. "Ah need to throw some clothes in mah bag. Be back in a jiff."

While she packed, I made her a ham sandwich from her well-stocked fridge. I was putting away the lettuce when Katrine appeared with an unzipped overnight bag in one hand and an envelope in the other. She didn't put her bag down. When she offered me the envelope, I exchanged it with her wrapped sandwich.

Katrine said, "Thanks, that'll come in handy on the journey." She grabbed the keys from a silver dish on the counter.

The envelope had heft. I slipped out two large, colorful bills with a twenty on the diagonal corners and tucked them in my pocket before leaving the rest behind.

Katrine drove us in her red Kia Sportage and parked it beside the café. The ferry approached at a distance.

"Ah'v got about ten minutes before ah board. Let's get a coffee, and ah can introduce ye to the island." We walked into the café. "Guid day, Trish. We'll have two coffees and a sandwich." Katrine turned to me and asked, "Will a ham sandwich do ye?"

I smiled. "Yes, thanks. That should quiet the beast nicely."

We sat at a round metal table with spindly folding chairs. When Trish arrived with the two handmade pottery mugs, she sized me up warily. I recognized her as the same redhead who told me there were no banks on Iona. Her eyes glanced toward Fiona's riding boots.

"Guidday, Kat. Who do ye have here? It seems ye picked yerself up a stray?"

"This here is Sarah. She's visitin' for a spell and will be takin' care of mah horses. Brìghde's gone into labor, and ah'm catchin' the next ferry."

She placed Katrine's coffee before her but withheld mine. "Such guid news—soon to be a nana. Ah heard Mary broke her hip yesterday in a fall. Ah could help ye with the horses if need be. Ah dinnae want ye to fash about anythin' here."

"Thanks, just the same, Trish. Ah was sorry to hear about Mary's fall. We're all sorted out, though. Sarah had a lovely ride with Saorsa this mornin', and they're fast friends."

Trish finally placed my coffee down on the table. She tipped her head to me. "Ah'll be back with yer piece."

I assumed that piece meant a sandwich. It felt like Trish had just vetted me and reluctantly accepted me, but it might not be a lasting truce. The taste of my first coffee in months erased the tension of our exchange.

Katrine had been holding her mug. The table wobbled when she put it down. "'Tis the end of our tourist season, and everyone's ready to have the island back to ourselves."

"You'd be the exception to that. You've shown me such hospitality from the moment we met. I can't thank you enough for inviting me in for tea and trusting me with your horses and now your home. I feel as though I've known you for years—not hours."

"Och aye, ah hear ye." She drummed her fingers on the table a few times. "'Tis been an uncanny day. When ah woke and saw the light on the water beckonin', somethin' long forgotten stirred in me this mornin'—it must've been mah grandchild passin' through the veil. Ye'r a godsend, and ah'm grateful to have met ye." Katrine pulled the keys from her pocket, and they clattered on the metal table. "Ah'll be off now, and dinnae want to be takin' these with me. Nae that ye have far to walk. Soon enough, Trish will let everyone ken ye'r a welcome stranger. Island news spreads fast, as ye can see with Mary's fall. Ah'v nae time to introduce ye properly mahself."

"Oh, don't worry about me. I'll be fine." It was the first time today that I actually believed it.

She took out her cell phone. "Do ye have a mobile number ah can ring you at?"

I squirmed in my seat. "Oh, no. I left without it." *Stick to the truth, Sarah, as best you can.* "Surprisingly, I've enjoyed not having it."

She put her phone back in her bag. "Ah'll ring ye on mah landline. Mah mobile number's written on the envelope. Ye'll be needin' more eggs and milk. The only grocer is next to the café. Nae one drives unless 'tis to the ferry with their luggage, so ye might as well pick up a few items now and fetch yer things. Ah never asked, where were ye stayin'?"

I didn't see the dreaded question coming. "At your place, remember?"

She tilted her head slightly. "That ye are."

"I can sort myself out." Katrine sat with her back to the café door, but I saw folks walking up the street from the dock. "I think the ferry's here."

She stood, taking the last sip of her coffee. "Och aye, ah'll be off then. Thanks ever so much." She squeezed my shoulder. "Dinnae get up."

"I'm the one who is grateful." I placed my hand upon hers.

Trish set my sandwich with homemade bread down and hugged

Katrine. "God bless."

Its diagonal cut bulged in the center, thick with ham and fresh tomato. Once I pinched the corners of the first half, it never touched the plate again. I feasted on it while I marveled at how my day had unfolded. Not one aspect of my plan had worked out, and for that, I was grateful. For the next week, I had a place to sleep, clothes to wear, and, best of all, two gorgeous horses to care for and ride. I even had an envelope filled with cash. If the island had a second-hand store, it might be enough for a pair of shoes and maybe even a change of clothes.

Trish asked, "Do ye want a tap off?"

"Yes, thank you. The sandwich is delicious." I raised my cup to her.

She poured. "Ye made fleet work of it. Do ye want somethin' else?"

"No, I'm set. Can you bring my check when you have a moment, please?"

She wiped her hand on her apron as she held the coffee pot before me. "Kat's already asked me to put it on her tab. Ye'r set for now."

I detected an undertone of suspicion again. Who could blame her? Maybe she—or someone else—saw me wash up on shore this morning, and I was already the talk of the town. *There's nothing to be done about it, so there's no point worrying about it.* What was their expression? Dinna fash.

I savored my coffee and glanced toward the beach. My thoughts turned toward my more immediate worries: Ian and anticipating our first conversation. He'd want me to come home immediately. Only a few hours ago, that was my plan. But that wasn't possible now, nor desired. I relished the idea of time to myself, time to land and integrate everything that had transpired on my odyssey, and most of all, time to love up Saorsa and Caim. The promise of riding every day caused an irresistible smile that broadcast my happiness.

How can I talk to Ian after all this time and tell him we still needed to be apart? He'll probably insist on coming here to me.

I felt uncomfortable adding another stranger to Katrine's home or even asking her if it would be okay. *Ian will have to understand.* I doubted he would. I briefly considered waiting to call him until the end of the week but dismissed it as too dishonest. More coffee had been a mistake. Jitters filled my chest and sitting still proved increasingly impossible.

The grocery store had two short aisles with an open refrigerated unit on the left wall that the cashier was restocking with more produce. At Katrine's recommendation, I filled my handbasket with eggs and milk. A loaf of homemade zucchini bread begged to be taken alongside a baguette. Carbohydrates have always been my comfort food. A bag of salty potato crisps jumped into my basket too. There was a scant selection of wine, and I chose a Sauvignon Blanc. As I placed my items on the counter, she rang them up without bagging them. After paying, I caught on. I was meant to provide a bag.

She offered me the box she'd unpacked the vegetables from. "Ye can have this today."

"Thanks." It was far larger than I needed but better than nothing. I stashed my items toward one corner, carried the lopsided weight to the car, and put it on the back seat. I stopped before opening the front door because there was no steering wheel.

Now was the time to notice and alter my unconscious patterns, like always trying to plan my future. *What if I became more like the hitch-hikers I'd dreamt about in the fox's den—living in the moment, relying on the kindness of strangers?*

A witness might have doubted my ability to drive a stick shift as I lurched out of town. Her car's clutch was more sensitive than mine. When I pulled into Katrine's driveway, my incompetence was forgotten as two bewitching sculptures of muscle, with manes and tails rippling in the wind, galloped along the fence. *Now, that's my idea of a welcoming committee.* A quiet gasp escaped my lips, followed by a sense of a déjà vu. A black horse galloping was the first image I'd seen when Faith held her hands over my eyes before she said goodbye. I parked the car and closed my eyes, attempting to recall the other images—a circle of black stones in the water, and a fire, not the wild kind—one contained in a fireplace.

Inside, I unpacked the groceries and more closely inventoried her refrigerator's contents. It held plenty of food for a week, so my remaining cash could be spent on other necessities. I counted the mix of fifties and twenties in the envelope, which came to nearly two hundred pounds. *Horse-sitting pays well.*

When I slipped it back in the envelope and placed it beside Katrine's stack of papers, I saw her mail with new eyes. The mail contained dates. I sorted through it until I discovered the year remained the same and exhaled. *Thank god.* Re-entry was hard enough without navigating the dynamics of a time warp. I ticked off the number of months since May on my fingers. Six months felt like a long time for Ian to wait without a word. I couldn't blame him if he'd moved on with his life. Before I'd left, we'd discussed marriage, starting a family, and buying a home together, but I told him I wasn't ready. Contemplating those commitments had put me in a tailspin. I was too young for a midlife crisis, but I was in the midst of one, questioning everything and worrying that I was somehow missing my life.

Six months ago, I'd been second-guessing the societal expectations I felt imposed on me: career, marriage, children, homeownership, and the iconic white picket fence. Now, my check-list was more basic. Date? Check. Shelter? Check. Food? Check. Money? Check. Clothes? Check. Relationships? Question mark. Job? Question mark.

I'd woken on the day that Faith appeared in our bedroom with the adage, *Be careful what you ask for; you may surely get it.* I sensed it needed a caveat—*And be prepared to make sacrifices.* I hadn't wanted to make any sacrifices. *Who does?* But what had I set in motion when I chose to leave with Faith? I'd likely lost my job and maybe even my relationship with Ian.

I flashed on the tarot card on my altar back home. *The Tower.* It portended a time of significant internal change, destruction, and regeneration. Suddenly, the full sweep of the last six months hit me behind the knees. Dizziness warned me that if I didn't sit down, I might fall down, and I moved toward the high-back chair overlooking the sea. I perched on the seat's edge, letting my head hang between my knees. My body flushed with heat, yet my hands felt clammy. A vortex of questions that didn't have easy answers swirled in my head.

What was the purpose of my underworld odyssey with Faith? How will I ever explain to Ian or my friends what happened? Will they believe me? What do I believe? If I don't tell them about it, is that lying? If I do, how will it impact our relationship?

My immediate inclination was to be protective and say nothing about my journey until I understood it. I feared subjecting myself to others' predictable disbelief and projections. Yet my close friends' opinions mattered to me more than I cared to admit.

Nausea threatened to upend my lunch. I lifted my head and pushed back into the chair for support, longing for my Peaceful Warrior's protection. My nose flared, and a lump rose in my throat. *Are you here?* Hugging my knees to my chest, I closed my eyes, trying to conjure her with memories.

I recalled our first embrace, when she transformed from Rage into a quiet, formidable strength, and the bars of her cage bent open, freeing her—freeing us. She resided somewhere within me, and I needed to summon her now.

Imperceptibly, at first, I felt her light touch on my lower back, as if a finger traveled up from the base of my spine, inviting me to straighten from my hunched posture. I uncurled, released my legs, and planted my feet on the ground. As the pressure landed between my shoulder blades, I tucked them closer together, letting my shoulders drop. My chest opened as I inhaled more fully, and her touch continued up my neck and vanished after reaching my skull. I rested with the accompaniment of my Peaceful Warrior at my back and opened my eyes to the sea, taking in the lovely surrounds of Katrine's home.

A wave of gratitude rushed in for arriving on Iona, a marked reversal from the anxiety that riddled my first hour here when nothing had conformed to my expectations. Now, I relished the space and time to reorient myself in this world, time to invite into my life the aspects of myself I'd begun to form a relationship with—Faith, Compassion, and Forgiveness. *I don't need to get ahead of myself. I need to slow down and listen.*

My right palm rested on my chest, my left palm on my belly. My hands rose and fell with each breath, and eventually, a weighted, settled peacefulness arrived in my body. Everything I'd gone through had a purpose, even if that purpose still eluded me.

This is my life, my story unfolding. I can take my time to discern what I share, how I share it, and with whom I share it.

CHAPTER 4

RESTLESS

SARAH'S MYSTERIOUS DISAPPEARANCE UPENDED Ian's world. To avoid questioning his sanity, he'd coped by burying himself in his work. His bank account was flush, but his peace of mind was depleted. He'd been running on fumes.

After making the rookie mistake of sleeping on the flight, his body hadn't adjusted to the time difference between Boston and Hawaii. Reading hadn't helped him drift off to sleep and the hotel's clock display indicated only twenty minutes had passed since the last time he'd checked, 1:47 a.m.

Accidentally dropping his cell phone in the Pacific during the sunset sail was somehow symbolic. Ian wasn't prone to interpreting signs from the universe like Sarah, but that one felt too obvious to ignore—*let go*. It was time to move on with his life, time to start piecing it back together, even if one of the central pieces had gone AWOL.

Forty-eight hours without a phone felt strange, reminiscent of the days when he had been unreachable after he left the office or home. The era of cell phones meant work was always at his fingertips, clients could find him anywhere, anytime, challenging him to maintain a boundary on billable hours so it didn't bleed into his personal time. Ian hadn't expected to experience such separation anxiety from an inanimate object until he realized it represented his last remaining connection to Sarah.

A future without Sarah felt unimaginable. He'd denied that possibility so far, but the fact that she hadn't reached out in six months had cracked his resolve, and doubts flooded in. *Is she still alive?* The thought made him ill. He couldn't go there.

Unwinding in Kauai's tropical weather offered a balm for his heartache. When faced with the option of driving to Lihue in predictable traffic to shop at the Verizon store or playing tennis or golf, he rationalized a phone diet was good for him, and he'd replace it when he returned home. It helped him break the habit of checking it in vain, hoping for a message from Sarah.

The day had started well, but the events of the afternoon and evening had unsettled him. It was the kind of thing he'd have talked through with Sarah. Ian relied on her to sense his unease and check in with him. She gently probed until he discovered how he felt. He and Jim rarely talked about what kept them up at night, instead they covered world events or politics on the tennis courts and golf course.

The night before he'd left, he ate dinner with Jocelyn and Jim. Jocelyn was shocked he still planned to take his vacation in Kauai without Sarah. Apparently, Jim hadn't mentioned it to her. Ian said aloud what he feared most: that Sarah was never coming back, and he'd put his life on hold long enough. He hoped this would finally put an end to Jocelyn's suspicion that he knew her whereabouts. Sarah's friends had deluged him with questions and, later, accusations that he found impossible to field. He nearly revealed Sarah's secret during their interrogation, but he'd stopped short of telling them about her doppelgänger.

The palm fronds rustled in the evening breeze. His book fell open on his chest while his thoughts strayed. Even though he put the novel on the nightstand, a sensation of weight remained over his lungs. Ian turned out the light and rolled over, but sleep evaded him.

His thoughts returned to the day. It had begun with an early morning run, a refreshing ocean dip, and reading at the beach till he dried off. He planned to repeat the sequence tomorrow—or more accurately, today, given the hour.

Yesterday at the driving range, he'd noticed a few parties of two teeing off. He'd meant to set up a tee time before going to lunch, but his hunger had sidetracked him, and without a phone, he couldn't call.

He walked to the pro shop and chatted with the young men behind the counter while he bought a sleeve of balls and a divot tool. The staff mentioned they were new to Kauai but not to golf, having played through high school and college. They accommodated his lack of planning by adding him to a twosome at 1:15 p.m.

His mind hadn't strayed from golfing while he played, and his time at the driving range had finally paid off when his short and long game had come together yesterday. Ian had brought the other players to their rental cars so they didn't have to carry their golf bags, before pulling up behind the line of empty carts near the pro shop. The golf attendant had been on his cell and Ian heard him say, "Gotta go," before he promptly greeted him.

"Aloha, sir. How was your round this afternoon? Would you like your clubs cleaned?"

Ian had noticed a trim, older Black man with graying sideburns waiting beside his golf bag when he drove up.

"Well, thanks, it's a gorgeous course. But I believe this man was here before me." Ian knew this was the last tee time of the day and noted the man strumming his club covers.

The golf cart attendant said to him, "What is it you need?"

"A cart—my tee time is now."

The blond attendant didn't offer to take his clubs. He curtly said, "You can have this one after it's empty."

There were several carts around and no need for the man to wait. If Ian had been treated that way, he'd have been miffed. He removed his clubs to expedite the process and headed for his rental car.

The golfer simply said, "Thanks."

Ian turned to him and said, "Enjoy your round. Watch out for the water hazards—they swallow balls."

"I'll keep it in mind." The man had a poker face while he put his clubs in Ian's dirty cart.

The difference between the attendant's courtesy toward him and the unnecessary, blatant rudeness toward the other man irked Ian as he walked away, leaving a sour taste in his mouth after an otherwise excellent afternoon. He assumed the white attendant was from the mainland because his racist attitude didn't embody the spirit of aloha.

The inside of his car had felt like an oven, irritating him further. Ian opened all four windows and blasted the A/C, replaying the scene in his head. What a shitty way to start a round of golf, given it was a mental game as much as anything. The guy was a guest on vacation. He shouldn't have to deal with that kind of crap on holiday—or ever. Then Ian realized his mistake, there was no vacation from racism. Maybe the Black man wasn't ruffled by it because he was used to it. If the attendant had acted that way with a witness, how might he have behaved if he'd not been there?

The residue of the racist exchange had stayed with Ian after his shower and nap—should he have called out the attendant's behavior even if it meant making a scene?

As he lay in bed, he considered the significance of his chance encounter at dinner, meeting the stranger again. Ian's shoulders tensed recalling the events of the evening.

He'd planned to eat at The Bistro's bar to avoid sitting at a table for two because staring at an empty chair only exacerbated his loneliness. Ian hadn't expected to chat with anyone other than the bartender and thought he'd managed to put the incident behind him during the drive.

At The Bistro, he snagged the only remaining seat at the end of the L-shaped bar. Shortly after he'd sat down, the bartender greeted him, and Ian put his attention on the menu. He had selected an Argentinian Malbec called The Seeker, and satisfied his fish craving by ordering their Fish Rockets appetizer and seafood gumbo.

While he waited for his wine, he spotted the Black man, who'd been given his cart, sitting two seats away. Upon seeing him, Ian's quandary returned. He'd treated the stranger kindly, the way he was raised, but he hadn't taken it a step further—that path was unfamiliar. When his wife stood to use the restroom, Ian noticed she was pregnant. The empty barstool between them provided a window for conversation.

Ian asked, "How was your round of golf today?"

After a moment, the man's face registered recognition. "The course has spectacular views, but my game was disappointing and there wasn't time to play another nine. When I stopped by this morning, that was the only open slot. I underestimated how popular it'd be this time of year—they said it's booked solid for tomorrow too."

"Really? I arranged my tee time after lunch and joined a twosome, so you could've played with us." An awkward silence hung in the air. "Hmm, after witnessing the racist treatment you received earlier, it seems you were denied access to the course."

"It's not the first time."

"What if I get a tee time for us tomorrow—will you join me?"

"Sure, I regretted lugging my clubs here just to play one round."

"If I'm successful, do you want me to raise the incident with the staff?"

"Thanks for your courtesy earlier today, but let's take it one step at a time."

"Is this your first time playing the course?" Ian asked.

"Yes, it's our first time to Kauai. We've just moved from Brooklyn,

New York, to San Francisco. The day before we flew out, our boxes left for the West Coast. We're still on East Coast time."

They commiserated over the challenge of adjusting to the time difference. When his wife returned, he stood to help her with the barstool and extended his hand to Ian. "I'm Darren. Janelle, this is the man I mentioned who noticed I'd been waiting."

Ian shook their hands. "Good to meet you. I'm Ian."

Darren took out his wallet and handed Ian his business card. "Let me know about tomorrow. I was so preoccupied with the move that I didn't think to book ahead."

Ian took the card and said, "I don't have a card on me, or a phone for that matter—it took a dive in the ocean."

Janelle had shifted in her chair and asked Ian, "What line of work are you in?"

"Consulting. How about yourselves?"

Darren replied, "We're both lawyers. It's a small miracle we managed to find vacation time. Normally, we go to Jamaica, but Janelle wanted to try something different. Neither of us has ever been to Hawaii."

When their dinners arrived, Janelle curtailed his hopes for company by saying, "Nice meeting you. Enjoy your meal."

The bartender was too slammed to chat, so Ian had eaten alone, reflecting on Darren's experience. The guys in the pro shop had been friendly and courteous to him today, but he was white.

Now, as he lay awake, he doubted they'd have treated Darren similarly. *If I get a tee time tomorrow, does it point to a pattern of racism? If I ignore it, am I being complicit? What good is all the reading I'm doing on anti-racism if I don't act on it?* If Darren was open to him addressing it, how would he go about it? Ian knew there wasn't a written policy to amend that directed staff to deny access to Black people. It was more invisible than that. It was people's attitudes and beliefs that required changing, and he also knew confronting the staff wasn't going to change their minds. *What can I do?* Mulling over it again wasn't going to change it. It was only robbing him of sleep.

He turned the light back on to read, hoping to distract himself, but it didn't work. His mind wandered from the words on the page back to the basketball courts, playing hoop, enjoying himself during last week's pickup game. There were two Black guys that regularly arrived together. Would they join him for a beer if he asked? He could only recall one of their names, John.

Ian's social circle lacked diversity, and Sarah's was only marginally better, given Veena had been born in India and Maggie in England. Their cultural differences surfaced more around foods and holidays. Whenever Veena cooked, his palate felt like he'd gone on vacation; the blends of spices delighted him. She invited them to celebrate Diwali, the festival of lights, when her home glowed with candles that symbolized our inner light. Veena and her daughter, Indra, dressed in colorful saris for Diwali, and sometimes her twin brother, Arjun, flew in from San Francisco to join them. Ian hoped Veena extended him an invitation even if Sarah remained AWOL. He recalled it was celebrated sometime between mid-October and mid-November.

Despite the setbacks that Veena endured, she managed to radiate a resilience he witnessed in few other people, including himself. Ian had come to know some of the Indian Gods and Goddesses, as statues decorated Veena's home. Lord Ganesha, sitting cross-legged with an ample belly, many hands, and an elephant's head, helped to remove obstacles. Ian wondered if he offered his prayers to a foreign god, would he be heard?

If he asked John and his friend for a beer after basketball one night, would his friendly gesture be received? Making friends had been easier in college, but when they went their separate ways for jobs, it left a hole in his personal life. Ian had filled that void with work, sports, and Sarah. Her friends had become his friends.

How is it I can talk to anybody, on planes, restaurants, or golf courses, but these connections never deepen? All his closest friends lived at a distance. His life lacked more than Sarah; it lacked intimacy.

When Ian had called his college buddy, Scott, to let him know he had client work in San Francisco, Scott invited him to come early to visit because he and his wife, Lucy, had plans afterward, but that timing conflicted with his trip to Kauai. Ian debated if he'd made the right choice coming here without Sarah instead of hanging out with Scott and Lucy. He'd met Scott in philosophy class so their conversations immediately veered into territory he rarely spoke with others about. They had the kind of relationship that didn't include talking by phone much, but when they saw each other again it was like they'd never missed a beat.

He had confided in Scott when he tried to find his father, twenty years after he'd left their family. The day Ian's letter was returned unopened, stamped 'return to sender, no forwarding address,' Scott came over with a bottle of scotch. He hadn't told his mother he'd reached out, not wanting to upset her, especially if it came to nothing. Scott and Ian sat on the front porch of his apartment, toasting all the memories that Ian never had with his dad and finally sealed the coffin on his absent father.

Ian imagined someday teaching his son how to ride a bike, pitch a baseball, do a layup, and throw a tight pass with a football. His mother had no athletic skills, which convinced him he'd inherited his ability from his father. The neighborhood dads had taken Ian under their wing and taught him everything he knew. He pretended it didn't matter, but it did.

The clock read 2:22 a.m. He pulled back the covers and left his sleepless bed, putting on the hotel's terry cloth robe and relocating to the lanai. Ian sat in one chair and used the other for his feet. The rustle of the palm fronds and chorus of frogs offered him something else to focus on as he closed his eyes. Eventually he felt drowsy and padded back to bed without looking at the clock or even taking off his robe. He hugged one of the pillows, curled into the fetal position, and drifted off.

The phone rang and startled me. *Should I answer it? What if it's Katrine?* After the fourth ring, I said, "Hello, Sarah speaking. You've reached Katrine's home."

A woman's laughter responded. "Very professional. 'Tis a side of ye ah'v nae seen yet."

I recognized Katrine's voice. Her ears must have been ringing.

"Ah'd forgotten to tell ye where the water shutoff is and the fuse box in case ye needed them for any reason. Storms are predicted later this week. If 'tis pourin', ah leave the horses inside. Otherwise, they have a rain blanket, but ah suspect ye'd of figured that out."

"True." I knew the place in me that attempted to control what I could, as if tidying my surroundings could tame the chaos within me. I surmised she was worried about her daughter, and leaving a complete stranger in her home to care for her horses wasn't easing her concerns. She told me the water shutoff was under the sink, and directed me to the cupboard where the fuse box hid. "Where are you on your journey? How long will it take to get there?"

Katrine said, "Ah came ashore a few minutes ago. Ah'm waitin' on mah bus to take me across Mull, then the ferry to Oban, and then the train to Edinburgh. Ah'm guessin' the same route that ye came here."

"Excellent guess." *Crap, I set myself up for that.* "I'm glad you called. Is there a second-hand store? I'd like a better pair of waterproof walking shoes."

"Aye, there's a clothin' swap in the church basement the first Wednesday of every month. Ye'll have to check their bulletin board. Ah'v nae been there for some time, and they may have changed the day of the week. There are wellies under the bench. Ye can muck the stalls in them."

I stared at my bare feet. "Thanks. Hmm, what if my shoes are in no condition to be swapped? Can I purchase an item?"

"Ah imagine they'd nae refuse ye, but we also have a fine cobbler. Ah'm sure he'd mend them. Nae much is thrown out—we've nae where to toss it. Our rubbish is ferried off the island, which reminds me ye'll find the bin in the back of the house. We bring our trash and recyclin' down to the dumpster near the ferry. Mah bus is pullin' up, ah best be off. Please eat from the garden. It'd be tragic to let it go to waste."

"One last question: Where should I sleep? Is there a guest bedroom or perhaps one of your daughter's rooms?"

"Ah doubt any one of them will be returnin' home, so it dinnae much matter. Ye can be Goldilocks and see which one's just right. Ye'v seen Fiona's room and Brìghde's the orderly one. Maeve's has a wall of bookshelves, which was never enough, so she has stacks coverin' the floor. Ah swear when ye nae lookin', they multiply like bunnies."

I chuckled.

"Ah'm off now. Thanks again."

After hanging up, the silence of the house settled in around me. Everything else had its place but me. I wandered upstairs to play Goldilocks. Brìghde's room was as described: orderly, bordering on sterile. Nothing was on her desk but a cup of pencils. Nothing was on her nightstands but reading lamps. I peeked in her closet. Nothing hung on the hook. The rod had only a few items on hangers. The pressed cotton shirts and creased khaki pants were evenly spaced apart. I sensed the precision of her mathematical mind. She had a lovely view of the fields and a handmade quilt folded neatly at the base of the bed.

I crossed the hall to Maeve's bedroom. Her floor-to-ceiling, custom shelves were stuffed two-deep with books, and even her nightstands held precarious stacks. Her corner bedroom offered a view of the sea opposite the bed. Across from the door was a window overlooking the neighbor's sheep farm. I recognized the pasture where I'd schooled Saorsa. A narrow desk was wedged below the window and beside the bed. Even with the chair pushed in, the access to that side of the bed was blocked. It didn't matter, given the floor was an obstacle course of book towers.

The wooden desk was littered with piles of papers, books, and pens—a mosaic of chaos begetting creativity. Two large photo collages hung on the limited wall space. I opened her closet, and a salmon-colored, boiled wool, knee-length coat caught my eye. Jeans hung on her hooks alongside a deep purple, plush robe. Her taste in clothes appealed to me. An abundance of sweaters spilled off the top shelf in various shades of green, from emerald to teal, cluing me in she might be a redhead.

I wandered into Katrine's corner bedroom, which had an expansive ocean view. A high-back chair and a tall lamp stood beside a window that overlooked her pasture. The partially unmade bed had a faded mossy-colored comforter pulled back on one side. A bud vase on her nightstand displayed a single lavender rose that spiraled open into a dusty cream hue. I bent to smell the bloom's faint fragrance and took a closer look at the framed photo of the girls sprawled in the grass in a kind of puppy pile on top of a man I assumed was their father. No one looked at the camera, only each other. The youngest child and man were redheads, the others were brunettes with red highlights.

A crumpled pair of men's boxer shorts claimed the floor on the opposite side of the bed and the nightstand had a paperback with soldiers on the front cover. It didn't strike me as her taste. *Apparently, she doesn't sleep alone every night. Good for her.*

I entered her bathroom and encountered myself in the mirror, along with a taped piece of paper filled with handwriting in stanzas, a poem entitled "Cleaning Your Heart" by Chelan Harkin.[1]

<u>CLEANING YOUR HEART</u>
by Chelan Harkin

There's crying
and then there's Crying.

Crying is the act of the true warrior,
the deep grief that cleanses the heart,
that wrings out the ancestral line
of its ancient pain,
that reaches back to the beginning
of every oppression
you've ever known
which shares a cord with all opposition
and finally kisses even the wound
with light.

Crying allows you to dive
into and beyond the dark
that has held back countless generations
from their gifts and desires
and truths,
Crying undoes the sickness
of secrets,

Crying no longer compromises
truth for comfort,

this Crying is the evolution of the soul,
it is the alchemy of the straw
of the old world

to the gold of the new,

it is the undoing of the body
from being cinched
to the past

it unties the corset
of worn-out contracts
your soul never wanted to live in,

Crying resuscitates
your breathless life,
it is the embodied refusal
to go on serving what no longer serves you,

Crying is light
taking the shadow's hand
and courageously walking
into the Great Unknown
trusting there's wholeness
on the other side,

it is releasing once precious handholds,
it is forgoing control,
it is the time of the end
and the time of beginning,
it dives you deep into new frontiers
that you may grab
a new handful of power,
it is surrendering deeply enough
all the structures you thought you knew

to re-home your soul in a more suitable
habitation,

Crying moves inner mountains
and slays illusions.

From the inside out
Crying undoes and remakes
the world.

I reread it out loud. It summoned memories from my underworld journey, the tear pool I'd dove into, and the dance of opposites between light and shadow. My conversation with the Hooks surfaced, challenging me to let go of what no longer served me. I recalled the lessons of surrendering to the Great Mystery and taking Faith's hand. I closed my eyes, and felt myself return to the darkness of the Fox's den, where I'd yielded to my night dreams and their wisdom, unearthing the secrets that had imprisoned me. I marveled at how revisiting those muddy memories mixed with shame and grief had opened a gateway for me to take up residence in my body again—*for if I am not at home here, I will not be at home anywhere.*

As I opened my eyes, Katrine's mirror reflected my centered strength. *I may appear mostly the same on the outside, but something seismic has shifted inside.* The corners of my eyes and lips lifted slightly, welcoming me like an old friend.

Katrine hung up and dialed Angus. "'Tis time! Ah'm goin' to be a nana soon! Brìghde's in labor. Ah'm on the bus."

"Congrats, Kat! Keep me posted on the wee one's arrival."

"For sure. The day's already been full of surprises. Ah wanted to let ye ken 'tis nae Mary at the house tendin' the horses. 'Tis Sarah... uh... ah dinnae ask her last name. We rode out together this mornin'."

"Aye, ah saw ye. Ah wondered who ye were with."

"Ah met her when ah went for a skinny dip. At first, ah thought she was an apparition, it bein' Samhain today—ah thought the veil had thinned. Do me a favor and check in on her. Let me ken what ye garner about her."

"Ah'll check in on her, but ah'll pay nae heed to a stranger's life. 'Tis a boundary ah try mah best nae to cross. Mah life's complicated enough without addin' their troubles to mine."

I wandered out of Katrine's room, wondering where I'd sleep, and leaned against Maeve's doorway. She was studying less than fifty miles from where I lived in Massachusetts. What were the chances of that? I chose her room, in a way swapping places with her. I'd wake to the view of the sea and share her bedroom with her books. They weren't an imposition since they didn't snore. I sat on the edge of her bed and the mattress was firm underneath me. *What now?*

I suspected it was five or six hours earlier on the East Coast, which meant Ian was still asleep, and I had more time to collect my thoughts. On a Sunday, he slept until at least eight. After a breakfast of pancakes and an espresso, he'd read and finally unpack his suitcase from the prior week and do his laundry so he could pack for the coming trip.

It occurred to me that I hadn't come across a utility room and wondered where Katrine kept her washer and dryer. I poked around until I found the tiniest front load washer I'd ever seen, hidden in a hall closet. At first, I thought it accomplished both tasks, but it was filled with damp clothes. A plastic laundry basket with wooden clothespins scattered inside sat on top, indicating the method of drying. I welcomed the opportunity to feel useful for a few minutes as I ventured outside to discover her clothesline near the vegetable garden. Hanging her underwear was an act of intimacy that couldn't be avoided, given the alternative of moldy clothes.

Next, I harvested kale, carrots, and cauliflower. The last cherry tomatoes were too precious to lose through the holes in the laundry basket, so I pinched the linen of my shift dress to create a fold for them to nest in. Ignoring the little specks of dirt, I popped one in my mouth. It burst with the sweet memory of summer.

Later, I changed back into Fiona's clothes, planning an excursion into town to buy a journal, shoes, and the toothbrush I'd forgotten earlier. My bare feet were my primary concern. Katrine's wellies were fine for mucking the stalls but too hot for walking. For me, a journal was as essential as footwear. I pictured myself with it, sitting at Katrine's bay window, in the high-back chair, capturing everything I'd experienced on my odyssey since I'd left home. The irony that here on Iona, I'd likely become the *rumored woman* who washed up on shore wasn't lost on me.

With the rest of my cash in my back pocket, I'd nearly departed to check the church bulletin board for news of the clothing swap until second thoughts stopped me. Sunday was the wrong day to go unnoticed to church. I pictured it swarming with people, and people asked questions. The only conversation I wanted was between myself and the page.

My search for paper yielded a yellow legal pad in Brìghde's top desk drawer. As I descended the stairs, the phone rang and I ignored it, assuming it was unlikely to be Katrine again.

Seated by the bay window, with my pen poised above the page, I had every intention to write, but I stalled. Nothing came, no traction, no doorway in. I admonished myself. *Just start anywhere.* The longer I stared at the lined page, the more my leg bounced. My hand went to Faith's pendant, my mind to the shipwreck, and the memory of composing my vow. She advised me to speak it out loud daily, affirming my commitment to myself. This morning, adrift on the sea, I'd only recited the opening line before my planning mind stepped in.

As I wrote my vow for the first time, I said it aloud. "To grow wild by the sea." *Wild is one word to describe today.* "To slow down and listen to what I am sensing and feeling and to act on it with authenticity and integrity. To know if I am purring or growling inside and to let myself be known." *My body and my heart can guide me, not only my mind. Right now, I'm decidedly purring.* "To give voice to my longings and follow them to a place of belonging, be-longing." *What are my longings? Where will they lead me?* "To be in reciprocity with all my relations."

Two grayish-brown geese waddled in the lower pasture, sinking their orange beaks and heads into the grasses, pecking, and occasionally wiggling their white rumps. They appeared to pay no mind to one another. Still, they had each other for companionship. Where was the rest of their flock?

Witnessing them had planted the thought of something to nibble on, and while I wasn't exactly hungry, I sought the comfort of a scone. Afterward, I licked the tip of my index finger and dabbed up the crumbs from the plate. Jocelyn and I shared this habit. We joked we were members of the Clean Plate Club. The ache of loneliness I'd felt earlier reverberated in my chest. Even if I could call or email my friends, what would I say?

Sorry to be out of touch for six months, I've been shape-shifting in the underworld.

Just imagining the conversation left me feeling restless, disconnected, and adrift, like I had on the boat this morning. *Has Ian mentioned anything about my doppelgänger to my friends?* Reestablishing my connection with Ian remained my priority and I wagered if I woke him, he wouldn't mind.

My whole body started to tingle from my toes to my scalp. I felt like a hive of bees buzzing, and I paced in front of the bay window, rehearsing what I'd say to explain why I couldn't come home immediately. I felt his imminent disappointment and hesitated. *Waiting isn't going to make it any better.* My sweaty palms gripped the phone and I dialed zero for the operator.

"Guid day. How can ah help ye?

"I'd like to make a collect call to the United States, please, from Sarah O'Sullivan. The number is 978-555-0119." I circled in the tiny space around the coffee table.

"Hold the line, please."

I held my breath as I heard it ringing.

The operator returned, "Yer party is nae answerin'."

"Could you let it ring a bit longer?" but I heard it click over to my voice on the answering machine again. "Never mind, I'll try later." I hung up and sat, deflated. If only I could at least leave a message; however, with collect calls, the charges had to be accepted before any speaking was permitted.

Why isn't he at home?

---

1. Chelan Harkin, *Let Us Dance: The Stumble and Whirl With The Beloved*, (2021), 79–82.

CHAPTER 5

SECRETS

I RESTED MY OPEN hands on my lap like Forgiveness had shown me. Next, I rolled my shoulders back and, with each exhalation, let the mounting anxiety drain from my body. *I'm safe. I'm clothed and fed. I have a place to sleep.* My eyes took in the beauty that surrounded me. On the next inhalation, I held my breath until I felt my pulse beating in my chest and then exhaled, repeating the pattern until a calmness filled me. *I'm going to be okay. I've got this.*

What now? Glancing at the pad, I automatically read my vow, the way billboards irresistibly captured my attention. Reading was another form of comfort that transported me to new worlds. I followed my impulse upstairs to Maeve's library. My eyes traveled along the spines and scanned the top covers of the stacks: *The O'Brien Book of Irish Fairy Tales and Legends, Fiona's Luck, Celtic Tales,* until my attention landed on the tattered maroon leather cover, *The Celtic Twilight* by Y.B. Yeats. As I read the opening lines, each sentence baited me to read on. Yeats named Hope and Memory as beloved daughters, reminding me of my guides, Faith and Compassion. I wanted nothing more than to climb into his pages until I reached the back cover. He'd written on the wavelength I felt called to explore. I brought Yeats downstairs with me, to my newly found nest, and tucked into a high-back chair with a view.

Angus hesitated at Kat's front door. Normally, he'd walk in, but he rapped lightly and waited. When no one answered, he detoured to the barn, but found it empty, so he returned to the house, and knocked again, shifting from foot to foot, and then entered. The house felt peaceful. He glimpsed the crown of a brunette's head, tilted to the side of Kat's favorite chair by the bay window, and approached quietly.

He gawked at her profile, cemented to where he stood. He recognized her—she'd appeared as a recurring character in his night dreams. Until that moment, he'd assumed she was a fictitious woman, who only existed in his unconscious. She'd challenged him in his dreams, and he'd been undeniably attracted to her, but he typically woke before anything transpired between them.

Angus sat on the edge of the other chair and roughly rubbed his face, then leaned forward as if she whispered to him. She smelled like a blend of the barn, the briny sea, and sweet strawberries. Kat had said she thought she'd seen an apparition at first. Her sensing was accurate—*this woman ken how to move between the worlds.*

Since she'd already visited his inner world, he decided to slip into hers. Kat would have her request fulfilled after all. His claim of disinterest in a stranger's inner life had dissolved upon laying eyes on her. He felt as if his bones had become kindling, and seeing her lit a fire within him, offering Angus a warmth he'd not felt for years, not since his relationship with Daphne.

He knew from his dreams that her lids hid dark chocolate-colored eyes that melted him. The ridged channel that bridged her pert nose and thin upper lip moved ever so slightly as she breathed. Her bonnie looks were merely the packaging of what interested him most. She felt like a precious gift he wanted to receive, to unwrap, if only she'd give herself to him. A strand of auburn hair had fallen from her side part across her cheek. He didn't dare tuck it behind her ear and risk waking her.

Angus closed his eyes and concentrated within as he asked permission to venture forth. When his body felt light and loose like a dandelion globe surrendering its seeds to the winds, he understood permission had been granted. Had it been denied, he'd have been met with a stone wall. Instead, visions of a mermaid resting on a reef beside a massive hook welcomed him and he wondered if he'd entered her dreamtime. He opened his eyes and pushed back in the chair, as the vision shifted into darkness, as if flying over a barren landscape of blackened lava flows and a single dead tree. He witnessed an owl's clumsy landing on a branch and heard the tirade of a caged woman below.

He'd seen enough and released the vision. Angus had learned how to rein in his abilities so as not to garner unbidden information from strangers. He'd assure Kat that she'd made a wise choice by offering this stranger hospitality and tell her that sitting beside Sarah was similar to visiting the standing stones, where the veil thinned, and he simmered with insight. However, the nature of his visions would remain confidential. It was Sarah's story to tell in her own time. Angus hoped she'd speak of it with him and wondered if she'd recognize him upon waking.

Even though he was impatient to meet her, he chose not to wake her. He needed fresh air to collect himself and regain his balance. He stood and delicately draped Kat's afghan over her, leaving Yeats resting open in her lap. The man who'd knocked on Kat's door only moments ago, set in his routines, had already departed, but he remained transfixed by this intimate stranger, as if she'd thrown him a lifeline when he didn't even know he was drowning.

I awoke disoriented, blanketed by an unfamiliar cream-cabled afghan. Convinced I hadn't put it on myself, I stood swiftly, turning my back to the bay window, as a thump near my feet made me jump and squeal at the book that had fallen.

I called out, "Hello? Is anyone here?" No answer. By the looks of the fading light, it was near sunset. Converting the afghan into a cape, I headed for the stairs, calling out again, but a note beside the plate of scones caught my eye. Crumbs decorated the handwriting. *Who's been eating my scones?* I read, "Call if you need anything." The note was signed "Angus" and included a telephone number. *Who's Angus? The owner of the boxer shorts?*

At the foot of the stairs, I yelled, "Hello?" but only an uneasy silence followed. Ascending the stairs, I repeated, "Is anyone here? Hello. Hello?" I kept making noise the way I'd hike in bears' habitat, not wanting to surprise anyone, but it appeared I was alone.

I borrowed a flannel shirt from the coat hook and wellies to go check on the horses and shake off the creepy feeling. Upon entering the barn, a man's voice caused me to stop. His back was to me as he stroked Caim's neck and spoke in gentle tones. I debated the merits of revealing myself or letting him think I was still asleep. He wore a faded denim shirt with the sleeves rolled up. His wavy hair nearly blended with Caim's chestnut coloring. It partially covered his ears and my father would've said he needed a trim. Curiosity got the better of me. I wanted to see who Katrine shared her bed with and hoped to dodge any direct questions about myself.

I called out, "Hello."

He turned his clean-shaven profile toward me and exited the stall. "Did ye have yerself a guid shuteye? Ah noticed what ye were readin', and dinnae want to wake ye in case ye'r havin' yerself an important dream, communin' with the fairy folk. Ah covered ye as the temp's droppin' fast. Kat asked me to check in on ye. She wanted ye to have mah number in case ye needed some help."

He seemed as nervous as I was. "Thank you, Angus. I'm Sarah. I saw the note."

Maybe Katrine doesn't trust me as much as I thought. Who could blame her? If she has any intuition, and I'm sure she has plenty, she knew something wasn't adding up.

He closed Caim's stall door. "Ah'v put the horses in for ye and fed them. The mares' tails are indicatin' a front is comin' through. It'll be bringin' back the season's cold weather."

"What do mares' tails look like when a front comes through?"

Angus gestured with a swirl of his hand. "All wispy-like."

Caim's tail was perfectly still, but we were inside.

He started laughing. "Come on, follow me. Ah'll show 'em to ye." Angus walked outside and pointed to the clouds, which admittedly resembled horses' tails blowing in the wind. I chuckled at my mistake. "Let me help ye put on their rugs. Kat was frettin' the weather would take ye by surprise. They're her bairns now, and she'll nae sleep worryin' that they might be cold."

Trailing him into the barn, I asked, "Any word on Katrine's grand-child?"

Angus entered the tack room. "Nae, 'tis a waitin' game now. Ah gather Brìghde has a few more hours to go. Mah ewe's take at least five hours to dilate."

I assumed Brìghde wouldn't like being compared to a sheep. The upper shelves housed two stacks of six blankets, one pile in navy, the other purple. His height enabled him to remove the top two from each effortlessly and he handed me the purple ones, which had heft. I'd forgotten blankets had different weights for different purposes and felt grateful for his assistance.

"Tonight we'll put on their lightweight stable rugs,"—he raised it in his left hand—"but ah'll keep their waterproof ones down as ye'll be needin' them when ye turn them out in the mornin'. Tomorrow night, if the temperature drops, switch to the heavier stable rug." He indicated with a glance at the remaining ones on the shelf. 'Those have more fill for warmth." He slipped Caim's turnout blanket on the rod, and the metal clasps at the end of the straps clattered against the ground, then he draped her stable blanket temporarily over the stall door.

I followed his lead and hung Saorsa's turnout blanket. "Thanks so much. Katrine left out these details during our quick walk-through."

Angus reached for the lightweight blanket I still held. "Here, ah'll help ye." He brought it to Saorsa to smell, getting his approval. "Tonight we give ye a wee bit extra help stayin' warm. Yer winter coat is comin' in nicely." He cast the blanket over Saorsa. "Ye want to start higher on his neck, so ye'r slidin' it into place down here, goin' with the direction of his coat. He's more sensitive than most. Ah heard ye'r already on good terms with him. Let's keep it that way. He can be a handful when he wants to be."

I came under Saorsa's neck, patting him, overriding my self-consciousness about talking to him with Angus listening. "You're no trouble at all." I fastened the buckles at his chest. "I don't believe a word they say about you."

Angus reached under his belly for the strap and clipped it on the diagonal. I tried to hand the other one to him, but he'd already retrieved it. "Tomorrow, if ye see any rub spots on their chest, use some detanglin' spray. 'Tis good for their coats, too."

I secured the straps around Saorsa's back legs. Clearly Angus knew his way around the horses. "Which one do you ride?"

"Ah'm nae fond of mah feet leavin' the ground. Ah leave the ridin' to Kat. 'Tis one of the few things she's never been able to persuade me to try. It dinnae mean ah'm nae fond of them. We're fast friends, eye to eye." We blanketed Caim next. "Kat tells me ye just arrived on Iona."

My stomach clenched. "I did."

"She says ye live near Boston, where Maeve is studyin'. How long are ye on holiday for?"

Caim's neck was between us so he couldn't see me biting my lip. "I haven't bought my return ticket yet. I'm taking it a day at a time during my sabbatical."

"Are ye a teacher then?" He'd finished fastening the straps and came around the front of Caim, locking his eyes on mine.

I patted her neck to steady myself and held his gaze as if nothing was amiss. "Yes, I am. I took a break from teaching this fall and am delighted to have met Katrine and be able to help her out this week. Some of my best childhood memories are on horseback, and Saorsa's every girl's fantasy. He was a dream to ride today. You're missing out. I confess I hoped to ride again this afternoon, but as you know, I fell asleep."

Angus walked out of Caim's stall and stood beside the door, ready to slide it closed. "Ye did at that. Ye must have needed it as you dinnae even stir when ah covered ye. Would ye welcome company for dinner? Sunday nights, Kat and ah often eat together. Ah guess ah'v become a creature of habit."

I felt like a deer in the dark, trying to cross the road with headlights bearing down on me. "Perhaps another night. I've not thought about what I'd fix for dinner, and now that I know it's likely to rain, I'd like to clear the pasture of manure." I bypassed Angus exiting the stall, heading for the wheelbarrow and pitchfork.

I heard Caim's door rumble on its runners and the scrape of the latch. "Sarah, ah dinnae mean for ye to fix mah dinner. Ah'll make it for ye and show ye some hospitality. Mah house is down the road toward the beach. Ye went through mah fields with the sheep when ye rode this mornin'." He pointed toward the direction of it. "Ah saw ye both headin' off, chatterin' away."

I pushed the wheelbarrow forward, focused on my task, but Angus blocked my passage at the barn door. "Ah'm nae chef, but ah ken mah way around the kitchen. Dinner will be ready around seven o'clock. That'll give ye plenty of time to muck the fields. Ah'll be glad for the company while we wait for news of Brìghde and the wee one." He looked at the sky. "Ye'll be wantin' to gather the washin'."

"Good idea. I'd forgotten about that." Apparently, he wasn't taking no for an answer. "Is there something I can bring?"

"Ah'd suggest a dessert of Kat's scones. She's a mighty fine baker."

"Okay, I'll see you at seven with scones in hand."

As I traversed the pasture in search of horseshit, I contemplated what I'd say tonight that wouldn't smell like it. My best defense was a curious mind, and luckily, I had one of those. *I'll be the one asking questions about his farm, his sheep, and his life. What man doesn't love talking about himself?* But what if that didn't work? As Yeats said, 'What garment of belief will I weave of my story?' What if I simply told the truth and didn't care if anyone believed me?

Mucking was deeply satisfying in a straightforward way. I saw a pile of shit and shoveled it. I filled the wheelbarrow and dumped it. My life had become more complicated, and my next moves weren't so obvious.

I retrieved Katrine's clothes from the line and folded them, leaving them on her bed. As I brought the plastic bin back to the washer, I wondered why I hadn't found simple chores so gratifying before. *Why did I resist them?* My answer was immediate. *You thought they were beneath you.* True, my preference was to pay someone else to clean my house, but that option wasn't affordable on my budget. *So why approach my daily chores of laundry and dishes with resentment?* I was the one making myself miserable. *Yet another aspect of my old shit story to rewrite. My friends would be proud of me.* We referred to our old shit story as the one we continued to drag around even though we didn't like the roles we played nor the scripts we'd written for ourselves anymore.

I went downstairs to try Ian again, but my mind was still on my friends, Maggie, Jocelyn, and Veena. *How will I ever explain to them where I've been and the new story that's unfolding?* Not being able to answer that question easily set me pacing between the kitchen and the front door.

How can I speak openly about my journey with Faith without them thinking I've gone off the deep end? Yet, if I stay silent about it, I'm essentially lying, which also jeopardizes our friendship. If I tell them about it, but they never believe me, it will eventually cause a rift between us.

The more I thought about this double bind, where neither option was desirable, the more tightly wound I felt. Either I spoke my truth and risked how it changed our relationship or lied and jeopardized my relationship with myself. Both my blessing and my vows invoked authenticity because I strived to live congruently. I'd stopped in the kitchen beside the phone. *Maybe the question isn't if I tell them but when and how I voice it.*

We told each other everything: our hopes, our fears, our relationship struggles, our imagined futures, and our night dreams. We delved further into our unconscious together during our monthly Authentic Movement sessions[1]. We'd practiced witnessing each other and ourselves and experienced the transformational power of being seen and heard without judgment or projection. *Could they bear witness to my speaking about my journey with Faith without judgment? I could request they use that muscle as they listened to me.* When I put myself in their shoes, listening to me, as I shared my tale, my Skeptic stepped forward. *They're probably pissed at me for leaving without saying goodbye or reaching out in six months, and likely worried about me.* What had Ian mentioned about my prolonged absence? Would he have risked speaking truthfully or kept my secret?

For now, this dilemma was on hold. First, I needed to talk to Ian. I reached for the phone. *He's the one person I can speak freely with. Thank god he witnessed me disappear with Faith.*

I tried him again, but only spoke to the operator. He rarely flew on Sundays for client engagements because he'd rather wake at an ungodly hour Monday morning and take the first flight out. *Why isn't he sleeping in our bed? Don't go there, Sarah, choose Patience. Choose Faith.*

Staring into Fiona's closet, I contemplated my wardrobe options for dinner. *What are the chances Angus will recognize her clothes? If he does, he'll either think I've taken liberties, which I have, or suspect I don't have any clothes of my own, which I don't.* I decided Fiona's jeans weren't dirty enough to discard and sniffed my pits. Nervous sweat had left me ripe. A clean T-shirt was required.

Mermaids have no need for bathing. Just the thought of a soak in a bath followed by washing and conditioning my hair felt blissful. I ran my fingers through my hair, but they snagged in snarls before even reaching my ears.

The bath water was hot but not scalding. Goldilocks decided it was just right and stepped in. With knees bent, ankles against my butt, I submerged my upper body and let my head sink below the water. My hair spread out, floating on the surface like Medusa.

After scrubbing myself from head to toe, I emerged groggy. Maeve's bed tempted me to collapse upon it. What if I called and canceled? The abbey bell chimed once. Was it five-thirty or six-thirty? I was incredulous there was no clock in the kitchen or bedrooms. I confronted another one of my habits, relying on my phone to tell me the time.

Reluctantly, I dressed to stave off the chill and surveyed Maeve's closet for another layer. My attempt to extract the olive-green knit cable caused a jumble of sweaters to tumble. The cardigan lacked a tag, so I assumed it was handmade and rummaged through the ones at my feet, looking for one that was less precious, but someone had knit them all.

I put on my first choice, planning to admit I'd borrowed it if Angus noticed. I could truthfully say that I hadn't packed warm enough clothes. He didn't need to know I hadn't packed any. After folding her sweater collection, I stacked them on the shelf. It looked too orderly; she'd know she hadn't left it this way. Well, playing Goldilocks involved more than sleeping in the bed. Hopefully, Maeve wouldn't be a bear about it.

Dressed as a mix of Fiona and Maeve, I called Ian. Again, it only rang and rang. At least the operator told me the time. It was six-thirty-five, so I treated myself to a few pages from *The Celtic Twilight*.

---

1. Lee Fuller and Lynn Fuller, "About Authentic Movement and Witnessing," July 25, 2022, http://leeandlynnfuller.com/about-authentic-movement-and-witnessing.

CHAPTER 6

PAIRING

THE ABBEY BELL CHIMED as I knocked on Angus's front door. When he opened it, a waft of Italian spices and garlic greeted me.

"Guid evenin', Sarah. Ye cleaned up well."

He had, too, but I kept that appraisal to myself. His locks were still damp ringlets around his face. I coveted his blue cashmere sweater that made his eyes impossible to ignore.

"Wow, it smells delicious here." I offered him my precious scones, minus the one I'd saved for myself.

"Grand, thanks for sharin', and"—he gestured with his free hand—"come in."

I noticed his bare feet and kicked off Katrine's clogs. I hadn't thought to borrow socks, and the tiled entryway felt like walking on ice cubes. A shiver traveled up my legs.

"Can I help with anything?"

His house layout was similar to Katrine's. It lacked the extra seating area beyond the kitchen, and only two oversized leather chairs flanked the fire—not enough for a family. I followed him past the dinner table, already set for two.

Angus placed the scones on the counter beside an opened bottle of red wine. "Ye can finish preparing the garlic bread. The butter's already melted in the pan and 'tis waitin' to meet the bread. Ye'll find the aluminum lives in the drawer beside the oven."

I'd heard him say, "al u MINI um," like Maggie said it, not the American pronunciation of "uh loo muh nuhm." A pang of missing Maggie's English wit was swiftly replaced by the realization she'd be the last person to believe me. Veena would probably think I'd had a nervous breakdown—therapists can't help but see everyone through a mental health lens. Jocelyn had a poker face from years of consulting; she'd privately simmer with the news.

"We're havin' spaghetti with lamb red sauce. Ah hope ye'r nae a vegetarian." Angus's accent was easy enough to understand, and the deep resonance of his voice comforted me.

"No, I'm not. I'm an omnivore without much chance of converting." I suspected we were eating his lamb and pushed the thought of those sweet creatures out of my head. A lonely glass of red wine sat next to the bottle.

"If ye enjoy red wine, that glass 'tis yers. It'll drink well with the meal and ye'll keep me from drinkin' alone." He sipped from his glass.

"Thanks." I wanted to start asking questions of him before he had me on my back foot. "So, how long have you known Katrine?"

He stirred the spaghetti. "Since we were wee ones. She actually babysat me for a while. We laugh about that. We grew up and attended school together till she left for university. Her family home's on the south side of the island near mine. Ah suspect ye'll have a steady stream of visitors, comin' under the guise of checkin' on ye." He put the metal strainer in the sink. "If ye'r lucky, they'll bring more scones. Kat learned her bakin' from her mum. They both have a talent for it."

I hadn't expected visitors and crossed my arms as I considered it. When he strained the pasta, a cloud of steam billowed up toward his face.

"When Kieran was lost at sea, everyone took shifts tendin' to her and the bairns." He ran water over the pasta and gave it a shake. "The islanders helped raise them. We're all waitin' on the news of her first grandchild."

Angus put a generous mound of pasta on both plates and ladled sauce over them, handing me mine. Apparently, he thought I ate like a horse. He was right. I was starved. We sat across from one another at his kitchen table. When he reached for my hands, palms up, arms straddling his dinner, I mirrored his gesture, clasping his calloused fingers. My face flushed; I attributed it to being overdressed.

Angus said grace with his eyes cast down. "We're thankful for the bounty of food, for the wellspring of the land, and our island community. We ask that ye hold Brìghde, bringin' forth a healthy wee one and the miracle of life for us to behold." He gently pressured my fingers, and I felt a tiny jolt. He'd yet to let go of my hands.

Did he want me to add to the blessing? I felt his lingering touch beckoning me. Uncharacteristically, I said, "Amen." Even though he released his hold, something about him still tugged at me.

Angus echoed, "Amen" and placed his napkin in his lap. "Mah brother's the local priest. Every week for a year, a mass was offered in Kieran's name. Kat spent the first week at the abbey prayin' her heart out, and when her prayers weren't answered, she hasn't set foot in it again. She's forgiven Kieran for fishin' that day, but she's nae found her peace with God for takin' him so soon from her and the bairns. Ah suspect she may never. That woman kens how to nurse a grudge. Ah stay clear of her bad side."

While he spoke I took my first sip of wine, tasting its smooth fruit-forward finish. I'd expected to celebrate my return with Ian, uncorking a fabulous bottle from his cellar, not sitting across from a total stranger. When I realized Angus had waited for me to eat first, I hastily twirled too much spaghetti around my fork. Instead of starting over, I stuffed it all in my mouth, but a piece dangled, which I slurped up. He pointed to his chin as his amused eyes stared into mine. I dabbed red sauce off my face, glancing down to check if I'd splattered my borrowed clothes and felt relieved, they remained clean, but blushed uncontrollably again under his attentive eyes.

The spotlight needed to move off me. "It's hard to imagine how excruciating that time must have been for Katrine. She's fortunate to have family and such a tight-knit community to help her through. That's less common nowadays in America. We're often more isolated, having relocated for a job far from where we grew up. Add to that the sixty-plus-hour work week most folks log and there's not much time to volunteer in the community and make new ties."

Angus offered me the plate of garlic bread before he took a piece. "Iona's a small island. Everyone kens yer business even if ye want to keep it private. It only took a few hours for word to spread that Brìghde's gone into labor and ye'r watchin' Kat's horses with Mary's hip surgery th'morra. 'Tis a lot of local excitement for the island."

It didn't sound exciting, but I took his word for it. *Just imagine the rumors that would fly if they knew how I actually arrived.*

Angus continued. "Dinnae be surprised to have yer suppers made for ye this week. Ah figured ah'd best get on yer dance card early and warn ye. Ye did look a bit terrorized when ah asked ye to dinner. Ah'm nae that frightenin', am ah?"

Frightening was the last word I'd use to describe him. His square jawline gave him more of a rugged look, like the island's landscape. "Oh no, it's not you—I'm not very social. I was hoping to do some writing while I was here." I took another sip of wine. "Is there a polite way to decline these dinner invitations?"

"Ah suppose ye could beg off sayin' ye tend to write best in the evenin's. Folks will respect that. Perhaps ye can offer us a readin' before ye go. Will ye be writin' about Iona?"

My full mouth gave me a moment to collect my thoughts. "I imagine Iona may figure in. I'm not in the habit of sharing my work, and I don't call myself a writer since I've yet to be published. Mostly, I write to understand myself better, so it's intended to be private."

"Ah can respect yer privacy."

I hadn't meant to rebuff his requests, but he seemed affronted, so I continued. "The only time I've read my writing to strangers was during a writers' retreat with my all-time favorite author, Terry Tempest Williams. She gave us the assignment to write from a childhood memory and requested we read it aloud the next morning. Everyone had two minutes to share it. I stayed up practically the whole night editing my two-minute debut. I realized then how different writing is when I'm anticipating a reader. Honestly, for me, it breaks the flow. In the end, I doubt what I read was that much better than what I'd started with—I did, however, lose sleep over it."

"Ah'm nae familiar with this author. What's she written?"

"Oh my god, you've been missing out. She's my muse. Reading her books inspires me to write. Her voice is so embodied, and she inevitably reconnects me to what I care about. In her book *Refuge*, she interweaves a sense of place, specifically the Great Salt Lake, with her mother's dying of cancer. Her family was exposed to the fallout of the atomic bomb test in the fifties.

"She's a naturalist, an activist, and she's written to help save our wild spaces. She wrote *The Hour of Land* about America's national parks. It's about what you would expect, what the land means to us, but she brilliantly adds what people have forgotten—what we mean to the land. She understands this inherent reciprocity we have with the landscape." I took a bite before continuing. Angus had asked me the one question that would get me talking, like asking Ian about wine.

He spurred me on, "What else has she written?"

"Oh, the one about her mom was amazing. It's titled *When Women*

Were Birds; Fifty-Four Variations in Voice. The week before her mother died, she gifted Terry her lifetime collection of journals, asking her not to read them till after her death. Later, Terry discovered they were all blank. The book is about her memories of her mother, reflecting on what it means to have a voice, on what is seen and unseen, on faith."

Angus had finished half his meal. "Ah'm intrigued. Where do ye recommend ah start?" He went to top off my wine glass, but I put my hand over it, and he only refilled his own.

"Oh, that's tough. Terry Tempest Williams's books are all quite different. However, a central thread is how she connects her observations of the natural world or art to a deeply personal inner landscape of discovery. I'd suggest *Leap*. It was inspired by seeing Hieronymus Bosch's Triptych, *The Garden of Earthly Delights*, at the Museo Del Prado in Madrid. She returned daily to study it and based the whole book on it. Terry was raised as a Mormon, and a museum print of this triptych was thumbtacked to the bulletin board above where she slept. However, Terry's grandmother only hung two of the panels, the ones depicting *Heaven* and *Hell*. The middle panel, *Earthly Delights*, was missing. She dives into that painting, her life, and our society in ways that address issues of faith and passion. I've underlined countless passages and written in the margins. Reading *Leap*, and many of her other books, provokes a conversation within me."

He smiled. "That's high praise for an author. She sounds almost like a companion. What's the conversation ye'r havin' with her now? Ah'd like to listen in if ye let me."

The wine had loosened my tongue, so I didn't edit my response. "Well, one of the underlying questions in my life is about faith, and I don't mean the religious kind. There are so many other dimensions to it, like what it means to have faith in myself, or faith in another person, or faith in the world. My..." I hesitated, searching for a word to encapsulate my journey with Faith. "My sabbatical has been an exploration of these questions." I felt overheated and swept my hair to one side so the back of my neck cooled off.

Angus left the silence between us, like a bridge we'd yet to cross.

"I've not found this kind of faith in the four walls of a church or in its doctrine." When I stopped speaking, there was another spacious silence.

Having a conversation that included pauses for silence was rare. Ian was usually ready with what he wanted to say, often interrupting me, and I'd lose track of what was arising within me. Angus listened attentively, drawing me out of myself and the protective shell I typically showed the world. I couldn't help but feel he heard more than what I said.

He'd already finished his dinner. My plate had plenty left on it and I felt overexposed for talking more than I'd intended. I overloaded my fork again, but this time, I let it all go and started over, twirling less spaghetti, feeling protective of my borrowed clothes and self-conscious of Angus's eyes on me.

He smiled knowingly. "Ah look forward to readin' her body of work. Listenin' to yer love of her has me keen to experience it mahself."

I needed to re-engage my plan to have Angus do the talking, "Who's your favorite author?"

He stood to get seconds. "Ah, there are a few. Neil Gaiman consistently impresses me. Have ye read anything by him?"

"Nope, do tell." I hadn't anticipated enjoying myself so much. Angus shared Ian's knack for pairing the wine with the meal and I took another sip.

Angus returned to the table with an insignificant extra portion, a gesture to keep me company while I ate. "*American Gods,* ye'd probably like. 'Tis a fantasy of sorts. 'Tis complicated. One of the subplots is that various Gods immigrated to America with people who were devoted to them. However, as people shifted their attention to watchin' television, they neglected their Gods, and various power struggles ensued. 'Tis an interestin' commentary on 'screen life' even before we all became dependent on our mobiles. Ah dinnae ken if he meant to raise the alarm about the moral imperative of where we put our attention, but it struck me that way."

Attention is the holy grail. I heard the Hooks' wisdom and also thought of the connection to the nonprofit, The Center for Humane Technology's work around the attention economy, but those were topics for another time.[1] "Sounds intriguing. Can I borrow your copy?"

"Aye, ah can surface it for ye." He glanced at my clean plate and raised his goblet. "To inspirin' authors and powerful narratives that influence how we live our lives."

After we clinked glasses, his remained suspended as his eyes held mine. Something unspoken passed between us. It felt flirtatious, like an invitation to what I didn't dare consider. "To the chef, who cooks as well as he listens. Thank you for a lovely dinner."

"'Tis been mah pleasure. Will ye join me for scones and a whisky? Ah ken most people like tea with them, but at this hour ah find a whisky's best."

My mother had taught me to drink scotch. I hadn't strayed from it until I met Ian and started drinking wine. "Sure, I'll take a splash." While my belly was full, my taste buds didn't want to leave without enjoying one more sacred scone. Besides, the pairing enticed me as an apropos celebration to end my first day on Iona, especially since it had begun with Katrine's scones.

We cleared the table, and Angus washed while I dried. He gestured toward cabinets, so I knew where to put the dishes away. His home had no feminine touches, no flowers, or flowing curtains, and no photographs of children that I could see.

After drying his hands, he checked his cell phone. "Ah'll start a fire. We can enjoy it while we wait. Ah confess, ah'd hoped we'd have heard somethin' by now." He took out two short glasses and poured a generous amount into the first one.

"Um, less than that for me, please. So, do you have kids of your own?"

"Och aye, about fifty-six of them before lambin' season. But if ye'r askin' about the two-legged kind, nae one. Ah'v nae married the one ah love." His longing hung in the air. I wondered if he was referring to Katrine.

He offered me my glass and the plate of scones. I glanced around for the butter and his hand was on it before I mentioned wanting it. The leather seat with a slight view of the front door was more well-worn, so I chose the other one, putting the scones on the coffee table.

Angus sipped his whisky before placing it and the butter beside the scones. He pulled a butter knife from his back pocket and handed it to me. "Ah'm a chosen uncle to a whole brood of bairns, and that's been enough thus far. Ah, like ye, prefer mah own company. Solitude is a kind of medicine for me. Kat respects that."

When he went outside for peat logs, I picked up the book beside his chair. Why were men so interested in war? I surmised it was better to read about it than be in one. He returned and built the fire, but his broad back blocked my view of his technique. I'd never used peat before, and my skills with wood were beginner level at best.

The white and green-hued rounded stones resembled Katrine's fireplace. "The stones are unusual. Are they local?"

"Aye, 'tis green marble, unique to Iona, the sacred stone of St. Columba. 'Tis prized by island fishermen for protection, though Kieran and his friends apparently were nae carryin' a large enough piece for the storm they faced. 'Tis said to have supernatural powers, for healin' and to protect against shipwreck, fire, and miscarriage. Ah'd nae be surprised if there's a pebble in Kat's pocket now or if she slipped one in the bed with Brìghde. She still believes in its protection." The fire blazed, and he sat back in his chair. "'Tis always on her in one place or another. Did ye see the jewelry she's designed with them?"

I'd just taken a generous bite of my scone. Angus waited for me to swallow. "She'd offered to show me her studio after we rode, but the call came in, and there wasn't time." I hadn't realized I'd reached for Faith's necklace until his eyes rested upon it.

"That's a bonnie pendant."

"Thank you. It was a gift." My index finger continually traced the infinity symbol as if it were braille. "I'd love to see more of her work. Does she sell it at the local jewelry stores?" My mouth was dry, and I swallowed the scotch instead of asking for water. It heated a path down my throat.

"Aye, they carry it. Katrine, like most artists, 'tis nae much of a businesswoman. 'Tis good that her needs are simple, and that Maeve earned a full scholarship to study abroad."

"That makes all the difference. The cost of tuition is ludicrous in the States. Many graduates are saddled with student debt on top of having to find a way to make a living. The focus becomes how much money one can make, not necessarily having a fulfilling vocation and life."

"We forget that money's a currency, nae a God. Ah sense ye'r nae enthralled by it."

"Not so much. It's a necessity for sure, but I was fortunate to be raised with the privilege of having it, so it doesn't have the same hold on me. Having enough food or a place to sleep was never an issue." *Until today.* "My parents warned me about the lure of money, encouraging me to do what I love and trust the money would follow. It was sound advice I've chosen to live by. I don't make much, but it's enough, and most days, I'm grateful to be a teacher." *How did he get me talking again?*

I took my last swallow of scotch. "I think people forget to ask: How much is enough?" It was so easy to talk with Angus, to reveal aspects of myself that I typically hid from strangers. The fire warmed me on the outside; the whisky warmed me from the inside, creating a pleasant buzzing sensation under my skin.

As Angus held the whisky bottle and gestured to refill my glass, I said, "I'll be on my way. Thanks for helping with the horses' blankets and for a lovely dinner tonight. Please let me know what you hear about the baby's arrival."

Angus stood to walk me out. "Ah'll come by with news in the mornin'. Guid night, lass."

I left Katrine's plate and scones, but I couldn't so readily leave Angus behind. Some men were immediately handsome, while others became more attractive as you got to know them; Angus was both. In the barn, his rolled-up sleeves had revealed muscled forearms; working the farm kept him in shape. There wasn't a hint of gray in his hair. I guessed his age was closer to mine than to Katrine's. Good for her! Men usually dated younger women.

After my eyes adjusted to the moonlight, it lit my way. I'd inadvertently left the front door light on but detoured toward the barn, giving in to the magnetic pull to check on the horses before I tried reaching Ian again. Demeter came purring up to me, rubbing against my lower leg.

Upon entering the barn, only Saorsa was visible at first and I tensed for a moment, afraid of mishaps on my watch. I peered into the stall to see Caim lying down. "Hey girl, stay there and rest."

Saorsa nickered and brought his head out to greet me. I only stroked his face and kept the door between us to avoid covering Maeve's sweater with horse hairs.

"Goodnight, handsome. Sleep well."

Seeing the peat pile near the front door prompted me to carry a few in for a future fire. The last thing I wanted tonight was to smoke up Katrine's house with my failed attempts to stay warm. Perhaps Ian could give me tips about how to start it when we talked. I sat before an imagined fire for my next attempt to reach him.

When the phone rang and rang, I hung up, a bit relieved. Something had shifted in me. *My future will work its way out even if it doesn't go as planned.* I fetched Yeats for companionship and looked forward to the novelty of sleeping in a bed. When I crawled in, I intended to read, but my eyelids were drooping after only a page, demanding I surrender to sleep.

---

1. Center for Humane Technology, http://humanetech.com

CHAPTER 7

TENSIONS

IAN FORCED HIMSELF OUT of bed shortly after nine and left for a run. He wished he'd dunked in the ocean afterwards because when he arrived sweaty and eager for a shower he had to shoo housekeeping from his hotel room. After a late breakfast, he jogged to the pro shop to arrange a tee time. While he was eager to golf with Darren, he hoped the schedule was actually booked so his suspicions of racist treatment would be unfounded. If he secured a time, he wasn't sure what his next move was or what outcome he could hope for if he tried to address it. None of his deliberations had yielded a plan, so he decided to wing it.

He held the door as two women walked out. Upon entering, Ian glanced around, recognizing the same staff as yesterday and feeling relieved that the pro shop was empty. Like all conflict-avoidant people, Ian loathed making a scene. His toes clenched against the ground where he stood at the counter.

"Hey, what are the chances of playing eighteen holes today? Another guest and I are hoping to get out. We're flexible on timing." Ian fingered the ball mark in his pocket.

"That shouldn't be a problem. Let me check." The young man

scanned the computer screen. "I have a twosome leaving in about an hour—if you can be ready—or there's one later this afternoon at two p.m."

Damn, suspicion confirmed. "Excellent. Can I borrow your phone to check if he hasn't already made other plans? Strangely, when he stopped by yesterday morning, he was told the course was booked for today."

Ian took Darren's business card from his wallet and rang him. Darren answered and conferred with Janelle before opting for the earlier time. They agreed to meet at the range twenty minutes early to warm up. When Ian asked if he should raise his concerns, Darren left the decision to him but told him to leave his name out of it; he planned to enjoy his vacation.

Ian hung up and said, "We'll take the eleven-thirty slot." He placed his fingertips deliberately on the counter to prevent himself from fidgeting. "Huh, I wonder why he was told the course was booked today when there's clearly availability?"

"I'm not sure, sir. It's odd. We haven't had any cancellations today. Do you know who he spoke with?" He glanced over at his colleague.

"No, and I'd rather address this matter without involving him further. It's complicated." Ian hesitated and took a breath. He was in unfamiliar terrain now. "The guest is a Black man. Yesterday, after I finished my round, I witnessed an uncomfortable exchange between him and the cart attendant. The guest had been kept waiting, and the tone of voice used with him was less than respectful. I probably wouldn't have said anything if I hadn't happened to meet him again last night at dinner and learned it wasn't an isolated incident."

His thumb started tapping on the counter, and words kept tumbling out of his mouth. "Why was he given the last slot of the day when he came by yesterday morning, and why was he told there was no availability today? You may recall I came here yesterday afternoon, and you offered me a twosome to join. He could have played with us." Ian pressed more firmly on the counter to stop his thrumming. Sweat had formed in his armpits. The staff person said nothing. "It appears that a white man has ready access to the course, but a Black man is consistently denied." He'd escalated the conversation without any path toward resolution in sight.

The young man had stopped making eye contact. "I'm sorry, sir. I don't understand how that happened. I can assure you we treat everyone the same."

"I'd hoped for that, but this has shaken my confidence."

He averted his eyes from the computer screen to look again for his colleague. "I can offer you both a complimentary pass today by way of apology."

"I appreciate that, and we'll accept. However, what happens the next time another Black person wants access to the course? What are the chances they'll receive fair and respectful treatment?"

The young man cleared his throat. "I don't know, sir. I'm not sure how to address this."

Ian sighed. "Honestly, neither am I, but staying silent didn't feel like a worthy option. Look, I've enjoyed excellent service from you these past few days, *and* it's not lost on me that we are both white. I know this is a difficult conversation. Ask yourself for a moment: What if it were true that Black people are being denied access? What if these aren't isolated incidents? Better still, what if you were Black? Might you feel differently about it then?" Ian clenched and unclenched his fingers. "I'd suggest bringing it up at your next staff meeting."

Tension crackled in the air. The young man replied, "Ah, yes sir. Is there anything else I can help you with?"

"No, I'm set." Ian felt heavier than when he'd arrived, like he carried a boulder in his hands and had nowhere to put it, and no one even acknowledged it was there. It was as if invisible vice grips were clamped on his trapezius muscle. As Ian walked out, he looked to the other staff person, but the young man kept straightening shirts on their hangers.

The confrontation had accomplished nothing other than making everyone uncomfortable. Ian doubted anything would change unless he spoke with management. Even then, he suspected the boulder would go unacknowledged. Ian shook his arms by his sides, but he couldn't shake the undertow of the conversation. Had he only made matters worse?

By the time he'd reached his hotel room, he concluded it wasn't urgent. After his trip, he planned to send a note to management describing the facts of the incidents. He'd offer his opinion that these were not three isolated events but rather indicative of a pattern of racism. Ian knew that the more it remained undiscussable, the more it operated unchecked.

Given they were in the hospitality industry, creating a welcoming atmosphere for all people of color was essential. He'd include the contact information for a few consultants specializing in equity, diversity, and belonging. At the very least, he'd have signaled that their behaviors weren't going unnoticed.

Making people uncomfortable wasn't something Ian aspired to, but in this case, he couldn't keep his commitment to not be complicit in the inequities of racism and stay silent, even if it meant fumbling.

Context mattered; if Darren hadn't been Black, Ian might have written off the staff's behavior as only rude. However, experiencing that same staff treat him with respect and dismiss Darren's presence, offering Darren poor quality service, and denying his requests for access felt like he had a front row seat to racist actions. Unfortunately, witnessing it didn't mean he had the playbook for what to do next.

In ten minutes, Darren expected him at the range. First, he needed to find an outlet for this pent-up frustration, so he dropped to the floor to do push-ups.

The twosome they played with were practically a stand-up comedy routine, joking their lost ball, and Ian's sides hurt from laughing so hard. When Ian offered to introduce Darren to Scott, his golfing buddy in

Marin, Darren said, "Until we find a house to buy, all my free time is spoken for. Janelle wants us moved in and the nursery set up before the baby arrives."

"That's understandable. If you aren't already working with a real estate agent, Scott's wife, Lucy, is the best."

"Introduce us immediately. Janelle will be thrilled to have the connection. She's been scouring online listings but insists on experiencing the neighborhood before becoming attached to a house."

"Lucy and Scott work together. He runs his own construction company, so if you need a remodel done, he's your man. I'll introduce you both by email later."

Driving back from the golf course, Ian's thoughts were directed toward a nap until the car radio played Sarah's parents' song, "Unchained Melody." He listened anew to it, and his hunger for Sarah's touch swept in like a tornado.

The last time he'd heard it, he'd been with Sarah, riding in the back seat of a cab, on their final night in Rome. Earlier that day, she had done a spontaneous healing ritual for her relationship with her parents on the Spanish Steps. Over dinner, she'd spoken about what she'd witnessed growing up between them, a tension between dependence and independence, and how she wanted to live differently, more interdependently. She shared that she wanted to experience a love that held her freely.

Ian had missed his moment at that dinner to propose because he'd mistakenly thought he needed the ring. Now he had the ring but no Sarah.

She'd sung in the cab, while tightly holding his hand, and teared up. They both agreed it wasn't a fluke—it felt more like a blessing from beyond.

Hearing the song, Ian yearned to hold Sarah in his arms, to know she was safe. His loneliness had escalated from an ache to boring a hole in his chest. For the first few months he'd self-isolated because he didn't know what to say to others. However, his spirits had flatlined. As an extrovert, part of his renewal came from being with people.

Today, he'd welcomed being the fourth in a round of golf, and unlike Sarah, he chatted with passengers beside him on a flight. She hated making small talk, which tended to happen with strangers. Out in public, she dropped a shell around herself and crawled inside. *Where is she hiding now? Is she ever coming back?*

Ian called the front desk and asked for a wake-up call in thirty minutes. He didn't trust his body clock to only nap, not when it thought it was near midnight. After lowering the blinds, he lay down, hugging his pillow.

I awoke in the dark, still tired. *Is it morning yet?* I had no idea what time zone my body was in, only that I was in someone else's bed. A full-on case of cottonmouth thwarted my temptation to roll over and go back to sleep. The direction of the bathroom wasn't immediately obvious. As I moved to sit on the edge of the bed, my inner thigh muscles complained, reminding me of yesterday's ride. Moments later, the simple act of sitting down on the toilet made me reach for the counter in support. I'd probably regain my riding legs just in time to fly home.

Wrapped in Maeve's plush robe, I navigated the stairs, with each step ignoring my muscles' protests and focusing on my reward—the scone I'd held back for breakfast. Everything was better with scones. I warmed it in the toaster oven and slathered it with butter and jam, savoring every last bite.

In the dim morning light, no raindrops fell, so a morning ride remained possible. I dressed in yesterday's dirty clothes and hustled to the barn. After feeding the horses, I embarked on mucking and was maneuvering around Caim when I heard "Guid mornin'." I turned to see Angus's face pinched with concern.

"Oh no, what happened?"

He leaned against the stall door, his hands tucked in his front pockets. "There were complications. Brìghde needed a cesarean, but she and her lad are braw, dinna fash."

"Oh, that's a relief. For a moment there, I thought it was bad news."

"Nae, all's well enough. However, because Brìghde had surgery, she cannae pick up the wee one until she heals more. Kat dinnae want to ask ye to stay on. She thought it would be an imposition, but ah told her about our dinner last night and that ah suspected ye'd welcome the extra time."

The air between us felt layered with an underlying, unspoken conversation. Last night, at times, I'd sensed a secondary meaning in his words but dismissed it. Maybe he had noticed I'd dressed in borrowed clothes and shoes after all. He hadn't pried, but he hadn't missed anything, either. I turned my back to muck the last of Caim's manure and composed myself. When I pitched it in the wheelbarrow, it landed with a thud.

Angus's hands gripped its handles, ready to move it for me. "Kat wanted me to see yer face when ah asked. She kens ah can read people well."

In other words, he was politely letting me know I'd not escaped his notice. "Please tell Katrine you're right. I'd be happy to stay on for however long she needs." I felt like a cornered barn rat, and he was the cat.

Angus pushed the wheelbarrow aside. Neither Caim nor I moved toward the opening. He took a step into the stall under the guise of rubbing Caim's face. I leaned on the pitchfork and patted her hindquarters. *Why does his proximity unnerve me this morning?*

He took a half step toward me with his palm out for the pitchfork. I handed it over to him and swiftly turned to busy myself with the clasps on Caim's blanket. The pitchfork clattered into the barrow. Angus came behind me, and I smelled peppermint on his breath as he said, "While ah'm here, ah'll help ye switch their rugs."

His emphasis on "ah'm here" beside me sent a rush from my crotch to my rib cage. *If I didn't know better, I'd think he was flirting with me. Do I know better?* I didn't trust that my voice wouldn't betray my unease. My body was picking up and transmitting signals that unsettled me. This wasn't the morning I'd pictured.

While he undid the buckles at Caim's chest, he said, "'Tis already rainin'. Ah'm guessin' ye'll nae be havin' that ride ye had in mind this mornin'."

I still felt flustered. I'd not mentioned my plans to ride this morning, or had I? "No, the rain is making other plans for me. It turns out you were right about the weather. Any other forecasts you'd like to share?" My tone had an unintentional edge of sass to it. I hadn't meant to bait him like that. What I needed was for the conversation to return to solid ground.

"Hmm, ah'd say that ye slept well but woke early, thirsty from last night's whisky, and already had the last scone this morning, probably around the same time ah had mine, with tea, nae sugar. Ah imagine yer legs will appreciate a day off from ridin' since they're a wee bit sore and that ye'll spend the mornin' by the fire with Yeats. Ah'm jealous. Ye'll be cozy while ah'll be out in the drizzle mendin' mah fence."

Angus was under my skin, far too intimate in conversation and physical space for my comfort. I quipped, "Are you sure you just arrived and haven't been spying on me? You do have an uncanny way about you. Don't let me keep you from the rain." I'd pulled off Caim's blanket and struggled to fold it as I walked away. "I can take care of the horses. It's my job, after all."

The blanket still held Caim's body heat, and its weight offered me ballast. I heard his footsteps behind me again.

"Here, let me help ye with it. 'Tis easier sometimes with two people. Ah'm sorry if ah'v disturbed ye. Ah dinnae mean to. Ah'v been told ah can be unnervin'. Ah normally keep to mahself." He sounded genuinely contrite, like his tail was between his legs. "Ah enjoyed our dinner last night. Ah'm nae meanin' to scare ye off. On the contrary, ah was goin' to offer to show ye around the island if ye dinnae mind walkin' in the rain."

I ignored his offer to help and kept the blanket hugged to my chest, as if needing its layer of protection. *Did he sense that flicker of attraction I'd had a moment ago?* The last thing I wanted was some romantic involvement here, especially with someone who could easily be Katrine's beau.

"Okay. I mean, I'm okay. I mean, I don't mind the rain." *Shit, stop tripping on my words.* "Thanks for your offer to help. I can manage on my own." I left the disheveled blanket over the saddle in the tack room. "For the record, yes, Yeats is calling, and you forgot I was planning to walk into town."

"Ah gather ye've a bit of shoppin' ye want to do. There's only one clothin' store, but the clothin' swap happens the first Wednesday of the month at the abbey. Between the two, ye can find what ye need."

Damn, he knows. How does he know? How many people know if he knows? I suspected at least Katrine. The rumor mill had likely spread across the island about my arrival. "Angus, you've got a remarkable ability to know things I've not spoken. What else do you perceive?"

He tossed the rain blanket over Caim. "Ah can read some better than others—ye'r like an open book to me. Ah gather ye'll be here for quite a spell. Though sometimes what ah sense and what ah hope for can get intermingled." He fastened Caim's chest buckle but left the rest to me.

"Ah'll be on mah way—leave ye to tend to Saorsa. He's nae the only one who's taken a likin' to ye." He tipped his head and turned to go. "Enjoy yer mornin'." While he walked away, he spoke without turning around. "Come by for lunch or a walk if ye like. Ye ken where ah live."

Angus felt the air crackle between them. He sensed Sarah had felt it too, but she resisted him because she thought he was taken. She was partially right. He'd been taken by her. She wasn't willing to flirt with him yet, but she'd sparked when he'd come up behind her, offering his help with Caim's blanket. Later, he'd set the record straight when she wasn't so concerned about asserting her independence.

Hearing Sarah agree to stay on longer than a week brought a mix of gratitude and relief that his prediction had proved correct. The extra time would give her a chance to be at ease around him, to speak honestly about her arrival and her recent past. She guarded her heart when she was awake. He'd hoped that she'd recognize him, the way he had her, but she showed no sign of it. He sensed she resisted their familiarity though, rationally dismissing him as a stranger.

Okay, that does it. He is flirting, and he's leaving the ball in my court. I wanted to know if he and Katrine were romantically involved and the nature of their relationship. *Though, why do I need to know? Nothing is going to happen—nothing more.* After all, Ian was in my life. At least, I assumed he still was. I wished he'd answer my damn calls.

Can Angus see my past, too? I'd heard of people having the sight but hadn't believed it. Didn't they need to have an article of clothing or a piece of jewelry to know intimate details about you? I fingered my pendant, attempting to call upon Faith, but it felt like she'd decided to offer me the silent treatment.

Saorsa accompanied me as I removed every tidbit of manure from his stall. "So, you and I are going to have more time together. That suits me. Though, I'm sorry for the way it unfolded. It's another reminder that life is more unpredictable than I care to admit."

I pushed the wheelbarrow to the aisle and stroked Saorsa's neck before unclipping his blanket at his chest. "You don't care that I washed up here in an oarless skiff, and if Angus knows, it doesn't seem to bother him. Is that kind of thing commonplace around here?" I unfastened the side clips and the ones around his hind legs. "And that's the tamest part of the story, which I imagine is ill-advised to admit to." I pulled the front edge halfway down to fold it while it remained on his back. "See, I've got this. All that's needed is a little ingenuity and patience.

"Accepting help isn't one of my strengths. It flies in the face of my fierce independence." I hung the blanket over the rod and ignored that it dragged on the floor since his stall door would remain open.

When I swung the rain blanket over Saorsa, it landed upside down. I pulled it off and tried again. "Besides, taking care of you is my job and it's my only job at the moment."

I could hardly sit still and read or write now. I needed to talk to Ian, hear his voice, and get my bearings.

Demeter sat on the trunk, swishing flies with her tail, and watching me. The steady rain didn't bother Saorsa or Caim as they left to munch grass for their second breakfast.

Without a raincoat, I jogged to the house and went straight to the phone. I didn't care if Ian was asleep.

The operator said, "Guid mornin'."

"I'd like to place a collect call…" I repeated the vital information only to hear it ring and ring and ring, so I hung up before she told me what I already knew—he wasn't home. The thought of him sleeping in someone else's bed nagged at me.

I recalled lying beside him in bed. If I wanted to cuddle, I'd rob him of the pillow he clutched and scooch my back up against him so he'd hold me instead. He'd wake enough to enfold me in his arms and bleat a soft sound as he snuggled in with me.

Determined to reach him, I dialed his cell number, planning to pay Katrine back, but all I heard was a pre-recorded woman's voice telling me the mailbox was full and couldn't accept messages. *Seriously?! Ian, how am I supposed to reach you? Carrier pigeon?* My writer's block temporarily lifted as I put my pen to page, and I decided to send an overnight letter.

Angus hadn't predicted my trip to the post office. *Maybe I'm being paranoid. He probably figures all women love clothes shopping, and doesn't know I hate it.* He must have counted the scones to know I'd held one back. It was a good guess that I'd wake thirsty and sore from riding. *I'm definitely being paranoid.*

I left the raincoat hood down as I walked to the post office, letting the drizzle dampen my hair. Walking past the abbey, the unique stone cross with an inner circle at the intersection of the horizontal and vertical lines shifted my focus of attention.

The bell chimed, seven, eight, and I waited for nine, but it was silent. *Shit*—the post office didn't open for another hour, so I wandered into the grocery store. There was a lined legal pad, and I bought it to replace the one I'd borrowed.

I walked south from the harbor along the road with an unobstructed view of the sea. The houses on the other side of the street enjoyed the same vistas and I wondered if remoteness made them more affordable. Similar-sized starter homes with no sea view, despite the name of the town I lived in, Manchester-by-the-Sea, sold for appalling prices. Buying a home felt out of reach on my teacher's salary and even more distant now that I'd lost my job.

One Sunday last winter, I spent hours on Zillow virtually touring homes. I'd get my hopes up after reading the brief descriptions, only to have them dashed upon scanning the photos. Everything in my price range bordered on being a teardown or a massive "fixer-upper." I couldn't picture buying a house project and living in a construction zone while we remodeled.

I pushed my concerns of home buying to the back burner to make room for my current priority, reaching Ian. The unexpected difficulty of it gnawed at my peace of mind. I reminded myself that nothing in the last twenty-four hours had gone as expected, nor for that matter, had my previous six months with Faith. My journey hadn't followed any plans, and it all turned out better than anything I could have imagined. *What if I'm learning to welcome surprises?*

What if Ian books a flight after reading my note before he's even talked to me?

I extracted his note from my back pocket and started to add a postscript about not making plans to come until we spoke, but mid-sentence I had second thoughts. After re-reading the note, I realized the tone of the postscript was terrible, and crumpled it up before stuffing it in my front pocket.

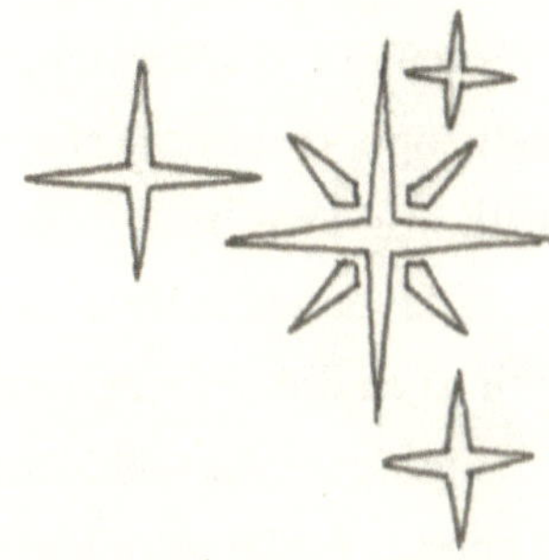

CHAPTER 8
RE-CONNECTIONS

I WANDERED SOUTH UNTIL I heard the church bell ring again, signaling it was time to turn around and a reminder that I'd never said my vow or blessing this morning. I surveyed the deserted shoreline for a place that called to me where I could rest my head and bow. Unlike sunbathers, I had no blanket to use that claimed my spot, no intermediary between me and the sand, other than my layer of clothing.

I knelt upon the beach and reached beyond my knees, touching both index fingers to the damp sand and simultaneously traced an arc around me, ending at my feet, enclosing myself in a temporary oval. I spoke aloud: "Amidst it all, I carve out sacred time and space to bow to the Great Mystery," and bowed with arms outstretched. When I rested my forehead on the sand, its grit greeted me, calling me immediately into my skin, and I imagined a few particles might stick there, anointing me on my third eye. My hair cascaded around my face, and a sprinkling of rain landed lightly, like kisses, all over the backs of my hands. Faith's pendant dangled against my chin.

The anxiety of not connecting with Ian drained away on my out breaths, followed by the nervousness Angus stirred in me with his presence. I exhaled more deeply, using my belly muscles to squeeze out all the old air. My rib cage expanded naturally like bellows, filling my lungs with new oxygen. After several more deep breaths, I felt the weight of my body supported by the ground. At that moment, I didn't need to hold anything—I was being held.

The sounds of steady waves lapping at the shore accompanied me with its endless rhythm, recalibrating me. Gratitude for the sea's companionship swelled within me. I pressed my palms into the sand, offering a squeeze of acknowledgment like the way one ends an embrace with a loved one. I sat up, filled with peacefulness, and spoke my vow aloud.

"To grow wild by the sea.
To slow down and listen
to what I'm sensing and feeling and
to act on it with authenticity and integrity.
To know if I am purring or growling inside, and
to let myself be known.
To give voice to my longings,
and follow them to a place of belonging, be-longing.
To be in reciprocity with all my relations."

The slow rise of waves rolled their way toward shore and moved back out. It was as if the sea was listening, carrying my vow into the great expanse. I imagined my spoken words floating along the outgoing waves and selected the crest of one wave to watch till it disappeared. *Will my sentences continue to float like hieroglyphics on papyrus, or will they sink to the sea floor?*

Only twenty-four hours ago, I drifted toward this island in the skiff, in no hurry to greet it, making plans to keep myself safe, to find an immediate return to the States, but now I felt settled here on this spot of sand, on this foreign land in the sea, in ways I'd never felt before at *home.*

My longing to ride daily, to write, to read, and even to learn silver-making were all within reach. *Can I let myself follow these longings?* Wasn't that the advice the Hooks had offered me—as a manta ray swam past—to follow my longings? I felt grateful I'd listened then. When I'd joined the ray, we had a magical encounter of somersaulting.

Recalling the ray's playfulness reawakened my sense of awe and wonder, offering a stark contrast to my tendency to worry about the future. *What if I spend more time following my longings and less time listening to my anxiety? How, then, will my life be different? Iona can be my practice field. Now is the time to learn what it means to live in accordance with my vow, to follow my longing to a place of belonging—be-longing.* My thumb rubbed against the backside of my ring.

White shorebirds scurried with their beaks in the sand, pecking their breakfast. Occasionally, they'd all flutter off at once, becoming an undulating white cloud. Suddenly, they'd switch direction in unison, temporarily disappearing from view and then reappearing moments later somewhere else, offering an illusion on the horizon. They mesmerized me. *What do I see? What am I blind to? What's mysteriously shifting in my life's direction? How important are the things I cannot see or even hear?*

I spoke my blessing aloud, sitting cross-legged with my hands resting on my knees, palms open, and fingers gently bent, cupping emptiness, receiving what was invisibly being offered, and invoking the qualities I wanted in my days, in my life. This morning, two stanzas spoke more loudly to me, nudging me to pay closer attention. The first was—*May I become patient with uncertainty, welcoming mystery into my life as my beloved dance partner, letting go of expectations, even with disappointment, to honor what is authentic in the moment.*

Mystery shrouded my disappearance and reappearance, blowing all my expectations about what was possible out of the water. Journeying through my inner landscape had introduced me to aspects of myself I'd been estranged from, inviting a new rapport and nascent ways of relating to the world and, yes, maybe even learning to dance with mystery.

The other line of my blessing that stood out—*May my experience be one of reciprocity with all my relations.*

My relations—*who are they?* I'd already expanded the definition to include four-legged, winged, and finned creatures. I felt the circle widening again to include the elements, the ocean, the rain, the sand on the beach, the wind, and even fire.

Spitting rain had dampened my hair but not soaked it—instead it curled with more bounce, the way it had in Kauai's humidity. I wiped the sand off my hands and composed a new note to Ian, writing from my heart. It flowed from a place of connection within, offering kindness. I tore it off the pad and folded it, slipping it in my back pocket. Standing, I swept the sand from my backside and forehead. The shorebirds flew off again and I silently bid them goodbye, along with the patch of beach that had hosted me, before strolling back along the sea.

When I arrived at the post office, the door was propped open. An elderly man behind the counter said, "Guid mornin'. How can ah help ye?"

"Do you have an overnight envelope to post a letter?"

"Indeed, we do, but that'll cost ye dearly. Is it pure urgent? It never arrives overnight. Ye must add at least a day to leave here and be processed on the mainland. Is America the destination?"

"Yes, Massachusetts."

"Och aye, a first-class stamp will get it there in about a week. Are ye sure ye dinnae want to save yer dosh?"

I assumed dosh was money. Ian might be away for work and not even receive the letter for days. My immediate needs for my *own* underwear, shoes, and clothes asserted themselves. "Thanks for your advice. A stamp will do."

He passed me a stamp, and I handed him a five-pound note.

He said, "Now ye can buy yerself somethin' bonnie," as he handed me my change.

I pocketed it and thanked him again. *Does everyone know I need to buy clothes, or merely assume that's what women do with their extra money?* Being the first customer in the shops felt unwise; it garnered too much undesired attention. Instead, the red phone booth beckoned. *Ian, will you answer me this time?* The operator's voice sounded familiar, but still no Ian, only the sound of our phone as it rang and rang and rang. This time I waited for her to tell me what I knew, so as not to be rude again. I thanked her and said goodbye. It wasn't her fault I couldn't make the connection.

Clothes shopping was a chore I dreaded, and the shop's racks offered slim pickings. My narrow feet meant the chances of finding a fit were even slimmer, but fortunately I found hiking boots with ankle support that actually fit, plus a white V-neck T-shirt, a package of bikini under-wear, and a bra. I only tried on the boots, willing the other items to fit.

When I spilled my selections on the counter, the cashier asked, "Is there anythin' else ye'll need?"

I shook my head. "No thanks, I'm set."

"What about socks? We have some crakin' wool ones here. They'll keep yer feet taps aff even when they're soakin' drookit, and the ones we carry have nae seams."

I guessed she was extolling the properties of wool to keep my feet warm when wet, and her sales pitch worked. "Yes, a pair of socks."

"We have them on special now. Buy one, and the second pair's half off."

"Yes, I'll take two." She was an exceedingly good saleswoman, and I wondered if she owned the shop. I selected the darker colors, figuring I'd wear them more than once between washings, and swallowed hard as I handed over a wad of cash. Since the shoe box wouldn't fit in my bag and I didn't want to carry it, I told her, "I don't need the box."

All her prior warmth disappeared with her glare as she handed me my change and said, "The cardboard recyclin' bin 'tis at the end of the road near the ferry dock."

I took my box. The green recycling dumpster sat a stone's throw from the phone booth. Trying Ian again felt futile. I'd invested my hopes in the post and needed an envelope. The gift shop's card rack displayed locally made cards with photos of island scenes. The one I selected resembled the boat I'd arrived in, and it cost me another three pounds. Handing over the last of my coins left me feeling nearly broke, only a few more colorful bills remained. While slipping Ian's note inside the card, and addressing the envelope, I prayed it reached him, and then dropped it in the red pillar box.

The abbey's bell rang once, signaling it was half past the hour as I walked to Katrine's. The question was half past what? Had it rung while I shopped to signal the hour, and I missed it? My grip on time had loosened when I traveled with Faith. It had been months since I'd felt compressed and hopelessly behind in accomplishing my to-do list. Time with Faith had become spacious, or was it that I'd learned to be present?

When I entered the driveway, the horses whinnied and trotted to the fence line. "I've nothing for you. Apparently, you don't mind the rain one bit." Their mud-splattered blankets wouldn't fit in Katrine's minuscule washer. Angus might know how she cleaned them.

I glanced toward his property before going inside. *Do I want to walk with him this afternoon?* My heart made a little jump of anticipation at the thought. After swapping Katrine's wellies for my boots, I went back outside, scuffing them in mud to diminish their new look. Anxiety stirred my insides. I'd depleted most of my cash with no prospects of earning more, and no access to my bank accounts. Having no proof of my identity had its limitations, but also felt oddly freeing, like the thrill of skinny dipping with nothing insulating my skin from contact with the silky water.

Hunger sent me back to the kitchen where I discovered a three-quarters full jar of peanut butter. I spread it on some zucchini bread and called it lunch. A dozen eggs assured me I could stretch my food supply beyond a week. I grabbed my purchases, eager to wear my own underwear and T-shirt. Thankfully, they both fit. The V-neck displayed my pendant perfectly. My ears still felt naked without earrings, but borrowing adornments felt wrong and risky.

The notion of reading *The Celtic Twilight* beside the fire sounded wonderfully cozy, except I had no clue how to make one. Besides, it made me a sitting duck for visitors who asked questions I wanted to dodge. I opted to be a moving target, so I borrowed a flannel shirt, Katrine's raincoat, and laced up my new hiking boots, eager to explore more of the island by myself. This morning's exchange with Angus had left me in a tangle and the beach was my nearest trusted friend; it would sort me out.

I strolled down the road to where Katrine and I had ridden. Just offshore, a remarkable outcropping of black rocks arranged in a near-perfect circle caught my attention. Had they been underwater yesterday?

Riding Saorsa had me so spellbound that I barely noticed anything else. My spine tingled again with déjà vu. Faith had shown that circle of stones to me when she covered my eyes. She'd known I'd land here.

As a child, before dozing off to sleep, a collage of images sometimes appeared. I had no idea what they meant or why they'd stopped appearing, and never connected them to my real life. The only time it had happened again as an adult was the day Faith had visited our home. Earlier that afternoon I'd uncharacteristically napped, and before I'd drifted off to sleep, the images had returned. That night, she implied it was one of the communication channels we shared. I tried to recall what images I'd seen—*had they been prescient?*

I closed my eyes and racked my memory the way I fished for a dream in the morning, reeling in a hazy shape. As soon as I remembered the outline of the owl on a bare branch, the image of a curled-up fox came swiftly. How could I have known then that I'd shape-shift into these creatures, gaining a new perspective and learning to trust my instinctual nature? The stone bridge I'd seen that spanned a verdant valley was exactly like the one I'd crossed with Faith, the same bridge where the beat of my heart became a rhythm that I danced to, swaying and moving between the opposing forces I struggled to reconcile. I'd come to think of that as "the dance of opposites." Curiosity had startled me out of it. I opened my eyes. *The images that day were prescient.*

The last image had been of a toppled queen chess piece. On that Saturday morning in May, my altar had a new configuration. Somebody had moved my queen chess piece from the periphery to the center. That night, Faith admitted to relocating it. I assumed it was still standing now since Ian wouldn't knock it over.

While my feet walked along the beach, my mind wandered. *Could cultivating my relationship with Faith bring back this gift of sight? If so, I'd welcome it—but what if I saw something tragic?* The thought spooked me, and my certainty faltered. As someone who wrestled with an inflated sense of responsibility, and how to respond with care without carrying around everyone's pain, knowing the future might incapacitate me. *It would give merit to my worries, which already have too much sway. It could hijack my ability to be present.* The only way I'd been able to tame my anxiety before was by telling myself I can't know the future. Until this moment, I'd believed that.

Well, I also believed in the Pygmalion Effect, in self-fulfilling prophecies.[1] As a high school teacher, I choose to believe in my student's abilities to learn and succeed, even when their behaviors might indicate otherwise. For some of my students, I wondered if I was the only adult who saw them in this light.

The experience of meeting my Cynic, face-to-face, even with Faith beside me, had disturbed me. Her conviction that nothing good ever happens had a way of sucking the oxygen out of the air and any remaining vibrancy with it. Faith stated she was her archenemy, and it made sense—a cynic outright rejected believing in possibility. Cynics stayed stuck in their pessimistic view of the world, a kind of cop-out. I welcomed critical thinking, knowing a healthy skepticism was sometimes warranted. It kept me safe. I had no need to banish my Skeptic. *I probably couldn't, anyway. My Cynic, however, I can live without. I know her line all too well: "Don't be a fucking idiot."* She'd tried to protect me from making a fool of myself, but she'd almost usurped a leading role in my life, the one I'd now reserved for Faith.

Maybe not knowing the future is a blessing. It offers me more freedom to be in the present. But would having a sense of the future impact my ability to influence it? Hmm—now I'm edging into the territory of fate, and I don't know what I believe about that. How does Angus cope with the glimpses he sees?

Angus mentioned he often kept to himself. Had it isolated him? He let slip that I'd be here for a spell. *How long is a spell? A few weeks, a few months?* I started to let myself entertain the possibility of staying on Iona beyond the week or two Katrine needed me. Ian likely wouldn't tolerate more time apart, *that is, if he's not already in another relationship.*

Iona's landscape cast its own spell on me. Even though it was cloudy, it didn't appear drab without sunlight. Occasional patches of honey-colored lichen swathed the shore stones. Clusters of tiny, lemon-yellow snail shells washed up near my feet. I selected one and checked to see if it was empty before tucking it in my pocket as a reminder to go slow. The steady pace of the waves lapping on shore instilled a sense of reliability.

I recalled my accomplishments over the last twenty-four hours: shelter, food, clothing, cash, and even my own hiking boots and underwear. *Let's not forget the two gorgeous horses in my care, available to ride when the weather cooperates, plus the attention of an equally dreamy man. Not bad for my re-entry. I'm gonna be okay.*

The sand's expansiveness felt like a canvas of possibility. Using a stick, I drew a circle and divided it into quarters with a vertical and horizontal line. Next, I gathered up the nearby abundance of pebbles, dried seaweed, and shells, and then plunked down beside my pile of riches to slowly arrange them in the quadrants, creating a mandala.

A line from my blessing arose as I admired the creation, "*May each day unfold with a priority on creative expression, sensing the deeper currents, and stalking the sacred.*" The mandala symbolized more than a creative act; it reminded me that creativity involved resourcefulness with what was present and that presence itself was a resource. My Peaceful Warrior accompanied me, protecting space for me to slow down and listen. This pace made it easier to make more conscious choices and offered time to tend to the sacred. My self-imposed urgency typically drove me to react. In contrast, this slower tempo felt more like the pace of embodied presence that I invoked in my blessings—allowing my heart, mind, body, and spirit to align.

Gazing at the mandala inspired me to create an altar in Maeve's bedroom. Faith's pendant, along with the yellow snail shell would adorn it. My journey with Faith offered me an opportunity to live into my blessing, to welcome mystery as my beloved dance partner. My blessing, like the conversation with the Hooks, invited me to shed the scripts and roles that no longer served me.

Why did I have to compose my vow before I returned? What if my arrival on Iona was my chance to live into my vow and integrate my underworld odyssey into this world? My vow felt similar, yet different from my blessing, but I couldn't grasp the distinction; they both oriented me when I started to feel overwhelmed and confused, reminding me of how I chose to live.

I spoke a line of my blessing out loud. "May I become patient with uncertainty, welcoming mystery into my life as my beloved dance partner, letting go of expectations—" I stopped mid-sentence when it clicked just how often my expectations misled me, preventing me from acknowledging the riches before me and causing me to ignore the present moment, and maybe even miss how the "Great Mystery" moved in my life as my beloved.

I want to learn to dance with Great Mystery in the lead. Landing here on Iona, not returning immediately to Massachusetts, to Ian, had wisdom in it. It prevented me from confusing the notion of the beloved with a partner, with Ian, or anybody for that matter. *What if I'm being asked to understand that no person can carry this longing for me?* Part of me wanted to lay back in the sand with my arms stretched wide, receiving the expanse of that notion, but sitting had turned me into a sponge. My jeans felt damp, and my body shivered.

I welcomed the third image Faith had shared: fire. The promise of drying out beside its warmth spurred me back toward Katrine's house. However, thoughts of filling her home with smoke pestered me. Instead of dwelling on my fears, I returned to my blessing and recited it to the rain and sea, "May my connection with the elements re-source my days, cultivating courage, faith, and a sense of belonging, be-longing." I substituted the word "conversation" in place of "connection" and repeated the new version. "May my conversation with the elements re-source my days, cultivating courage, faith, and a sense of belonging, be-longing." My conversation with the rain, however, felt a bit too intimate at this point. I was ready for shelter and eager for fire.

Gusts of wind bent the tall grasses in waves, imitating the rippled surface of the ocean. It blew through Fiona's jeans, despite their skin-tight nature. I jogged to the gate secured with a mint green rope, and since Angus remained out of sight, I slipped into his pasture to take a shortcut.

The unexpected stirring I'd felt toward him rushed in again as I crossed his land. I didn't want to acknowledge it nor act on it. I wanted to know where things stood with Ian. Not knowing how much longer before we'd speak only intensified my impatience. *So much for befriending mystery.* I put myself in Ian's shoes—he'd been waiting six months not knowing when we'd connect. At least, I hoped he'd waited.

A barking Australian shepherd bounded toward me. I paused to let him smell my hand, but he continued voicing his opinion that I didn't belong here. He'd ignored Katrine and me when we rode through yesterday. A sharp whistle silenced him. He ran toward the barn and Angus, who'd already begun striding toward me. My chest fluttered, and I felt my pulse thudding against my rib cage. *Get it together, Sarah.* After a deep breath, I walked toward him, feigning more confidence than I had.

---

1. Ben Solomon, "The Pygmalion Effect: Communicating High Expectations," *Edutopia*, December 16, 2014, Edutopia.org/blog/Pygmalion-effect-communicating-higher-expectations-ben-solomon.

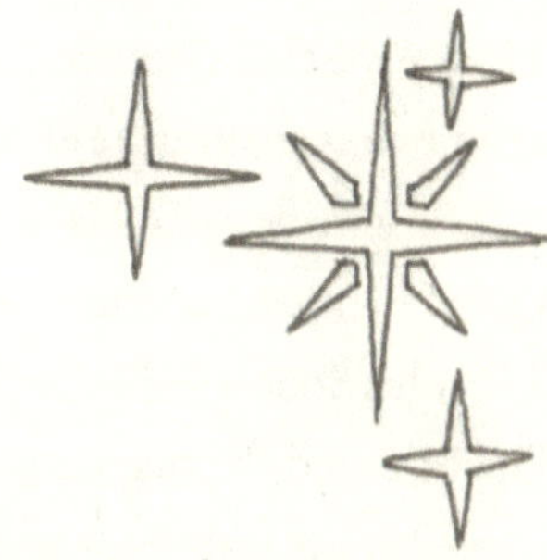

CHAPTER 9

FIRE

"YE VENTURED OUT, AH see. Do ye fancy a cuppa to warm up by the fire?"

A fire is exactly what I want. Did he know that? "That'd be lovely. Thanks." *Especially since I haven't had the confidence to start one myself.*

We walked side by side, with his well-heeled dog. I asked, "How big is this island? It feels like I could traverse it in a day."

Angus hand-signaled for the dog to return to the flock. "That ye' could lass, maybe twice. 'Tis only five kilometers long, about half that wide. The trick is some places are nae that passable. Ye need a bit of local knowledge to nae get yer new boots stuck in a bog."

I'd hoped he wouldn't notice. "Yeah, I was lucky to find them in my size. They fit like a glove."

"Ye'll still be wantin' to break them in to avoid blisters by tradin' off with yer older shoes for a wee bit."

Is he baiting me? Does he know I don't have any other shoes here? "I wanted something to keep my feet dry. I've never heard of this brand, but it's all the store carried. The limited selection was kinda refreshing. Back home at REI, there's a wall of hiking shoes and about six different brands, each with three or four different styles. It's overkill."

We'd arrived at his door, and he opened it for me to go in first. "'Tis a bloody waste of resources, is what 'tis! Dinnae get me started. We've all become consumers instead of citizens."

His tone declared his irritation and I imagined a rant might follow. While I bent over and unlaced my new boots, drops fell from my hood all over his floor. He'd kicked off his stained work boots but not moved. When I stood, he helped me remove my coat, hanging it on a peg. I shivered again, but not from the cold.

"A wee nip will take the chill out of yer bones."

Scones and scotch, tea and scotch. Does he have it with his eggs in the morning?

He took a flask from his back jeans pocket and held it up. "'Tis a way of life here, ah'll admit to that, but ah dinnae have it at breakfast."

Damn, there he goes again, reading my mind. "How do you do that? Respond to what I'm thinking before I say it."

"Ah dinnae ken any other way. Usually ah'm better at holdin' mah silence, but somethin' in me wants to be honest with ye. Do ye mind that much?"

"It's a bit unnerving, but I've had some recent practice with this. You remind me of a dear friend I've been missing. I never expected it to happen with another person. Then again, there's been a lot of things I've not expected lately."

He handed me his flask with the top already off. I took a nip, and a fire lit in my mouth. Angus raised one of his eyebrows as he took it back from me. "Well, that's a sign ye'r alive, nae a programmed machine. Ah fancy the unexpected, but it dinnae show itself that often on the farm. Everythin' plays out within a more predictable range—until ye washed up on these shores."

I wanted to believe that was a turn of phrase, that he didn't know I arrived in the hull of a boat. "A fire sounds fabulous right about now.

I've never tried to light peat before, and I'm afraid to smoke up Katrine's home. Can you teach me?"

"That'd be mah pleasure. There's a trick to coaxin' a good fire from yer peat. 'Tis all in the way ye stack it. It requires the right amount of air around it, freedom to breathe."

Don't we all? We'd safely switched to another topic, leaving how I arrived on the island alone, at least for now. His home wasn't any warmer inside than it was outside, and my borrowed flannel shirt felt insufficient. I wrapped my arms around me, rubbing my palms on my forearms to kindle some heat and followed behind him. Angus bent beside his fireplace that currently only held charred bits and gray ashes. I noticed a pail filled with little, odd-shaped oval cups.

"Ye take these starters"—he displayed the cut-up cardboard egg boxes he held in his hands, each section partly filled with wax and a wick. "They're a wee bit unusual but work like a charm. Ye place them on either side of yer center brick, two in front and two more in back. Then add two more peat logs next to the starters, so ye have a row of three across. Frame them with two more peat bricks in front and back. Now ye'v built yer square base, and last ye tip two more to the center." He propped them up like a triangle. "The trick is lightin' the cups. When ye do it, begin with the back ones." He struck the four-inch-long matchstick. "Lass, hand me another one of those starters from the pail."

I offered it to him, but instead of taking it from me, his hand gripped mine from below. The heat of his palm infused the back of my hand as he lit the cup. A rush of warmth escalated through my body as if he'd lit me, too.

"We melt down old candle bits combined with shredded cardboard and use it as fire starters."

I had a hard time paying attention to anything but the effect of his touch.

"Ye can see they light easily and burn slowly."

Is he talking about me or the starter?

"'Tis about time for me to make another batch. Ye can help if ye like—'tis more enjoyable with two." He bent toward my hand to blow out the flame, maintaining eye contact with me. His breath on the inside of my wrist sent an involuntary tremor up my arm. As he slowly withdrew his fingers, his calluses brushed over my knuckles, triggering a fierce heat that jettisoned through my chest, up my neck, and across my cheeks. I had no way to hide and he undoubtedly knew the effect he was having on me. Thankfully, he briefly turned his attention to the fireplace, disassembled it all, and said, "Now ye give it a go."

Angus only moved slightly out of the way, making us more intimate than we'd have normally stood or sat together. Distracted by his presence, I reached for the middle brick, and the next step gradually occurred to me: *four egg cups on either side—two more bricks in parallel and two more, one in front and back for my base.* I propped the last two peat bricks against one another, forming a tent and leaving access to the starter cups.

He handed me the matches. "Go ahead. She should light up nicely. She might smoke a bit at first, dinna fash—'tis normal, till she properly catches fire."

Again, I couldn't help but wonder if he meant me or the fire, noting he spoke of it as female, the way Katrine referred to the sea as if she were a woman. *Are any elements masculine?* I lit the back starters first and progressed to the others, tossing the used matchstick into the fireplace. "How's that?"

He stared at me as he said, "She's bonnie. Give her a moment to catch fire." I turned away from him to watch the tendrils of smoke, already feeling ablaze. My body responded to his flirtations, even if my mind struggled to ignore him.

The scent of the peat differed from wood fires, more like sticking your face in a pile of moss; it offered a grounding, earthy smell. I waited for him to move before toasting my backside, fearing standing so close before him, lest my hips have a mind of their own. Just the thought of it made me quiver. I heard him in the kitchen and wondered how his tea ritual varied from Katrine's. She hadn't added whisky to her tray, at least not in the morning.

He called from the kitchen. "Are ye peckish?"

It sounded like an odd question, as if I was a hen. "No. I'm good." Then I realized he'd asked if I was hungry, which I was, but my stomach hadn't announced its demands yet. He brought bread and cheese on a wooden cutting board with a bright yellow mustard called Coleman's that reminded me of the snail shell in my pocket. Angus returned with a tray containing a jar of honey, his flask, and two teacups. Inside the cup floated a slice of lemon pierced by cloves, and a cinnamon stick. He liberally poured a splash of whisky into both cups before handing me one.

"Ye can sweeten it to yer tastes. A proper hot toddy will drive out the chill."

I dipped one of the spoons into the creamed honey and mixed it into my cup. The steam delayed me from taking my first sip, and I ignored the temptation to taste the honey plain.

"Go ahead. The honey's produced on the island, and ye'll nae find any better. Plus, 'tis a natural antibiotic, but it loses its healin' properties when ye put it in boilin' hot tea. Medicinally speakin', ye'r advised to have it plain."

Oh my god, does he sense all the impulses I'm repressing? I sampled the honey; it tasted like ambrosia with a hint of wildflowers. Angus grinned.

"It doesn't seem fair that you can read me like an open book, but you remain a mystery to me. What's going on in there? Do you know the expression, 'A penny for your thoughts?'" The cup warmed my hands, but sipping the hot toddy scalded my tongue.

"Mah thoughts will cost ye more than a penny—ah can promise ye that. Are ye sure ye want to hear them?"

My pulse quickened and forewarned, I decided to ease in. "Let's start with the cheaper ones and see what I can afford. I'm on a budget during this trip. My teacher's salary doesn't stretch very far."

He sipped his hot toddy. "Och aye, ah imagine it dinnae since ye had to forego the more expensive travel fare."

Ignoring his reference to my arrival, I asked, "Have you traveled much?"

Angus leaned forward and poked at the fire. "Aye, ah'v been to various countries, mostly due to destination weddings—ah believe that's the word for them. They're bloody expensive, but ah'v seen places ah'd nae normally have chosen."

"Really, like where?"

"Southern Italy, where the food was intoxicatin'. Mah time there was too short. Ah hope to return as an Italian in mah next life. Hawaii, but ah'd nae return. The sun is unkind to a fair skinned Scotsman."

My mind drifted from the conversation. *That's where Ian is, Kauai—on the vacation we planned together. He still went without me, or with someone else. No wonder he's not answering the home phone.*

"It seems ah'v lost ye to the islands. Have ye been to Hawaii?"

I attempted to make my mind a blank slate but couldn't. Answering his question, I pictured Ian in Kauai. "I have. I love swimming there, but I've got to hide from the sun. As a kid, did you have those watercolor sets called 'paint by numbers?' I call it tanning by numbers. At the beginning of a trip, I start at 50 SPF and work my way down slowly to 30 SPF. Inevitably, I miss a spot and a red lobster patch appears that itches and later peels. The SPF shirts are a godsend. I can snorkel without burning my backside." I prattled on trying to think about snorkeling, not Ian. *Why don't I want him to know about Ian? What makes me think he doesn't already?* "Where else would you want to travel?"

"Ah prefer the cooler climates, hiking in the landscapes of Aotearoa or Iceland is on mah wish list."

I noted he used the Māori name for New Zealand. "Me too. I've only flown over Iceland, and the views from above are stunning. They run this promotional inflight video on Icelandair—which is brilliant because they have a captive audience staring at the screen. After watching it, I'd wished I'd arranged the stopover they wisely let travelers do for free." I sipped at my hot toddy that was already half gone. *Time to slow down and eat something.* "Is there a movie theater on the island?"

"Aye of sorts. We convert the community center occasionally to show pictures, but 'tis never what's recent. Netflix tends to have us watchin' from our livin' rooms. 'Tis nae the same as the big screen but offers a distraction when ye need it."

"Do you have internet at your house?"

"Och aye. Ah dinnae live in the Dark Ages. Ah like to be able to video chat mah friends overseas. Kat's bound to get it now that her grandchild is born. She'll be wantin' to have a chance to see the wee one."

"Could I borrow your computer to send a message? I didn't bring my laptop or cell, and I'm missing the ease of communication with the time change."

Angus put down his hot toddy. "Sure, ye can log on whenever ye like. Do ye want to message someone now? 'Tis right over there." He pointed to his kitchen table.

I'd nearly finished my hot toddy and felt suddenly overheated. "Thanks. It'll only take a moment." I shed my flannel shirt as I walked toward his computer, draping it over the chair's back before sitting down. "It's locked."

Angus didn't get up. "The passcode is Daphne2018 exclamation point, only the D's capital."

It worked. I couldn't help but ask, "Who's Daphne?"

"The one ah scared away."

"Angus, you're not a frightening man. On the contrary, you're quite the gentleman." I looked at him, but he wasn't looking at me for a change as he stared into the fire.

"She dinnae want to live with what ah ken about her, especially when she was nae tellin' it to me herself. Ah could nae read her all the time, but it proved too much for her. Ah cannae lie and pretend ah dinnae ken what ah did. It came between us." Angus stood, picked up his cup, and walked directly toward me at the kitchen table. "Bein' with me requires total honesty. Many folks say they want that, but the truth is, they dinnae. As ye said, 'tis unnervin." He tapped the kitchen table gently twice and picked up my teacup. "Kat reminds me 'tis a lot to ask of any woman, but ah cannae live otherwise. Ah suspect nor can ye." His eyes locked on mine.

Angus was calling me out, gently telling me he knew all about me. And if he did, Katrine probably did, too. A surprising sense of relief arrived with the thought of coming clean. "I've been trying to reach my partner, Ian, but he's not answering because he's traveling. I just realized he's in Kauai, and I promised to let him know when I arrived safely. I'm sure he's worried about me. I'd love to include Katrine's telephone number so he can call me, but I don't have it. Can you tell me in a moment?"

I logged on to my Gmail account and was daunted by the volume of unread messages. Ignoring them, I quickly typed an email to Ian with the subject line: "I'm back, call me."

Aloha Ian,

I'm back—long story. I'm not at home, and I suspect you aren't either because I've been trying to reach you. I'm sorry I missed our trip to Kauai. I'm on a different is-land—Iona—off the coast of Scotland. I'm okay, better than okay—I'm fabulous and currently house and horse-sitting for a few weeks. I'm borrowing a neighbor's computer and can't check for messages that often, so don't expect a swift reply. Call me. Her number is...

I was about to say, "I'm ready," when Angus rattled off the number as he moved about the kitchen. I typed it in and repeated it back.

Please don't leave a voicemail because I can't check messages and won't know you've called. I can't wait to talk to you and share my mind-blowing adventure. What did you tell everyone about my absence? I can't believe I've been gone six months.

I hope you're well. FYI your voicemail is full! I couldn't leave a message.
Love you and miss you,
—Sarah

I hit send. "What's the time difference between here and Kauai?"

"They're eleven hours behind us. 'Tis only three in the mornin' there now. Ye'll be needin' to call on patience before ye speak with him. Ye'r free to use mah computer whenever ye like. Ah ken what 'tis like to have a loved one at a distance." Angus walked over and handed me a refreshed hot toddy. I felt more at ease taking it, knowing I really wasn't hiding anything from him. He asked, "A pence for yer thoughts?"

"Do I need to say them aloud?" I blew on the hot toddy, stalling for time, knowing it was too hot to enjoy.

"Aye, plus ah like the sound of yer voice. Come sit back by the fire with me and let me get to ken ye the old fashioned way." He paused while my imagination made the leap he inferred. "Ah meant talkin'—Sarah, nothin's goin' to happen between us that ye dinnae want. Dinna fash, ye'r safe with me. Ah ken ye'v quite a tale to share."

I did—an unbelievable one. We returned to our seats by the fireplace, and I felt lightheaded as I reached for some bread and cheese, liberally spreading the mustard.

"Ye'll be wantin' to go lightly on that. She's as spicy as she is bright."

Again, with the feminine pronouns. "I like it spicy."

He half-smiled. "Ah like spicy, too, with a bit of sass and spirit mixed in."

I took my first bite and realized Angus wasn't just flirting. It carried the heat of wasabi and my sinuses burned, making me wince as my eyes watered.

He laughed. "Ah warned ye."

"You did. My bad. I'm guessing you know how I arrived on Iona. Does Katrine know, too?"

He tore off two pieces of bread, preparing both with ample mustard and cheese. "Och aye, ah told Kat, but she already suspected. Ye arrived on Samhain, a sacred day when the veil thins. She saw ye walkin' in the early mornin' wearin' that linen shift dress, and at first, she thought she was seein' a ghost. Later, there was a rumor ye'd washed up in one of the fairy crafts. There's many a rumor bein' told about ye on Iona. She called me to check up on ye, and to check ye out."

He took a bite and let his words sink in. "Kat's nae afraid of ye. She thinks ye'r a blessin'. She may nae attend mass, but it dinnae mean she dinnae believe in the Greater Mystery, as she's fond of callin' God. She keeps to the old ways. Kat's mum and her grandma were wisdom keepers of Celtic tradition. 'Tis in her soul, and her daughter Maeve's uncanny in her ways." He finished the first piece of bread and brushed his hands on his jeans. "Now ah have a confession to make."

Angus leaned forward toward me. "When ah saw ye had fallen asleep readin' *Celtic Twilight,* ah could nae help but sit with ye and watch ye for a spell. Part of yer recent past came to me. Ye'v had quite a journey, and ah'd be honored if ye trusted me enough to share it. Ah dinnae mean to pry."

His head tilted down, but he still looked sheepishly at me. I'd settled into the corner of his wonderfully oversize leather chair with my knees up. Unsure what to say, I held my tongue.

"Ah doubt there'll be many ye can share this tale with aside from me and Kat. Ah dinnae ken if this will bring ye closer together or drive a wedge between ye and yer man. The unexplainable has a way of seperatin' folks who cannae bide with it, as it did with Daphne and me. Ah dinnae love her any less, but she's nae at ease around me, and that's nae way to live yer life."

Until this moment, I hadn't worried about how Ian would relate to my journey. He'd joked that Rumored Woman was a good witch when she appeared in our bedroom that night, and he'd let me go. *Well, maybe he didn't have a choice in that. I didn't exactly ask for permission.*

"Ah dinnae think 'tis an accident ye find yerself on Iona. Nor that ye met Kat on the very day Brìghde went into labor, and Mary had broken her hip. She dinnae let anyone ride Saorsa, except he took to ye, and he takes to very few." He settled back in his chair, extending his long legs and resting his elbows on the armrest.

I couldn't read his mind, but his open body language gave me cues. I sighed. "It's a relief not to try and dodge questions that should be easy to answer. It's all been wild, otherworldly, and yet wonderful." I felt uncorked. "As for speaking about it, I don't even know where to start. I tried to write about it today, but it's hard to describe in words. It's still reverberating in me. I know it happened"—I fondled Faith's pendant—"but at the same time, it doesn't seem real or even possible."

He handed me the other bread and cheese he'd made like a peace offering and I took it.

"Dinnae try so hard, dinnae fight yer own story. Let's sit a spell. If ye conjure the memories in yer mind, it'll be like offerin' me a picture show. If ah have questions, ah'll ask ye."

Sipping on my hot toddy, I stared into the fire and replayed the night that Rumored Woman appeared in our bedroom. Angus repositioned himself in his chair. I turned to see his face flush at that R-rated scene; I should have started later.

He said, "Dinnae skip any parts on account of me. Ah'm enjoyin' mahself. Ye'r a bonnie lass, and ah'll nae lie about mah attraction to ye. Ah ken ye feel it, too. We can sort that out later—let's get back to yer journey."

Now all our cards are on the table. So, he's admitting to flirting, and he knows I'm drawn to him. I felt released from trying to keep myself hidden. *There's freedom in being myself. Why do I ever try to be otherwise?*

I longed to be back with Faith and closed my eyes to conjure her. The image of the stone bridge spanning the verdant valley arose. Faith had led me there and encouraged me to cross it. I stood up before the fireplace to fully embody the memory of pausing midway on the bridge, letting my hands spaciously hold the invisible ball of light that pulsed between my palms. Slowly, I began to sway, shifting my weight from foot to foot. My hands followed, tracing an infinity path that stretched from hip to hip. The more I repeated this simple gesture, the stronger the sensation grew until my whole body vibrated.

When a new movement arose, it surprised me. My hands slowly separated, my left palm turned down, as if it rested on a geyser of energy that floated it upward, and my right palm turned up and received a waterfall of energy that pressed it downward. My hands continued to interact with an invisible current until an impulse arose to bring them back in front of me. I rotated both palms to face one another, and slowly moved them toward each other. The air between my hands felt dense and thick. With bent elbows I held my staggered hands so my left fingertips almost touched the center of my right palm, and the base of my left hand hovered near my right wrist. They nested without touching—forming an elongated S-shape of an oscillation, a channel of energy rippling through them. Then I bent my wrists upward, as my hands traveled skyward in a slithering motion like a snake until my bent elbows straightened and my hands traveled above my head. Waves of heat blanketed my chest. I opened my eyes and let my hands drop to my sides. The fire's flickering flames relentlessly darted up and disappeared, reminiscent of the energy that had moved within me.

I recognized Angus's living room, but moments ago, I'd been elsewhere. *I can still go there. It's still unfolding—it's not over.* It felt as if all my cells were on high alert as I turned around toward Angus. His look beckoned me to continue, but I sat instead, because it felt like more than enough for now. He didn't press me.

I reached for the cup to have something tangible to hold in my hands.

"Thank ye, lass, yer movements continue to reverberate in me, as if a channel has been delicately carved, creating more fluidity. Ah feel spacious and awakened inside."

"Me too. It started as my memory, but it shifted to something new." I took a sip of the hot toddy to return more fully into the room.

"There's an aliveness to ye that's mesmerizin'."

I knew what Angus meant. At times, as a witness in Authentic Movement, a mover captivated me such that I couldn't pry my eyes away, awaiting her next gesture and letting it stir me even as I sat still. Sometimes, if she spoke of her movements, I'd discover the congruence between what I felt as a witness and what she experienced as a mover.

"Do you think I can learn to read you the way you read me?"

"Likely, if ye want to experiment with it."

I leaned forward. "Can you teach me?"

He shrugged. "Perhaps. 'Tis a degree of intimacy ah dinnae ken either ye or ah'm ready for yet. Let me sleep on it."

I already trusted Angus's judgment. His grounded presence felt similar to Ian's. My thirst sent me to the kitchen for a glass of water and my antsiness kept me from sitting down again. Rationally, I knew Ian was sleeping, but I still hoped for a message. "Do you mind if I recheck my email?"

Angus gestured toward the table. "Help yourself." He ran his fingers through his hair, intertwining them at the back of his head, leaving his elbows in the air. "Ah'd very much like to spend more time with ye as ye recall yer journey. What ye'r wrestlin' with is familiar to me. Ye may find it odd, but ah'm already benefitin' from yer experience." He let his arm fall back to his side.

"I'd like that." I bent over the back of the dining chair, resting my forearms on Katrine's flannel shirt, as I checked for Ian's reply. Nothing. He'd likely sleep until at least seven, leaving me several more hours to practice patience. I felt unburdened, realizing how much my secrecy had been weighing me down. Maybe it had even contributed to my writer's block. I put on Katrine's shirt and gathered my hair out from under the collar as I walked to the door to put on my new boots. "Thanks for the fire and hot toddy"—I paused at the threshold—"and for listening."

Angus walked toward me at the door. I sensed him not wanting our time to end. "Can ah help ye with the horses later?"

"Sure."

His face broke into a smile that rivaled the sun.

CHAPTER 10

SUNSET

Tɪʟᴛɪɴɢ ᴍʏ ʜᴇᴀᴅ ᴛᴏ the sky, a few raindrops kissed my cheeks. As I neared Katrine's pasture, Saorsa and Caim raised their heads from eating grass, and their ears aimed forward. I clucked for them and they sauntered toward the fence when they saw me offering a handful of longer grasses that grew beyond their mowing reach. They lipped it gently from my open palms as I chatted with them across the top rail.

"Katrine will be back soon enough—meanwhile, I've got you covered. She has her first grandchild, so you'll have to get used to being second and third fiddle. I don't know the little one's name yet. I'm sure you'll meet him. Patience for dinner. We all need to practice patience."

After drawing a hot bath, I slipped in, eager to conjure my time as a mermaid. I'd begun to sense another realm when the phone startled me. Eager to speak with Ian, I scrambled to wrap myself in a towel. The ringing came from Katrine's bedroom.

"Hello." My tone was anxious.

"Hello Sarah, ah'm ah disturbin' ye?"

"No, Katrine, I was only delayed getting out of the tub. How is Brìghde and your grandson?"

"That's what ah'm callin' ye about. They're well, thanks for askin'. But ah need to stay on longer than ah planned. Will that be okay with ye? Did Angus speak with ye about it already?"

"Yes, it's my pleasure to stay on. Everything's fine here. Honestly, there's no place I'd rather be."

"Guid, ah appreciate it. Ah'll be back later in the week to get a few things ah forgot, but only for the day. Likely ah'll stay on another week until her mother-in-law arrives. Soon Brìghde will be beggin' for mah return. Ah ken they dinnae get along so well, but ah can hardly keep her away much longer. There's only one guest room, and ah'v had squatters' rights."

I chuckled. "I'm set here. Angus has seen to it, and the horses have their rightful rugs on. He helped me decipher them yesterday." I tried my best Scottish accent, "Dinna fash." It was Katrine's turn to chuckle. "I never heard what your grandson's name is?"

"Finlay, they're callin' him Finn. 'Tis a powerful name, but ah think he'll live into it. Ah'll let ye towel yerself off properly. Thanks again—ye'r a Godsend. Bye for now."

A little puddle had formed on her bedroom floor where I'd stood. I mopped it swiftly with my towel, along with the trail of drips I'd left in my hasty exit. Sinking back into the tub, the water wasn't warm enough anymore to chase off the chill. I turned on the hot tap, letting a waterfall of warmth cascade over my feet. My legs moved together and apart, making chaotic little waves that collided with the tub walls until the heat engulfed me.

After turning off the tap, a few final drips from the faucet punctuated the silence. I closed my eyes and floated my left hand, palm down, on the water's surface, and my right hand, palm up, rested below the surface. I waited in silence and asked for guidance, wondering if I'd see or hear my guides. As my hands moved slowly toward each other, the water caressed my skin. I rotated my wrists, thumbs up, and lifted my hands out of the water, as I brought them closer together, palms staggered without touching, in the same gesture that had arisen before Angus's fireplace. I opened my eyes to see the channel of space between my hands that resembled a sine curve. I felt a current of energy pass between my palms and undulate beyond me. I had no explanation for it, nor did I need one. I simply enjoyed the mysterious sensation.

I turned both palms upward, still cupped, in the gesture of receiving that Forgiveness had shown me before we swam as mermaids together. Was the tingling sensation from the water's heat or my attention? Rotating them to face each other, I sensed an invisible, pulsing ball of energy. Slowly, I moved them wider apart without the sensation dissipating. The tangibility of my hands had a way of convincing me that they were real. *What if the intangible, invisible energy between my hands is equally real and at least as important? It's so easy to dismiss the things I cannot see as inconsequential, yet my growing sense is that they are of utmost significance.*

I let my hands rest on my thighs. Clear impulses had directed the motion of my body, even as I questioned where that guidance came from. Receiving guidance required me to be open and vulnerable. *Could I learn to reframe vulnerability as a strength, not a weakness, and remain receptive?* I sensed a new rhythm entering my life, shaping me, and teaching me the power of surrender.

My students' ability to learn correlated with their willingness to meet me with an open mind. When they didn't, it spelled drudgery for everyone. Even knowing how essential receptivity is for learning in my professional life as a teacher, I'd failed to translate it into my personal life. The state of my body, heart, and mind could more often be described as closed off, disconnected, or absent, especially when I dismissed my longings.

The abbey bell chimed, and I counted two, three, four. *Time is another invisibility.* In theory, there were always sixty minutes in an hour.

Sometimes, those minutes moved faster, and at other times they dragged. I couldn't hasten time any more than I could rush the season.

I pulled the drain and stepped out, using my damp, rough towel to briskly dry off. While I dressed, I contemplated borrowing a different sweater, but the olive-green cable hung over the desk chair. *Proximity wins.*

I realized I didn't want that to be true in the case of Ian. *Shared history wins.*

However, I'd begun sharing my recent history with Angus before telling Ian. *Cumulative history wins.*

Why am I trying to qualify this? It's a sweater, for god sake. Just put it on and stop making it more complicated.

What if Ian called when Angus was here? Given his radar, he'd know I preferred to be alone. It'd be awkward, but we'd deal with it.

My radar told me Ian had intended to propose in Kauai. I wasn't ready and felt grateful to have more time to sort myself out. The blue sapphire on my right hand sparkled at me. After my divorce, I'd repurposed the gem from my wedding ring to symbolize my commitment to myself. When I approved the red wax design of the setting, the parallel curved lines that enfolded the oval sapphire appealed to me. The gem was tucked into one corner where the curve rounded down. After it was cast in gold, it resembled a stylized Egyptian eye. Now, this blue eye looked back at me and reminded me of the vows I'd spoken at the end of my time with Faith, to grow wild by the sea. *I'm ready to lean into my instinctual, sensual nature, claiming this rather than sidelining it. That's the kind of life I choose to create.* I'd worn this ring for three years but never thought to invoke a vow to myself. A ritual bubbled up inside me. The time had come to sanctify this symbol. I was about to speak my vow again when I heard Angus's voice downstairs.

"Guid evening. Ah'm ah too early?"

My ritual can wait. I came downstairs saying, "No, you're just in time to watch me make the fire."

He'd already removed his shoes and hung his coat on a peg, but he fished for something inside his jacket's pockets. The back pocket of his jeans had the familiar bulge of his flask.

"Grand." He offered me a handful of starters. "Ah brought ye some to make it easier."

"Thanks." Even though his hands didn't linger on mine *this time*, the memory from before was enough to stir me again. I didn't try to suppress it, not now, not moments after vowing to act as more of an inlet than a brick wall.

Angus's lips curved slightly. "Ah was bein' a bit forward with ye then, testin' if ye felt the same way. Ah ken ye'r spoken for now, and ah'll respect that till ye tell me otherwise. Have ye heard from yer Ian yet?"

"No, but Katrine called. She let me know she plans to stay another week. Am I being redundant, telling you things you already know?"

"Ah told ye before, ah enjoy the sound of yer voice. Ah dinnae care if ye tellin' me what ah already ken. There's nae harm in confirmin' it. Plus, things change." He walked into the living room and sat on the couch.

"I enjoy the sound of your voice too. You probably know that—but I'll confirm it for you." I put the starters down by the fireplace and turned back to him. "Now, will you answer something for me? What's the nature of your relationship with Katrine?"

"She's mah dearest friend."

I focused on the fire, building the base, and stacking the peat. I heard Angus in the kitchen when I expected him to watch my setup and paused before lighting it.

He came over and said, "She looks fine. Dinnae hesitate. Trust what ye'v created. Remember the back starters first, then the front."

When I lit it, smoke followed. "Oh no." I started frantically fanning the air with my hands.

"Dinna fash, Sarah, ye'v done it right. A wee bit of smoke is normal.

There's nae need to fret." I noticed Angus had brought two glasses from the kitchen and took his flask from his back pocket. "A spot of whisky for ye tonight?"

I nodded. I'd already developed a taste for it.

"Ah like to bring mah own. Ah also noticed ye have some zucchini bread. It goes surprisin'ly well with whisky."

What doesn't go with whisky? I didn't stifle my laugh. "As well as scones? I'll get us some." I brought the loaf with a knife and the Irish butter on a plate.

"Have ye harvested Kat's garden yet today?"

"No. I meant to, but I forgot."

"Let's check it and then take a walk to catch the sunset."

We returned to the kitchen with a massive green zucchini I'd missed yesterday.

Angus held it up. "Ye can make yer own zucchini bread next."

I caught myself admiring his hands, not what they were displaying. "Given I don't bake very well, it would taste better steamed with butter."

"The skin becomes a wee bit tough when 'tis left to grow too long. Ah can transform it into a loaf for the two of us. 'Tis nae that tricky."

Learning when to harvest was a skill I'd never practiced. My fruits and vegetables came from grocery shelves. Our garden excursion had clued me in to the cooler twilight air, so I grabbed another layer as we walked out the door. When we reached the road, the strangest sound interrupted the quiet, as if someone had pulled their finger through a plastic comb.

"What's that?"

"'Tis a corncrake. One lives in these fields, though he should have flown off by now, and he's tellin' us this is his territory. They migrate an impressive distance from Africa."

"What's a corncrake?"

"'Tis a timid bird. Ah'm nae surprised ye'v never heard of it. Few have, and even fewer have ever seen one."

The sun was putting on a spectacular show tonight, and I had an impulse to see it slip into the sea. "Angus, can we walk up that hill?"

"Aye. That's what yer new shoes are for. Ah was plannin' to take ye there earlier today. Dun I 'tis the highest point on the island and our best view. 'Tis guid to get yer bearin's and have some perspective."

We walked in an easy silence, like the kind that arises when two people are enjoying reading in each other's company. I mostly watched the placement of my feet, listening to the corncrake's occasional odd call, until I heard what sounded like bagpipes. I asked, "Do you hear that?"

"Aye, that'd be Padraig playin' for the sunset along the coast. He's a bit of a fixture on the island. Ye'll meet him someday."

The hill's steepness sent the path into switchbacks and loose stones covered the trail. I wasn't looking forward to coming down in the dark.

"Dinna fash. Ah'll lend ye a hand on the way back down if ye need it."

The idea of physical contact with Angus felt more dangerous than the slippery slope. I focused on the ground, listening to the bleating of the black sheep peppering the hillside. As we neared the top, another flock awaited us. The peak had a round stack of stones, but the stunning backdrop of the three-hundred-and-sixty-degree view distracted me from asking about it.

If gratitude could glisten on our skin's surface, I'd have had a sheen that rivaled the blazing globe approaching the sea. The sun cast a reflective golden path on the water that reached toward us. From our perch, the grassy hillside rolled into the outline of the rocky shoreline. It was beyond glorious. Angus offered me his flask, and I took a nip. After he sipped, he poured a splash to the ground; his offering summoned a sense of reciprocity.

He asked, "Shall we sit a spell and enjoy the show?"

"I'd like that." I welcomed the chance to catch my breath.

We watched in silence, as if looking over the shoulder of an artist painting on their canvas, careful not to disturb the beauty they created. Below us, a small pool of dark water shaped like a heart briefly captured my attention.

"Another time ah'll take ye to her, ye'll nae want to rush yer visit there. We'd be wise to walk down the hillside soon while there's still some light."

I stood in acknowledgment. "Agreed." Angus sensed my apprehension about walking down without falling. I recalled Ian's advice from many hikes together: take small steps, put your heel down first, then toe, heel toe, heel toe.

"Step where ah step. Use mah back if ye need to lean on somethin'."

We took our time and I sighed in relief when we reached level ground. Darkness had descended quickly, along with the temperature.

The horses needed tending, and Angus helped. I hung Saorsa's wet turnout blanket over the rod and rubbed him down. "You're not so wet, nothing a brisk toweling can't remedy." I realized my mistake as Saorsa kept nudging my side with his head and stamping his hoof. "You're hungry. You'd rather be eating. Okay, big fella, you've made your point. Who says I can't read minds?"

Angus had already switched Caim's blanket and was fetching their grain. I peeled hay for each of them from a bale, shaking the flakes as I tossed them in their stalls. They shape-shifted mid-air from a rectangle, landing as a toppling golden pyramid. We blanketed Saorsa together. Angus closed their stall doors, and I fed Demeter. I squealed upon seeing the decapitated mouse near her food dish. Angus came quickly and laughed when he saw the cause.

"A present for ye?"

"A present I could do without. Does your offer to help include disposal services?"

"Aye, ah'll take care of it. Ye'r meant to be more grateful for her huntin' services. 'Tis better dead than alive. Ah can only imagine how ye'd holler if it ran across yer feet." Angus picked it up by the tail, dangling it in front of me, and I backed away.

"I'm only grateful you're here to deal with it." We walked out together, and Angus tossed it beyond the hedge.

The fire-warmed house welcomed our arrival. I hesitated to embark on dinner together in case Ian called, so we made a meal of zucchini bread. Although Angus and I spoke for nearly an hour, my mind wasn't in the conversation.

Eventually, the phone rang, and I bounced up to answer it. "Hello, this is Sarah at Katrine's home."

"Sarah, my god, it's finally you."

"Ian, oh darlin', what a relief to hear your voice. I've been calling you at home until I realized you might be in Kauai. You went on our vacation without me."

"Yes. I've done everything without you for the last six months. Believe me, it wasn't my first choice. I was just reading the news during breakfast and almost didn't check my emails. Thank god I did."

"Yeah, especially since your voicemail is full. I've been desperate to talk to you."

"Me too, but my hotel bill will be astronomical. I dropped my cell in the ocean. Can you return to the computer so we can see each other?"

"Yes. Yes. I think I can." I glanced at Angus, and he nodded. "Send me a Zoom link. Oh my gosh, I'll see you in a few minutes. Bye for now." I felt myself hovering at the ceiling. Angus waited at the door with his jacket on.

"Thanks, Angus." His scotch glass was empty, but mine was hardly touched. I grabbed it along with the monster zucchini and I handed it to him. "Here, take this. I look forward to tasting your baking skills." After I said it, I regretted it. There was no way to make this moment less awkward. We exited and walked in stiff silence. The jitters inside me intensified with each step.

When we arrived, he said, "Ah'll give ye yer privacy," and he retreated upstairs, leaving the zucchini on his entry bench.

I returned to his computer, typing in Daphne2018!, but when I typed in my email password, it was wrong. The little dark circles the letters hid behind left no clue to my mistake, only denied me access. I deleted them all and started again. Each moment of delay felt like gridlock at a green traffic light. Even though Angus had left the room, I took his computer into the bathroom for privacy and closed the door. Ian's face waited for me as I logged in.

He launched into conversation. "Oh god, what a relief to finally see you! It's been too long, darlin'. I can hardly believe it's you! You look wonderful and too far away. I need you in my arms."

I took his pause for breath as a chance to respond. "I know, darlin', me too. So much has happened. I don't even know where to start. First, tell me—are you well? Any big news on your end?"

Ian shook his head. "I'm much better now. I've missed you terribly. Nothing new to report, same, same." My fears that Ian had moved on were only fears; there was no truth in them. He leaned toward his screen as if he could reach me through it. "I have a thousand questions about your adventure with Rumored Woman. I want to hear all about it in person, not like this. I can't bear another minute apart. God, you look so good. When are you coming home? I can arrange your flight and overnight your passport."

I felt his passion steamrolling over me. I'd forgotten what I'd written in the email. "Ian, slow down a moment. It's more complicated. I can't fly back, not right now."

His brows furrowed, creating a cavernous crease between them.

"I'm caring for two horses and staying in the home of a woman who's away tending to her daughter. I told her I'd be here as long as she needed me. Ian, this is all out of context. Let me at least tell you about the last forty-eight hours. It's equally unbelievable."

"No. Sarah, I can't wait any more weeks to see you. I've already started looking into flights to Scotland. I'll cut my trip short here and fly home to Boston to pack some warm clothes. I can be there in a few days if I reschedule my client commitment."

I shifted back on the toilet seat. "Ian, please slow down. So much has happened since I left and after I arrived here. I sent you a card. The image on the front resembles the boat I awoke inside early Sunday morning. I washed up on shore—the boat had no oars, no drinking water, only a blanket." I sped up as I spoke. "I arrived with no money, or identification, just wearing a linen dress, not even shoes. It turns out there are no banks here." I sensed Ian's impatience. "I guess these details don't matter. What matters is I met this woman going for a morning swim, and she invited me in for tea. Her name's Katrine. I didn't tell her about my circumstances. How could I? Instead, I kept her talking by asking questions about her family."

Ian interrupted me. "Sarah, I don't care about her. I want to see you."

"Let me explain." I spoke even faster. "I learned she had horses, but not just any horses—Friesians. She loaned me her daughter's clothes and riding boots and trusted me to ride with her. It was like an incredible dream riding through the fields and along the beach, but it was real. It reminded me of my time with Faith."

Ian asked, "Who's Faith?"

"Oh, that's what I came to call Rumored Woman. God, there's so much to catch you up on. Back to Katrine for a moment. Her friend, who was supposed to care for her horses, broke her hip. I volunteered to watch them for her—because I didn't have any other place to stay and I hadn't reached you yet. I was broke and barefoot. Katrine was a godsend, opening her home to me. Not only has she given me a place to stay in exchange for feeding and riding her two gorgeous horses, but she's also paid me! Though, I've already spent most of that money on necessities. I'm so grateful for her and want to help her in return. She trusted me as a total stranger in her home. It doesn't feel right to leave now or ask her if I can have you as a guest." I stopped, breathless.

"You're like a cat, always landing on your feet. Okay, I get that it would be awkward to ask if I can join you. Sarah, I don't give a shit where I sleep. Sleep is the last thing on my mind. I can stay in a hotel. I'd love to go on hikes with you, watch you ride, drink fine scotch, and hear all about your adventures with... Faith. We can make love on a deserted beach or in the afternoon in my hotel room. Now, can we get back to making plans for me to visit you? And then you can fly back with me."

"Ummm." It became clear that time zones weren't the only thing that separated us. We were coming to our reunion from two totally different perspectives. I felt his compulsion to be with me and have me home, but I didn't share his urgency to return yet. Torn between the need to be honest but not come off as selfish, I called upon Faith to help me communicate what staying here longer meant to me. I heard her advice, *Give voice to your longing,* and glanced around the bathroom but saw only myself in the mirror's reflection.

"Thanks for understanding the need for a hotel room. When I woke in the boat, I was shocked and disappointed that I hadn't arrived home with you, but so many things have unfolded here with such grace. Now, I'm not ready to rush my return. I want to take some transition time to integrate all that's happened away from my familiar habits, time to sort out who I am now and who I am not, how I want to live. Iona offers me space from the routines I could so easily pick back up." I followed the advice of the Hooks and my vows: to listen to what I am sensing and feeling, and act on it. I felt emboldened to speak my heart the way Faith had encouraged me only moments ago.

"Wait, what are you saying? You're not planning on coming home?"

"That's just it, Ian. I don't know yet when I'll fly back to Boston. I feel strangely at home here. It's hard to explain. I just fit. I'm living by the sea, riding horses with space and time to reflect on my time with Faith. I want to enjoy this for a while. Oh, and Katrine's a blacksmith. I could learn jewelry making or make the silverware I've dreamed about. I can write. I can—"

"Hold up. It sounds like you're not coming back anytime soon. What about us, our relationship? You've hardly mentioned us. I don't want to see you virtually. I want to be with you, inside you. For Christ's sake, it's been six months! We were supposed to be here, now, in Kauai together." Ian had been leaning into the screen but had pushed back in his seat. "Sarah, we're meant to be together, not on separate continents. The sunset sail I went on wasn't the same without you. I was taking a picture of it to share with you and lost my footing. That's when I dropped my cell phone in the goddamn Pacific Ocean. I started to cry amongst a group of total strangers. It wasn't because of the phone. I could replace it. It represented my last thread to you, and I feared it had snapped. When I read your email after breakfast, I cried again in the restaurant. You know me, I don't cry easily. I'm a wreck. I've been on a hellish emotional rollercoaster and want to get the fuck off. Now, I finally see you, and I'm over the moon. I'm ready to move heaven and earth to get to you, but you're pushing me away. I can't even see your full face—you sat back and didn't fix the screen."

I leaned back in.

Ian continued. "I prayed you'd return in time to fly to Kauai with me. I wanted a different place to unwind with you, to hear what had happened. But I had to decide if I'd go alone when you weren't back in time. That's when my fear that you might never return sunk in. Initially, I told your coven you left on silent retreat without your phone, but they didn't believe that lie. They've done their best to interrogate me. They wanted to report you missing to the police! It's impossible to answer their questions when I have no answers—not even for myself. I had to tell the school you wouldn't be teaching this fall. I don't think you'll have a job waiting for you anymore. I can't keep covering for you."

Ian's voice kept getting louder and louder. I turned the volume down on Angus's computer. He often raised his voice when upset, but if I mentioned it, he'd shout back that he wasn't yelling. I felt Ian's vulnerability briefly surface when his tone softened, but within a breath, his tone hardened, barbed with anger. I remained silent, letting all his emotions move through me.

Ian exhaled, sighing. His voice shifted again to his professional, authoritative tone. "I'll fly back home, repack my bag with your passport and warm clothes, and we can return together after your horse-sit finishes." I felt him imposing his plan, taking control. I held my silence like an empty vessel. Ian filled it. His voice was pleading now. "I want to see you. I need to see you, to hold you." He waited, and his tone shifted. "But it sounds like you don't have the same urgency to see me. This is so far from what I imagined—I imagined I'd walk home and find you at home, not that you'd return halfway around the fucking world." I felt him pulling away as he shook his head.

I doubted Ian was in a place to listen to me. He wanted what he wanted and felt justified in demanding it. "Ian, I hear you. I understand nothing about this has gone to plan, and it's not what either of us expected. I want to see you and hold you. I miss you. I'm sure the waiting and not knowing if or when I'd return has been rough on you. I'm sorry I couldn't call you. It wasn't possible. There were no phones in the underworld. Besides, it wouldn't have made sense to you. I can hardly understand it myself, and I lived through it. Sometimes, I think I dreamt the whole thing up." I touched Faith's pendant. "I'm afraid I'll forget what I learned. I need time to integrate and recalibrate so I don't revert to my old habits of being overly productive and prioritizing everyone else's needs over mine. On Iona, I only have myself to take care of and two horses that help me ground and center. I don't want to fall back into old patterns. Can you understand this?"

"Sarah, it sounds like you're saying I'm an old pattern with needs that overshadow yours, that our relationship isn't something you're sure you want to fall back into. Tell me I'm wrong—because that's what I'm hearing."

"Ian, please don't make this about you. I'm trying to understand how you feel. I want to see you too. It's just I'm not ready to leave Iona immediately. I don't know what I want, and I want the time to sort myself out. Can you understand how I feel?"

Ian's voice turned to steel. "Honestly, no. I don't know why you can't sort yourself out at home. There's space for you there—a home, our bed, your life, your friends, and most of all, me." He ran both his hands through his hair and gripped his skull. It pulled back the skin around his eyes. "Sarah, what am I supposed to tell your coven? Do I keep lying for you when folks ask? Or shall I say she turned up on an island in Scotland, and she's not coming home yet?" He let his hands fall. "What the fuck? No, I don't understand." Ian slammed the computer screen down.

He'd disconnected us. I stared at the blank screen in disbelief. It felt like the bathroom walls were closing in on me. I waited for him to have second thoughts and tried to join the meeting again, but it said the host had to let me in. He wasn't letting me in. I wanted a do-over. I'd not been skillful in my communication, but I'd been truthful. I hadn't allowed myself to think beyond staying here for a few weeks, but as I tried to explain myself to Ian, it became more apparent that I wanted to stay on longer. My life here was unfolding with a sense of freedom and sanctuary. Saorsa and Caim were more than horses to me. They were symbols of the life I wanted for myself. It felt too soon to make plans to depart. I waited to hear Faith's voice again, but the silence felt hollow.

I rechecked my emails, but there was nothing new from Ian. I was the one waiting now. *Should I reach out again?* Ian tended to short-circuit after a heated exchange. He'd need a nap or to hide out for a bit, but he usually wanted me to find him. I sent a message with the subject line: "Hide and Seek."

> *Hey Darlin,*
>
> *I know you're upset. I want to give you space, and I want to connect. I want to find a way through this impasse—please don't assume I don't want to see you—or be with you. I don't know where home is right now. My sense is I have to find it within before I can rely on it being outside myself. I want to belong inside my skin the way I have with Faith. While I can't see her anymore, I believe she's within me. Please try to understand.*
>
> *I know this all seems irrational, and you probably think I'm being unreasonable, selfish even. I'm sorry. I can't make sense of it to you if I haven't made sense of it to myself. Maybe I'm meant to steer with a different rudder than reason. I'm telling you how I feel and what I'm sensing, and I want that to count as much as what I think. I can't justify my feelings to you. That's impossible.*
>
> *It's getting late here, and I'm sitting in a neighbor's bathroom for privacy. I'm going to head back to Katrine's in another five minutes. I'm exhausted. I want to check in tomorrow and I'll be back at this computer tomorrow at 7:00 a.m. Kauai time, 6:00 p.m. my time.*
> *I love you,*
> *Sarah*

I hit send and waited to see if he would reply. There was so much more separating us now than continents. We both held vastly different expectations about what would come next. I stared at my inbox, overwhelmed by all the unanswered messages, but nothing new arrived from Ian. It felt like he was punishing me for being honest. I feared the connections that once held us together had frayed over the last six months.

After leaving Angus's computer open on the toilet lid, I studied myself in the mirror. I felt different from the woman I was before my journey, but I appeared the same. Appearances can be misleading. I turned on the tap, holding my cupped hands below it, waiting for it to warm. It spilled over the edges of my fingers, bringing my attention back to my skin, my body as a vessel. I splashed my face and gently rubbed it, peering at myself, running my wet fingers through my hair, letting my nails lightly scratch my scalp. I gathered my mane of hair and swept it to my right shoulder. It had grown. Maybe I'd matured too. I sensed my Peaceful Warrior had my back, and I didn't feel alone. I stood taller, choosing to be patient.

The dram of scotch beckoned, practically untouched, and I drank it all. It burned down my throat, heating my chest and strengthening my resolve. *I want to be here. For how long? I don't know. I don't want to make plans for a change, nor have Ian make plans for me. I don't want to get ahead of myself. I want to move at the tempo my heart, mind, body, and spirit can move—the pace of embodied presence.*

Sitting on the toilet lid, I typed another reply, as the low battery message flashed on the screen, warning me if I didn't plug in, it would shut down. *Ain't that the truth? Time for both of us to re-source ourselves.*

Chapter 11

Re-Source

S LAMMING THE COMPUTER SHUT only temporarily satisfied Ian. His fury vanished as fast as it had arrived, leaving him deflated. Sarah's engagement ring blared on the nightstand. He fixated on it as he paced in the small space of his hotel room until he misjudged the corner of the bed frame and clipped his shin. "God damn it." The mattress sagged under his weight as he assessed the damage—no blood, only a scrape and inevitable bruise.

Ian lay back, staring at the ceiling fan making its steady rotation. Their exchange had flattened him. He'd been soaring after reading her email. When he heard Sarah's voice and finally saw her, he assumed their separation was nearly over until she implied she intended to extend it. Ian's heart plummeted. He felt like Icarus, flying too close to the sun, scorching his wings, and crashing into the sea. Regret flooded in for ending the call abruptly, but not enough to reach back out. He required time to lick his wounds. *Why does she need more time to get to know herself? Why does she have to be alone?* He rolled over on his side and clutched the pillow to his chest.

Ian preferred the driver's seat. For the last six months, he'd been an unwilling passenger, or worse, forced to sit in the back seat while Sarah had her hands on the wheel. He was done being at the mercy of her timetable. It was time for her disappearing act to end. Ian had kept his part of the bargain, caring for the cat left in his charge. At least *she* was thriving. Persephone had been a welcome companion but not a substitute for Sarah.

His head kept shaking. How had their call turned into an argument? It was so far from what he'd expected to happen—from what he wanted. She caught him flatfooted. Usually, he rebounded better and still sank the basketball. This one he couldn't even touch.

Ian sat up and checked his emails. She'd reached out as he expected. The subject line, "Hide and Seek," pissed him off again, so he didn't even open it. *She's the one hiding, for god's sake. I'm the one seeking.* His finger had found a nub in the sheets, and he scratched at it.

She'd implied she wasn't coming home, not now and likely not soon. Sarah had changed for sure. But Ian couldn't pinpoint what was different. He'd imagined hearing all about her journey in person, over meals and fine bottles of wine, during walks, or in their bed, not over Zoom for god's sake. Work required excessive screen time and he refused to have a virtual relationship with Sarah.

Her gold engagement ring continually hijacked his attention. No matter what he said to himself, he couldn't deny he wanted to hand-deliver everything she needed. *What if I don't listen to her? What if I just show up? Why does she get to decide what I do?*

Iona was less than five miles long. Sarah couldn't hide from him if he wanted to seek her. Two Friesian horses would be easy enough to recognize, given all the videos of Friesians she'd shared with him over the years.

Their engagement ring was too painful to see, so he tucked it into the side pocket of his briefcase, but out of sight wasn't out of mind. He had hoped, beyond reason, that he could propose to her in Kauai, even though the odds were stacked against him. Typically, Ian wasn't prone to irrational acts. But his notions of normal dissolved when Sarah departed with Rumored Woman through the mirror. Naming her Faith was apropos. *Faith, have I lost mine? Have I ever had any?*

Ian believed things would work out and thought of it more as optimism than faith. Whenever he couldn't find his keys or a tool, which was admittedly often, Sarah would say he'd lost them. She insisted if he didn't know where they were, that that was the definition of lost. He disagreed. They were misplaced. Eventually, they'd turn up. He'd clung to this habit when Sarah disappeared, telling himself she'd turn up and their life would return to normal. He was half right. She wasn't lost—she'd turned up, but nothing was normal.

It didn't matter that he couldn't see their engagement ring. It was all he could think about.

If he proposed, he'd find out where they stood, but he suspected she'd say no, since Sarah wasn't ready even before she left. He'd fantasized that when she returned she would be. Clearly, he was wrong. *Would she ever be ready?* Ian refused to give in to the tears that threatened.

He grabbed his room key, pulled on his sneakers, and took the stairs instead of the elevator. The balmy air greeted him. Running helped him regain his equilibrium. Today, he skipped his warm-up and sprinted until he was out of breath and slowed his pace.

Ian felt fed up with solitude. He wanted to relax with Sarah. At least he knew she was alive and well, which was more than he knew when he woke this morning. At least he could stop worrying about her, but he didn't want to stop imagining his future with her.

I closed the computer, taking inventory of my life. *Here I am, sitting in a bathroom in a stranger's home on an island in Scotland. Seriously.*

Why am I trying to defend my right to stay here, arguing with Ian, the one person I want most to connect with? I wasn't purring inside. I'd given voice to my longing, as Faith had advised. *Could I follow my longings to a place of belonging?*

I hugged myself, waiting to hear if Faith would speak to me again. Out of the silence arose the impulse to listen to Sarah McLachlan's song, "Answer."[1] I reopened Angus's computer and prayed for enough battery life to hear it. It felt like the balm my soul needed now to calm my doubts and desperation. At first, I listened, humming, then by the second verse, I sang along with her, choking back my tears.

> *"Cast me gently into morning*
> *for the night has been unkind*
> *take me to a place so holy*
> *that I can wash this from my mind*
> *the memory of choosing not to fight.*
>
> *If it takes my whole life*
> *I won't break, I won't bend.*
>
> *It will all be worth it, worth it in the end.*
>
> *I can only tell you what I know*
> *that I need you in my life.*
>
> *When the stars have all burned out*
> *you'll still be burning so bright.*
>
> *Cast me gently*
> *into morning*
> *for the night*

has been unkind."

My voice cracked as I sang, "...that I need you in my life..." Tears rolled down my cheeks as I gazed upward and called upon Faith, my faith, to be with me now. *She is my answer. She is the source for me to return to, my re-source, my burning light.* Angus's screen went dark. When I blew my nose, the sapphire caught my eye again.

I emerged from his bathroom, to a roaring fire, feeling both drained and fortified. Part of me wanted to linger before it—to sway in the easy rhythm, weaving between the opposing forces I'd sensed, swept up in how the dance of opposites had evolved. I wanted to know what came next. I wanted to believe the opposition between Ian and me could be reconciled.

Angus's computer cord peeked out from under his kitchen table. I crawled under it like one does for shelter during an earthquake. Heavy footsteps signaled him coming down the stairs. I must have looked like I was hiding. In a way, I was.

"Did ye lose somethin', lass?"

There were so many ways to interpret that question. I hoped I hadn't lost Ian, myself, or Faith. "I was retrieving your computer cord." Recharging to reconnect was the essential move at the moment.

"Ah'll take care of it. Sit a spell. Let me refresh yer glass."

Standing quickly after downing my full shot of whisky had made me feel lightheaded. "No thanks." Tears threatened to spill over again.

Angus kept his distance, leaning against his leather chair. "Get some rest, lass. Everythin' will look better in the mornin'."

The fire's comfort called to me, and I stood before it with my back to Angus. Under my breath, I said, "I just want to go home."

"'Tis okay, lass, ye can go. Ah can tend to the horses. Kat will understand that ye..."

I interrupted Angus. "No, not that home. I meant Katrine's house, which somehow feels more like home than the one I left. I'm at sea again, adrift between two places"—*between two men*—"belonging neither here nor there." The ease of communication with Angus after failing to feel heard and understood by Ian disarmed me. *Why is the pull toward Angus so strong?* I hardly knew him, whereas Ian and I had been together for nearly five years. I worried Angus knew what I was thinking. How was I going to sort myself out before talking to Ian again? The barn felt like the safest place for me, accompanied by two horses: sanctuary and freedom.

"Ye'll come through, lass, have faith and patience. 'Tis yer life, after all, nae one else's."

I turned around. "Exactly—it is my life. I need time to listen for what's true. Why can't Ian understand? Well, that's not exactly fair. He's been understanding, but I've stretched him to his limits. For months, he's wondered if I am okay or ever coming back, and now I've enacted his worst fear only minutes after he knows I've returned."

As I turned back toward the fire, my heart felt heavy. I placed my right palm on the center of my chest, touching Faith's pendant. I knew how much I'd been asking from Ian and imagined how hard these last six months must have been for him, how he'd pictured a different reunion. I, too, never expected to return to anywhere else but our home. However, expectations were about living in the future, a future we can't know until it has become our present.

I heard my blessing again. *May I become patient with uncertainty, welcoming mystery into my life as my beloved dance partner, letting go of expectations, even with disappointment, to honor what is authentic in the moment.*

Am I willing to disappoint Ian if that's what it takes not to betray myself? My answer felt firm and clear. *Yes.*

Staring into the fire, my recently edited line from my blessing surfaced. *May my conversation with the elements re-source my days, cultivating courage, faith, and my sense of belonging, be-longing.* The Hooks' and

Faith's advice was to follow my longings. *I can trust my heart. It won't lead me astray.* I'd always thought a fireside chat was between people near a fire, not between the fire and a person. My conversation with it tonight illuminated my old patterns of avoidance, even toward what I wanted, in an attempt to sidestep disappointing others or myself. I hadn't recognized how it confined me within invisible walls. *I imprison myself in a cell of my own making.* Standing before the fire reminded me of my choices. I've so often held these kinds of silent conversations near the sea. The image of fire I'd seen when Faith held her hands over my eyes returned, and I silently thanked the flames and turned to Angus. His eyes were filled with compassion and something else I couldn't grasp. I figured he, like Faith, had listened to my unspoken conversation.

"Goodnight, Angus. Thanks for listening and letting me use your computer." He tipped his head and blinked slowly at me. "I offered Ian six o'clock tomorrow evening as a time to reconnect. Would arriving a few minutes earlier to use your computer be okay?"

"Sure, ah'll be out in the barn. Ye dinnae have to hide in mah bathroom. Ye can sit by the fire, have yer conversation here. Ah'll light one for ye."

I put on my new boots and tied temporary bows. "Thanks."

Angus followed me to the door. "Sweet dreams, lass. Do ye want a torch to walk back with?"

"No, I'm set."

When I heard the door click shut, I stopped and pulled the bows of my laces, slipping off my boots and socks. The cold, stiff grass poked the soles of my feet as I walked cautiously, finding my footing in the dark, on the level ground that didn't quake—the only trembling came from within me and there was nowhere to hide from myself. I had to become my own shelter and find my own solid ground.

I stood still for a few minutes in the dark. The clouds obscured the stars, reminding me that sometimes what I know to be true can be hidden from sight but not gone—like Patience and Faith. *Okay, Ian, take all the time you need. It's the same thing I'm asking for—I have to be willing to give it. Transition time is what's called for now.*

During Authentic Movement, the silent time between moving with eyes closed and speaking as Mover or Witness was called transition time. I experienced it as a time to recalibrate and often drew or wrote about the subconscious material I'd been surfacing. It built a bridge over the liminal threshold I'd crossed. *What if being on Iona is my transition time? Time to establish a new rhythm for my life.* Typically, I moved from one activity to the next, never taking time to transition—like teaching all day and immediately engaging with Ian. If I heard a series of tragic news reports, I rarely allowed myself time to settle or release its impact. I carried that disturbance into the next activity of fixing dinner, correcting papers, or reaching for the remote to watch a show before bedtime.

My toes felt numb. I wiggled them and continued toward home. When my heel landed squarely on a hard pebble, I shifted my weight to the ball of my foot, stepping more gingerly. I'd been barefoot on my journey with Faith, and I'd arrived here shoeless. *Was that a hint? Stay in direct connection to the earth—invite a conversation.*

The final line of a poem by David Whyte whispered to me. "...fallen in love with solid ground."[2] I paused in the darkness and closed my eyes, trying to recall its title as if it were written on my lids. As a child, I'd fallen in love with the sea, lying on my belly on the sailboat's bow, mesmerized by the spray of the water and its patterns as it rushed by in a frothy tumult. The ocean revealed its secrets to me then, and we'd been inseparable since. *Could I fall in love with the earth in the same way?*

An irony washed over me as I recalled the poem's title, "The Opening of Eyes," and as I opened mine, I sensed the pulse of the ground beneath my feet. Was this the same energy I'd felt surging into my left palm earlier today by the fire? I tilted my hand toward the earth in the same gesture of receiving, offering a conscious invitation for a relationship as

I continued in the dark toward Katrine's home. My other hand held my hiking boots, which bumped against my thigh as if knocking.

The earth is always under my feet, but I ignore it. When I rode, I kept a keen eye on the ground to ensure safe footing for the horse. Yet I was more negligent where I placed *my* feet—no wonder I'd turned my ankles so often. My toes told me I'd arrived at the edge of Katrine's driveway. *Turn left to the house or right to the barn?*

Saorsa nickered when he heard me enter the barn.

"Hello, my friend. I thought I'd come and say goodnight." His head waited for me outside his stall door. I left my shoes on the ground and offered him my hands to smell before I fondled his velvet muzzle. He snorted softly. "Let's make a date for a ride as soon as it's not raining."

I fetched the spray bottle and joined him in his stall, trusting him not to trample my bare feet. After letting him sniff the bottle, I unbuckled the front of his blanket, lightly spraying his chest. His heat warmed my hands as I rubbed it in; his solid muscles gave me strength. The smell of sandalwood and lavender soothed my nerves. Before leaving, I leaned my face against his neck, letting him support me for a moment.

In the bedroom, I took the yellow snail shell from my pocket and placed it on the nightstand. Removing Faith's pendant felt premature; it risked severing our connection. I crawled into bed, welcoming the dark. *What kind of conversation have I been missing with the earth, like I've been missing with fire? Could I also fall in love with the air by following my breath?*

My final thoughts were of Ian, and his eagerness to return to what we had in our past, but I also noticed my reluctance to go there. I intended to move at a snail's pace, noticing the ground beneath me. If the seedlings in me were to bud and blossom, I needed to plant myself in rich soil. I didn't want to feel rushed or crowded by Ian, nor confine myself to his needs. I wanted time and space to listen to my inner voice and trust my life's unfolding.

Angus had wanted to comfort Sarah in his arms, but he kept his distance. Thankfully, he'd misunderstood her reference to home. Relief had flooded him when she said she wanted to stay on. He'd faltered again in his ability to read her. Earlier, he'd been caught off guard when she mentioned Ian's name. Discovering Sarah's committed relationship humbled him, and cautioned him that she wasn't a completely open book. While he welcomed an element of surprise in his life, Ian was a surprise he would have preferred to live without.

It was time to take his own advice to her. Patience and faith were called for now. Some part of him knew she had to be the one who came to him, on her own terms. If he pressured her, she'd surely pull away. In the last forty-eight hours, she'd turned his life upside down, and he was struggling to find the horizon line.

While Ian ran, he pondered his options for seeing Sarah. Clearly, he was going to have to go to her, but *when* was the question. Running under palm trees with his T-shirt soaked with sweat, it was hard to believe Thanksgiving was only a few weeks away. Ian knew that fall was a time of letting go, but while he didn't want to let go of Sarah, he wasn't sure if he had any choice in the matter. She was recreating her life, rewriting it, and he feared he was losing his coveted role as her leading man. Getting back on the scene meant flying to Scotland.

Breathless, he peeled his T-shirt off to mop his face before dropping it in the sand and kicking off his running shoes. He shoved his socks inside them along with his hotel key, eager to swim. Two-and-a-half foot waves were rolling in, in sets of three. As he dove into the curl, he felt the force of it ripple over him before he came up for air. Ian bodysurfed until a wave thrashed him into the sand.

Bare chested in the balmy air, he gathered his things. It was time to leave Kauai. Now that Sarah had returned, all he wanted was to be with her. After a quick shower, he researched the route to Iona and discovered it was a trek. Upon arriving in Glasgow, he'd need to take a three-and-a-half-hour train ride to Oban, followed by a ferry to the Island of Mull, plus a bus across Mull to catch the final ferry. Delta's flight schedules made making all those connections in the same day impossible, so an overnight stay in Oban was essential. He eliminated the option of renting a car when he learned the island didn't allow tourists on with vehicles unless you had a medical pass.

There wasn't enough time to fly to Iona before his client commitment in San Fran, but he could leave immediately after it. *When will she start to feel homesick, to discover her fantasy about island life wasn't what she imagined? Waiting another week might be perfect timing.*

When Lucy and Scott had learned he had work in San Fran, they'd invited him to go wine tasting on the weekend prior. He'd declined because it conflicted with his trip to Kauai. Regrettably, they weren't available the following weekend, so he had intended to wine taste alone. He sent them a quick email telling them he was cutting short his time in Kauai and asked if they were still up for him to visit this coming weekend, adding that he'd met a couple who needed a real-estate agent and he'd introduce them via a separate email. By leaving today he had time to head home first, gather warmer clothes for Scotland, and send a care package to Sarah.

Ian optimistically packed while speaking with the Delta agent to change his return flight. He was zipping his bag when she reiterated his itinerary that hopscotched across the Pacific Ocean from Lihue to Honolulu to Los Angeles. The good news was she'd upgraded him to Premium Select on the final leg from Los Angeles to Boston. The bad news was that the first flight with availability departed Kauai at seven-thirty that night.

Jocelyn and Jim's daughter, Sam, had been cat-sitting for him, so he'd have to confess his change of plans. He'd tell them a half-truth, that he wasn't cut out for vacationing alone. Explaining Sarah's reappearance felt fraught with the same challenges as her disappearance. It was ultimately up to her what story she chose to tell. The truth was unbelievable and whatever she made up would be more plausible.

Ian decided traveling without a phone was a hassle he could avoid; his plane didn't board for several more hours, and the Verizon store wasn't far from the airport. First, he stopped at Hanalei Coffee Roasters for a double espresso and a dark chocolate macaroon. Waiting in line, he saw a couple wearing different colors of the same T-shirt: "Slow yourself down. Hanalei Kauai."

Ian wished there was a fast-forward option that had him boarding the plane to Glasgow, but he had a half-dozen flights to take before he used his passport and hand-delivered Sarah's.

Traffic had been sparse on the road, and when Ian crossed the Kalihiwai River bridge, he intentionally slowed down because he knew to look up to the right to glimpse the cascading waterfall. Sarah had read about Kauai's eleven amazing waterfalls, and they'd planned to visit several together. On their last trip, they'd hiked the Kalalau trail's first leg to see Hanakapiai Falls. Most hikes saved their reward till the end, but that trail hugged the Napali Coast and offered breathtaking views all along the way. Sarah had insisted on frequent stops to enjoy them, afraid to take her eyes off the trail since she tended to turn her ankles. This made the two-mile trek take much longer than if Ian had been alone. In fairness, the path was treacherous in places, especially after it rained—which it did most days.

As he neared Lihue, traffic slowed to a snail's pace. By the time he arrived at the Verizon store, he brimmed with impatience. The chatty salesperson recounted how people drop their phones in the water all the time and warned against using back pockets in a bathroom. Ian didn't correct her assumption because he wanted to keep them on task. Next, he stood in line at the Hertz desk to ensure his charges were adjusted.

After clearing agricultural inspection and checking his golf bag, he only had a half hour before his flight boarded. It was too early to call Sarah and risk waking her—he wanted their next call to be an improvement over their last. He intended to call her during his two-hour layover in Honolulu.

Ian sat in the boarding area booking his flight to Scotland. He'd decided against checking with Sarah. It was too much like asking for her permission. It wasn't like she was too busy to see him since she wasn't even working. He even booked a return flight for Sarah with miles, knowing he could cancel it without penalty. The prospect of sharing Thanksgiving dinner with Sarah and their friends filled him with hope for rebuilding their lives together.

It wasn't lost on Ian that his actions were incongruent with his professional advice. He taught the consequences of a "decide and announce" leadership style. Its drawbacks surfaced during implementation in the form of resistance—disguised as formal compliance, or worse, as passive-aggressive behavior. Not including people in a more participatory decision-making process meant they had less ownership of the outcome and brought less commitment to enacting it.

By the time his plane touched down in Honolulu, he was starved. He located Kona Brewery as his best option for dinner, ordered a Longboard beer and ribs, and felt human again upon finishing it. He tried calling Sarah, underestimating how early she started her day, and his call went unanswered.

Ian's next flight left the gate on time, but they sat on the tarmac for mechanical reasons.

1. Sarah McLachlan, "Answer," YouTube LIVE, The Official Sarah McLachlan, 4:19, https://youtu.be/1lV33Na_N7Q?si=6SneCxBo9qjdass5.

2. David Whyte, "The Opening of Eyes," in *River Flow: New & Selected Poems,* Revised Edition, (Langley, WA: Many Rivers Press, 2012, 31, line 20.

CHAPTER 12

CONDITIONING

A DREAM FRAGMENT SURFACED as I kept my eyes closed. I was oceanside, sitting on a driftwood log, watching a blue heron hunt in shallow water. Her legs remained still, but her elegant neck stretched downward slowly until, without warning, she thrust her beak like lightning into the ocean. She shook her head and tipped it back as I watched a lump travel down her throat. The sharp bark of a dog startled me, so I turned to see where it was coming from, but I couldn't find it. When I looked back, the heron flew off, squawking like a prehistoric dinosaur with her long, spindly legs dangling awkwardly behind her.

It felt so real. There was nothing out of the ordinary that typically happened in dreams. At least, I used to think the impossible was relegated to night dreams until my journey with Faith. It was my first dream snippet on Iona and I pondered the symbolism of the heron. *Who is the part of me seeking nourishment that must go slow and hunt alone? Is her counsel to act decisively, without hesitation, when I see what I want? To act cautiously amidst intruders and relocate if necessary? Who is the barking dog in me that I can't see?*

Upon opening my eyes, blue skies offered the promise of a morning ride. My mood brightened at the thought but faltered upon recalling last night's conversation with Ian. I threw back the covers, determined not to let his anger toward me ruin my day. *I can't control his feelings. I need to accept them. He may feel differently tonight when we speak—if he's ready to talk, or he may still be hiding.*

My legs hurt even more than yesterday, and it was obvious not stretching had been a mistake. Wearing Maeve's robe, I gingerly descended the stairs to put on the electric kettle. Some things were easy in life, requiring only the push of a button. A hunk of zucchini bread sat on the counter, broadcasting thoughts of Angus. I pinched a corner and ate it while I waited for the water to boil. Usually, I wasn't that patient. I'd have scampered upstairs to get dressed, making better use of my time, adhering to the adage, *Don't just stand there, do something*. Well, technically, I was eating.

The sunbeams stretching toward the water captured my attention, reminding me of the day I'd arrived. I brought my tea and the last of the loaf to the chair by the bay window to let myself wake slowly to the day. Yeats sat here too, waiting for me, and Saorsa and Caim kept each other company in the barn. I was hardly alone.

The abbey bell rang once. Before it rang again, I had dressed, including wearing my own underwear. Such a simple pleasure delighted me. The air felt crisp with the freshness that comes after a storm. I opened the barn door, and a chorus of whinnies greeted me, buoying my spirits.

"Yes, yes, I know you're hungry. While I was taking my time this morning, you were here waiting for me—patience, patience." I had the routine down: feed first, muck after. I decided they didn't need their turnout blankets, but their blankets needed the sunshine, so I draped them over the fence rail. I groomed and tacked up Saorsa while he ate. A ride on a spirited, thousand-pound beast was the perfect way to take my mind off last night's call with Ian. I was dusting off my memory of how to lunge, sending Saorsa mental pictures. "Are you paying attention? Will you cooperate without Katrine here?"

Thankfully, he was a prince. The only interruptions to our lunging session were my fault. I kept getting the excessively long line tangled in my unpracticed hand. I had to halt him and loop it back up again so it moved freely when I needed to lengthen it, and felt grateful I didn't have an audience. When we finished, he lowered his head to make it easier to remove the cavesson and bridle him. I praised him, tightened the girth, released the stirrups, and led him to the mounting block for our moment of truth. He remained steady as I put my weight in the stirrup and eased onto his back. "Good man, Saorsa! Can we go three for three at the gate?"

My nervousness contributed to the frustration that ensued. Saorsa wouldn't stay still as I reached to unlatch it. He kept tossing his head. Likely, I'd asked wrong, or he was choosing not to listen. When we finally managed to get out and close the gate, tension gripped my muscles. Given the proximity of Angus's flock, I had zero interest in practicing again with his gates. Those fluffy little obstacles presented another challenge I didn't need underfoot.

We walked along the road. "How do you feel about cars coming up behind you? Does it spook you?" I kept contact with the reins following the movement of his head. "So, skipping the pasture means finding a place on the beach to practice our walk-halt transitions." Saorsa sighed and stretched his neck low. Our few minutes of walking had worked its magic to relax us both.

Since we still needed to get to know one another, I circled him asking for a halt after a few paces of a walk, and again after a trot, to notice how he responded to my seat and the engagement of my core muscles. It never ceased to amaze me how such subtle movement translated into him moving differently; I didn't even need to use my reins for him to stop. I praised him, "Good fella, Saorsa." We practiced different walking gaits, and his hoofprints in the sand revealed two overlapping circles, a Venn diagram. I attempted to create the Celtic Trinity knot with a third circle, but it lacked the symmetry I'd imagined.

We tried our sand art in a new location, trotting in a figure eight. When I stopped at the center point to gaze at the mysterious circle of stones in the sea, Saorsa shifted his weight and stamped at the ground. "Are you impatient to move? Well, we're all warmed up." I sat up straighter and turned him parallel to the shore where a long stretch of deserted beach awaited us. He responded immediately to my request for a canter and the surge of his first strides caught me by surprise. There's a reason we referred to cars as having horsepower. I had a powerhouse beneath me revving to go, but it was our first date alone, and despite how much I craved the freedom of a full-out gallop, cantering was more prudent.

I followed the rhythm of his stride, enjoying how his long mane undulated in the wind until we reached the distant jetty, where we transitioned to a trot and slowed to a halt. *Why would I ever want to leave here? Do I have to?* After turning around, I asked for a canter again, but this time I rose from my seat in a balanced position, so he didn't have to carry my weight on his back and gave him his head. It didn't take much leg to urge him to gallop. He tore down the beach toward the infinity sign of his hoofprints. Before we reached it, I sat back in the saddle, engaging my core muscles, signaling my request to slow down, and vibrating my hands upwards. He listened. Katrine had trained him well, making Saorsa a dream to ride.

The internal rush from experiencing his power, coupled with our ability to understand one another was more than a marvel; it was orgasmic. I bent over and hugged him as we walked through the image of infinity and our failed attempt at a Celtic Trinity knot. I hadn't set out today thinking Saorsa and I would become sand artists as we created my sacred symbols on the beach. If I ever chose to have a tattoo, the infinity sign topped my list. The line from my blessing had come to life. *May each day unfold with a priority on creative expression, sensing the deeper currents, and stalking the sacred.*

I stroked Saorsa's neck again and asked for a posting trot, which on Friesians, felt more like a floating prance. The lift of their legs was a beauty to behold and a blessing to ride. His propulsion translated up and through my body.

When we returned to a walk, I reached down to check his chest. We'd both worked up a sweat, so I turned us toward the barn for a cooldown and let out the reins. The sheep had moved further down the field, but there was no sign of Angus, and a twinge of disappointment surfaced. I could always head over early under the guise of checking my emails, but I knew that was a ruse. I wasn't ready to communicate with my friends and doubted Ian had responded. *Nope—today is my solo day. It's time to embrace my inner heron.*

Caim had trotted to the fence and I tried my gate skills again, trusting she wouldn't seize the moment to escape. We were better at it but had lots of room for improvement. After untacking Saorsa and grooming away his girth marks, he joined Caim by cantering down the pasture, his tail waving goodbye. I hadn't recovered as swiftly and had the rider's waddle.

I quelled my grumbling stomach with ham on a baguette for lunch, and despite protests from my thighs, decided in favor of another ride. Eventually, my legs would rejoice at the thought, too. When the abbey bell chimed once, I wondered if it was one o'clock or half past the hour? I enjoyed tracking time in half-hour intervals rather than minutes. It felt more spacious.

Ian occupied my mind as I groomed Caim. When she snorted, I realized I'd hardly spoken with her, which wasn't the best approach for our first ride. I also hadn't bowed yet today and left her in the stall, sliding the door closed.

In the tack room, I knelt upon an extra saddle pad, saying, "Amidst it all, I carve out sacred space and time to bow to the Great Mystery." As I rested my forehead on the pad, I kept my arms along my sides, feeling my chest rise and fall against my thighs with each breath. I exhaled the residue of feeling responsible for Ian's emotions, letting go of my regrets about disappointing and hurting him. My shoulders dropped closer to the floor. *I don't need to figure everything out to be safe. The earth and sea hold me. I already belong.* The familiar smells of saddle soap and leather comforted me. After speaking aloud my vow and blessing, a sense of connection resided within me. When I stood, a wiggle traveled up into my hips, rib cage, and shoulders. I replaced the saddle pad and returned to Caim, ready to cultivate our connection.

Saorsa crowded the aisle and whinnied. "I know, fella, you're entitled to your opinion. We had a lovely ride this morning—now it's your mum's turn. There's no need to be the jealous type." I shooed him off to the pasture as Caim waited for me to lead her out.

Caim stood still while I mounted her, despite the persistence of Saorsa hovering nearby. Knowing Katrine must have left him behind many times before, I suspected this routine was familiar, and he fussed because it was part of his nature to fuss, not unlike Ian. I conjured an image of us returning as I told him, "We'll be back soon enough. Don't miss us too much." Animals were mind readers, paying more attention than humans to pictorial thoughts and emotions, sometimes more than words. Angus was an exception, and his skill intrigued me. His ability to read minds and experience premonitions might have drawbacks, but it didn't dampen my desire to learn how he did it. He reminded me of my connection with Faith and how our communication went beyond words.

Saorsa continued snorting and crowding the gate. Clearly, the pictures I sent him weren't working. I waved with my hand, wishing I'd taken a crop. "Okay, Saorsa, back up, back away. You've had your turn. The last thing I need is an escape artist." Saorsa trotted off into the pasture, leaving us space, whinnying, and Caim responded.

My gate skills improved on Caim. However, I attributed it more to her than to me. Saorsa protested being left behind with another loud, more piercing whinny. Caim gave him the silent treatment.

Caim wasn't as demanding as Saorsa, but no less deserving of my undivided attention. Soon I arrived at my next challenge, Angus's gate, the one I'd shied away from this morning when we walked the road. Avoidance wasn't practice, so I tried. My approach was decent, but as soon as I leaned over to grasp the ring, she took a step before I could reach it. On our second attempt, I unlatched it but had trouble swinging it open. It wasn't graceful when I tried to shove it, but it moved wide enough for Caim and my knees to pass through. By some miracle, we closed and latched it on the first try.

The Australian Shepherd arrived underfoot, and Caim lowered her head to say hello. If he had a tail, it would've been wagging. Instead, his entire back end swayed from side to side. I appreciated that he didn't bark at horses, and assumed he and Caim were long-term friends.

Angus whistled and waved from across the field, where he repaired the fence line, and his dog departed. I waved in response before I circled with Caim. It only took a slight shift of my weight to have her attention. Why weren't humans this easy to connect with? Well, Angus was remarkably easy, too easy.

Stop, Sarah. Don't compare Ian to Angus. Everyone's different. Relationships aren't always comfortable, but working through the challenges deepens the intimacy. I aspired to keep the lines of communication open between Ian and me, especially when it felt difficult.

When we trotted toward the next gate, the sheepdog joined as if gates were his domain, and as soon as I closed it again, he returned to the flock.

At the beach, we stood beside the mandala I'd created yesterday. Even though it had escaped the high tide line, the winds had dispersed its seaweed bits. *Everything changes all the time.* I needed to become better at accepting those changes and letting go of my attachments to the past or some imagined future. Bowing meant surrendering to the present moment, letting go of control—*given it's an illusion anyway. The only choice I have is how I respond.* I sat up straighter, the gesture I'd come to associate with my Peaceful Warrior. She reminded me to pause long enough to discern my conscious choice, curtailing my knee-jerk reactions.

My relationship with Faith kept evolving, from the unquestioned intimacy as my childhood friend, to a prolonged estrangement until she appeared as my doppelgänger six months ago, to guiding me in the underworld. She continued communicating with me even during our estrangement, offering me images before I fell asleep and those phrases she'd admitted to sending me in my twenties like an equal and opposite force. Even though I couldn't see her anymore, I no longer questioned her existence.

I wanted to cultivate our channels of communication, tending my night dreams, watching for images when I closed my eyes, and listening for her guidance. Last night's dream of the heron counseled me on the necessity of stillness and solo time to stalk the sacred. Shifting the tempo of my life felt like an invitation I could cast for Faith to accompany me more often.

Seeing the stone circle amidst the waves reminded me of the images Faith had shared in the underworld before we parted. All those images had revealed themselves on Iona, and all but one of the images she shared before our journey had come to pass in the underworld—the toppled queen chess piece remained unseen. The queen represented the archetype of sovereignty, of authority that tended to the whole kingdom, offering blessings. Unlike the magician or warrior, the queen symbolized partnership, partnership with the landscape and human community. If she's toppled, what's usurped her power?

How do I reawaken this dormant ability to glimpse my future? My riding legs weren't the only muscles that needed exercise and conditioning. *Could I learn to ride my mind like I ride a horse?* It offered an interesting metaphor for meditation and cultivating consciousness that had never occurred to me. *I'll be riding every day on Iona, rain or shine, off or on a horse.*

I brimmed with gratitude for Caim's gentle companionship, letting me take in the scenery and forgiving me when my thoughts strayed from her. She turned her neck and head toward my knee, reminding me of her presence. "Okay, let's go." She promptly walked on.

We trotted a few strides before I asked for a canter, traversing the expansive beach. Caim's rocking gait was easy to sit, plus Katrine's saddles were exceedingly comfortable, like well-made Italian shoes. I didn't want to work up a sweat on her, so we slowed to a walk, and I loosened the reins.

We meandered along, admiring nature's artwork. Strands of seaweed strewn by the receding tide were eye-catching in their composition. I imagined them framed in a triptych that I'd call Surrender. Without a camera, I practiced impressing them in my mind.

The power of images. Angus had seen the images I'd recalled on my journey with Faith. I wished he'd teach me how he did it, and wondered if distance made any difference. If I sent him an image, could he receive it even if we weren't together? My guess was yes based on the times I've thought about friends, and they've called, or I've called them, and they'd said they'd just been thinking about me. Long-held relationships formed tendrils of connection that defied space and time, even if it wasn't working at the moment with Ian. *Or is he willfully ignoring it? Angus is different. We're essentially strangers and yet so effortlessly connected.*

As we turned toward home, we approached the mandala. This time we walked through it, embodying the idea that every act of destruction brings on its heels an act of creation, if we have the patience to wait, and the eyes to see it.

The season of fall was a time of letting go. I missed the vibrant color of our Japanese maple at home and how its cranberry leaves announced autumn. I'd gather the first few leaves that fell for a centerpiece on our kitchen table. Last year, it transformed overnight. One afternoon, I admired the maple's stunning display of elegant beauty while checking the mail, but that night's high winds stripped her, and the next day all her leaves blanketed the ground in a crimson halo. She stood bare, displaying her previously hidden architecture of branches, a different kind of beauty. Back then, I only expected to wait another year for her return to full glory. Maybe if the winds hadn't already fleeced her, Ian could send me a picture.

Could I imitate the season's wisdom of letting go this fall and welcome the stillness of winter? Winter's bare branches easily fooled the uninitiated, those who had no appreciation of dormancy—to them the plant may appear dead. Yet, the sap invisibly rose in springtime when green buds burst like commas all along the line of the branch, eventually becoming exclamation points proclaiming the blooms to follow.

Where would I bloom this spring? Could Ian and I let this next season of our relationship unfold? I felt his expectations pressing in on me, trying to rush the season. *What if he shows up unannounced?* I'd deal with it, if it happened.

We arrived at the first of two gates, and it only took me two passes to unlatch it. I saw a flash of black and white bounding up the field. As Angus's sheepdog neared, I said, "Hey buddy. I'd like a table for one by the window with a view, please?" He ran up ahead. My writing beckoned, so we trotted to cover the distance more quickly. Tourists strolling up the road snapped pictures of Caim, who was undeniably picturesque.

Another wave of gratitude washed over me to have landed amidst Iona's beauty. *I have a chance to grow wild by the sea with two blessed horses to ride, who, by my caring for them, are caring for me.* The intention of my blessing—*to be in reciprocity with all my relations,* had become my experience. I started composing a thank-you note to Katrine in my head. She mentioned she'd only return for a day, and since her priorities wouldn't include me, another ride seemed unrealistic. We might not even have time for a conversation to acknowledge the circumstances of my arrival and I wanted to thank her again, in light of that, for her radical hospitality. I'd also mention Ian's pending visit—in case he showed up unannounced.

Caim's four-legged friend waited at the next gate, wagging his invisible tail. "Okay, buddy, you can score our performance." We opened it on the first approach and walked through easily. However, replacing the mint-green loop over the fence post took two more tries. I said to the dog, "How about you give us points for execution, not for style." He dashed off toward his flock.

If only I'd paid closer attention to how Katrine had made it look so easy. I scratched Caim's withers. "You were splendid, doing exactly as I asked."

Saorsa pranced back and forth, posing an unnecessary challenge at the paddock gate, so I dismounted upon arrival. Caim rubbed her face on my leg as I shooed Saorsa away, waving my hand and saying, "Back up." He swung around and trotted a few paces away, then spun around once we'd entered, and stopped abruptly before Caim to touch noses and snort.

We all sauntered into the barn together and Saorsa lingered as I untacked and groomed Caim. I pictured feeding them a carrot as I said, "I'll rustle up a treat for you. Give me a minute."

Katrine's garden displayed flops of carrot tops, and I pulled up two, but they were still on the small side. Determining the hidden progress of root vegetables stumped me; apparently I'd harvested them prematurely. I didn't want to make the same mistake with my process, but patience wasn't my strength.

Both horses waited at the fence line, as if they'd understood my intention. I snapped the greens off and offered them, unsure if they'd like the tops. Their lips happily groped them from my flat hand. I halved the carrots, feeding Caim first. "Thanks again." Turning to Saorsa, I said, "Patience, my friend. We all need to learn patience. Let's say we do this all again tomorrow. Rinse and repeat."

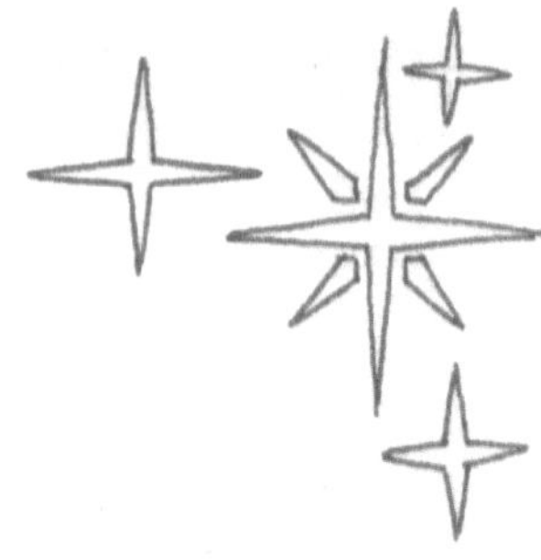

CHAPTER 13

SPACE

T HE KITCHEN COUNTER OFFERED a treat for me—another plate of scones with a hand-written note on the back of an envelope.

Thanks for easing Kat's mind by tending her horses and home.
Enjoy,
Margaret

Just the sight of them caused my mouth to water. I presumed Margaret was Katrine's mum, and that I must have just missed her delivery. My timing had been perfect. At least the rumors about me on the island included my love of carbohydrates. Recalling last night's dessert of scones and scotch brought an irrepressible smile.

After finishing a glass of Katrine's glorious well water, I slathered a scone with butter and jam, taking my first bite while still standing. Delicious. Maybe I'd learn how to bake these? I left the jam jar behind, so I wasn't tempted to reapply it as I sat overlooking the sea. It had already become my favored spot where my paper and pen awaited.

I imagined Katrine's life, and how her beloved had relocated to create their home here. *It would suit me too if I weren't so far from Ian and my friends. I'm a tourist, a stranger to these lands, a rumored woman. Where do I belong?* The question gave me a way into writing.

Belonging. How is it the same or different from where I call home? So often, home is thought of as an outer structure. What if it starts first within my skin? What does being at home within myself even mean? Is it another way of saying embodied presence—when I'm fully inhabiting my heart, mind, body, and spirit? How do I even sense my spirit? To do all of that, I have to slow myself down. The pace of life here is a tempo that allows me to know myself on all these levels. What if this pace is my norm, not the exception, not only lived on retreat or vacation?

The words 'presence' and 'prescience' sound and even look similar, being here now and knowing the future. Is presence a precursor, a requirement for prescience? It also sounds like presents. Is being here now the gift I give myself?

If I'm fully here now, perhaps my consciousness, which is no longer split with multitasking, becomes available to be in relationship to the future in a clairvoyant way rather than anxious about an imagined future. There's a reason my collage of images revealed themselves to me just before sleep, as I was still and quiet, more undefended and open. I can be still and quiet anywhere. Iona isn't essential for this. What's essential is being in my body—fully—my soft, supple body, the one that flows with the horse's movement, yet stays centered. The stillness that can be found even amidst movement, for life is always moving.

I paused, listening intently for what called my attention next. Gratitude. Gratitude to Katrine for offering me such kindness. Gratitude to have landed in her home. Gratitude to feel such a pervasive sense of well-being. I penned a thank-you note to her and found Scotch tape to stick it to her bedroom door in case she returned while I wasn't here.

My stomach craved protein, so I boiled two eggs and made a salad with buttered baguette for an early dinner. When I returned to the bay view window to eat, the water called me, so I listened. *Why not have a picnic dinner at the beach?* I stuck my fork in my back pocket and draped my blanket around my neck. The gusts of wind made it nippier than I'd imagined, so I didn't spread out my blanket on the sand to sit on. Instead, it became a shawl around my shoulders as I leaned against the rock jetty, eating my meal.

I felt Ian's longing to be with me, but I couldn't return it. Like a solo heron, I longed to be with myself, finding and sourcing my own nourishment. *How could I make vows to him if I'm not honoring my vows for myself? Maybe it's time to shift our relationship from lovers to only friends.*

The wind caused rippled patches on the ocean's surface that morphed like saltwater clouds and glinted with sunlight, the way my sapphire sparkled in my ring. Throughout my dinner, my mind repeated the single thought: *this is my life, this moment, this is my life.*

After dinner, I pulled off my ring and dipped it in the ocean before kissing it, and then held it to the center of my chest as I spoke my vow out loud.

"To grow wild by the sea.

To slow down and listen

to what I'm sensing and feeling and

to act on it with authenticity and integrity.

To know if I am purring or growling inside, and

to let myself be known.

To give voice to my longings,

and follow them to a place of belonging, be-longing.

To be in reciprocity with all my relations."

I made the sign of the cross with my ring before putting it back on. For me, this gesture integrated the vertical line of spirit with the horizontal line of matter, reminding me that these realms intersected in my heart, in the place of infinite capacity and transformation. I wanted to tap into the well of my heart and drink from it like the cool, clear waters of Iona.

Ian ran toward his flight's gate. He saw the boarding area vacant and sprinted the last bit, hoping the ramp door remained open. He boarded immediately, breathless and parched, and took his assigned window seat in the empty row. The flight attendants clicked shut the overhead compartments, indicating the door would close at any moment. If no one else qualified for an upgrade, he'd have to entertain himself for the final leg of his journey home to Boston.

Sarah's six-month disappearing act had forced his hand to spend more time alone since he couldn't explain her absence to others. He tried not to think about it because it made him doubt his sanity. The light at the end of that exceedingly long tunnel was finally in sight. Ian called Sarah again, but she didn't answer. Before he turned off his phone, he emailed her to let her know he was in flight and that he'd call as soon as he landed.

The last passenger to board stopped at his row and slipped off her open shoulder bag onto the seat beside him. Ian perked up seeing her natural beauty. Her chin-length blonde hair framed a lightly tanned oval face, and a form-fitting tank top revealed her athletic frame. She effortlessly lifted her carry-on luggage to stow it above. He furtively glanced as she rummaged in her bag, taking out various items and piling them on the seat—a turquoise shawl, a massive hard-backed book with wine bottles on the front, and a black case of Bose noise-canceling headphones that obscured the book's title. Lastly, her reading glasses precariously topped the pile and then tumbled when she removed her bag to put it under the seat. Ian retrieved them and placed them on their shared middle table.

She glanced at him for the first time and said, "Thanks." Next, she wedged the book in the front seat pocket, draped her shawl over her shoulders, and held the headphones while sitting down.

Ian couldn't help but notice her vibrant blue eyes. "No worries." She appeared close to his age, and he noted no wedding ring. He intended to introduce himself, but within moments she'd put on her headphones, the traveler's sign of "Do not disturb."

The same sign Sarah hung when she decided to remain on Iona, conveying she didn't share his eagerness to be together. As a Libra, Ian valued balance in all things, especially matters of the heart, which hardly described the emotional seesaw of the last forty-eight hours: depressed to be on Kauai alone, elated to finally speak with her, and crushed that she planned to stay on Iona. Why was she keeping the Atlantic Ocean between them? He found it easier to be furious with her than to let his sense of rejection sink in.

Ian scrolled through the movie selection, but given the frequency of his flights, he'd seen most of them. In the documentary section, he found a series on Picasso and while the opening credits played, Ian used his peripheral vision to glance at his seatmate. Her closed eyes permitted him a prolonged assessment that she wasn't asleep—her lips were too tight.

He read the book's title, *The Sommelier Prep Course.* Studying wines and their regions appealed to Ian, even if he never planned to take the exam. Later, when she opened the book, she appeared to have read half of it, and had highlighted some of the text. She piqued his curiosity more than Picasso.

I clucked twice for the horses as I slipped between the fence posts. Their heads raised, and soon, their hooves were clopping in the aisle as I dispatched their grain. Ian preoccupied my mind as I accomplished the routine of feeding, blanketing, and closing up the barn.

Before heading next door, I made a small plate of scones for Angus. No one answered my knock and the door was unlocked, so I let myself in, and called out, "Hello, I've come bearing gifts." Nothing. A fire blazed in the fireplace, and I toasted my backside to dispel the chill. After setting the scones beside his computer, I typed in his password, thinking Daphne a fool for discarding a man like Angus.

His computer's clock told me I was early, 5:54 p.m., and I knew Ian tended to be late. My inbox had a new message from him entitled "Seek," that informed me he couldn't talk until his flight landed, which I presumed meant in Boston—at least I hoped it wasn't in Scotland.

My rib cage felt tightly laced in a corset until I took a deep breath, realizing I'd been bracing myself for the conversation.

I resettled on the hearth, checking in to sense if I felt disappointment or relief, and both surfaced, with a mix of irritation. His cryptic email withheld information, which I attributed as intentional, a form of control. *Is he consciously or unconsciously making me wonder if he is coming here, giving me a taste of what it's been like for him these last six months?*

I'd been afraid our call might be a repeat performance of last night. Our pattern of hide and seek needed to stop. I didn't want him to seek me—not yet. But I couldn't exactly write that, so I only wrote, "Safe travels, talk later."

The fire was inviting, but this wasn't my house. I left in search of Angus, so he'd know he didn't need to stay outside to give me my privacy. His dog announced my presence, persistently barking.

"Hey buddy, good job. I know I am a stranger here. Where's Angus?" He kept barking until a whistle silenced him, and he bounded off. I followed his dog around the corner of the house and saw Angus near his barn door, arranging fence posts. He waved and I told myself it would be rude to turn and leave. As the distance between us shrunk, the flutter in my chest quickened. The gradual slope of the hillside deposited me to where he waited.

"I'm on my way. It turns out this timing didn't work for Ian."

"Ah'm sorry he stood ye up, lass. That's got to hurt."

"Oh, he didn't stand me up. He's in-flight. So, he's calling me later tonight. I wanted to let you know I was gone, so you didn't stay outside on my account."

"Dinna fash." He took off his leather work gloves.

"Thanks for the fire. It was lovely to sit beside it for a brief conversation."

"Shall we listen for what else it has to say? Ah'm in nae hurry on this fence repair."

As appealing as that sounded, I fought it. "No, not tonight. Do you mind if I come by tomorrow to check my emails in case Ian and I don't connect later?"

He nodded. "How about we agree—ye come by whenever. Ye dinnae have to keep askin' mah permission or makin' plans. Mah door's unlocked. Consider it a standin' invitation. Ah dinnae want to impose on yer need for space, and at the same time ah want ye to ken 'tis mah pleasure to see ye."

"Thanks, Angus." I turned to go and hesitated. "I do need one more thing?"

"Anything, lass. What can ah do for ye?"

"I haven't been properly introduced to your dog. What's his name?"

"Och aye, that's Jake. He's a fine herder and a decent doorbell, more bark than bite."

"He does make it difficult to surprise you. Enjoy your fence repair." *He's not the only one who needs to mend fences.* "I'll see you tomorrow." As I walked up the incline, it was as if I was swimming against the riptide that pulled me toward Angus. I continued to resist it, attempting to walk faster, but my muscles protested, still hobbled from riding. Slow was my speed today. New muscles and new capacities were forming in my life, muscles that required intentional conditioning and, yes, some pain.

Walking back to Katrine's in the dark, I contemplated the shifting dynamics between Ian and myself. A line from a Kahlil Gibran passage I'd memorized years ago surfaced: *But let there be spaces in your togetherness.*[1] My recall lacked the elegance of his phrasing. Something about the winds of heaven, a dance, and how love wasn't a bond that binds. It was more about being held freely, like the sensation I had with Faith as she embraced me—that there was room for all of me. Gibran advised alone time. He hadn't written about a heron, but that image came to my mind. He wrote about the art of being together and also apart, the way oak trees can't flourish in one another's shadow.

I longed for a soak in a hot bath and started it while I poured myself a glass of wine and undressed. The bathroom mirror had steamed up, and the tub was nearly full. My foot only lasted seconds in the scalding water. There was no chain on the plug and no room for more cold water. I growled inside, impatient to be submerged in my element. *What if I took a dip in the sea?* It had been calling me closer all day. I'd considered a swim during my impromptu dinner picnic, but it felt too compressed, given my plan to speak with Ian. So much for that plan. Nothing stopped me, and the darkness offered privacy.

In case I encountered a stranger, I wore my shift dress, so the island rumors about me didn't include streaking. The sand felt cooler than the grasses. A brief check to the left and right confirmed the beach was mine tonight, so I stripped and waded into the frigid water. My breath caught in my chest as my inner thighs got wet, testing my resolve, but

I persevered. When it reached my belly, my elbows involuntarily raised, and I squealed. *Deep enough*. I dove in. The shock took my breath away. I surfaced and had to consciously calm myself down, shifting from successive, short intakes of air to smoother, slower breathing. Pins and needles prickled my skin. After a few strokes, the sensation dulled until numbness ensued. Swimming in Kauai's tropical waters with Ian would have been far more enjoyable. Still, at the moment, we had followed Khalil Gibran's advice, and there was plenty of space between our togetherness. I had a feeling Ian planned to close that distance soon.

The remedy of a cold saltwater soak for my sore legs swiftly lost all appeal compared to the thought of a hot bath. I beelined to the shore and felt relief as my feet reached the sand, barely stopping to wrap myself in the towel and grab my dress before dashing over the fence and up the hill.

Inside, I bounded up the stairs two at a time. Sinking into the bath, hot water stung my skin. I was moving between opposites. *Is my capacity to find the centered place between them improving? What would it take to shift the strife between Ian and me back to a sense of ease?*

Meeting Ian had rekindled the passions I'd tried to extinguish in favor of playing it safe with my marriage to Arthur. *Maybe it's time to direct that passion toward me, to lean into my longings, trusting them, even if it means I fall for them—even if I'm scorched. If I am, those will be sacred scars, tattoos of a life well-lived.*

I reached for my wine. It didn't taste great, but it was good enough for toasting a day well-lived. *More days like this, please.* I lingered until the tub water turned lukewarm.

Angus kicked himself for assuming Sarah had been stood up. He'd projected what he wanted to be true and missed what was actually happening. Claiming he could read her like a book proved a hollow boast.

His spirits lifted when he saw scones and a note on the table. Sarah's handwriting acted like a lure, tempting him to reach out to her. However, he also respected the distance she needed.

The fence repair had proved more complicated than he anticipated and occupied his entire day. He foraged in the fridge for dinner and ate leftover spaghetti by the fire with his book in hand, but his mind wandered from the page.

Kat had phoned earlier and mentioned her plans to return later this week, but only for a day. She expected to be away another week. *What then—will Sarah stay on? Will Ian come to fetch her?* He had more questions than answers. He stared into the fire, hoping for clues, but none were forthcoming.

Angus prayed Sarah remained longer. *She could stay in mah guest room if Kat prefers her house to herself.* But he dismissed the thought as inappropriate. It was hardly the space Sarah needed. He felt himself falling for her. *Why ah'm ah settin' mahself up to be disappointed?* Before she arrived, he'd been happy, or at least he'd thought he was. Maybe he'd just settled into a routine, unwilling to risk his heart again in a relationship. Some part of him still believed Daphne and feared that every woman he'd be with would eventually find him too intrusive.

Given the island's slim pickings, he'd toyed with the idea of online dating. Kat and he had joked about it when she started using eHarmony. After a half dozen dates that were, at best, a waste of time, he was about to gloat and say, "Ah told ye so," but then she met Roary.

They'd been together for nearly a decade. Angus had to admit he liked the guy, and she'd never have met him in the limited trajectory of her life. Their arrangement was ideal. Roary commuted to Iona for a few weekends in the month, and she combined her errands in Edinburgh with overnights at his place. Those nights, Angus took care of her horses. Saorsa had come to accept him. *Maybe Kat will stay with Roary more*

*often, giving Brìghde her privacy but still bein' close to Finn. Perhaps that
would encourage Sarah to stay on longer if she was helpin' Kat and had
space to herself.*

He knew the chances of Sarah staying on Iona were a long shot, and
he wasn't a betting man. Angus suspected he was setting himself up for
another heartbreak, but he couldn't resist his attraction toward her, nor
deny the foothold she already had in his life. Sarah had an uncanny way of
making him feel off balance. Angus hadn't mentioned it to Kat. He only
now admitted it to himself. Would he tell Sarah he recognized her from
his night dreams, or was that degree of intimacy better kept on pause?

Closing himself off without closing himself down was a fine line
to walk that Sarah needed to learn. Her openness left her unguarded.
Maybe that's part of what makes her so attractive. That, plus she was
intelligent, sassy, and gorgeous—an irresistible combination.

Angus had yet to turn the page, so he put the book aside. Tonight
he was reading his heart to discern his next move. He wondered how
Sarah's day had gone. Her handwriting was no substitute for hearing her
voice. When his phone rang, he eagerly answered it and tried to hide his
disappointment upon hearing his brother's voice.

John picked up on it immediately. "Were ye expectin' someone else?
A lovely lass, perhaps?"

His jest was closer to the mark than he knew. No sooner had he hung
up with him when the phone rang again. Angus's heart leapt for a second
time, as late-night calls were unusual.

He heard Kat's voice quavering. "Angus, 'tis Finn. He's been havin'
seizures. We're back in the hospital." His heart clenched as he held the
phone more tightly. Everything in him resisted the thought of Kat losing
her grandson. She'd already had enough loss for one lifetime and was
crying openly.

He sat forward on the seat. "Oh, Kat, that's awful. Ah'm so sorry.
How can ah support ye?"

"That's why ah'm callin'. Angus, can ye sense anythin'? Will he be alright?"

"Kat, ye ken it dinnae work that way." He pressed his palm to his forehead, then ran it over his skull and tightly held the back of his neck, tipping his head toward the heavens. "Ah'v nae got the sight any more than ye. Ah'll pray for all of ye. The wee ones are more resilient than we ken. What are his doctors sayin'?"

Kat blew her nose. "We dinnae ken anythin' yet. We're waitin'. Ah can nae leave from here. Do ye think ye could bring me some more clothes and yer mum's remedies? Ye can meet Roary at the train station in Oban. Ah left so fast ah dinnae have time to bring her tea and tinctures for Brìghde. Ah'm goin' to phone her next to see if there's anythin' else she recommends for Finn."

"Of course, ah'll be there." Angus released the hold on his neck and stood. He poked at the peat until the flame rekindled. "Text me a list of what ye need and where to find it. Ah can be on the 8:00 a.m. ferry th'morra. Ah ken there's a bus shortly after ah dock that'll get me across Mull. Ah'll look up the ferry schedule and text ye and Roary the arrival time in Oban. Ah'd be happy to come the whole way to see ye, Brìghde, and meet Finn." He started to pace in his living room.

"Thanks, Angus, but there's a restriction on visitors. God willin', ye'll meet him soon enough." She sniffled.

"Aye, tell Roary ah'll wait for him in Oban. Ah'v got some errands to do before ah turn back around. Ah'll be at yer house around seven o'clock to pack whatever's on yer list. Kat, be faithful. Call on Kieran. Ah'm sure he's watchin' out for his grandson. He'll nae let any harm come to him." Angus heard Kat sobbing again and felt the full force of her ruptured heart. He stood still and waited as she wept.

Her voice faltered. "Ah miss him so. Roary's been wonderful, but 'tis Kieran ah want by mah side in these moments."

He heard her blow her nose several times and then inhale deeply.

Some wounds never fully heal. They may lay dormant for years until they split open again without warning, revealing an abyss. Angus recognized the territory, and tonight he stood on its periphery, knowing he couldn't prevent her descent, but he could stand on solid ground and offer her a hand when she was ready to take it. She'd done that for him. "Of course ye do, Kat. Just breathe. Ah'm here for ye. We'll get through this together. Does yer mum ken what's happened yet?"

Her voice became firm. "Nae, ah'm waitin' till ah have more news before ah tell anyone besides yer mum. Angus, could ye call her for me tonight and tell her about Finn? Ask her to hold her tongue. Ah dinnae want this news movin' across the island yet—ah cannae speak of this again. Just puttin' it in words makes it more real than ah want it to be."

"Och, aye, ah'll call her when we hang up. Keep me posted. Ye' ken ye can ring me at any hour for anythin'. We dinnae need to talk. We can just breathe together."

"Thanks, Angus, ah may."

"Ah'm holdin' ye close in mah heart, Kat." His hand rested on his chest, and tears spilled down his face. "Godspeed on Finn's recovery. Mah prayers are with ye. Ye'll have the whole island prayin' for ye when ye'r ready." He wiped the tears with the back of his hand.

"Bye for now."

Angus rang his mum next. She carried generations of knowledge from her maternal line about the medicinal properties of plants, and most of the island relied on her. They agreed to meet at the docks by 7:45 a.m. As he readied himself for bed, he couldn't help thinking this would mean Sarah would stay longer. His wondering if Kat would opt to stay at Roary's had been prescient. If only Finn's health weren't the reason. Sometimes Angus couldn't distinguish between his hopes and his knowings. He didn't dare predict Finn's recovery, but he'd pray for it. Soon, the whole island's prayers would be in full force, and he had no doubt that would help.

I came downstairs in Maeve's robe to refresh my wine and build a fire, eager to sit beside it, listening for what conversation might arise. All was quiet. Yeats offered me his company for a while, almost lulling me to sleep, but I resisted my drowsiness, trying to stay awake for Ian's call. I swapped Yeats for the legal pad, re-reading the passages I'd written earlier in the day on what home meant to me and how it intertwined with my sense of belonging. I followed Rainer Maria Rilke's advice to go into myself.

Even though Rilke wrote to Kappus over a hundred years ago, when I read *Letters to a Young Poet* for the first time, it felt like he spoke directly to me. I missed my dog-eared copy of the book. His advice "to live the questions" became my prompt for my journaling.[2]

> Patience with uncertainty. Not my strength. That's why I'm consciously choosing to cultivate it with my blessing. Is my blessing powerful enough to invoke patience with all that's unresolved and, in many ways, unfulfilled in my heart? Will I have the courage to stay true to my longings and continue to listen to them even if the destination is unknown or maybe even unreachable?

> Yes. I refuse to abandon my desires on the roadside, walking away as if they don't matter. I choose to walk alongside or even behind my longings, letting them lead, not having to be out in front, pretending I know where I'm going. I'm enjoying life at a slower pace, learning to belong inside my skin.

What part of me authored my blessing? Faith? Did she inspire it as a way of inviting me back into a relationship with her, given I'd closed off most of our other communication channels? My blessing is essentially an invitation for congruence. It names the qualities and behaviors I want to characterize my life. Can I treat my blessing like a home to inhabit?

Inhabit and inhibit are only one vowel apart. Inhabit: to dwell or reside within, perhaps to relax at home within the self, the cell of myself. Inhibit: to prevent, hinder, discourage. If I'm inhibited, I'm overly self-conscious and unable to act naturally. My blessing is about living without inhibitions and overcoming the societally imposed ones, to remain faithful to what's most important to me: sacredness, reciprocity, and loving.

Why did Faith encourage me to compose my vow before I could return? A vow is a sacred commitment I keep with myself. It creates the space to invoke my blessing, the qualities I want to inhabit in my days. The power within it is its fluidity, in living in accordance with it. Just as the declaration of love as a statement—I love you—is so different from experiencing loving as an action.

Ian's hanging up on me wasn't loving or kind. My telling him I didn't want to return yet wasn't kind either, at least not to him. I'm asking a lot of his love for me. Love can't be presumed. It's not a given. It changes. Sometimes, our actions diminish that love, sometimes enhance it. Am I acting like our love is not at stake here? What does it mean to live into my vow to myself in the context of our relationship? Isn't my relationship to myself, to Faith, also at stake?

Treating my blessing and vow like drafts, editing and honing them, is an act of vitality. Thus far, I've only edited my blessing from 'connection' to 'conversation' with the elements. It reflected the emerging relationship I'm finding with the earth and with fire. What about air? After all, breathing is a condition of living.

I often stumbled in speaking the stanza in my blessing that invoked a relationship with my breath. I tinkered with a simpler way to convey my intentions.

May my breathing and pausing be a reminder to slow down, ask for guidance, and melt with breath. Better. Air is essential for fire, and fire transforms—like the phoenix moments of my life, when I thought all was lost, only to discover a rebirth on the other side. I want to trust in this inevitable cycle of destruction and renewal, not try to shield myself from it or only experience half of it.

I edited the stanza about venturing into terra incógnita.

May I be willing to be lost, to venture into terra incógnita, letting go of my need to know, my need to figure it out to be safe, trusting life even in the darkest moments, believing in renewal.

It was an improvement but still didn't quite capture the sentiment, so I let it rest until more clarity arose. I felt myself within one of these cycles of destruction and renewal, dismemberment and remembrance. *What skins am I shedding that are no longer essential?*

I flipped to the last page of the legal pad and wrote "Draft Blessing, Version Two" as a title and rewrote my blessing so I could more easily reference it until I'd memorized the new stanza. Reaching for my blanket from the back of the chair, I decided it would become my prayer mat. I laid it before the fire and knelt on it, tracing the space before and around me, saying, "Amidst it all, I carve out sacred time and space to bow to the Great Mystery." I bowed before the fire. My heart swelled within my chest as I spoke my vow out loud. While I couldn't see Faith, I sensed her presence, convinced she was listening as her pendant dangled against my chin.

I sat up briefly to grab a throw pillow from the couch and curled on my side to watch the flames ascend and disappear.

Eventually, I closed my eyes, inviting the collage of images to return, but none came. At some point, I drifted off to sleep. I awoke later with a stiff neck and sore legs. The fire was out. If the phone had rung, it would have woken me. I assumed Ian's flight was delayed as I padded back upstairs to crawl under the covers, returning to the blessed darkness of sleep.

Movements woke Ian to an empty seat and a full bladder. The red sign on the bathroom door read occupied. When his seatmate came out, she flashed a smile, saying, "Oh, I hope I didn't wake you when I got up." Her voice had an accent.

"It's okay."

When he returned to their row, she wasn't wearing her headphones and as he waited in the aisle for her to let him in, he seized his chance for a conversation. "I noticed your book. How long have you been studying to be a sommelier?"

She stood beside him at his same height. "About a month so far. I've toyed with the idea of taking the exam for years."

After they'd settled into their respective seats and buckled in, the announcement to prepare the cabin for landing interrupted their chat. Ian's ears started to pressurize on their descent. He asked, "Are you heading back home?"

"Yes, Boston is home for now."

"Were you born in New Zealand? I've been trying to place your accent."

"Yes, I came to the States for college, and when my internship turned into a job offer, I stayed."

"What kind of work do you do?"

"I'm in marketing." She began putting her belongings back in the bag under her seat.

When she held the tome of a wine book, Ian asked, "Can I take a look at that?"

She handed it to him. "A couple of my clients are in the wine industry and grew up around vineyards. On a lark, I enrolled in the class and decided to get a jump start on the reading list."

The class intrigued Ian. "Who's offering it?" Ian reluctantly handed her back the book, knowing his travel schedule made it impossible to complete any courses. He and Sarah had tried to take Argentine tango lessons but never progressed beyond the beginner's level with all the nights they missed. Sometimes, she'd go without him. Even when they attended together, they rarely danced with one another because the instructor believed that strangers were often more polite and forgiving of mistakes.

"Boston University Metropolitan College. It's a nine-week course that meets at night."

The wheels touched down and they both reached for their cell phones, turning off airplane mode. Various ring tones sounded in the cabin. Ian saw Sarah had briefly responded about talking later.

The seatbelt sign dinged off, and his seatmate stood to exit the plane. She turned to wish him well and walked the short aisle out the door. A few passengers separated them as he exited behind her. An unexpected pang of regret surfaced that he'd never see her again, especially since he hadn't asked her name or where she worked.

Waiting at the carousel for his bag, Ian spotted her at the oversize luggage door. He hustled over to fetch his golf clubs, intending to help her and introduce himself. However, before he arrived, she'd already collected her bike box with ease and rolled it away. She hadn't even noticed him. Ian dismissed his disappointment and all it implied as he gathered his baggage and trundled off with it to his car.

Traffic was thick. He'd been cut off once and nearly side-swiped when he started to call Sarah. He hung up before it rang, since it was after eleven for her, and concluded their call would go better when they were both rested. The twenty-two hours of travel had taken its toll. Tired and hungry, he detoured to pick up a pizza.

When Ian arrived home, Per glanced at him from her cat tower but didn't budge to greet him. She had no idea he was actually home early. Using the pizza box as a plate, he sprinkled the packet of chili flakes liberally before taking his first bite.

While he ate, Ian texted Sam to tell her she was off cat duty. When he stood to open a bottle of wine, Per was underfoot, rubbing against his shin.

"Oh, have you forgiven me for abandoning you? I missed you too, but I'm afraid your days are numbered. Sarah won't tolerate you given her allergies. Maybe Veena was serious, and she'll adopt you."

Next, he emailed Sarah, letting her know he planned to overnight her phone tomorrow and asked what else she wanted him to add to the box. He saved the details of his intended visit until they spoke.

---

1. Kahlil Gibran, *The Prophet* (New York City: Alfred A. Knopf, 1971), p15.

2. Rainer Maria Rilke, *Letters to a Young Poet*, translated by Anita Barrows and Joanna Macy, (Boulder: Shambhala, 2021).

CHAPTER 14

UNCERTAINTY

Wednesday morning, Angus was up before the sun, tending the sheep and making a thermos of tea for the journey. Kat had already texted her packing list. He hadn't rung Sarah to give her a heads-up, hoping he could sneak in without waking her.

He told Jake, "Ye'r on duty today. Ah'll be back later," and left with an empty overnight bag in hand and backpack over his shoulder.

Kat's door was unlocked. He walked into the living room and saw the blanket, pillow, and an empty wine glass on the floor in front of the fireplace. The house held the silence of sleep. He ascended the stairs quietly, pausing on the ones that creaked. Peering into Fiona's room, the bed was made.

Standing at Maeve's bedroom threshold, he watched Sarah sleep. She lay curled on her side, facing the door. Her eyelids were like crescent moons, and her dark hair splayed across the pillow like roots. Angus ached to wake next to her. With each breath, he imprinted her image in his memory to conjure again and again until he forced himself to tiptoe away.

In an attempt to muffle any noises, he slowly closed Kat's door, but it squeaked loudly. He froze and listened to a rustling of sheets—maybe Sarah had rolled over. He didn't dare move the door again to check.

Angus focused on Kat's list: *top drawer, five underwear—next drawer, five pairs of socks—bottom drawer, two long sleeve shirts, two turtlenecks.* She hadn't mentioned which colors, so he peeled off what was on top. Next, he gathered her blue cashmere sweater and a robe from the closet hook. He was bent over, tucking her slippers in the sides of the overnight bag, when he heard the bedroom door squeak again.

He stood and turned to see Sarah, sleepy-eyed in a purple robe, with a quizzical look on her face. "I thought I'd heard something. Angus, what are you doing here at this hour? Is something wrong?"

"Morning, lass. Och aye, 'tis Finn. He's in the hospital for seizures. Kat phoned late last night. She's wantin' to stay close and needs some more warm clothes."

Sarah rubbed her eyes. "Oh, that's awful. They must be distraught. Can I help you gather anything?"

"Nae, ah'v got it all." He put the bag on the bed. "Ah noticed a note taped to the door for her. If ye like, ah'll add it to her things."

"Yes, please." She removed it, peeling off the tape, and handed it to him.

Angus enjoyed seeing her with her morning hair and wished he didn't have to run off. "Ah dinnae mean to wake ye. Ye do look as though ye slept well." She tucked her hair behind both ears. "Ye'r a vision of loveliness, dinna fash."

Sarah cast her eyes down before asking, "What ferry are you catching? I can give you a ride."

"That'd be grand. If ye did, we'd have time for a cuppa. Ah appreciated the scones ye shared yesterday. Any chance there's another one?"

She'd already turned to go and spoke over her shoulder. "Yes. I'll start the kettle and throw on some clothes so as not to scandalize myself further on the island. When you talk to Katrine, please tell her I'm happy to stay on as long as she needs, and there's no need to pay me further. She's the one doing me a favor."

Despite the circumstances, Angus smiled. He dialed Kat's number, but there was no answer, so he texted he'd be at her house for a few more minutes if she wanted anything else, and that he hoped no news was good news. Angus was descending the stairs as Sarah came up. He pivoted his back to the wall and moved the overnight bag to the side so she could slip by him. His heart beat faster at the proximity of her passing, only dressed in her robe. It had fallen slightly open, revealing a hint of her breast's contour, kindling his desire. He leaned against the wall to recover his balance.

Sarah had tidied the living room floor. Her notepad had been turned face down on the coffee table, and the wine glass waited in the sink. The familiar acts of reheating scones and making tea settled his nerves.

Standing in front of the bathroom mirror, I looked like I'd just crawled out of bed—because I had. My hair needed taming. I pulled it back into a ponytail, *not flattering,* and removed the band. The tap required more time to warm than I had, so I splashed cold water on my face and quickly finger-brushed my hair and teeth. I desperately needed to buy a toothbrush. How had I kept forgetting it? I hastily put on yesterday's dirty clothes.

Angus sat with the tea and scones at the kitchen table, but he hadn't started eating. I jested, "Thanks for making breakfast, honey. How'd you sleep?"

"Fine, nae thanks to ye. Ye were a cover hog all night, swimmin'. That must have been some dream."

We both laughed. *How did Angus know Ian always calls me a cover hog?* We turned our attention to eating our scones, and an awkward silence ensued.

When the landline rang, I prayed it wasn't Ian as I answered it. It was Katrine. "I'm so sorry to hear about Finn. I'm here as long as you need me. How is he?"

"He's stable in the ICU and they're runnin' more tests. The doctor still dinnae ken the cause. Can ah speak with Angus?"

"Of course." I handed him the phone.

The horses needed feeding. I didn't want them to be anxious when they heard the car leaving, so I grabbed the keys and dashed to the barn. The absence of gray storm clouds held the promise of a sunny day and eliminated the need for their blankets. *Is a two-ride day like yesterday too much to ask for? Will it include a call with Ian?* I planned to check my emails after my trip into town and was mentally composing my list of toiletries when I felt Angus's presence. Saorsa nickered, and I turned to see him watching me take off Saorsa's blanket. "Hey, I'm guessing it's a no-blanket day?"

"Och, aye, but watch for the mare's tails later today. Another front is comin' through. Tonight, the temperature will drop, and they'll need a warmer rug." Angus went to take off Caim's blanket. "Best be on our way. Ah'v got to fetch somethin' before ah board the ferry."

"We're set. Is there anything I can do for you? I'm not so savvy with sheep, but I follow instructions well."

"Nae, they'll be fine. Jake will tend to them." We arrived at the passenger side door together, another awkward morning moment.

Angus asked, "Did ye want me to drive? Do ye ken how to drive a manual?"

"I'll drive. I've got a standard at home, but the steering wheel is on this side." I walked swiftly to the driver's door as he put his bags in the back seat.

Angus buckled his seat belt for the short trip. "Luckily, there's nae many cars on the road. Just watch out for the sheep."

I laughed. As I started the car, I realized I'd forgotten to grab the last of my money on our way out the door. The damn toothbrush would have to wait. *Never mind, I'll walk back to town later.* "How long will it take to get to Edinburgh?" I'd forgotten what Katrine had said.

"Och aye, ye arrived by other means. Ah'm nae goin' the whole way, only to Oban. Kat's beau, Roary, is meetin' me there. He's takin' the train from Edinburgh. Ah should be back in time for dinner. Ah was plannin' to pick up some Thai food since there's nothin' like it around here. Would ye care to join me when ah return?"

I momentarily took my eyes off the road to look at him. "I'd love it. I was going to offer to make you dinner, but it wouldn't compare."

"Ah'll take a raincheck on that. What can ah bring ye back?"

"Chicken pad Thai, medium spice, please."

"Consider it done. Ye'll have to be patient. Ah'm nae sure when ah'll be back."

"Patience is on my list today. I plan to pick some up."

The parking space Katrine had chosen on my first morning was empty, and I chose it, already becoming a creature of habit. Angus exited the car and walked toward an older woman holding two small brown bags outside the café. She gave him a familial embrace and then handed him both bags, gesticulating what seemed to be instructions. They hugged again, and she watched him walk off until she stared directly at me.

I smiled but didn't wave as I leaned against the car with his backpack and overnight bag at my feet. Angus surprised me by handing me one of the bags. "This one's for ye. More spray for the horses, body oil for ye after yer bath, and a tea ye'r to drink twice a day—steep it in the mornin', then add more hot water to the herbs at teatime, and dinnae strain the herbs till the afternoon tea."

"For me, why? Who was that?"

"That's mah mum. She kens plant medicine. Ah was only expectin' to pick up her concoctions for Brìghde and Finn. She says ye need strengthenin' after yer journey. Ah'm nae in the habit of arguin' with her on such matters. She wanted to meet ye, but ah told her under different circumstances when we're nae so rushed. Ye'll be here for a spell. Let yerself be shrouded in mystery a bit longer. That 'tis if ye'r successful at dodgin' today's visitors. There's bound to be at least one lookin' to meet ye."

"Thanks for the warning. I plan to be on horseback most of the day." *Maybe I'll hide at Angus's house to avoid further contact.* Though I wouldn't object to another baking delivery.

Passengers started boarding. "Ah'll be on mah way." I resisted the urge to hug him goodbye. "An embrace from ye would really have ye the talk of the town, nae that'd ah'd mind. Ah'll see ye later." He turned to walk down the slight hill toward the ferry.

His mum still watched me; no doubt she'd scrutinized our exchange. I ducked back into the safety of the car and drove off.

Angus couldn't get Sarah out of his mind, even with the mission at hand. After he boarded, he turned to wave to his mum. She always waited to see him off. Today, she'd witnessed how he related to Sarah. His body language probably revealed volumes she wouldn't miss reading. Later, she'd extract a confession from him.

When he'd handed Sarah the oil, he tried to erase the image of her massaging it over her arms, breasts, hips, and long legs. Now, as the shore grew more distant, the intimate moment came rushing back. Angus rested his elbows against the railing, letting his lids stay closed to enjoy his daydream until the overhead announcement startled him.

As they docked in Fionnphort, he was already anticipating his return journey when he realized he'd forgotten to arrange a ride home.

Schlepping back after a long day, weighed down by his purchases, wasn't appealing. He considered calling a friend since it would give him the chance to shower and shave before their dinner date, but he wanted to see Sarah waiting for him. *That, for sure, will cause a stir on the island.*

Angus hadn't been seen with a woman since Daphne. All the eligible women on Iona had given up on him when he continually rebuffed their flirtations. He'd concluded his romantic relationships would inevitably all end poorly, as his and Daphne's had, since transparency wasn't what most people aspired to twenty-four seven. Time would tell if Sarah accepted the challenge.

Even though he was on a mission of mercy, Angus found it hard to suppress the smile inside at the thought of sharing dinner tonight with Sarah. It pleased him that she'd been planning to make him supper, and he looked forward to it more than he cared to admit. He'd always treasured his solitude. However, since Sarah's arrival on Iona, he was ready to trade it for as many hours spent with her as possible. The attraction he'd felt toward her in his night dreams had only intensified in her presence. How she'd transited between those realms remained a mystery to him.

I had been debating about mucking stalls or enjoying a scone when I heard the phone ringing inside. My leg muscles hurt as I hustled to answer it.

"Hello," I said eagerly, hoping it might be Ian.

"Sorry lass, ah dinnae mean to make ye run, ye sound breathless."

"It's okay. The exercise is good for me."

"Ah forgot to ask if ye'd fetch me. Ah plan to do some resupplyin' in Oban, and ah'll be a bit of a packhorse." He added, "Or ah can ask someone else."

"No, I'm happy to pick you up. What time will you arrive?"

"Ah'll call around five o'clock when ah ken which ferry ah catch in Fionnphort. 'Tis only a ten-minute ferry."

"Sounds good. I'll be there."

"Aye, that ye will, thanks."

I retrieved my bag of goodies from the car and unpacked the contents on the counter. More horse-detangling spray was a boon; I could give in to the temptation to try it on my own mane. *I have more to untangle than my hair.* I spritzed the air, and the aroma of sandalwood and lavender reminded me of Faith. After unscrewing the top of the blue glass bottle labeled body oil, I dabbed a bit on my inner wrist and brought it to my nose. Hints of jasmine, vanilla, and sandalwood greeted me.

The bag of loose tea had orange petals, mysterious herbs, dried berries, and something resembling bark. It smelled medicinal. *Not promising.* My insides were still jittery. The surprise of waking to Angus in Katrine's bedroom had started popcorn popping in my chest. Learning about Roary reassured me the boxers next to Katrine's bed weren't Angus's and inadvertently opened a door I was trying to keep locked.

Yesterday, I'd flown solo as a heron all day and would be a hermit again today. I told myself it was okay to look forward to Angus's companionship at dinner. Except my next thought was of Ian. *When will we speak today?*

The electric kettle had rumbled to a boil, and steam billowed from its spout. I prepared a pot of my new tea and let it steep as I sat in my spot by the front window. It was easier to be patient, staring at the view. A half dozen goldfinches, with their distinctive red mask and yellow and black wings, had lined up on the fence rail. Were they enjoying the view, too?

After pouring myself a cup, I brought the tea to my nose; it was intensely herbaceous, hardly an inviting smell, and my first taste was nasty. My attempts at sipping it brought the dance of opposites to mind. What was good for me and what I liked were not necessarily compatible. This kind of tea was better cold and downed swiftly, sipping involved unnecessary torture. I saved a bite of scone to change the taste in my mouth when I finished it.

While the tea cooled, I returned to my daily practice of bowing, kneeling on my folded blanket before an imagined fire, tracing my fingers around me, saying aloud, "Amidst it all, I carve out sacred time and space to bow to the Great Mystery." My hands stretched out front, and my forehead rested on the ground in Child's Pose. Concern for Finn's health met me first. I let it seep away knowing these fears wouldn't change the outcome. Next, this morning's ripples of excitement from Angus's proximity spilled out, and finally, my anxiety about speaking to Ian eventually ebbed. After giving it all back to the earth to hold, a blessed emptiness filled me. In that quiet place, all I heard was my breath. My rib cage pressed against my thighs with each intake of breath, receding as I exhaled, and I listened for how my body wanted to move.

When I knelt, resting on my feet, a gentle sensation rinsed through my skull, and my left ear cleared. As I spoke my vow, a feeling of lightness, almost buoyancy, had me rise a bit, expanding my chest with my next breath and lifting my weight off my feet. On my next inhalation, I raised my chest skyward and tipped my head back, feeling a tautness in my throat as I paused. Upon exhaling, I tucked my chin to my chest, rounded my back, and then exaggerated these movements for a few more breaths, accentuating the curve of my spine, arching and hunching, then grad-ually lessening these moves until they were barely perceptible— until each breath gently played my spinal cord like an instrument as if it were a hollow reed that my breath sang through. When I shifted my weight to sit on my butt, something released near my tailbone.

A single word arose—rhythm. *What about rhythm? A snake em-bodies rhythm visually as it slithers, that same sine curve is the pulse of my heart. Seasons are a form of rhythm, along with the moon's waning and waxing. How do my days embody rhythm?*

I spoke my blessing, hearing the reference to the tempo of my life with new ears. After reciting it, I changed positions to lie on my back, feeling my thighs, butt, and shoulder blades meld into the earth. Rest was the essential ingredient for rhythm that I'd neglected to add in my days, which were usually in perpetual motion. Stillness was reserved for computer work, book reading, or sleep. I was rarely horizontal during the day. It wasn't that I didn't get tired. It was more that I resisted napping. What if each day I surrendered my whole body to the earth, in supine position, for a few minutes of stillness on the floor, the grass, or the beach? My childhood had included countless hours of staring at the clouds as they morphed their shapes.

Even if I'd stopped growing, my cells still needed time to regenerate. Why had I confined rest to bed and sleeping?

The answer presented itself swiftly. My mind judged it as a waste of time. I had more important stuff to do than sit idle. I could always accomplish one more thing and not feel so far behind on my ever-expanding to-do list. Yet, even now, when that list was too short to preoccupy my mind, my attention still left the present moment.

I was already contemplating tomorrow's fireside yoga practice. My monkey mind was everywhere but here, now, lying on the floor. Again, it fled to the future, anticipating eating Thai food with Angus and sitting by the fire afterward with scotch and scones.

Should I light a fire before I pick him up so we can return to it? But I don't know if he'd prefer to eat here or at his house. He'll probably need to check on his sheep. It doesn't matter to me. I can be flexible. Stop. Stop getting ahead of yourself, Sarah.

What if I waited until he called and asked him where he wanted to eat? *Could I let my day unfold? What if I didn't have to think about it all ahead of time? A head.* I heard my culprit named again. My mind's controlling habits. *My mind flees the present moment and takes over in a futile attempt to control the future and keep me safe.* I relied on control when I disconnected from the resourcefulness of residing in my body, listening to my heart and gut instincts. *When I'm connected within myself, another conversation becomes possible, one I can trust.*

Conversely, when I've been divorced from myself, I've been less present and less trusting of myself, others, and the world. That disconnection, that disembodiment, legitimately created both a lack of safety and a fear, especially of the unknown. Which in turn caused me to become more fearful than faithful, more indecisive, sometimes to the point that I didn't even sense how I felt, and I've defaulted to numbness, going through the motions of my life—until my postcard moment, 'Wish you were here,' invited me back home.

The outer world gains more authority when I lose touch with my inner life. Ugh. Furthermore, when I'm disconnected, it's more likely that I project my fears onto others, the situation, or the future, and that my attachment to plans and the need for control escalates. The less embodied I am, the more rigid I become, both physically and mentally, as I cling to my beliefs.

Control is no substitute for not having a relationship with Faith. Faith isn't a rational construct. The sayings "can't get there from here" and "things are not what they seem" echoed in my head.

Plans are helpful, even essential, to coordinate actions and resources with others. Can I learn to hold them more lightly, let them morph? Maybe faith isn't about the future as much as the ability to be present, less attached to outcomes and plans, flexing more. Who am I to know what should happen? Faith and humility go hand in hand. Everything is so interconnected that figuring it all out is impossible.

I sighed. *Isn't that why I bow to the Great Mystery each morning? Why my blessing welcomes uncertainty as my beloved dance partner?* I snorted at how obvious it was, yet I regularly failed to see it.

May I experiment with venturing into terra incógnita, letting go of my need to know for the rest of my day between now and dinner. It felt like a luxury, hours stretching out in front of me with Saorsa and Caim—freedom and sanctuary. *What would it take to design my life with this quality of spaciousness? Why isn't this part of the rhythm of my week, weekend, or month?*

I returned to my cup of tea and tested its temperature on my lips. It had cooled enough, but I didn't intend to savor it. I took a deep breath and held it while I swallowed continuously, then chased it with my last bite of scone.

CHAPTER 15

ESSENTIALS

THE TASTE OF UNKNOWN bitter herbs clung to my fuzzy teeth. My non-existent toothbrush would've been handy. I huffed at myself as the dishes clattered in the sink.

How could I keep forgetting something so essential? What else have I failed to remember? With my list in my back pocket, I trekked into town, mulling over my attraction toward Angus and my need to pull away from Ian. Neither felt healthy.

I assured myself I'd done nothing wrong. My feelings were simply that—feelings. I aspired to stay in touch with them. Feeling them didn't mean I needed to act on them, and I hadn't. My foot accidentally connected with a stone on the road, and I sent it tumbling ahead.

The attraction between Angus and myself had been acknowledged and I didn't plan to pursue it. I followed the stone and kicked it again further down the road. I wasn't going to pretend my feelings weren't there. That amounted to denial, another form of lying to oneself and others. Pretending I didn't have a feeling didn't make it go away. Instead, it came out sideways, in shadow. This time, as my foot struck the stone, it veered into the grass on my right, out of sight. I left it there, noticing how my shadow stretched ahead, accompanying me to town.

My vow required self-witnessing, an awareness of whether I was purring or growling inside, and courage to let myself be known. I aspired to living authentically and congruently, dropping the need for a mask to hide behind. *Masks are for birds, like the goldfinches on the fence today or for opera singers who made a living off high drama.* I was done with high drama. I wanted moderation. *Is there enough room in my heart for both Ian and Angus? There must be. My heart is the place of infinite capacity. Yet, even if my love can be bountiful, I only want one lover in my life. What if I choose to be my own lover for now, celibate, relegating both Ian and Angus to friends? I could already hear Ian's protests amidst the bleating sheep.*

Any romantic involvement with Angus would be reverting to my old pattern of no space between relationships, no time alone, no heron time. I'm here to break patterns, not repeat them. I resolved to keep my relationship with Angus as friends, nothing more. *Well, maybe an occasional flirtation to release the tension, but no more physical touch.* That boundary had to hold firm.

My connection to Ian felt tenuous, and only partly because he'd hung up on me—mostly because I wanted to feel seen and heard by him, but instead, I felt steamrolled. Had this always been the dynamic between us, and I'd been oblivious to it? How often had I let myself be steered in a different direction to accommodate his needs or desires? *Why don't I assert my own needs—my wants—more often, or even admit to them? Sometimes, I don't know what I want—or is that a cop-out?*

I'd perfected the action side of my life, but it wasn't necessarily tied to what I most wanted. I tended to sedate myself with a hefty dose of busyness combined with a shot of fogginess. It was my version of a cocktail for protection against disappointment—except it didn't make for happy hours or a contentment in my days. I hadn't been willing to risk knowing and asking for what I wanted, fearing it would be denied, withheld, or used as a bargaining chip. I'd witnessed those power dynamics between my parents and concluded vulnerability was for foolish losers.

It didn't matter if Ian hadn't deployed those tactics. *It's not Ian's fault if I go along with him and don't let him know I want something different. He's not a mind reader—but Angus is. Am I being seduced by the ease of not having to speak my heart and mind?*

How do people in committed relationships navigate the tension of wanting different things, specifically, mutually exclusive things? In the past, I'd tended to take the less risky path and went along with what Ian proposed. My heart clenched at that word "proposed." I felt it looming.

At the grocery store, I focused on procuring the necessities, but upon paying, I realized that I'd forgotten the necessary shopping bag again. My toothbrush and razor fit in one back pocket, my toothpaste in the other. I held the box of tealight candles and deodorant as I strolled home along the beach for more privacy.

The boat that brought me here had disappeared. Even on land, I still felt adrift and without oars. While I'd addressed my immediate needs, my future remained uncertain. *Isn't it always uncertain?* Maybe, but typically, I had a plan to steer through life and avoid the shoals. Not having a plan, even if it was a false sense of security, made me feel vulnerable. My last six months hadn't been planned, but I'd had guides: Faith, Compassion, and Forgiveness. I presumed they were still my guides, *and* I wanted a plan.

My mind left the present moment once again as I imagined how good it would feel to brush my teeth and have freshly shaven legs before rubbing in my new body oil. *Does Angus's mother harvest plants according to the phases of the moon or while the dew is still on them?* I'd dismissed these practices as ridiculous until I discovered that a rose cut in the morning before the sun reached its petals lasted longer than one cut at midday. I'd made enough last-minute table arrangements before summer dinners, cutting my roses at the wrong time, only to see them limp and losing petals by morning. It might not always be convenient to respect and act in alignment with the cycles of the moon and sun, but it mattered—another reminder of the importance of the things we cannot see.

Again, I walked inside my head. The conversation the shoreline had to offer was lost on me. I'd hardly even noticed my surroundings until I recognized Angus's home. Jake met me at the door without barking, even with Angus absent.

Typing his password, Daphne2018!, continued to pique my curiosity. *Would Angus reveal more of this history to me?*

A new email from Ian awaited me with the subject line, "Packing List." It began like a postcard, minus the picture. Ian wrote, "Missing you—wish you were here." The rub was, I was glad to be here and speculated that Faith had sent me to Iona, so I'd stop missing myself—my life.

He let me know he'd arrived too late to call last night, but neglected to tell me when he wanted to talk today or to send a Zoom link. Apparently, he thought I could read his mind. He planned to pack my phone, wallet, and any other small items that would fit in an overnight box he'd ship today and wanted my packing list for a suitcase.

He's coming. Once again, he'd been cryptic. *When is he coming?* In my reply, I let him know that I'd be at the computer at 1:00 p.m. and requested a Zoom link. At least I could establish a time to talk. My jaw tensed from being spoon-fed information. I felt him controlling me from a continent away and swung futilely at the air around me as if I could cut the puppet strings.

Angus had Sarah's parting comment on repeat, "I'll be there." He took comfort in the simple statement, even if it only referenced today. Gazing out the bus window, he experienced the unfamiliar sensation of moving swiftly through the landscape. He rarely rode as a passenger in a car and didn't bike or ride a horse. He preferred taking his time with everything, moving slowly, unwilling to be rushed. Maybe that partly explained why Sarah unnerved him. She'd arrived out of the blue from his dreamtime to his daytime, taking up residence in his heart and mind. He found himself considering her even when she wasn't near. Would he move fast even if she were available? Unlikely.

His relationship with Daphne had soured him on impulsivity. They'd met the day she arrived on Iona, sharing the same ferry. A wheel on her suitcase had broken, and she'd been struggling to steer it when she ran up against his Achilles tendon. She apologized profusely. He assured her he was fine and even offered to carry her bag to the hotel, but that was before he'd discovered she'd packed it full of books. He sympathized with the wheel. It had buckled under the weight. They chatted with a polite distance between them until arriving at the St. Columba Hotel. She offered to repay him with dinner that night and wouldn't let him brush her off. When she touched his arm, a charge passed between them. Angus listened to his body and relented. He'd expected it to come to nothing, a shared meal after which he'd never see her again. He was wrong. It was a good reminder he didn't always have an accurate read on the future. She painfully drove that point home later, impaling his heart with it.

Daphne's laughter and affable nature unwound the tightly coiled spring he hadn't realized he'd become. When she invited him to her bedroom, he accepted without hesitation. He was still there in the morning. Over the next week, they ate every meal together, never sleeping apart. They shared the unedited stories of their lives, their hopes and dreams the way one might tell a total stranger, inadvertently entwining their stories.

On her last night, he finally admitted to himself he wanted her in his life. He said, "Ah want to see ye again and again and again."

Daphne had seductively kissed his lips and then his palm before she wrote her address on his skin, saying, "See, my flat isn't that far away. London's an easy reach."

Their time together compressed into her island visits and his few trips to the city, when they hardly left her flat. A year went by quickly, and he fell in deep with her. He'd introduced her to Kat, his mum, and friends, and everyone agreed he had found "the one."

The day he stared at her new suitcase in his bedroom on what would become her final visit, he marveled at how one broken wheel had changed the trajectory of his life. But Daphne wasn't herself on that trip. She had a sharp edge he'd never felt before, and he couldn't say or do anything right. He couldn't get a read on her either. It was like she had dropped a cloak over her body, bristling at his touch.

The hallmark of their relationship, the ease with which they moved together, had been hijacked. The broken wheel was back. He watched her pack a day earlier than he expected, taking everything she typically left behind: her toothbrush, hair dryer, and extra shoes. She emptied her underwear from the top drawer and piled in her accumulated books. Daphne never traveled without half a dozen books. He suddenly knew why her suitcase had been so light on arrival.

She stonewalled his questions and ignored his growing desperation for an explanation. She wouldn't even let him carry her suitcase downstairs. The air had turned frigid between them despite the roaring fire in the living room.

She said, "Don't touch me. I'm leaving for good." As if he hadn't noticed.

He repeatedly asked, "Why?" but she refused to talk about it until she finally dealt her devastating blow. In retrospect, he wished he hadn't pushed.

"I was wrong to come, to start a relationship with you. I can't abide by your intrusive ways."

She actually called him an intruder. None of it made the slightest bit of sense to him. She had arranged for a taxi and left him standing, gobsmacked at her reversal. She never returned his calls or letters. Silence, deafening silence, was all they shared.

Angus had let her nest in his heart. Every item she extracted from his home felt like she ripped the twigs from within his chest. He felt like a world-class idiot—first because he, who could read her and nearly everyone he'd ever met, hadn't seen this coming. Secondly, he couldn't find any explanation, anything he'd done wrong or even differently. But most of all, he rebuked himself for giving his heart away to her so quickly in the first place. He vowed never to make that mistake again. Slow and steady was his speed, and he planned to stick to it.

His eyelids rested longer with each blink. It had been an early morning start to the day, and the motion of the bus lulled him to sleep. A passenger's bag bumped his shoulder, rousing him from his nap. He heard them apologize and replied, "Dinna fash. Ye'v done me a favor. 'Tis time ah wake."

The bus's engine had downshifted and soon stopped in the parking lot. His long legs had been crammed up against the seat. Standing offered relief. He grabbed his backpack and duffle bag, following the other passengers down the aisle, feeling like one of his sheep being herded to the barn. Everyone headed for the ferry to Oban in a straggling line.

My foul mood precluded riding Saorsa, so I tacked up Caim and focused on my breathing until I was a worthy companion. We ventured further along the beach and into the fields, studying the safety of the footing as I planned to retrace our steps with Saorsa later. Today, there were cows in the fields beyond the beach, so even the farmers trusted the solidity of the ground. I carefully observed how far their hoof impressions had sunk in the mud before assuming it would support our weight. Grazing in different fields has its wisdom. Giving time for life to replenish itself wasn't only healthy for horses, sheep, and cows, it was wise for humans to vary their routines. Ian and I had varied our habituated patterns, but the footing beneath us felt unstable.

Typically, I stayed home; he was the one who traveled for work. After teaching and the surround of people all day, I needed time alone to recover. The rub was when Ian had been home, all day alone, he expected to spend time with me, and I tended to accommodate his needs, not mine. It was easier when he was out of town because I didn't have to ask for space and time to myself. I needed to learn to tend to myself, like my roses, sensitive to what helped me thrive.

What was I harvesting in my life this season on Iona? I welcomed the turning inward which fall and winter naturally offered. Ian was more of a perpetual spring and summer personality. Our planned trip to Kauai was a respite from the onset of New England's colder weather. He relished client work in California's sun; those were his different pastures.

While Caim and I headed back to the barn, a platoon of red-beaked, black-and-white-uniformed birds scurried along the shore, pecking at bits. They made high-pitched, sharp calls as we approached. Caim paid them no mind—she wasn't as tightly strung as Saorsa. I scanned the beach for the figure eight I'd made yesterday riding him, but it had disappeared, only lingering in my memory.

It occurred to me that time spent outside every day offered more than exercise. Humans weren't meant to spend our lives indoors; it limited the possibilities for conversation—watching and listening to the birds—getting to know their calls, their migrations. They weren't decorations, they were an essential part of the fabric of life, each one had their role to keeping this Great Mystery in balance. I'd lost that balance in my life, my role in its fabric, thinking I was more important than the creatures that cohabitated the earth. Island living created a kind of unavoidable intimacy. *Am I ready to welcome a close encounter with it all? Maybe.*

I managed to unlatch and latch the gate on the first try and sensed Jake's approval. He probably considered me a risk, or at least job security. I caught myself wondering if I'd try the pasture gates with Saorsa today or walk the road and reminded myself to decide in the moment. There was no need to get ahead of myself.

Saorsa trotted along the fence line, giving us his welcome prance. I couldn't imagine ever tiring of watching him move or of riding him. He joined us in the barn as I untacked Caim. They hung out as I mucked the stalls, then trailed behind me, more like dogs, as I cleared the pasture. Staying ahead of their deposits meant less need for removal from their hooves, bodies, and blankets. I welcomed their companionship as their presence grounded and settled me. Then it occurred to me I'd forgotten their treat. Maybe they'd been sending me pictures. "Sorry, my friends, I've been a bit dense. I don't have this part of the routine down yet." I pictured a bruised apple in the fridge. The carrots needed more time in the ground. As if on cue, they both walked away. Really? Had they only been waiting until they conveyed the message?

I chuckled at the thought of trying my thought experiment with Saorsa and Caim. After emptying the wheelbarrow, I raided the fridge with my boots still on. The floor needed sweeping, and today was my last dry day for laundry. My tiny, borrowed wardrobe would fit in her washer, and after it hung dry I could keep wearing it until my belongings arrived with Ian. *When is he coming?*

While composing my packing list, the memory of Angus gathering Katrine's clothes swept in, filling my chest with a flash of heat, reminding me my body had a mind of its own.

I quartered the apple and walked back outside to where my massive message transmitters, Saorsa and Caim, waited for me at the fence line.

"Well, you two aren't just pretty faces. Okay then, game on. Elders first." I fed Caim and her lips felt like velvet on my palm. Saorsa groped more greedily. "That was fast. You didn't even drop any bits." Both their noses sniffed my hands, expecting more. "Yes, round two, then it's gone."

They remained nearby to munch grass, and I sat on the top fence rail, enjoying their proximity.

Chores awaited me, but I didn't have to rush off. I heard the recently edited lines of my blessing: *to pause, receive guidance, and melt with breath. Where does that guidance come from? Am I conversing with the sun, like my roses, or are my parents watching over me, sending inklings?*

I sent Saorsa a picture of me lunging and riding him this afternoon, saying aloud, "Your turn's next." He lifted his head slightly to relocate to new grass or perhaps nod. I had no way to know for certain what he was thinking and it didn't matter. *Connection and non-attachment—this is the dance of opposites I'll move with today.*

I swung my legs around and jumped off the fence. Laundry time. At this pace, even chores were enjoyable. My blanket also needed washing. Who knew where it had been before? Starting Katrine's washer was neither easy nor intuitive. Why were the symbols used on European appliances so indecipherable? Everything was in Celsius, and even finding the cold setting baffled me. I'd mixed the whites with darks and hoped my new T-shirt wouldn't emerge tie-dyed.

Lunch was an amalgamation I ate standing. I scrambled an egg but sent my stomach more appealing images of pad Thai for dinner as I sliced some cheese and finished the last of the ham on a hunk of baguette. Ian wouldn't have approved. Meals were more important to him than to me, so when we were together, I spent more time fixing them and cleaning up afterward. When he was gone, I ate at random hours, waiting till I was hungry, listening to my internal rhythm, not the routine established by the clock.

What if I didn't always accommodate his food needs and some nights were simple meals? I could at least let my desires be known. What Ian chose to do about it was up to him. I predicted he'd fuss about it. *Could I ignore his fuss instead of reacting to it? I can certainly try.*

How often does Ian accommodate me? I surmised sometimes those instances were invisible to me if he didn't object to my preference. I'd need to ask him.

With no dishwasher to unload, cleaning the kitchen went swiftly. I'd been cycling the same plate, cup, and utensils from the strainer. Dishwashing was another area of friction between Ian and me. He often stayed seated at the dinner table after we finished eating while I tended to get up to clean. Alternatively, he'd announce he had to make a call or send an email and disappear while I finished the dishes. Ian's timing was impeccable. He'd surface when I was wiping the counters to say, "Sarah, you didn't need to do that. I was planning to take care of it."

It didn't land in me as genuine. If he'd planned to do it, why not mention that before he left or while he sat there watching me do the dishes? Furthermore, why say it at all? A simple thank you or an offer to clean up the next night would be more believable. After all, I'd chosen to clean up and he'd chosen to let me.

Some nights, I remained at the table with him or headed off to do something else, but the next morning, I'd wake to a sink full of dirty plates and pans, a sight that made me growl. Ian knew this—I hadn't left it a mystery. He wasn't fond of cleaning the kitchen, and I knew this, too. We needed to find a way to work it out as the dishes didn't do themselves, even with a dishwasher, and it was a daily navigation that caused a fuss. Some part of me knew it wasn't really about the dishes anyway, that it signaled a hidden dynamic of roles we'd not addressed.

Ugh. I'd become the resentful woman standing in the kitchen, like my mother, while Ian, like my dad, went off to enjoy himself. I wiped my hands dry on the tea towel and looped it over the handrail of the oven. It was time to edit this old shit story.

What did Katrine do when her family was here? In my fantasy, everyone pitched in to help. *Why do people like to be waited on, served, and cleaned up after? What if it were an invitation for fun rather than a chore to avoid? Would some good dance music shift the mood? So much of my life is spent handling the necessary logistics: laundry, dishes, cleaning, cooking, and grocery shopping. What if all that time could be enjoyable rather than futilely avoiding it or resenting doing it?*

If I hired someone else to maintain my life, I'd have to work more to pay them. In the right state of mind, chores offered me moments of reflection or simple pleasures and sensations. Washing dishes was like a tub bath for my hands as warm, soapy water cascaded over them.

I found the broom and swept the floor, listening to the swish of the bristles. My mind contemplated Socrates's advice, how the unexamined life wasn't worth living.

The abbey bell chimed once, indicating twelve-thirty. I penned my packing list and brought an envelope from Katrine's counter to have her mailing address handy for my call with Ian. I briefly debated contacting my friends, but hadn't discerned what to say to them about my absence. I doubted they'd believe me if I told them the truth and worried they'd think I'd lost my mind. The thought of arguing with them about my sanity felt troublesome, but I also didn't want to lie. The bind was paralyzing, so procrastination won out.

After discovering there was no new email with a Zoom link from Ian, I emailed him Katrine's address and my short list. Angus still had a landline, so I used it to call Ian collect. This time, the operator was successful, and a groggy Ian answered, accepting the charges.

"Hey darlin', sorry to wake you, but I didn't want to miss you again."

Ian's morning voice was unusually raspy. "What time is it?"

"In which time zone? I think it's 2:00 a.m. in Kauai. It's one in the afternoon here and just after eight for you. Rise and shine. You apparently have packing to do. That was some change in plans."

"Yeah, turns out I didn't want to be in Kauai without you after all. Hey, I feel terrible for hanging up on you. I needed time to sort myself out."

"It's okay. I understand the need for time and space."

Ian's voice was conciliatory. "I hear you. Your wish is my command—time, and space. I came to my senses when I realized I didn't have much choice in the matter. How does the saying go, *'If the mountain won't come to Muhammad, then Muhammad must go to the mountain.'*"

I laughed. "In your eternal wisdom, you've now become a prophet and a ruler?"

"Indeed, I foresee a large white bird carrying me to the shores of Scotland, followed by every other means of transportation known to man, short of a motorcycle and skateboard. I researched the trip, Sarah. Consider yourself lucky you washed up in a boat. I can't believe how hard it is to reach you. After my flight, I take a train, a ferry, a bus, and another ferry. For god's sake, could you be any further away if you tried?"

"I guess not."

"They don't even allow rental cars on the island. Do they still use a horse and buggy over there?"

"No. It's quite civilized. Only the bare necessities and a beauty that's hard to describe. You have to see it."

"I plan to—how else will I see you?"

"Good point. When are you coming? You left that detail out of your message."

"I'd prefer to be there now, but my flight tomorrow is to San Fran. I'm going early to see Lucy and Scott to wine taste in Napa before working till Thursday. My Friday morning flight leaves at an ungodly hour and hopefully lands two hours before my plane departs for Glasgow, so I'm not heading back home. I have to stay overnight in Oban because the train schedule is so limited. You could meet me there."

While I appreciated his willingness to come to me, I breathed more easily knowing our reunion wasn't imminent. "I'd rather meet you here and introduce you to enemies number one and two, Saorsa and Caim."

"Ah yes, my rivals for your affection. I have a suggestion: ride me instead."

"Wise ass. Thanks for sending off my cell and wallet. I emailed my list, but now that we're talking, I can walk you through which jewelry I want."

"Hey, can you give me a minute? I need to pee like a racehorse. I'll send you a Zoom link in a moment."

"Sure. See you soon."

"Not soon enough."

After we hung up, I sighed. If I pushed back on Ian for not talking with me first about the timing of his visit, I risked ruining the connection we had reclaimed. When we logged back in, I opted to keep the conversation light.

"How was your flight back?"

"Long, with too many stops. I'd hoped to call you from LA, but I had to sprint before the gate closed. You'll get a kick out of this—I was upgraded to premium class, and the woman seated beside me was studying to become a sommelier."

"You do have a knack for attracting wine lovers to you."

"Yeah, I wanted to look at her book, but we didn't start chatting until we descended. She kept her headphones on the entire trip. The kind of move you'd make. I watched some of the Picasso documentary series and fell asleep."

I made a mental note of the potential for a good Christmas gift for Ian. We went through my list, and he found it all. "I'll let you go—wait. Is that the cat lying on my pillow in the background?"

"Ah that's Per, short for Persephone. You remember her. She appeared the night you disappeared. I've often thought her sole purpose was to remind me I wasn't hallucinating that night. She likes your side of the bed and is keeping it warm till you return. I'll oust her in a heartbeat."

"Yeah, and buy me a new pillow—*not to mention deep cleaning the house*. I'd forgotten about her and can't believe you named her that. Maybe some part of you knew I'd be gone for six months in the underworld."

"I confess I thought about that myth, but I expected you to return in a few days. When those days turned to months, I started doubting if you were ever coming back. It's such a relief to see you in this world and to put this whole ordeal behind us."

"I'm not sure it's behind us, but let's not get into that now. Here's a weird coincidence for you. Katrine has a black barn cat named Demeter. However, she's an outside cat. No coming into the house or lying on my pillow." I heard myself say weird and knew it was the wrong word choice. In the past, I'd referred to these coincidences that way, pulling back or distancing myself from them. Something had shifted in me and they didn't freak me out anymore. *A better word is wild. When weird becomes wild, and wild becomes wonderful. That's what I'm welcoming now after my journey with Faith, and what I'm inviting here on Iona as I grow wild by the sea.*

Ian had walked back into the kitchen. "That is weird. Just think—soon, we will be able to text and call one another at any time. Let's plan to talk tomorrow, before I leave, in case there's something else you want in your suitcase. It'll be parked at Logan while I'm in California, so it's now or never on your packing list."

We agreed to speak at nine, offering him another hour of sleep. I returned to Katrine's and checked on the clothes. The washer still had twenty minutes left on its cycle. I couldn't ride Saorsa until I'd hung everything to dry.

My legs were still painfully sore, so I snooped around for a yoga mat and discovered one under Maeve's bed. I guessed from its faded blue appearance that it had been left in the sun some days for its own salutation. After unfurling it in front of the fireplace, I stretched with random yoga postures until I lay on my back in Savasana. This small act was proof of my learning to oscillate between movement and rest. As I let myself sink into the earth, a light slumber blanketed me until a loud buzzer startled my eyes open.

The washer had finished. I rolled up the yoga mat and extracted the slightly damp clothes into the basket. When I stuffed my wool blanket in the stainless-steel drum, the risk of shrinking it felt imminent. I pressed the start button anyway. Hearing the rush of water, immediately followed by jostling and sloshing, I wondered if it would come out felted.

At the clothesline, I practiced my nascent skills at hanging laundry. I'd used up all the clothespins before the basket was empty. Apparently, three clips per item were too many. The line had become a spiky deterrent to birds, with wooden V's everywhere. I figured it might be an advantage. What prevented birds from resting on my clean clothes and shitting all over them? Using the great outdoors as a dryer had its risks.

I kept my date with Saorsa, and our gate practice only showed marginal improvement. The decision to be inside the fence line was advantageous when a car slowed with the window down. At first, I thought the driver might have mistaken me for a local and wanted to ask for directions. I was off the mark.

She said, "Hello, Saorsa," and waited a moment before adding, "Ye must be Sarah."

"Hi. Yes, I am."

"Angus mentioned ye might be ridin' today. Ah was hopin' to catch ye for a cuppa."

I noted she didn't introduce herself, but the square shape of her face and set of her eyes resembled Angus's features. "Perhaps later in the week. Given this is our last day of sunshine, I'm not sure when I'll return."

Her lips barely smiled. We both knew I'd wiggled out of the interrogation for now.

"I didn't catch your name."

"Och aye, that's because ah dinnae mention it. Ah'm Angus's sister, Deirdre. Enjoy yer ride. We'll find another time." She drove off with a wave.

A twinge of regret arose, as sisters were always a fountain of knowledge, though our snippet of exchange warned me Deirdre was deft at directing a conversation. This morning I'd felt his mum's maternal eye on me, and guessed she'd sent her daughter as her emissary to check me out. When Angus foretold potential visitors today, it had provoked an unsettling feeling and the compulsion to escape. The notion of hiding appealed to me. *Maybe I am hiding from Ian, too.*

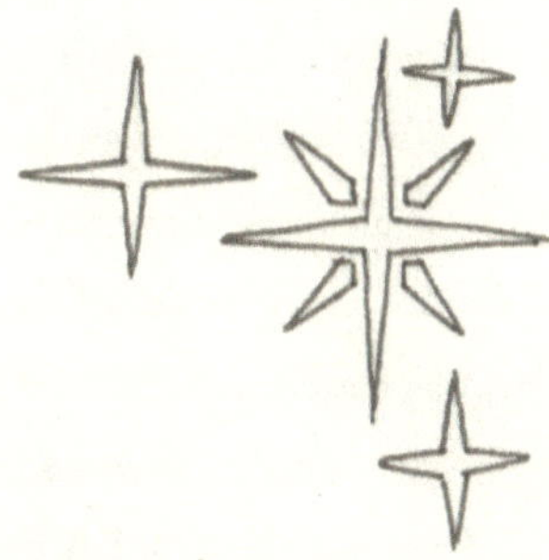

CHAPTER 16

PEREGRINE

ANGUS DISEMBARKED THE FERRY and began his two hours of errands before meeting Roary at the train station. His first stop was one of Scotland's oldest active distilleries, Oban, to replenish his supply of whisky, and then on to the wine shop to procure a New Zealand Sauvignon Blanc for Sarah.

En route to the bookstore, he passed a cashmere shop and Angus recalled how all the women in his life loved cashmere. It might be too soon in their relationship to come bearing multiple gifts, but he decided to look. He breezed in, and a pair of black cashmere gloves sat on the shelves near the door. She'd need them soon, and since they were one-size-fits-all, it was one of the least risky items he could buy. The saleswoman had him in her sights and closed in on him.

"Would ye like a scarf to go with it?" Not waiting for his answer, she continued. "What color hair does yer lady friend have?"

"She's a brunette."

The saleswoman selected an array of plaid scarves with deeper shades of greens, purples, and blues. He preferred the one with indigo, creme, and gold, selecting it from her hands. "Ah'll take that one." *Will Sarah still be here at Christmas? If not, Deirdre will become the happy recipient. Nae, if Sarah leaves sooner, ah'll still give it to her as a goin' away gift. Somethin' to remember me by.*

At Waterstones bookstore, he relished the time to browse the shelves, landing in the poetry section. Angus had lost himself in the pages of *Drunk on the Wine of the Beloved: 100 Poems of Hafiz,* translated by Thomas Rain Crowe, when his phone dinged. Kat had texted, requesting he pay Sarah, and saying she'd reimburse him.

To avoid handing her cash, he perused the card rack. It held images of dolphins, corncrakes, and beaches. Nothing felt right till he saw a sunset and then a peregrine falcon. He couldn't choose between the two, so he bought both, along with three books. They didn't all fit in his pack, so he stowed Hafiz in the extra bag he'd packed for their meal and phoned in their Thai food order.

The train must have arrived early, because Roary stood by the station's entrance where they had agreed to meet. They greeted each other with a single-armed embrace. "What's the news of Finn?"

Roary shuffled his feet and looked beyond Angus to the crowd. "The doctors are still runnin' tests. His blood work revealed a deficiency in glucose and magnesium, but they haven't ruled out other causes."

"The waitin' is torture. How's Brìghde's health? Has she been able to have the wee one on the breast? Ah imagine that would be the best for both of 'em?"

"Ye'd have to ask Kat. Ah'v nae inquired to that level of detail. Thanks for comin'. We'll let ye ken as soon as there's news to share. Let's hope our next meetin' will be cause for celebration." Roary held out his hand for the bag.

"Och aye, ah pray for that." Angus gave him the overnight bag and gripped Roary's shoulder goodbye with his free hand.

The ATM was only a block away from the Thai food restaurant. At the ferry terminal, the boarding line had already formed, filled with a women's football team carrying duffle bags with the Glasgow City F.C. emblem. He'd stood behind them, entertained by snippets of their conversations, jesting, and frequent laughter. It was a respite after his somber exchange with Roary.

He found a private corner of the upper deck, putting his pack on the booth bench across from him, a not-so-subtle barricade to discourage folks from sitting there. His mind wandered back to Sarah, wondering if she'd spoken with Ian today. He felt protective of her, as if she were a freshly emerged butterfly from its chrysalis and her wings were still wet.

The initial guardedness she'd erected before they'd established the circumstances of her appearance had vanished and her transparency acted as aphrodisiac. While he longed to drop his defenses, the thought also terrified him. He felt snared in a tension of opposites and doubted he'd sort it out before he arrived home.

Staring out the ferry window toward the dark waters below, Angus explored his reluctance. *What am I so afraid of? What's the worst that can happen if I let my guard down?* The answer surfaced immediately; he'd fall for her even deeper than he already was, and he was already well over his head. *Would that be so terrible? Nae, it'd be heavenly if she's in the depths with me, surrenderin' to the feelings between us.* But she wasn't. She was holding on to the ledge of her former life, a future with Ian. There wasn't an engagement ring on her finger, but he sensed it wasn't far from her mind. What he couldn't see was if she wanted to wear it. *Would a brief encounter of depth be better than nothing at all?* Despite his vow to himself to go slow, he sensed he'd have regrets if he held back.

Angus had played a fair amount of football. It was the one time in his life he'd befriended speed. He thrived on the intensity and had a way of sensing his opponent's moves. As a striker, he didn't hesitate. His footwork was deft, and he took every shot on goal, sticking to his opponent with pressure, increasing their chance of making a mistake. *Sarah's arrival on Iona could be the most important match of mah life. Ah dinnae want to watch it from the stands. Why start hesitatin' and second guessin' mahself now—when timin' is crucial?*

When he'd discovered she was spoken for, he told her he'd respect that. *How can ah honor mah word but nae be left on the sidelines? What if ah dinnae seek out any romantic involvement? What if ah focus on cultivatin' our friendship? Let her experience what's possible between us and pray that 'tis more enticin' than what she shares with Ian.*

Ian. Angus had no interest in meeting him. *He'll pick up on mah feelin's for Sarah and think of me as his competitor. That'd be Ian's mistake.* He wasn't sure why, but he knew it was true. Ian wasn't his opponent. He wished the man well in his life.

The steady hum of the ferry's engine shifted, indicating docking maneuvers. Angus gathered his bags as the overhead announcement prompted other passengers to do the same. He was in line before the Glasgow City F.C. players clamored behind him. They were beyond rowdy; obviously, they'd spent their time finishing off a few pints. Several passengers exchanged disapproving glances at their raucous laughter, but the players carried on unfazed.

The bus waited with the luggage doors open like side wings. Angus heard the team following him across the parking lot. He'd expected their paths to diverge. Yet, they tossed their bags in the luggage hold.

Angus boarded with his bags, fishing out his new murder mystery before stowing his pack overhead, leaving the Thai food on the seat beside him. He thought he'd taken a discreet nip from his flask until one of the players plunked down across the aisle from him.

She asked, "Did ye nae learn yer lesson in school about sharin'?"

Her green-flecked eyes flirted with him. She was bonnie, and he surmised she was used to having her way. He took his flask back out and offered it to her.

However, after she took a nip, she passed it to her mates instead of returning it to him, saying, "Now dinnae be rude and finish it, or we'll have to buy him a dram in Mull. If they even have a pub where we are stayin'."

Angus let go of any thoughts of hiding in his book or even another nip. He only felt attached to the flask; it had been his father's.

She held her gaze on him. "Hello, neighbor. Where do ye live on Mull?"

"Nowhere—ah continue on to Iona. What brings ye to Mull?"

"We have two weeks before our next match, and Coach has rented a few homes for us to do some team buildin'. 'Tis what makes us champions. Ah swear, some moments on the pitch ah get a sixth sense of what mah mates will do before they do it themselves. Ah love it when that happens. Sounds odd, eh?"

Angus nodded. "Och aye, ah'v had that experience. Ye'r blessed. Ah think of it as grace."

She leaned in toward Angus. "Do ye play?"

Angus nodded. "Ah played at university."

She perked up. "Really, what position?"

"Ah was a striker. Sometimes ah ken where the ball was goin' to be, and ah planted mahself there to receive it. Ah'd already seen where it was goin' to land inside the goalpost, and ah aimed for that spot. The goalie rarely ever touched it."

"Ah'm a striker. Ah ken just what ye mean." She handed his flask back to him noticeably lighter.

Angus raised it to her, saying, "Sláinte," and took the last sip.

"Ah can smell yer takeout. Ah dinnae suppose ye'd be willin' to share that too?"

"Nae, that's spoken for, but ah'd be willin' to refill mah flask if ye dinnae make a habit of offerin' it up to the whole bus."

She replied, "Ah'd be happy to keep this round between ye and me, Striker."

She unabashedly flirted, and Angus warmed to her attention. "It just so happens ah'v replenished mah supply." He took down his backpack and selected the fourteen-year-old whisky, turning his shoulder to offer a modest screen of the maneuver, questioning his wisdom of refilling it on a moving bus, but his hands proved steady enough. He only filled it halfway in case it made the rounds again and trusted her with his flask while he put the bottle of Oban away.

"Sláinte," she said as she raised it to him. "Mah father likes this brand, too. Ah recognized the label." She passed it back. The reference to her father reminded Angus of the age difference and signaled the limits of her affection. "So, who are ye eatin' yer Thai food with tonight?"

"She's a friend—for now."

She gestured with her open palm, rolling her fingers, beckoning for his flask. "Life's short, Striker." After a stiff swig, she said, "That's for mah younger sister. She died of cancer this year," and abruptly stood to go, handing his father's flask to him. "Bye, Striker. Remember, always take yer shot. Ye may nae get another."

Angus hadn't seen any of that coming. He'd adjusted to the idea of her company for the remainder of the ride and was no longer interested in the distraction of his murder mystery. He screwed the cap back on his flask and tucked it in his pocket, knowing tonight he'd open the eighteen-year-old bottle of whisky to share with Sarah. *Tonight, ah'm comin' off the sidelines.* While stashing the mystery back in the bag with the Thai food, he spied Hafiz waiting for him.

There was no better companion for a conversation than a mystical poet. He randomly opened the book to the poem entitled "In the School of Truth" and read it.[1]

"Don't sit there thinking;
go out and immerse yourself in God's sea.
Having only one hair wet with water
will not put knowledge in that head."

The stanza lingered with him and emboldened him.

I was about to turn Saorsa around for home when a soaring bird caught my eye. I knew it was a falcon and guessed it was a peregrine from its blue-gray coloring, dark head, and white neck. Last October, I'd invited my friend Bret, a falconer, to visit my class. He brought a hooded peregrine, allowing us a rare intimacy as it perched, tethered to a ring on his leather glove. The students exclaimed in awe as he demonstrated his flying skills. Afterward, he stood with it on his arm and closed with a poem—"A Tethered Falcon," by Hafiz. It was all the more memorable because Bret didn't read it to us. He recited it. He embodied it. The irrefutable truth of a few lines left a searing impression on me, especially, "My soul endures a magnificent longing."[2]

Bret inspired me to adopt the practice of committing poems I loved to memory. Today, as I watched the peregrine swoop and dive at lightning speed, I felt swept up by its undeniable magnificence. Saorsa wasn't much of a bird watcher and took advantage of the moment to eat grass. I let him, breaking the rules, because I hoped to glimpse its nest in the cliffs.

Another line was resurrected, "Quivering at the edge of my Self And Eternal Freedom."[3] *What is freedom anyway?*

I asked Saorsa, "Given freedom is the meaning of your name, any insights you want to share for our walk home?" As I gathered the reins, he lifted his head.

The sun cast our elongated shadows across the grasses as it neared the horizon. The abbey bell announced it was already four. My spacious afternoon suddenly felt compressed, with only an hour before Angus called.

We trotted or cantered as the ground allowed, giving us both a workout, then walked the last distance along the road to cool down, skipping our gate practice. I leaned forward to check Saorsa's chest temperature. He'd recovered. As we approached Caim at the gate, the abbey bell rang again, marking four-thirty.

"Did you miss us?" I popped off Saorsa to enter the paddock more quickly and caught a whiff of myself. I was ripe. A shower would be essential after gathering the washing and hanging my blanket out to catch the last rays of sunlight. Caim and Saorsa touched noses. It was as if they downloaded their day's adventures by scent.

Taking off Saorsa's tack, his bit was coated in foamy green gunk because I'd let him eat grass. Even though it would be a dried mess later, it had to wait. I mindlessly brushed him down, pondering my wardrobe choice for the night and the necessity of snatching my underwear from the line to avoid the embarrassment of having it blowing in the wind when Angus arrived.

After feeding the horses, I skipped wrestling their blankets on and scampered to the clothesline. Unclipping two items, I discovered my first error. There was nowhere to put the clean clothes nor the half dozen clothes pins. *Damn.* I ran inside to retrieve the basket, tracking dirt from my riding boots on my cleanly swept floors. It wasn't until I started removing the other items that I noticed my next mistake. They were still damp. *Shit.* They needed more time. I fingered the jeans I'd planned to wear tonight. The crotch and front pocket weren't dry. *Plan B.* I took only my bikinis and the partially filled laundry basket of damp clothes. I'd rehang them after I showered and dressed.

The rose bushes had called to me, so I searched the kitchen drawers for pruning shears but only found scissors. Not ideal for roses, but they would do.

I trotted back out and hastily clipped three as their thorns pricked my fingers. Finding a vase would have to wait. I stashed them in a glass. Despite being downright furry, my plans to shave were jettisoned. No one would know that but me. The abbey bell started to chime. I didn't have to count. I knew it was five. Thankfully, Angus hadn't phoned yet. I prayed he was also running late.

I started the shower and stripped, but after I'd dunked my head under the spray, the phone rang. *God help me if that's Ian. It'd be just my luck.*

Dripping wet and barely wrapped in a towel, I answered. "Hello, this is Sarah at Katrine's home."

"Sarah, 'tis Angus. Ah wanted to let ye ken ah'll arrive at half past five, so see ye shortly. How was yer day?"

I could tell Angus wanted to chat while he waited. *Why, of all times, did he pick now to stop reading my mind?* "I'll be there to fetch you. But right now, the water's running for my shower and I promise you'll be grateful you didn't keep me from it."

He laughed. "Ah'll take yer word for that. See ye soon."

With only time for a quick shampoo and no conditioner, my hair was a wet snarl. I was quivering at the edge of lateness, not the eternal freedom Hafiz wrote about. Well, rushing around had its upside—it kept my anxiety about dining together in check. At best, I had five minutes left to dress. The phone rang again and I made a strategic decision to ignore it. If it was Katrine, she could call Angus. If it was a local, I didn't have time to talk. If it was Ian, now wasn't the time for us to speak again, either. He'd have to wait till tomorrow.

I exhaled and took a stolen moment to massage the body oil into my skin. It'd have been so much more enjoyable with smooth legs, but so be it. The smell of jasmine transported me.

Capping the bottle reminded me I'd not had the second dose of the miserable tea. I put on my underwear and dashed back downstairs, allowing the oil time to absorb before I finished dressing. The tea was cold, which couldn't have made it taste any worse. I poured a cup and winced through it, eager to brush my teeth, but the abbey bell rang.

Damn. I had to leave now.

Instead of raiding Fiona's closet again, I searched Maeve's drawers and grabbed a pair of black leggings and a black cotton mock turtleneck, then aimed for her coveted coral felted-wool jacket in her closet. With no time to look in the mirror or reconsider, I rushed downstairs, swiped the keys, and slipped into Katrine's clogs. Again, I approached the wrong side of the car.

The horses trotted along the fence line, accompanying the car's departure. I sent them a mental picture saying, "I'll be right back." Thankfully, Iona had zero traffic. I intentionally pulled into a different parking space. All the passengers had already disembarked the ferry. I scanned the tiny town and spotted Angus talking on his cell phone, leaning against the stone wall, and gazing at the shore.

Suddenly, I felt self-conscious about Maeve's jacket. Everyone on the island would probably recognize it as borrowed if I got out of the car to greet him. I'd only meant to wear it inside the house. I could take it off, but I wore leggings and the only time I wore leggings was if my top covered my ass. The whole outfit went together. I regretted not wearing the damp jeans and yearned for my own clothes.

Even though I was late, I sat in the car and resisted the urge to toot the horn. When he turned around, he couldn't miss Katrine's red car. He wore his backpack and another bag rested at his feet as his left hand held the phone. Was he also left-handed? Angus twisted at the waist, looking in my direction. I waved, and he nodded in acknowledgment, picking up his bag while talking on the phone. I stayed in the car, convinced prying island eyes watched me.

The car windows were down and I heard half of the conversation as he swung his backpack off and put the bags in the back seat. "We'll light a candle tonight, Kat. The news will be better in the mornin'. Ah'm glad they're lettin' Brìghde sleep the night with him. They both need each other right now. Call me when ye ken anythin' more." He paused after he sat in the passenger seat, his feet still on the pavement, his back to me. "Och, aye, ah took care of it—dinna fash, we're set here. Go have a stiff whisky. Ye need it. This is in Kieran's hands now, ah'm sure of it. The wee one must be havin' quite the conversation with him, gettin' the lowdown of how he's to carry on the Reid family's traditions, probably tellin' him all the best fishin' spots." He folded his legs inside. "Let me tell folks what's happened. Ye'll be wantin' all their prayers said on Finn's behalf."

---

1. Shamsuddin Muhammad-i-Hafiz-i-Shiraz, "In the School of Truth," translated by Thomas Rain Crowe, *Drunk on the Wine of the Beloved: 100 Poems of Hafiz*, (Boston: Shambhala, 2001), 18.

2. Shams-ud-din Muhammad, "A Tethered Falcon," translated by Daniel Ladinsky, *I Heard God Laughing: Poems of Hope and Joy*, (Penguin Books, 2006), 50.

3. Ibid.

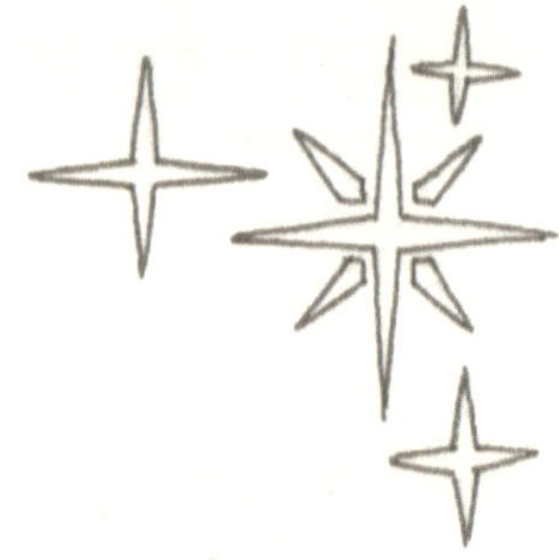

CHAPTER 17

EDGES

TEARS STREAMED DOWN THE side of Angus's face. I hadn't heard them in the strength of his voice. He'd been so reassuring to Katrine, but the man before me was clearly hurting. I reached out my left hand and put it on his shoulder.

He'd switched the phone to his other hand and closed the door, wiping the trail of tears on his cheeks. "Bye for now. Try to get some rest." Angus placed a heavy hand on top of mine and gently squeezed as he said, "Let's be on our way."

I drove and asked, "How bad is the news about Finn?"

"We cannae be sure. His seizures have stopped, but they think he may have had some brain damage durin' the birth. 'Tis still a mystery they may nae ken until he's grown. There's a risk of runnin' any more tests on him as the brain scans can cause cancer later in life. They've decided to stop the diagnostics."

Tears welled up in my eyes as a lump formed in my throat. What they were going through was unimaginable.

"Kat agreed to let me tell folks. She cannae bear to speak of it over and over again right now. Ah'll need to make some calls, check on the sheep, and hearin' ye were about to shower, planted the thought in mah head. Nae only showerin' with ye, takin' one mahself."

I could tell he was trying to lighten the conversation. "We're in no rush to eat. Do you still want to have dinner together, or would you rather be alone, talking with friends and family about Finn?"

"Nae, lass. Ah'd much rather have dinner with ye. To be honest, ah'v been thinkin' of nothin' else all day. Dinnae take the one bright spot in mah night away."

"Okay, please take your time. I have a few chores I didn't finish, and I still have to blanket the horses."

"Ah noticed they were still out. Ye'r goin' to want the warmer rug tonight. Can ye reach it? Ah can help ye."

I'd pulled into his driveway. "I'll manage fine on my own."

Jake waited at the passenger side door and started to bark. "Ah'm sure ye will, lass. Let me grab mah things." Upon opening the car door, Jake was at his knee. Angus patted his head. "Did the sheep behave for ye? Ye dinnae lose any while ah was away." He stood, and Jake followed at his heels. As he slung his pack over his shoulder, he said, "Ah'll leave ye with the Thai food. Ah'll nae tarry."

The sun was behind Dun I as I entered the barn, and the horses could sense something. Demeter meowed in the aisle. She jumped on the trunk and rubbed her back against the blanket hanging from the rod.

Inside the tack room, I reached on my tippy toes for the blankets, but my fingers only grazed them. I used a riding crop in the fold to tug at them until they sagged over the edge far enough for me to grab a corner and pull each blanket down. Their weight was more like a rug than a blanket. Angus's help would have made it easier, but I managed.

To protect Maeve's jacket, I'd taken it off. All my worrying about what I wore was suddenly in stark contrast to the news of the night. *It's so easy to get caught up in what doesn't matter.*

Tending to the horses settled me. Afterward, I brought in the rest of the washing and fetched our Thai dinner from the back seat. The heft of the bag surprised me and unpacking its contents revealed two books. Only the book of Hafiz's poetry tempted me. I resisted checking to see if the falcon poem was inside, knowing if I started reading, I wouldn't want to stop, so I saved it for when I was ready to sit by the fire with a glass of wine to savor it.

My cupboard search turned up a drawer with woven placemats and colorful cotton napkins, garden shears, and more tealights. Still no vase, so I opted for a small pitcher and recut the rose stems so we didn't have to look through the arrangement. I debated if candlelight would be misconstrued as a romantic evening but concluded the candle would be lit on Finn's behalf. After all, Angus had told Katrine he would.

There were two containers of chicken pad Thai, so I dumped them in a single pan. I whipped up a salad and put out some cheese, bread, and a jar of Coleman's mustard. After lighting the fire, the peat smoke thankfully abated. I'd been missing listening to music but hadn't done enough snooping in Katrine's house to know how she played it. The house wasn't completely silent; the fire occasionally crackled. I tucked in beside it with Hafiz and my wine. A few poems later, Angus's voice was at the door.

When I greeted him, I reined myself in before offering a hug. He held a bottle of scotch in one hand and a white wine in the other. Was he planning to drink his dinner?

He smiled. "Ah'd welcome an embrace after the news of Finn."

I hugged him briefly, feeling the hard bottles at my backside. It would have been too intimate if he had pressed his palms against me, but I noted I'd broken my rule of no physical contact twice already in the last hour.

Angus pulled away first and displayed the label on the wine. "Ah guessed ye might like a Sauvignon Blanc."

"You guessed exactly right. I love any from New Zealand. Thanks, that was thoughtful." I noticed his accent had lightened with his mood. "Can I pour you a glass?"

"Nae, ah'm afraid ah already started on the whisky, and ah won't be turnin' back. Ye can save yer stash. Ah fetched this today." He held up the bottle. "An eighteen-year-old Oban for ye to try."

"That wasn't all you picked up. I enjoyed reading Hafiz. It's uncanny. Earlier today, I recalled a line of his poetry while a peregrine falcon spellbound me."

"Did ye now. Which poem was that?"

" 'A Tethered Falcon.' I only know a few lines from it."

"Let me fill mah glass first so ah can listen properly."

My mind suddenly went blank. The lines I'd recalled earlier were nowhere to be found. Angus had poured his glass and waited. I shrugged my shoulders. "I forgot them."

"Dinna fash. Maybe it's hidin' in the book."

"Were you able to reach the folks you wanted?"

"Och aye, ah only needed to place a few calls for the word to spread. We'll be holdin' a mass for Finn th'morra mornin' at the abbey. Would ye like to accompany me?"

I squirmed at the thought of meeting the whole community, and arriving with Angus, but I set it aside as petty, given the circumstances. "Sure, thanks for including me."

Angus tipped his head toward the fireplace. "Ye made yerself a bonnie fire. Ye'r a quick study."

He'd left the door wide open for my request. "I am and I'm eager for you to teach more about how you read minds."

"Minds and hearts, lass, but nae always as well as ah'd like. We can try an experiment to see if ye have the knack for it. Ah promise to make mahself an open book if ye have the specs to read me."

"Really? Shall I heat dinner? Are you hungry?"

"Ah'm famished, and ah need some food to offset the head start ah'v had on the whisky."

Would whisky make him easier to read, drop his defenses?

"Ah have nae defenses from ye, lass, even though ah'v tried. Ah'v only respect for ye and the journey ye'r on. If ah can accompany ye, it'd be mah privilege. Faith has been elusive in mah life. Ah'd welcome us bein' on better terms, especially now with all that's unfoldin' with Finn."

After turning on the stove, I brought over the tray of cheese and bread.

"Thanks, lass. Ah' see ye found Kat's mustard?"

I sat down beside him on the couch. "I did. It's habit-forming, like a number of things around here."

He turned toward me with a slightly raised eyebrow. "Is that so? What other habits are ye referrin' to?"

"Well, for starters, this daily view of the ocean." I rotated and gestured toward shore. Even though the windows were dark, there was no doubt of its presence. "Plus, having Saorsa and Caim to tend to and ride. Sometimes, I wonder who is caring for whom. I'm also fond of homemade scones for breakfast, scones paired with scotch for dessert, conversations with fire, and having the space for my inner life to blossom and reveal itself to me." I paused. "And being so fully understood and seen by you."

"Ah'm fond of bein' one of yer habits. Promise me if we come close to crossin' an undesirable line, ye let me ken."

"Hmm, yes, I will." I heard the noodles sizzling in the pan. Being unfamiliar with Katrine's stove, I'd turned them up too high and stood to adjust it. The heat between Angus and I also needed to be dialed back to a simmer. Following my longings and desires had its limits. I suspected Angus was aware that more than one recalibration was needed at the moment.

The noodles were stuck together, so I poured a splash of water over them, which immediately turned to steam as I stirred them apart.

I snitched a morsel and focused on my breath, trying to settle myself down. Maeve's boiled wool coat was no longer needed, but I'd missed my window for a wardrobe change. *If you can't take the heat, get out of the kitchen.* I heard Angus putting more peat on the fire. He was bringing on the heat.

I'd forgotten to make salad dressing and searched her fridge for a bottle while enjoying the respite of cool air. I closed the door empty-handed and pivoted to discover Angus had planted himself in my path, waiting for me. My temperature rose again with his proximity. He was intentionally within the invisible boundary of personal space.

He handed me an envelope. "Kat wants ye to have this—'tis yer payment for next week, and the note is from me. Ye can open it later. We both figured some cash would come in handy. She wants to pay ye as she would've Mary or anyone else. Ye best take it and say thank ye." He hadn't moved an inch.

I'd not seen this direct side of him. It didn't bother me since he was advocating for something in my best interest, not his. "Thank you. Sometimes, I can follow instructions. Now you're standing between me and the salad. If you want to eat, you'll need to move."

He didn't move. If anything, I sensed he wanted to close the distance between us, and salad was the last thing on his mind. Had the whisky I smelled on his breath emboldened him? I trusted Angus was a gentleman and held my ground until the stalemate ended with him stepping back.

My face had turned the color of the wool jacket, but not in a way that camouflaged me. I busied myself with the last of dinner prep by taking Katrine's olive oil and balsamic vinegar in either hand, drizzling them directly over the salad, and then tossing it. Angus always referred to her as Kat, and I hoped there'd come a time when she and I were on more familiar terms with each other. It was unreal that I'd known her for only hours before I was living in her house, using her condiments, riding her horses, and wearing her daughters' clothes.

Angus said, "Kat looks forward to gettin' to ken ye too."

Right. No thoughts are private here. "Can you get the plates? We're ready to eat. Also, what does Katrine do for music?"

"She has an old record player in the credenza over there. Ye'v nae done much sleuthin' around the house. Is there anythin' else ye'r missin'? Did she tell ye where the house key is in case ye wanted to lock yerself in?"

"No, she didn't mention it, and honestly, I didn't think of it. I don't lock my house at home either."

Angus made a barely audible sound. I served him first, offering him a plate full of pad Thai. "Is this enough to start?"

"Och aye, we're off to a lovely start. Ah'm enjoyin' the evenin' with ye. Where have ye been all mah life, Sarah?"

He waited near me as I served myself. "I'm here now, and I suspect if you met me a few years ago, the conversation we'd be having tonight wouldn't be half as enjoyable for you." That did it. I had to strip off Maeve's coat. What had I been thinking? This wasn't inside clothing.

There was no sense hiding my body when I couldn't even hide my thoughts. After I put down my plate, I'd started to slip out of it when I felt Angus's hand lifting its weight off my shoulders. My blood rushed feverishly around my chest as if competing in the Indy 500. He draped it over the chair beside me.

As I went to sit, he said, "Here, let me help ye." He'd pulled out my chair and pushed it lightly against the back of my knees, which had already gone weak. I was sure the heat coming off my body now rivaled the fire. The embarrassment of being unable to hide my flaming cheeks only made me flush more.

Thankfully, Angus had walked back into the kitchen. The sound of the fridge door opening and closing was followed by his muscled arm appearing over my left shoulder to refill my glass. I wanted to press the wine bottle against my face or the back of my neck as an ice pack. He probably saw that image and was pleased with himself.

I aspired to his ability to read minds—and hearts—as he had corrected me. He was certainly making his intentions and feelings known. I'd have to be dense not to pick up on it. He could make the experiment a bit more difficult.

When Angus sat, he reached for my hands. "Let's say a prayer for Finn." I offered him mine to hold. "On this night, in yer home, Kieran, ah' call on ye to tend to yer wee grandson. Finn needs yer strength and Brìghde yer guidance. Kat needs ye too, as ye ken. Dinnae hold back, mah friend. We are all holdin' Finn in our hearts, and we call upon this current of love we dwell within to see us through." Angus squeezed my hand.

I squeezed back before letting go and saying, "That was beautiful, the way you invoked Kieran." He nodded in acknowledgment and waited for me to take my first bite. The spice was initially enjoyable, but the heat continued to build in my mouth. I searched for the culprits to avoid—those little red flakes or red pepper fragments—but there were none. "Was all well with your flock while you were away?"

"Aye, Jake had it under control."

Control was better suited to sheepdogs than between people. "Do you name your sheep?"

"Some cannae help but earn a name. They're all different, even though they may look the same to ye. Ye must be more intimate with them to notice their personality, their markings, and habits. Ye'r wonderin' if ah butcher them too. Nae personally, but ah raise them for their meat, nae so much their wool. They live a good life, and they die with dignity. Ah source some of the finest restaurants in Scotland now that farm-to-table is all the rage."

"I've always been an omnivore but never actually knew the fowl or four-leggeds I'd eaten." My stomach started to do somersaults, thinking too closely about my protein source. "The Thai food's delicious. Thanks for thinking of it."

"Is it too spicy for ye?"

"I'm on my edge." *In more ways than one.* I took another sip of wine. There was no danger of my overeating.

"What other edges are ye on, lass?"

Clearly, Angus wasn't trying to steer this conversation into safer territory, so I needed to take the reins. "Well, today I contemplated terra incógnita, testing my willingness to venture into unknown territory with Saorsa and trusting I'd be safe." I didn't mention the line from Hafiz that sprung back to mind—*Quivering at the edge of my Self And Eternal Freedom.*[1] "Your sister invited me to tea. Luckily, I was on my way out for a ride—oh, that comment didn't come out how I meant it. It's not that I don't want to meet your sister. It's just I was hoping to learn more about your family from you."

Crinkles appeared around the outer edge of his eyes. "What do ye wanna ken?"

"How many brothers and sisters do you have, and where are you in the line-up? Are both your parents still alive?" *Why am I so nervous? This isn't an interview, Sarah. Relax.*

"Ah can see we're easin' into the more difficult terrain later. Ah'll indulge yer curiosity a wee bit, but ah might as well test ye. Ye said ye wanted to read me. Ye'v seen mah mum and met mah only sister, and ye ken mah brother is a priest. Is mah dah still alive?"

I stared into his eyes, and the answer was a clear "no." "I'm sorry for your loss. How long ago did he die?" Angus held a tender silence. I guessed. "It wasn't recent, more like five years ago, maybe?"

He nodded. "Closer to seven. What else can ye sense? Dinnae think about it too much. Say what first arises from yer heart, nae second guessin' or doubtin' it. That's a sure way to shut yerself down."

I heeded his advice. "It wasn't sudden. He was sick for a while. His death was a blessing. You'd lost him years before he died."

Angus nodded again. His eyes welled with tears. He let them spill over and raised his whisky. "Sláinte."

I raised my glass of wine. "Sláinte." This was hardly the subject I wanted to be correct about.

Angus put down his glass and offered more context. "He had a stroke and never fully recovered. He hated bein' dependent and unable to speak his mind and crawled further and further into himself until we could nae reach him."

"I'm so sorry, Angus, for bringing this up, especially now."

"'Tis okay, lass, dinna fash. Ye'll find 'tis easier to read a person when the information is more meaningful, in matters of the heart. However, sometimes, if ye'r too emotionally involved it becomes muddled. The day-to-day thoughts take a whole other level of skill and practice."

I'd changed my mind and wanted to get to know Angus the old-fashioned way. "Tell me about your mum and your relationship with her. Witnessing this morning's brief exchange, you appear close to one another."

"We are. We always were, but we grew closer when mah dah grew ill. Ah'm the oldest. Ah became the man of the family, an odd mantle to carry when yer dah is still alive. He ken it. He dinnae resent me for it. One day, he reached into his side drawer and gave me his flask. It was somehow symbolic. He wanted me to carry it with me, with his blessin's." Angus stood, "Can ah fetch ye a glass of water? Ah need to hydrate."

"Sure, thanks." I heard him at the sink and felt more moving than the water flowing from the tap.

He returned to his seat and resumed sharing his past. "His nae bein' able to communicate with words honed mah skills at readin' minds to another level and deepened the intimacy between mah mum and me. Ah'd sit with them a few nights a week over dinner. Mah mum would talk to mah dah. He'd look at me and try to offer a few words, mostly speakin' to me in pictures. Ah started to see the images he was sendin' me, and ah'd offer mah response while watchin' mah dah's face to see how close ah was or if ah needed to adjust the story ah was seein'. He'd nod in agreement or shake his head if ah misinterpreted him."

"Angus, that's remarkable. What a way to turn adversity into a blessing."

"At times ah think it a curse. Sometimes folks dinnae want ye to ken their mind or their heart. Like now with ye, ah feel ye pullin' back. How much do ye really want me to ken about ye?"

His directness made me squirm again. "It's a good question. It's complicated." The air between us crackled like the fire. I'd stopped eating and stared at my hands. My fingers were interwoven in the way that felt most natural. "Who I've been and who I'm becoming feel like they are diverging in ways I've not noticed before." I intentionally separated my fingers, shifting my other thumb and index finger on top before closing them again. It felt awkward and unfamiliar and somehow fitting. "Sometimes speaking about my history feels like it cements my life in its mold and establishes the scaffolding for my future. I can't help feeling confined by it, even when it's comfortable. I know my life experiences are what have shaped me, but I don't want them to define me. I don't want to cling to my memories because I feel unmoored. I want my identity to be more fluid. Am I making any sense?"

"Aye lass, more than ye ken."

I wondered what he was alluding to but wasn't brave enough to ask. My thoughts turned to Ian, our shared history, and how he was pushing me back into it. *If only he would wander alongside me and wonder with me who I am now and who I'm becoming.* I felt Angus wanting to come to know me, and knew he was right—I was pulling away. I took another bite of the last of my meal.

Angus held the pregnant silence between us and stood to get seconds. As he sat, he spoke. "Yer history, yer family life, all yer relationships shape ye. Ye can nae forget ye have a choice in the matter. How about yerself? Would ye let me ken more about yer family?"

"There's not much to tell. My parents are dead, and I'm an only child like my father. My mum was one of seven. We moved away from where she grew up and only saw her family on some holidays. I have more chosen family than blood family." A fierce ache for Jocelyn, Maggie, and Veena overtook me. I used my napkin to wipe my mouth and kept twisting it in my lap.

"Kat's mah chosen family. Ah'm closer to her than mah sister, Deirdre. Ah had a feelin' mah mum might send her around today to meet ye. Th'morra ah'll be sittin' with them at mass. Ah'll introduce ye properly then."

The thought was overwhelming. I shifted my focus to the roses.

"Does Katrine leave the old roses on the bush till they turn to rose hips or cut them to encourage more blooms?"

"Ah cannae be sure, but she coaxes them long past their season. Kieran gifted them to her. 'Tis one way they stay connected. She'll be glad ye'r carin' for them, and 'tis bonnie to see them tonight." He picked up a fallen petal and rubbed it between his thumb and forefinger. "Yer glass is empty. Are ye ready for yer whisky?"

"I am. You finish, though. I can get it myself."

"Bring me over another glass if ye would, and ah'll pour one for Kieran. Ah should've made the offerin' sooner when ah invoked his name, but he's the forgivin' sort." He poured a dram for me and then for Kieran, which he tucked beside the candle and roses.

"From what little I've gleaned, it sounds like theirs was one of the rare marriages filled with love."

"Och aye. 'Twas overflowin' with the kind of love we all long for." He stared at the flame on the candle. "They were truly beloveds to one another." Angus raised his glass. "To Kat and Kieran, to love that kens nae barriers, nae even in death."

I mirrored his gesture as we both took a sip. The scotch was smooth and warmed my mouth and throat, with a hint of peat, like drinking liquid earth blended with fire.

"Have ye had that kind of love in yer life, Sarah?"

His question brought Ian to mind. "I don't know. I thought I did, but now I'm not so sure."

"What about yer parents? What kind of role model did they offer ye?"

"I wish I could remember more of my childhood and what they were like with each other in the early part of their marriage. The expressions of love on their faces in their wedding album aren't the memories I have of how they looked at one another later. I witnessed how the little divots of careless remarks, deliberate sarcasm, and grooved arguments weren't addressed until it created a gulf between them. They had a kind of civil truce, upholding their roles and duty to one another, but the vitality and vulnerability that comes from passion and cherishing fell away." I took another sip of scotch. "I fear most marriages have this fate. That time erodes love, and only a few know the secret of keeping it fresh." I thought of my failed marriage. "Perhaps Katrine and Kieran lost each other while their love was still devotional, before time wore it away. Oh, listen to me. I sound like such a cynic. I believe my parents loved each other as best they could, but it was no anam cara."

Angus seemed surprised I knew the Gaelic term for soul mate. His eyes fixed on me. "Some relationships ye cannae deny, nor dilute with time. Sláinte." He clinked Kieran's glass and then mine. "To welcomin' love into our lives. A stranger reminded me today that life's short. We cannae hesitate to make it the life we long for."

I fingered the rim of the glass. "How about you, Angus? What's the life you long for? Are you living it?"

"Och aye, lass. Ah ah'm tonight, ah ah'm tonight."

The color rose in my cheeks again.

"Let's wash up and sit by the fire."

A man offering to do dishes. He has no idea what an aphrodisiac that is, or does he? "Sounds good. Any chance you could put some music on? I'm going to change my top. I'm too warmly dressed to enjoy the fire."

Angus stood swiftly and was behind my chair, pulling it out. "Allow me to help ye."

His body spoke directly to mine, bypassing my brain and sending my blood to throb at the surface of my skin.

"Thank you. You're quite the gentleman tonight."

"Aye, ah'm at that. At times ah' wish ah' was more of a rogue." He pushed the chair into the table, keeping his grip on the back of it.

"I'll be right back. Surprise me with some music."

He took me at my word. As I went upstairs, Angus flipped through Katrine's records. By the time I'd descended, he'd placed the needle on the vinyl. The opening notes stopped me in my tracks.

I recognized the song immediately: "Unchained Melody." A tidal wave of emotion made me reach for the banister. *How did he choose my parents' song, and tonight of all nights?* Hearing it brought up my earlier wish to have witnessed their relationship when their longing was still palpable. It couldn't be a fluke. I'd just spoken of their marriage—or what little I understood of it.

Angus watched me freeze. "Ye dinnae like it. Ah'll change it."

"No, I like it very much." I walked toward the fire instead of the kitchen. "This song means a lot to me. It was my parents' song." I sat on the leather chair and listened to the lyrics freshly. "My dad was in the merchant marines and shipped out to sea for months at a time when they were first married. Later, he became an international salesman and traveled extensively for work. Their relationship had long periods spent apart." I couldn't help but think of Ian again and our months apart. Time must have gone slowly for him. This was the yearning I'd heard on our call: hunger for my touch. Except now, it also brought up how my body had hungered for Angus's touch only moments ago.

I am a tangled mess.

Angus sat on the corner of the couch nearest my chair. I felt his eyes on me. As the song ended, he went to the kitchen to clean up.

I joined him, putting the leftover pad Thai back in the container. "You can take this home with you."

"Do ye want me to leave, lass? Ah can tell the song struck a chord in ye. Are ye wantin' to be alone now?"

"Honestly, I'm not sure. Let's keep cleaning up. I'd pictured us sitting by the fire, but this song threw me for a loop. Why did you choose it?"

"Ah almost put on some sax, but when ah saw it, ah was thinkin' of Kieran and Kat—'twas their song too. Ah dinnae mean to bring ye to yer edge."

"That you did, Angus. You have an uncanny knack for it."

"We invoked Kieran tonight and even spoke briefly of yer parents. Whether we mention him or not, Ian is with us as well. Ah been tryin' to contain mah feelin's for ye all day since ah was watchin' ye sleep this mornin'."

"What? You were watching me sleep this morning?" I took a step back.

---

1. Shams-ud-din Muhammad, "A Tethered Falcon," translated by Daniel Ladinsky, *I Heard God Laughing: Poems of Hope and Joy*, (Penguin Books, 2006), 50.

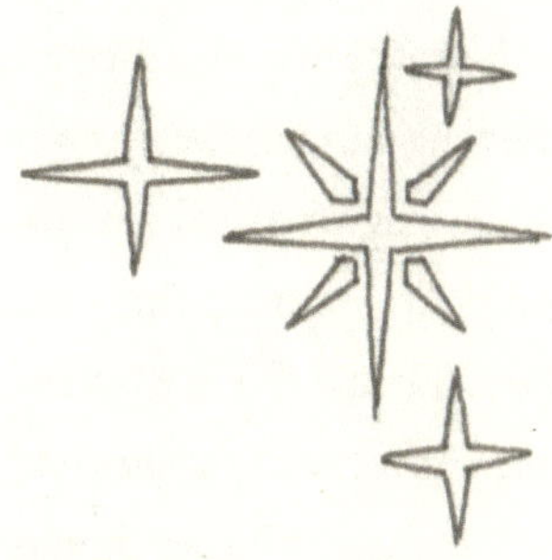

CHAPTER 18

CONFESSION

HE'D REALLY PUT HIS foot in it. He should have kept that to himself, but his tongue had a mind of its own. "Och aye, for just a wee minute, from Maeve's threshold. Ah'm nae stalkin' ye, Sarah, only admirin' ye, longin' for ye from afar." He stopped washing. There was no turning back to the sidelines now.

"Angus, you don't even know me. I hardly know you. This is crazy-making." Sarah put the dish towel down and folded her arms across her chest, gripping her elbows.

He didn't have to read her mind to know she'd erected a barrier between them. How could he tell her he recognized her from his dreams? That she'd already nested in his heart?

Drops of water flung from his fingertips as he gesticulated. "Sarah, nae everythin' makes sense in this world, at least nae always from a rational place, ye of all people ken this. How did ye find yerself on Iona? What was yer journey with Faith about if nae bein' willin' to believe in somethin' ye can't always touch or see, but ye ken to be true?" He didn't wait for an answer, but he lowered his voice and tapped his temple twice with his index finger as he continued. "Yer strategic mind is fabulous. It'll serve ye well in life for so many things, but on this particular threshold, it will nae carry ye through." Both his hands moved in unison as he signaled in the space between their rib cages, attempting to bridge the distance he knew he'd caused between them.

He figured he'd already prematurely ended their evening, so there was no point in holding back now. "There's a terra incognita between us. We call it the Great Mystery for a reason. 'Tis unfathomable, untouchable, except with our hearts." He placed his right hand over his heart and held it there. "Please dinnae close yer heart off—nae to me, nae to yer life. Ye'r so open in this moment." He felt himself pleading with her. Not only had he come off the sidelines, he'd immersed himself in the sea of his longing with no mind to his inability to swim.

I'd not seen Angus this animated before and felt his restraint in wanting to reach for me. I studied his face while I sensed his intentions. All I felt was warmth flowing toward me. I let my arms drop to my sides.

"I'm trying." I mirrored his gesture momentarily, pressing my hand to my heart. "There's an undeniable current moving between us. At times, it's hard to navigate and even harder to swim against, which scares me. At other times, there's an ease between us, and it's more like drifting down a river in an inner tube, dangling my feet and hands in the water. The hitch is it switches without warning. Everything in my life is in flux, and I'm scrambling to find solid ground. I don't know what to make of you or what's going on between us, and I feel exceedingly self-conscious even raising it." The fire in my core blazed again, making my underarms sweat and my face flush crimson. There was nowhere to hide from Angus, so I met his gaze.

He'd tucked his thumbs in the front pockets of his jeans, elbows bent. His head tipped back as if the ceiling held answers, and he closed his eyes briefly and sighed. When he returned his gaze to me, I felt him looking directly into me. "Do ye ever watch an infant sleepin'?"

I nodded, wondering where he was going with this.

"There's this feelin' like ye'r watchin' an angel before yer eyes. That's how ah' felt this mornin'. 'Tis how ah felt when ah first met ye. Ah cannae deny it. Ah will nae deny it. Life's too short to pretend otherwise. Ah need ye to ken that about me, about how ah view life. Ye asked me about what ah long for. 'Tis someone who will meet me there, someone who has ventured into the territory and wants to build a life that includes a relationship with the holy, unfathomable aspects of livin', and for the record, ah'm scared too—bloody terrified, but ah'm also more alive than ah'v been for years." He bit his lower lip. "Ah'v said enough. Ah best be goin' home. If ye'r still willin', ah'll come by and bring ye to mass. If ye want to stay home, ah'll understand."

I didn't protest the ending of the evening. We'd finished washing the dishes, but Kieran's glass remained by the roses and lit candle.

"What do I do with Kieran's whisky?"

"Ye can leave it out for him until the candle burns down and then pour it out in the rose garden. We dinnae blow out candles after a blessin' when our ancestors have been invoked." He ran his fingers through his hair, from his temples to the back of his head before his hands dropped by his sides. "Sleep well, lass. Thanks for yer company and for lettin' me peer over the edge with ye. Ah'll walk alongside ye, nae pullin', nor pushin'."

He'd seen the image I conjured, my unspoken request of Ian. His acuity about my desires unsettled me. The whole night had unhinged me. I handed him his bottle of Oban. "Goodnight, Angus. Please come by in the morning. Remind me what time to expect you?"

"Half past seven."

I walked him to the door. The rain had already started. "Would you like an umbrella? It's wet out there."

"Nae, ah enjoy heaven's blessin's."

I closed the door behind him and turned off the lights, but the room glowed with Kieran's candle and a beckoning fire. I sat on the hearth for a few minutes, hearing the refrain of "Unchained Melody" play through me and humming the tune until I returned to the record player and turned it on again, singing along with it.[1]

> *Oh, my love, my darling*
> *I've hungered for your touch*
> *A long, lonely time*
> *Time goes by so slowly*
> *And time can do so much*
> *Are you still mine?*
> *I need your love*
> *I need your love*
> *God speed your love to me*
> *Lonely rivers flow*
> *To the sea, to the sea*
> *To the open arms of the sea*
> *Lonely rivers sigh*
> *"Wait for me, wait for me"*
> *I'll be coming home, wait for me...*

Had Kieran made a request tonight via Angus to hear it played? Had my parents requested it? Was that kind of conversation with our ancestors even possible? *It seems anything is possible on Iona.*

My parents' relationship, like most, was complicated and impossible for me to judge from the outside. The last time I'd heard "Unchained Melody," I was in a taxicab with Ian in Rome. The timing then was also uncanny. I had reached for Ian's hand when it started because I had invoked my mum and dad in an impromptu ritual on the Spanish Steps earlier that same day.

I'd stood between the fountain at the bottom, Fontana della Barcaccia, and above the Roman-made Sallustiano Obelisk, in front of the Trinity de Trintá del Monti church. At first, I thought I'd selected the spot based on availability, as tourists were everywhere. Later, I noted I was midway between the archetypal symbols of the feminine and the masculine. Below was the curvaceous water fountain resembling a vagina, and above me, the phallic obelisk. Standing visibly between these forces helped me to tap into the same invisible energies that resided within me, to call upon them to move in a more balanced and integrated way. I was ready to lay down the guardedness and defenses I'd erected that prevented me from receiving love. At the same time, I wanted the freedom to continue to pursue my dreams unfettered while still giving love. I kept my hands discretely low, with my palms turned outward, till I felt tendrils of energy from both directions that I could braid together with a mysterious third strand. My eyes took in the surroundings with a soft focus. I continued the movement of braiding until the golden cord felt solid and thick in my hands.

Later, I shared the image with Ian as a symbol for a new model of relationship, one of interdependence, not dependence or independence. I told him I wanted to be held freely in a spacious love and learn to offer that same kind of love. Now I wondered if Ian and I were capable of that kind of love, the loving I imagined Katrine and Kieran had shared.

The fire's embers and the centerpiece candle still burned. I regretted not cutting a rose for my nightstand when I rushed around earlier. The reverence surrounding the arrangement on the kitchen table kept me from breaching it, and I ascended the stairs empty-handed with my heart full.

I lay awake in bed, staring at the ceiling, pondering the difference between desire and longing. Longing felt tied to something holy, invisible, and maybe admittedly unattainable, yet the longing was partly fulfilled by remaining in a relationship with this ineffable eternal quality. My blessing was an articulation of my longings. Desire felt more like a relationship with another person, a thing—or even myself—and was potentially attainable if I persisted. My desires propelled me like horsepower. I'd better learn to ride it, lest it run away with me.

Longing informed me in surprising ways, often disrupting my plans. It moved more slowly, like a drop of honey. The glancing taste of sweetness was enough to fuel it, yet the hive where the honey resided was elusive. Longing felt connected to Divine Will as if hitched to a constellation of stars by a subtle golden thread that pulled me along, asking me to be faithful and trust it.

Hearing my Cynic speak of marriage tonight had brought a sour taste to my mouth. I recognized the power she had to rob me of love. The antidote to Cynicism's hold on me was compassion for my parents' challenges and forgiveness for my failed marriage, for my breaking of vows. I'd divorced my husband, but ultimately, I hadn't divorced myself. I repeated my vow in my mind, like a mantra, until sleep claimed me.

I awoke still weary but ignored the temptation to roll over and go back to sleep. The horses needed feeding before Finn's mass. My bedside table had the start of an altar but no clock, so I delayed bowing. Rain was coming down in buckets. If I'd forgotten the laundry on the line, it would have gone through another rinse cycle. I dressed for the barn, wondering what I'd wear later for church.

Downstairs, the whisky and roses reminded me of the possibility of a conversation with ancestors. If I had their attention, what guidance would I ask for?

Finally, my inner thigh muscles didn't protest. I'd recovered my riding legs in time for a week of storms and bolted to the barn, closing the door behind me, keeping out the miserable weather, but inadvertently leaving myself in the dark.

"Hello, my friends. Where's the light switch hiding?" I groped the perimeter of the walls and discovered one outside the tack room. I flicked it on, saying, "And then there was light." Almost simultaneously, the abbey bell rang seven times. "And thankfully, the time. Only breakfast for you. Trust me, you don't want to go out in this downpour."

Back at the house, I called Angus for advice on the church dress code to determine if pants were acceptable. If not, I needed more time to find an alternative and shave my legs.

Angus picked up on the first ring. "Guid mornin'."

"Good morning, Angus. How'd you sleep?"

"Fine, lass. Have ye changed yer mind about comin' this mornin'?"

"No, I'm planning to join you. I wanted to ask about the horses. Does Katrine still let them out on a day like today? I've kept them locked inside with last night's blankets on them."

"Guid question. There's nae hard and fast rule here. 'Tis fine to leave them in till after mass, then sense what the weather is decidin' to do for the day. Her barn's design gives them a choice of shelter. The weather's fickle here, but ye can trust their judgment. What else is on yer mind?"

"It's along the same lines. What do women wear to church here? Is it okay if I'm not wearing a dress?"

Angus laughed. "Ye can wear whatever makes ye comfortable, lass. Dinna fash on such matters. Be warm and dry."

"Thanks. I'll be ready shortly. Bye for now."

"See ye in a wee bit, ah'v got to put on mah Sunday's finest."

I heard the sarcasm in his tone and assured myself it wasn't like anyone would even see what I wore under the trench coat. I found a pair of Fiona's wool pants since my mom would give me an earful if she saw me wearing jeans to church. Maeve loaned me a white turtleneck, and Brìghde's drawers yielded my favorite find, a plum-colored cashmere scarf. Wearing an article of clothing from each daughter was like bringing them all to mass today.

Angus found Sarah in the barn. Seeing her devotion toward Saorsa, he was envious. Last night, he'd laid himself bare, letting his longings for her be known. While he had no regrets, he wondered if he'd overstepped his bounds and was anxious to sense if there was an awkwardness or guardedness between them this morning. Angus hoped she was making space for him in her heart. It was clear that Saorsa had taken up residence there, the way she rested her face along his neck.

Saorsa gave his presence away with his whinny, and Sarah turned around to see him leaning against the stall door.

"I didn't hear you come in. How long have you been here?"

She sounded guarded. He only hoped it was because her unbridled affection had an unexpected witness. "Long enough to be envious of Saorsa."

She patted Saorsa's neck. "Dinna fash. My heart has unlimited capacity."

Angus chuckled at her attempt at a Scottish accent and breathed more easily. "If ye stick around, ye might improve yer Scottish accent. Come on, if ah'v timed it right, we can hold off all the introductions till after the mass. Ye ken ah'm considered quite the catch on Iona? Walkin' in on mah arm today ye'll be makin' all the other lasses jealous."

"Undoubtedly. Let's go then."

The rain fell steadily in drops, not the drenching sheets like before. Angus's stride was swift and long. I had to hustle to keep up, which helped me shake off the jitters that had been building all morning as I anticipated meeting his family and the rest of the island. "I take it there's been no more news of Finn."

"Ah spoke with Kat this mornin'. Finn and Brìghde had a guid night together. He's out of ICU, and they're takin' him home again today."

"That's good news."

"In a manner. 'Tis a waitin' game. We'll pray Finn has nae more seizures. That 'twas blood and nae brain related."

"Well, the whole community is praying for him, and his grandfather is watching over him. Let's imagine the best outcome." I felt like embracing my inner optimist. Ian and I were on better terms, and I planned to take a long walk to clear my head before we spoke again.

"Ah'd be happy to show ye around the island's south end if ye'll walk with me? We could go to the marble quarry, perhaps find ye a stone for protection?"

"Sure, I'd like that. I was just thinking about a trek in the rain, but you picked up on that, didn't you?"

He nodded. "We'll see if the weather holds. Let's nae get ahead of ourselves. We can tend to the horses and maybe pack a lunch. The St. Columba's café sells soup and bread."

Could I emulate his approach to staying in the moment and plan less? Doubtful. "Not getting ahead of ourselves sounds wise, though I wouldn't mind having a plan in case someone invites us for tea. I'm not up for socializing with strangers yet."

"Ye can say ye have other matters to tend to. 'Tis mah favorite line, and ye can borrow it."

I'd borrowed clothes and shoes; why not borrow excuses? "It's true. I do have other matters to tend to. Ian and I planned to speak later this afternoon."

"Well, ye have yer excuse then, that'll cover ye for the horses and Ian."

I felt Angus's effort to be magnanimous but sensed something else in his demeanor. Islanders waved to one another as they approached the abbey from various directions. "Guid mornin'" echoed back and forth. We waited to let the folks enter while Angus held the door for them. He came alongside me, slipping his arm in mine as he ushered me up the aisle toward the front. My rule about no physical contact was breached again before 8:00 a.m., in church, no less.

He stopped before a pew on the left, dropping his arm. I imagined each family had their designated spaces. Angus uncharacteristically entered first and introduced me briefly to his mum before taking the seat beside her. I said hello and thanked her for the tea and oil. Deirdre sat on the other side of her mother and offered me a "guid mornin'."

I sat in a tiny space on the bench between Angus and the wooden panel at the end. It was snug. My left hip pressed against his right hip the way the back seat of a car compresses three adults together, except the bench didn't have safety belts. I didn't realize then they'd be necessary.

The priest entered, and we all stood, giving our hips more breathing space. He said, "Let us pray." I bowed my head, aware I'd missed my morning practice again. For the next hour, I followed the familiar prompts to sit, kneel, stand, make the sign of the cross, and echo "Amen." Even though it had been years since I attended church, the familiar rhythm was easily resurrected in my body until I froze when I heard the prompt for the *kiss of peace.*

Angus pivoted to his mum first, and I stood stiffly in place until the older man in front of me turned around to embrace me with the wooden seat back between us. *That made more sense, a hug, not a kiss.* Angus faced the back of the church, offering a hug to the man behind us, and I followed their example with another tent hug. Next, Angus waited for me to be available. Nothing was between us when he pulled me closer; our hips meshed. His freshly shaven face was smooth against my cheek, and he smelled of vanilla. A tingling, pulsing sensation began in my crotch and swept up to my chest as he pressed against it. My lips parted, and the quick intake of breath was audible. His arms squeezed me briefly again before he released me. My hips begged for more.

I felt immediately guilty. I'd broken my rule of not touching yet again. On the surface, the *hug of peace* was acceptable. After all, everyone had done it. The residue of guilt came from how much I'd enjoyed it. My thoughts went to Ian next—that I was betraying him—then to the reality that I was standing in church, aroused. I tried to focus my mind back on the mass toward Finn, but my body was tuned to Angus, carrying on its own conversation. Sitting back down in the packed pew didn't help matters.

I was acutely aware of how our thighs rested against one another. Being wedged on the bench hadn't been an issue for me moments ago. Now, it made me overheat and squirm inside. I loosened the cashmere scarf from my neck, but it wasn't enough to vent the furnace he'd stoked. I tried to remove my coat, and Angus, always the gentleman, grazed his hand on my shoulders to help. He knew once again the effect he was having on me. I was grateful when it was time to kneel. I bowed my head, praying for guidance—and a chastity belt.

The people in the pews before us stood to go for communion. I hadn't anticipated this moment either. *Should I go?* I assumed receiving the sacrament was prohibited since I'd not been to confession in years. I stepped aside in the aisle to let everyone else proceed before I sat visibly alone. My lapsed Catholic status offered up juicy fodder for the rumor mill, and I had no intention of rectifying it by going to confession, especially since Angus's brother was the priest.

Katrine and I were alike in that our sacred practices resided outside these walls. My self-confession was enjoying today's mass, sitting so near Angus. Our *kiss of turmoil* still reverberated in me. Maybe sitting within the sanctioned walls of a holy church added to the thrill of it. I refused to let the initial seed of guilt take root in me. Yes, I desired him, but I hadn't acted on these feelings, and I wasn't planning on it. I planned to be conscious and watchful.

Meanwhile, the line from "Unchained Melody," *"I've hungered for your touch,"* kept playing on repeat in my head, testing my resolve. My hunger for his touch was powerful but not as powerful as my reservations about acting on it.

I stood again to let Angus's family file back to their seats, forcing my attention to Finn. The good news was that he arrived home today. I bowed to the wisdom of taking life one day at a time, not worrying—instead, having faith and trusting everything would eventually be okay even if, at the moment, it appeared anything but. I respected that Brìghde and her husband had stopped running tests on him. *Sometimes, looking for a problem can cause a problem.*

I planned to tell Ian to stop looking for a problem between us and to trust time because, as the lyric from "Unchained Melody" implied, *"Time can do so much."* I needed him to try to understand me. I needed him to want to.

I imagined people came to church for the comfort of being amongst others who believed what they believed. However, the prevailing beliefs of those around me weren't comforting to me. I wasn't on board with the elevation of men over women, nor the church's stance on gay relationships or reproductive rights, nor their proclaimed need for a priest as an intermediary. I believed I had direct access to the divine, the Great Mystery, or whatever anyone chose to call it. Today, I made the sign of the cross, naming it the Father, the Son, and the Holy Ghost.

There was room in me for people to hold beliefs different from mine without making it about right and wrong. More people believing something doesn't necessarily make it true. It does, however, make it more powerful. I shared their belief that praying on Finn's behalf made a difference. I also believed that it mattered when Angus called on Kieran last night as an ancestor. *Can we ever really be alone? Are our ancestors always with us, bidden or unbidden?*

After the mass concluded, each row emptied one at a time, starting at the front and following the priest down the aisle. Angus helped me with my coat and lay his hand on my lower back for a split second, guiding me to join the procession. Our prior intimacy still swirled inside me as I navigated countless introductions to strangers.

I said hello to what felt like half the island. Their names and faces were a blur, except one. I recognized Trish, the waitress from the café. She asked, "So tell us, what brought ye here so late in the season?"

The truth, an oarless boat, was decidedly the wrong response. As a teacher, I knew how my students stalled when they didn't know the answer. "Good question. Curiosity, I suppose—plus I wasn't available sooner. I had a prior commitment." Trish wasn't appeased. Her continued interrogation was interrupted by a gray-haired woman who introduced herself as Katrine's mother. I thanked her for the scones and was praising her baking skills when Angus appeared by my side. His touch on my lower back caused me to flinch. We said our goodbyes promptly, leaving the mulling townspeople behind.

There was a loaded silence between us for the return walk. Angus already knew what I wrestled with; he'd provoked it amidst witnesses. I couldn't bring myself to ask, "Why were you flirting with me during mass?" His behavior wasn't the issue. What it stirred within me was what troubled me. My well-crafted armor had turned to putty with his touch. Was he escalating because he knew I was about to speak to Ian again?

The rain was only spitting, so we stopped at the barn, and Angus helped me swap the horses' blankets so they'd have their freedom. I said, "I want to put on jeans before our walk."

He replied, "Ah'll fetch mah pack and come by shortly."

Even though it only took me a few minutes to change, the wind had picked up, and the rain was pelting when I answered the door. I pulled up my hood, sequestering myself within it and signaling my resolve to forge ahead. There was no attempt on either of our parts to converse. We briefly stopped at the café across from the St. Columba Hotel. Angus offered two thermoses to the woman behind the counter, requesting the day's soup. I estimated this operation would take a few minutes, so instead of browsing the shelves' provisions, I popped across the street to see what the hotel was like inside and if I'd recommend it to Ian.

No one was behind the front desk. I skimmed the menu for the restaurant and glanced outside at the sprawling garden. The place was beautiful. I sensed Ian would be happy enough with the accommodations. Whether the visit met his expectations was another matter.

Angus leaned against the lobby wall, watching Sarah intently, waiting for her to notice him after she turned her attention from the menu. He'd been so focused on Finn he'd missed that she'd reconnected with Ian. It was a humbling moment, reminding him he didn't always know what was happening with her.

Upon seeing him, she said, "Thanks for buying lunch today and dinner last night. I promise to torture you with my cooking at some point."

"If ye insist, ah'll oblige." Angus surmised Ian might be arriving soon, sensing his presence around the hotel, and was eager to leave it behind. He refused to share Sarah any sooner than he had to.

Sitting beside her at the abbey had offered him stolen moments of physical intimacy. Her responsiveness to his touch was undeniable. It erased any lingering doubts he'd harbored. He couldn't recall a mass he'd enjoyed more. Admittedly, he'd held her a bit too long and too closely during the kiss of peace—if only it had been a kiss. The impulse to tangle his fingers in her hair as he tipped her head back and tasted her lips was nearly untamable. Being in church was the only thing that saved her. His mum was probably fending calls from half the island by now, wanting to know the details of their relationship.

The weather was inhospitable. There was no sign of humans anywhere. Even the livestock were huddled or hiding in barns. We silently walked through the village, past the dock and the furthest point I'd explored. It was *terra incognita* ahead.

How long will I reside on Iona? My agreement with Katrine only lasted another week; beyond that my clarity blurred. I'd not opened the envelope Angus handed me last night nor read his note, but I was clear it was the last money I'd accept from her. If she was willing to let me stay on, I preferred to barter—a place to live in exchange for caring for her horses. It was a bargain for me.

Remaining longer required a way to make money. I assumed I'd lost my job and, with it, my medical insurance. My options for earning an income were slim and undesirable here—cleaning houses or waiting tables. Teaching was unlikely. I didn't know their curriculum and I'd not seen a school. Maybe I could work as an online tutor with some of my former students or help with college essays, but virtual work required internet access. I'd offer to pay for it if I could convince Katrine to install it. Again, cash flow was a priority, particularly the inflow.

If I stayed through the fall, it offered the possibility of learning jewelry-making from Katrine and maybe even actualizing my dream of creating flatware. More importantly, remaining here offered me time to integrate my odyssey with Faith and what it meant for my future. *Will I still be here at Christmas?* I pictured Katrine's home packed with family, especially with Finn's arrival. *Where would I sleep then?*

I peered around my hood at Angus, wondering what was on his mind. Before I could ask, he pulled open the blinds on mine.

"Ah think Kat would be happy to have ye stay on. She's said as much. There's scant work here for the locals, so tutorin' an American clientele would be best. Besides, ye dinnae have a work visa. Ye can always work at mah house if Kat's unwillin' to leave the Dark Ages and get Wi-Fi. Ye can also stay in mah guest room. Does that about cover it?"

"Yes. You smart ass. I really want to learn how you do that. You said the logistical thoughts are harder to pick up on." Sarah stopped walking. "Shit, what you said is true. Not only am I without a work visa, I'm not legally in Scotland! I never came through customs."

"Nae, ye dinnae. Ye can stay as long as ye like then, but once ye leave, ye can only visit. That 'tis unless ye marry a Scotsman. Ah might ken a candidate if ye'r interested in a proposal." The words were out of his mouth before he'd thought to edit them. He felt himself suspended in time, awaiting her response.

Sarah's eyes went wide, and her voice shifted an octave higher. "Did you just indirectly propose to me?"

Angus's heart pounded an escape route from his chest. "Och aye, ah believe ah did. Ah surprised mahself. But ah stand by it. Nothin' would bring me greater happiness. Shall ah drop to one knee and do it properly?"

Sarah took a step back. "No! Angus, I'm going to pretend that didn't happen. I was afraid Ian might propose, but I never expected you to jump the line. You are brazen!"

"Ah'll give ye that. Someday, it'll be a grand story to share with our bairns."

"You're over the top. Stop toying with me."

"Ah'm nae, Sarah. Ah'v seen it in mah heart. Ah' dinnae ken if 'tis real or only mah hopes."

"You're the one who said not to get ahead of ourselves. For god's sake, you have us married off with kids! How's that not planning ahead? I don't even know where I'm sleeping next week! I've no plans for my immediate or distant future. You don't even know my last name."

Angus couldn't help himself; a grin spread across his lips. "Ah'll nae argue with ye, though ah do fancy this fiery side of ye. Standin' here in the rain ah think ah' can see steam risin' off ye."

"You really are a smart ass." Sarah walked away from him.

He noted she hadn't said no to him. She only took issue with his timing. He felt a flicker of hope ignite in his heart that he kept sheltered from the rain. She had no idea where she was going, but he let her lead anyway, falling in for a few steps behind her.

---

1. Righteous Brothers, "Unchained Melody," 1955 North Melody Publishing, LLC.

CHAPTER 19

TREASURE HUNT

*H*ow is this my life? *I'm wandering in the rain, arguing with a Scotsman who takes my breath away. In a matter of hours, I'll be talking, hopefully not arguing, with Ian, and he'll be here in a week. My life's an epic tangle; I've got to sort myself out before he arrives.*

I stared at the ground, watching my feet take the next step when his leather work boots came in sync with my stride. "Let's go in search of this green marble since I'm in need of protection, especially from premature proposals."

Angus led us down a hillside into a bay with cliffs towering on either side and a shore filled with stones. I had expected more of a quarry and cautiously picked my footing down the sloped path. When I took my eyes off the ground, Angus was already leaning against the cliff wall that offered shelter from the wind and rain. His pack was at his feet, and his eyes were on me, gauging my mood. I growled inside but wasn't going to snarl or snap at him. Hungry for comfort food—as if eating could quell the restless beast roaming inside my skin, I acted more civilized than I felt.

"I like your choice of restaurants. It's not crowded, even with this lovely view of the ocean. I understand today's special is soup and bread?"

"Aye, are ye eager to try it?"

"Yes, I'll lighten your load before I fill your pack with rocks."

"Ah'll have to speak with the maître d'. The tables and chairs seem to be missin'."

"All I require is a spoon." I hoped an early lunch would ground me.

Angus offered me a thermos. I temporarily put the spoon in my mouth, needing both hands to unscrew the lid. The smell of rosemary, garlic, and onions had me eager to taste it. I balanced the lid on a rock and took my first taste of pure bliss. "Is this your lamb by chance?" It was tender and flavored deliciously, not gamey at all.

"Aye, most likely. There's nothin' like eatin' locally."

"It's amazing." I wandered a distance away before sitting on a larger boulder to eat. My eyes hunted for my protection. The green stones weren't obvious to me. I turned a few over with the side of my shoe. A shiver spurred the thought of hot tea and brought me back to Angus. He hadn't budged, and his gaze still beheld me.

"What's yer pleasure, lass? Tea or whisky? Ah dinnae pack water. Or perhaps ye want yer second course of bread and butter?"

The idea of another nip of whisky to warm my core appealed to me. Scotch, bread, and butter—another pairing I'd yet to try, but I resisted the temptation. "Tea, please. Where have you hidden the bread and butter?" I capped the stew and propped my spoon on top. Angus handed me a brown wax-paper sleeve with a thick cut of bread, then a green- and gold-wrapped pad of Irish butter with a knife. After spreading most of the butter across the crusty homemade bread, I tore it in half and offered him the larger portion.

"Thanks, lass. Ah'll trade ye." He handed me the converted lid of the thermos turned teacup.

My first bite reminded me of the simple pleasures in life, and my lips involuntarily smiled. I took shelter next to the cliff beside Angus.

When he pivoted toward me, his broad shoulders offered an additional buffer from the winds. The sip of tea that followed my second bite wasn't as effective at warming my core as whisky would have been. Angus continued to watch me intently. I didn't return his gaze. Instead, I looked beyond him to the expanse of the sea and relished my last bites of heaven. After finishing my tea, I thanked him and gave back the empty lid before walking away.

"Ye'll have to dig a bit to find the green marble. They sometimes hide a layer deep. Protection has a price."

He confirmed my suspicions that this would be more of a treasure hunt. *Ian would love this place.* If only I'd paid better attention to how to find it again. In Kauai, I was sure he'd spent hours bent over searching for Kahelelanis, the tiny pink shells that washed up from the island of Ni'ihau. Ian was remarkably patient, given his yield would only partially fill the small black film canister he saved for this activity. *How patient could he be with me? Don't most men prefer the chase to the catch?* I thought it best not to get caught.

The quarry was the first place I couldn't hear the abbey bell ringing. The term headwinds took on new meaning—with the persistent winds buffeting my hood, they drowned out every other sound, offering an unrelenting opportunity for an exclusive elemental conversation. It remained one-sided, more like a lecture.

I squatted to paw through the stones. Eventually, I began to recognize the green-marbled ones. It helped that they were wet, so the streaks of olive were more apparent. My search yielded a small pile of rocks that called to me. I planned to leave with at least six, one small enough to carry around in my pocket, one for my altar, another for Ian, and gifts for Maggie, Jocelyn, and Veena.

Angus was bent over using both hands to extract much larger stones by the water's edge. He clearly had a technique and a favorite spot. We kept our distance for the better part of an hour. I heard him exclaim,

"Now, she's bonnie!" as he held it out for me to see in the palm of his hand. Its recognizable heart shape was the find of the afternoon.

I surveyed the ones I'd surfaced and selected six. The one for Ian had an hourglass shape of a woman. She wasn't as smooth as I would have liked, but in a way, that was perfect, too. She needed more time by the water to take off the rough edges. I paused for a moment, quietly asking permission to take the stones with me. No contradictory inklings arose, so I slipped them into my front pocket, keeping my treasures close to my body.

I returned to the backpack for the other piece of bread, convinced it'd be criminal to let it get stale. My numb fingers managed to butter it. Sharing the last half was an act of discipline, as I offered it to Angus at the water's edge. His flask was out, and his eyes said what his mouth left silent. I took a generous swallow, feeling it warm me. A hot bath was on my mind. I was ready to go.

"Shall we pack up? Ah gather ye have other plans for the afternoon." He handed me the last bite of bread, but he didn't accept his flask back. Instead, he brushed off the stone heart and brought it to his pack. I happily finished the bread and wanted to chase it with lamb stew, not scotch.

"Ye need more meat on yer bones if ye'r goin' to stay warm outside in the winter here."

The idea of being warmer appealed to me, but I could do without the weight gain. My hip bones were visible again, and I wanted to keep it that way, despite my newly formed habit of scones, zucchini bread, and my most recent discovery, St. Columba's bread baking. I wasn't planning on denying myself carbohydrates. They were essential mood regulators.

If possible, the stew tasted even better than before. Finishing it filled me with regret. When I'd read the hotel's rate sheet, it indicated they closed at the end of November. Given they owned the café, I worried it might also close. Likely, everyone else made their version of lamb stew and wouldn't need it provided. It wasn't lost on me that I saw myself here for the winter.

"Lass, if ye'r still hungry, there's some left in mah thermos."

"No, I'm fine. My stomach is satiated, but my taste buds are looking for more. Do they keep the café open even when the hotel closes for the season?"

"Aye, they have quite a followin' with the locals who can nae afford to eat at their restaurant but enjoy a meal they dinnae have to fix themselves."

"That's a relief. I'll be an avid customer." Of course, that would require an income. The realities of the world kept pushing in on my island retreat.

Angus had slung his backpack on. "Ye'll heat up once we start walkin' up that hill. Watch yer footin'. Step where ah step if ye like."

I followed in his footsteps as best I could. He was right. By the top of the hill, I'd stopped holding my arms tight to my body, attempting to brace myself from the cold.

We walked in a distant silence most of the way back and parted ways when Angus said he wanted to check in on his mum. I visited Saorsa and Caim and swiftly mucked their stalls. The chill had returned to my bones even though I was out of the wind, and I counted the minutes before I'd be submerged in warm water.

Demeter rubbed against my shin. "Okay, if you stick with me now, I'll put out a saucer of milk." She scampered alongside me with her tail up and waited at the door as I took off my boots and coat. Instead of heading upstairs to start my bath, I kept my word and brought Demeter her treat. Afterward, I started a fire, picturing myself beside it with Yeats before my phone date with Ian.

I grabbed the legal pad and pen on the way to the tub, hoping I could melt my writer's block and begin to capture my journey with Faith. However, it was as if the blank page repelled ink. I stared at it, not knowing where or how to start, so I switched to compose a note to my friends and stalled again—I couldn't exactly write, "Hey, I left through my bedroom mirror, and now I've washed up on the shores of Iona."

What could I write? My outreach to them remained a dilemma. I soaked, pondering it, and what surfaced was compassion for Ian and the awkward position I'd put him in with my sudden departure and lack of communication. It was time for me to put an end to my mysterious disappearance. This was my story to tell. And while I aspired to honesty, another dilemma arose.

How can I explain my experience with Faith to anyone else if I still haven't made sense of it myself? I felt stranded. It wasn't quite like the morning when I'd awakened in the oarless skiff, it was more like I'd been windsurfing when the wind changed direction to an offshore breeze while I was far from the beach. The only way back was repeatedly tacking, zigzagging my way home. What tack could I take? It wasn't my nature to lie, but composing a sentence that told the truth eluded me.

Admitting defeat, I shifted tasks to one I could accomplish: a packing list for Ian. I missed my jewelry. It was more than an act of adornment. It represented a symbolic source of strength I consciously called upon. My silver drop earrings and the white freshwater pearls were already on their way to me in the package with my phone. I'd been attracted to earrings in the shape of drops for years. It wasn't only my love of water that they signified. It was also my longing to drop into my life and to inhabit my skin. I'd spent so much of my life beside myself, only paying attention to my mind, not to the language of my body. I yearned to live a more sensual life, slowing down and caring less about being productive.

Be careful what you ask for—you may surely get it. I had the choice to stay longer on Iona. *Will I accept the invitation to live a slower-paced island life? Can I find a new rhythm with work?*

My body wanted to dive into the sea and return to the sensation of swimming as a mermaid, invoking forgiveness for myself and Ian. I set the paper and pen aside on the bathroom floor, letting my hands drop beside my thighs, bending my knees, and sliding down till my head was underneath the water. I didn't dare try to inhale. When my lungs ached, I surfaced for air and submerged again. The confines of the tub were no substitute for the sea, but it appeased me for the moment.

I doubted there was a pool on Iona, and the frigid waters were hardly inviting for me, even as an avid swimmer. *How does anyone learn to swim on this island? Does Angus know how to swim? Is that why he prefers to keep his feet on land, for fear of drowning?* It seemed risky to live on an island and not know how, especially if you were a fisherman. I put Kieran and Angus out of my mind.

Angus hadn't planned to check in on his mum when they had set out to the quarry, but when they passed the road to his family home, he felt the pull to visit. Likely, she was summoning him, especially after having met Sarah at mass. She'd be full of questions, but she'd pay less attention to what he said and more to how he said it. There was no hiding his desire for Sarah, certainly not from his mum. Besides, he needed some female advice and wasn't likely to ask Deirdre. Usually, he'd turn to Kat, but she wasn't available.

He walked in the front door to the smell of herbs. He'd hoped for the aroma of baking. His mum was at the stove stirring, surrounded by various mason jars and bottles. The kitchen was a holy mess.

"Angus, ah was wonderin' if ye'd turn up today. Ye dreepin'—come in and dry off by the fire. There's a pot of freshly made tea under the cozy." She didn't stray from her concoctions.

He hugged her from behind, and she tilted her head to momentarily rest on the side of his cheek. A hot toddy was more to his liking. He added a splash from his flask and left it on the table beside the pot in case she wanted to join him.

She turned and smiled at the sight of it, "Ye'r like yer father. 'Tis guid to see his flask now and again. 'Tis like he's sayin' hello to me. So, speak to me of Sarah. What's between the two of ye?"

She doesn't miss a beat.

"That's why ah'v come. Ah need yer advice, or at least a chance to talk it out. Ah find mahself feelin' things ah'v nae felt for anyone before, sayin' things even ah can't believe when ah hear them. Ye may want to sit down for this next bit."

His mum took a seat and reached out to lay her hand on his. "Say what ye came to say. Ah ken ye'v fallen in deep with her in such a short time. Ye'v lost yer bearin's."

"Och aye, ah'm in over mah heid, and ye ken ah cannae swim, ah cannae even find mah footin'. Ah indirectly proposed to her today on the way to the quarry."

"Angus, ye dinnae. Are ye tryin' to scare her off?"

"Nae, just the opposite. Ah'm tryin' to be patient, to give her space, but ah'v made a mess of it. 'Tis complicated. She has another man in her life that ah gather 'tis quite serious. She's nae wearin' his engagement ring, though, 'tis only a matter of time. Mah window of opportunity is a wee crack. She said as much when she hollered at me."

"Tell me what prompted ye to propose on such a dreich day. Ye'll nae get any points for settin' or romance."

"We were talkin' about how she might earn money if she stayed on. Ah mentioned she cannae be employed here without a proper work visa, but she could stay as long as she liked if she never left—or if she married a Scotsman."

"That's nae a proposal, Angus. Ye were only circlin' the territory."

"Och aye, if ah'd stopped there, ah'd nae have raised her ire. Instead, ah plunged on tellin' her ah knew a candidate if she wanted a proposal and offered to drop to mah knee to say it properly."

"Ye'r right. Ye'r off yer heid."

"Ah could nae stop the momentum once 'twas out of mah mouth. Ah said it'd be a guid story to share with our bairns someday." Angus rubbed his face with his hands. "Mah heid's mince."

Angus's mum reached for the flask, tipped it into her cup, and poured more into his. "Well, ye have laid yer cards out bare. What'd she say?"

"She essentially told me ah was off mah rocker, which we can all agree 'tis true at this point. However, she dinnae say nae. She referenced needin' the green marble's protection from premature proposals, and that ah was brazen to have cut the line. Ah suspect that when her man comes to visit, a ring will be in his pocket. She senses it, too." He paused, shaking his head. "Ah can feel her attraction toward me. 'Tis thrown us both for a loop. Ye ken ah'm nae one to move swiftly on matters of the heart, nae after Daphne. Ah thought ah was happy here before she came. Now ah have to admit ah only buried that longin', pretendin' it dinnae matter to me, but it does."

His elbows were on the table, and he rested his eyes on the base of his hands; his fingers held his forehead. "Ah'v seen us together here with wee bairns. Ah dinnae ken if they're ours. They could be Kat's future grandchildren. Her bond with Kat runs deep. Kat's told me as much. She says Sarah and Saorsa light up together. Ah'v seen it too. If she wanted, she could make a home here." Angus got up and unzipped his pack, fishing out the heart-shaped marble to show his mum.

His mum cooed. "She's a bonnie one, Angus. She's a keeper."

"Och aye, ah dinnae suppose ye have a remedy for this?"

"Ah dinnae think ye want a cure. Give her time to ken her own heart and heid. Be yerself, Angus. If she dinnae choose ye, she's a fool, and ye'll be better off without her."

"Ye have to say that—ye'r mah mum."

"'Tis what she's awakened in ye that's important for ye nae to forget again. 'Tis what ye have to listen to now, but sometimes it only speaks in whispers. Ye'v been deaf to it for years since Daphne left ye. Stay faithful, Angus, and bide yer time. Grace has been on yer side so far." Her eyes went to the stone. "Let me have a closer look." She took it in her hands and ran her palm over it to brush the remnants of sand, admiring it. "This here almost looks like a lifeline. Bring her by for a cuppa. Ah want to ken the lass who holds yer heart in her hands." She stood and gave him back the stone. He felt the cool weight of it. His mum went back to tending her herbs.

"Do ye need help with anythin'? Ah'm grateful ye sat a spell with me."

"Aye. Ye can deliver this tea here"—she lifted a jar in the air—"to Kat's mum on yer way home. She needs to keep her strength up to meet her first great-grandson. This news of his seizures has taken a toll on her. She was already in a delicate way."

Angus finished his toddy and put away his flask. He was ready to be on his way home, but he couldn't say nae to her requests, either of them. "Ah'll take it with me and bring Sarah around soon for a cuppa." He gave her another hug, and this time, she turned to embrace him, her love enveloping him.

CHAPTER 20

SWORD

THE BATH WATER WAS tepid, and I'd already reheated it once. My puckered fingers indicated it was time to extract myself and get dressed. Clothing decisions. If I had access to my own clothes, what would I reach for? I often cycled through the same jeans and T-shirts. So why were my closet and drawers stuffed with items I rarely wore?

I put Fiona's sweatpants on and eyed her cream cashmere sweater longingly but instead found a soft tunic sweatshirt that was cozy enough for post-bath attire. Downstairs, the warmth of the fire greeted me and I felt pleased with myself for taking the time to build it earlier. My thirst brought me to the kitchen for a big glass of water. On the counter waited the bulky envelope Angus had handed me last night.

The card featured a close-up image of a peregrine falcon. I admired his round, dark eyes and hooked beak. Yesterday's sighting replayed in my mind as I removed the money to read his note.

Dear Sarah,
Though you're house-sitting now, I hope you ken you always

have a place to land on Iona. There's no need to migrate or
call anywhere else home.
With love,
Angus

He named the tension I've been feeling: the pull of home in two places. I was incredulous that he'd practically proposed to me today. *What would he have done if I called his bluff? What if he meant it? I could see myself calling Iona home for a season, maybe even a year. I can't see myself accepting any marriage proposal from Ian or Angus.*

My independence was paramount. I wanted to enjoy it, along with my freedom, in this sanctuary. This much had become crystal clear. It was time for me to listen to my inner guidance and I hankered for my tarot deck, more eager for its arrival than my phone. The communication channel it provided me with my unconscious mind was vital.

Would Maeve have a deck in her room? I scampered back up to search her bedroom. *If I were a tarot deck, where would I be?* Nightstand drawer. I tried the one nearest me with no luck. I crawled over the bed and checked her other one. *Score!* She even had the same deck I used, Thoth. I searched her shelves, convinced the book was wedged in there somewhere. Different titles caught my eye, and I tipped down the spines of the ones that appealed to me. *The Ancient British Goddesses, The Mist-Filled Path, Walkers Between the Worlds, The Spiral of Memory and Belonging, Fire in the Head.* I could get lost here for the winter, never to be seen or heard from again, except, of course, to ride Saorsa. I saw the familiar ankh symbol first. If I'd had to turn up anywhere else, Egypt would have been intriguing. After plucking it off the shelf, *Tarot Mirror of the Soul,* by Gerd Ziegler, a spontaneous wiggle of delight burst forth. I brought my treasures with me to sit before the fire.

While shuffling the deck to warm it up to me, I pondered my question. It wasn't about staying or not staying on Iona. I already knew I wanted to stay and delay my return to the States. What I needed was guidance on communicating my intention with Ian without wavering or doubting myself when he pushed back. The abbey bell chimed once, indicating one-thirty, leaving me a half hour before we spoke.

I pulled the Ace of Swords. A green sword pointed upward into a crown of golden light with another golden sphere behind the blade, perhaps the sun surrounded by blue sky. Below the hilt was a cloud layer, and wrapped around it was a coiled snake with two crescent moons mirroring one another. I knew a snake represented transformation. The moon and sun were forms of light, symbolizing unconscious and conscious energies. The element of air ruled the suit of Swords, which related to the mental plane, having perspective. Something was written on the blade, but it was too small to see.

The tarot book offered several keywords as descriptors of the card. The phrase I related to was "intellectual clarity." It mentioned that the blade's engraving was the Greek word for clarity.[1] After reading its description, I felt affirmed in my decision to stay on Iona. It predicted that intellectual clarity would eventually make way for the release of creative energy. Several creative endeavors awaited me on Iona—improving my riding skills, writing, and maybe learning jewelry-making. My journey with Faith had explored the territory of my unconscious. If I remained on Iona, it would offer me space and time to make meaning of those experiences in the light of day, to consciously choose how I wanted to live my life.

I continued reading the indication. "You will be able to recognize facts and call by name things which other people would prefer to sweep under the carpet. This entails a great responsibility on your part. Be sure never to express your insights heartlessly. But when you are fully in contact with Love, use your sword without sparing yourself or others."[2]

It was highly relevant advice for my conversation with Ian. Ziegler asked me to reflect on "what supports or hinders clarity." I recalled my conversation with the Hooks on this subject. *My clarity is hindered by my fear of disappointing others—in this case, Ian.* Time alone helps me to know what I want. When I can patiently listen in silence and look within for guidance, I'm less swayed by society's expectations and the expectations of those I love. I needed to call on my Peaceful Warrior to help me pause and make conscious choices rather than react.

The book's suggestion initially stumped me. It said, "Meditate on this statement: The truth which you speak has neither past nor future. It is, and that is all it needs to be."[3] The asterisk indicated it was a quote from Richard Bach. I discerned it was reminding me to be present, specifically advising me to stop getting ahead of myself or justifying myself with a lens of the past. Was it also echoing that my longings were enough, and I could trust them? *I don't know what the future holds. I'd like to let it unfold without allowing my past to define me.*

The book's affirmation confirmed I could trust my clear perceptions. It was clear to me that all proposals of marriage were off the table. I wanted my independence and freedom in this sanctuary. The only proposal that served me now was the one I planned to make to Katrine, to board here in exchange for horse care. *Saorsa and Caim will be the recipients of all my affection. Maybe I'm clearer than I give myself credit for.* Even without the green marble stone in my pocket, I felt its protection. Maybe sitting amongst them today, I'd soaked up more than the rain.

It was time to create my altar on Maeve's nightstand. I retrieved the small Iona stones from the front pocket of the crumpled jeans on the floor. There was an indigo-blue scarf I'd seen earlier in Maeve's drawer that was reminiscent of the backdrop of the tarot card, so I borrowed it as a tablecloth and arranged the pebbles in a line like a sword pointing to the yellow snail shell, which reminded me to go slow. I lit the tealight and bowed before it, letting any lingering self-doubts drain away until I sat up straighter in my clarity to speak my vow and blessing. *Better late than never.* I blew out the teardrop flame and tucked one stone in the sweatpants' side pocket for protection.

I wondered if Angus would be home for my call with Ian and had second thoughts about wearing the baggy, clean sweatpants in case Jake's welcome included muddy paw prints. Plus, they weren't flattering. *Stop it. My clothes are irrelevant.* The trench coat was still damp but kept me dry as I trekked over with my list for Ian. The wind boosted me along at my back. Jake hadn't seen me, so I knocked. No answer.

I walked in and called out, "Hello." Still no answer. Angus's place had a chill. It begged for a fire, which I successfully lit with minimum smoke. There was a new message from Ian, with a Zoom link and a short note: "Can't wait to talk. I wish I were delivering your phone in person."

Yes, with a phone, I'll be accessible at any time. My cocoon from the outside world was about to be breached. I hadn't realized how much I enjoyed being without a phone until its arrival loomed. *Just because I'll have it doesn't mean I have to always have it on me.* I felt Ian's ulterior motive, and I prepared to set boundaries. My spine straightened, and I felt the presence of my Peaceful Warrior protecting my space. *Yes, I'm clearer than I realized.*

I logged onto the Zoom call, and Ian promptly let me in. He sat with a cup of espresso at our kitchen table. Seeing our home again created an unexpected tug.

"Hey darlin', I checked on the weather. Shall I pack sunshine for you?"

"Very funny. Yes, it's on my list. Shall I read the rest to you and help you find things or type it up?"

"Your assistance might be wise, given your closet and drawers are... how shall I say... less than organized."

"It's an intuitive system. It works for me." For the next ten minutes, I guided his hands to retrieve what I wanted.

"I looked into places to stay on the island and have a choice of two hotels, The Argyll and St. Columba, but only St. Columba has Wi-Fi in the rooms, so unless that flies in the face of local knowledge, I'll make a reservation."

"It's a good choice. I had lamb stew from their café today, and it was heavenly. I'm sure you'll love the restaurant menu."

"I read it already and laughed at 'Haggis Tatties and Neeps.' Their wine list has promise, but I'm still packing a few bottles in my luggage to celebrate with you: Mollydooker's Carnival of Love and Enchanted Path. There couldn't be a worthier occasion to raid my cellar. I want to hear everything about your enchantment while I'm there." I heard Ian imply he didn't want to hear about it now. "I'm gonna be forced to do some whisky tasting during my overnight stay in Oban. Are you sure you don't want to join me?"

"Whisky is a way of life here. You'll fit right in. How about you explore Oban first and tell me about it? Hey, you haven't mentioned how long you're staying."

"I think it's about a week. I have to check my tickets."

Angus walked in and signaled he was heading upstairs. I contemplated fleeing to the bathroom, but the fire's pull was stronger. It felt awkward talking with Ian now that Angus had arrived home. "I appreciate your willingness to make the trek. Hey, I forgot to ask you to pack my fox pelt."

"I'll add it to the pile. Speaking of creatures. I've got to ask Sam to house-sit for Persephone while I'm there. When do you plan to tell the coven you're back?"

"Soon. I'm not sure what to say yet." My attention was split between the call and Angus upstairs.

"Do me a favor and wait till I fly to California. I don't want a repeat performance of their last interrogation. This is your story to tell."

"Agreed."

"I can't wait till you have your phone, and we can talk without scheduling it. I miss you, Sarah. It's torture having the Atlantic Ocean between us."

I felt the ache in his voice but didn't want to go there, not now. "I miss you too, Ian. I'll ring you tomorrow when I have my phone." We ended our call before it went off the rails. I hadn't wielded my Ace of Swords. It was still in its scabbard.

It was quiet upstairs, and I wondered if Angus was waiting till I left to come down. The reality that Ian was coming soon was finally starting to sink in. I felt myself vacillating between excitement and anxiety. A hive of bees flew around in my chest again. Part of me wanted to be with Ian, but an even larger part wanted to hold him at bay. *What's that about?*

I imagined he'd expect me to spend all my time with him, including sleeping together. *Did I want that?* I knew he'd protest shifting our relationship status from lovers to friends, and would pressure me to fly home with him. *How can I show him why I want to stay? Introducing him to Saorsa and Caim won't hold any sway with him.* I wanted him to understand me and accept my decision, but it felt like a long shot.

Would Katrine be back? If not, I'd have an excuse to stay at her house. Why do I need excuses? Why not state what I want and let it stand on its own? I don't need Ian's permission or agreement or even understanding. But the truth was I wanted it. *Stop. Stop looking outside yourself for a source of authority—it's time to grant myself permission from my inner authority. And stop getting ahead of yourself and worrying about Ian's visit.*

I pictured my Peaceful Warrior with the Ace of Swords, the Sword of Clarity, inhabiting the archetype in me that's not reactive. If I could access that centered place within me, everything else would flow from there.

I called upstairs, "Hey, I'm off the call. There's no need to hide." I heard the tub water slosh. How much of our conversation had he overheard? Angus had surprised me when he peeled off our return walk to visit his mum. Maybe he still wanted some time to himself. I returned his computer to the kitchen table and placed another peat log on the fire, so it'd be warm when he came down from his bath. My fire awaited me. I was pulling on Katrine's wellies when I heard him say, "Ah'll be down in a minute."

His voice sounded so near, and it startled me. Angus stood at the top of the stairs, bare chested, with only a towel wrapped around his waist. I gawked, before I stammered, "I can—can wait," and sat on the bench to collect myself. The shock of seeing Angus nearly naked short-circuited me and I stepped outside to get a blast of cold air, the closest thing to a cold shower I could think of.

A few moments later, he opened the door barefoot, wearing jeans and a cream cashmere sweater. His wet hair curled in tiny ringlets that enticed my finger to twirl them. "Ye confused me, lass, ah thought ye said ye'd wait, but ah heard the door close. Ah thought ye had second thoughts and left me, but Kat's coat still hung on the hook." His mouth opened as if he was about to question why I was standing in the rain.

"No. I needed a bit of air, that's all."

He undoubtedly saw through my excuse and stepped away from the door, gesturing for me to come in.

"I should be on my way. I've got to go feed the horses."

"There's nae rush for that. Are ye still cross with me from earlier?"

"No. To prove it to you, I'll make you dinner. I have a fridge full of vegetables from Katrine's garden that I've not had a chance to use."

"Ah'd luv nothin' more. Ah'll help chop and provide mah lamb. Now, come sit by the fire to warm up. Ye were nae dressed for standin' outside in that flimsy cotton sweatshirt. Tonight's a night for cashmere."

"Oh, I agree. Fiona's cashmere called me, but I didn't want to borrow it. It's too precious. I was just thinking about a Scottish cashmere sweater of my mum's I asked Ian to pack for me. He's coming in a week." I watched the news register on Angus's face; his Adam's apple moved as he swallowed.

"Well, ye shouldn't wait that long to wear yer cashmere. Ah'v got one ye can have now. Ah shrunk it by mistake. 'Tis sure to fit ye as it dinnae fit me anymore, and ah cannae bring mahself to throw it out." He walked upstairs and returned with a black V-neck sweater. It appeared to be my size as he held it up before me.

"For me?"

He nodded, dangling it as an offering.

"It's irresistible. I'd be delighted to take it off your hands." And I did. "If the way to a man's heart is through his stomach, the way to a woman's heart is surely with cashmere." I practically skipped toward the bathroom to put it on.

It was a perfect fit, still long in the body and arms, enough to drape over my hips but not slipping off my shoulders. I predicted I'd live in it. Walking back to the living room, I pretended to be on a fashion runway, giving a twirl in front of the fire. "It's divine." I wrapped my arms around myself in delight. "I doubt I'll ever take it off. It's so luxurious and warm. Thank you, Angus." I leaned over and gave him a peck on his cheek, then sat beside the fire.

My brief display of affection left him speechless. Sitting, watching the fire, I felt my clarity crystallize. I'd keep my independence for the year. *I'll not ask Ian to wait any longer for me. If he becomes romantically involved with another woman, I'll have to accept the consequences. I'm embracing the unknown. I'll have my space and freedom to listen from within, not afraid that he or Angus, or anyone, can take my freedom away with their feelings toward me. No one can squeeze me out of my life unless I let them. The choice is mine.* I realized I trusted myself enough to choose me. Plus, my savings account had enough to cover my expenses if tutoring was slow. I sat up straighter, ready to wield the Sword of Clarity.

"Ye seem quite pleased with yerself. 'Tis as if mah cashmere sweater was a superwoman cape. What's come over ye?"

I laughed aloud at the image and stood, imitating her familiar stance: feet shoulder-width apart, hands resting on my hips, elbows out, shoulder blades back, spine straight. Coursing inside me was a newfound surge of power and clarity. My Peaceful Warrior had my back.

Angus laughed along with me. "Ah see the headlines now. 'Wonder Woman Turns up on the North Shore of Iona.' "

I grinned. "Yes, rumors were flying around about that woman." I flopped back down. "All joking aside, I have arrived at a point of clarity. Your not-so-disguised proposal this afternoon nearly drove me over the edge. I've been torn between my life in the States and Iona. It's wild that I arrived here via an oarless boat and even wilder that my body feels more at peace in this landscape in less than a week than anywhere I've lived to date."

I hesitated, pondering the edge I'd yet to name. "I'm also torn between the relationship I left with Ian and the relationship I'm finding here with you. I've been shocked at the chemistry between us, but my intuition says it's more than that, or that it could be. I'm afraid the physical attraction will overshadow the potential for our friendship. I know I want you in my life, Angus. I simply don't know in what capacity. I hope that we can become friends."

I scooted back, burrowing into the comfortable seat. "It's unsettling to me how I feel when I'm with you. I feel stretched between my former self who left on a journey with Faith, who I became while I was with her, who I am now, and the sense of who I'm becoming. I'm betwixt and between. I've been feeling pressure to decide, to know what I want or what I want to do or who I want to be with. I've felt like I owed Ian and my friends an answer and explanation of where I've been, but I have no idea what I'll say. I've felt like I should keep myself from getting to know you even though I want to, which has made me feel a muddy mix of guilt, shame, and fear that I'm missing out. Our embrace in church stirred my body in ways I've not felt for months or maybe ever. It's hard to say. I know now is not the time to go down that path." I exhaled in relief. It was all out in the open now.

"Ye, sound a bit tortured. Ah'm glad to hear ye'v come to a decision then—dinnae leave me hangin'. Ah'm keen to hear where ye'v landed. Ah'd like nothin' more than to take ye in mah arms, Sarah, and kiss ye properly, but ah fear that's nae where this conversation is goin', so have mercy on me and tell me where ah stand."

"It's true. I'm feeling less torn now. I don't know if this will make sense to you, but I've decided not to decide—to give myself a year, a year of freedom. If I can figure out a way to stay here, I will. I want to ride and read and write and listen to my dreams. I want to learn how to bake and knit, and if Katrine will teach me, make my own jewelry..."

Angus interrupted me with an urgent tone, sliding to the edge of his seat. "That all sounds grand, Sarah. Ah'v seen ye bein' here through the seasons. Ah'm still nae clear what this means for ye and me. Ah heard ye say out loud what ah felt as well, long before our embrace." He leaned forward. "Ah'm ah allowed to hold ye, to take ye in mah arms like ah'v been longin' to since ah met ye?"

I didn't hesitate or mince my words. "No. No, that's not going to happen now. We can be friends, Angus, but nothing more for the year. If our friendship is a foundation for something else, so be it. If it's not, we'll still have our friendship." I waited for him to say something. As he pushed back in the seat, I felt him pulling away from me. A vacancy filled the air. "Hey, are you still here? It feels like you've left the room, like all the guards you were letting down have now flown up, and I'm on the other side of the fortress moat. Put down the drawbridge, please."

"Ah dinnae ken what ah can say."

I'd wielded the Sword of Clarity but left out the love part. "Hey, Angus, did you hear all of what I said or only the word no? Do you not want to cultivate a friendship first, keeping the romantic entanglements out of it?"

Angus felt like she'd lifted his heart in the air and dropped it from a height that shattered it. After Sarah said no, everything else was simply noise. He couldn't trust himself to speak; his lips could barely form words. The grip he'd held on the chair's armrests released as he crossed his arms and clutched his sides. Angus stared at the floor, wishing it would offer a trap door for him to disappear into.

"Ah only heard nae. Repeat the rest in a minute." Sarah offered a friendship. It wasn't the end of the world, so why did he feel like it was? Because he'd hoped for more, so much more, and had sensed it was possible when only the stairs separated them. The lust he felt for her wasn't one-sided; he felt the longing in her eyes. It had taken everything in him to turn away and get dressed. When he saw her walk out in his cashmere sweater, the V dipped between her creamy breasts, and he couldn't help but grow hard for her. She woke him in ways he never wanted to let fall asleep again. Angus wanted her. He wanted her now, and hungered for her touch like the lyrics in the song last night. His left hand had become a loose fist that he brought to rest upon his chin as he bit his thumbnail. *What did she say about a year? What will I do over the next year? How does Ian fit into this?* He spoke without removing his hand, his knuckles pressed against his chin, lifting his gaze to stare into the window of her eyes. "Okay, lass, tell me the part ye said after nae. Ah'm listenin' now."

"Angus, you know I'm drawn to you. I love spending time with you and I'm eager to share with you what happened to me with Faith. You may be the one person I can talk it through with and not have you look at me like I lost my marbles. That means more to me than I realized. I want to have walks and dinners with you. However, I'm drawing a boundary at any romantic involvement—a very firm one. It's the same line we've had the whole time, but I've crossed it."

Sarah continued, "So much is unsettled in my life. I need to get to know myself better. The me that has arrived here is not the one who left home. I'm grateful to have landed on an island outside the mainstream culture. I'm reveling in the space and safety I feel here. The one thing I know is if I'm involved romantically with you or Ian, I'll start to accommodate my life to your needs and wants, and I don't want that influence right now. I feel like wet clay. I want to be the one choosing my shape, not you or Ian."

Angus could see a silver lining in this. His fist had opened with his index finger propped on his cheekbone, and his thumb held his chin. "Are ye tellin' me 'tis hands off for Ian too? Is this a level playin' field? Have ye told him that as well?"

"I've not said anything to Ian about it. I just arrived at this clarity standing here before your fireplace. When I was on the call talking to Ian, and you were upstairs, I felt cleaved between you both. The split was untenable. I don't want to live a divided life anymore. Your nearness electrifies me at times. Seeing you after your bath, practically naked, I'm sure my jaw was hanging open. It's embarrassing. I had to walk out in the cold rain to get hold of myself."

Sarah folded her legs up to her chest and hugged them with her arms. "I don't know if I can even be attracted to two men simultaneously or if my feelings for Ian have changed. I need to have this conversation in person with him—he deserves that, too. He's sure to be as hurt and confused as you. I don't want to take responsibility for his or your feelings. I need to break this bad habit of accommodating others if it means betraying myself. It makes so much sense to me now. I don't want to choose not to be with Ian, only to choose to be with you. I want to choose me. For the next year, I choose me! It's what I've been saying all along, but not with the same conviction. I want space and time to connect with myself." She sighed.

Angus did his best to practice restraint and accept the terms she'd laid down. He pushed up the sleeves of his sweater, letting his hand rest in his lap. "Ah hear ye, lass. If 'tis a friendship that ye are offerin', 'tis a hand in friendship ah'll gladly take. The drawbridge is down, and the boundary is clear. Ye'r right, once ah ken ye were spoken for, ah gave ye mah word ye were safe with me. Ah stand by mah word. But ah confess, ah dinnae want to lose ye without lettin' ye ken how ah feel.

"Ah'v meant to have ye feel torn, to nae make yer decision so easy. Ah sensed yer Ian was comin' with a ring in his pocket, how all yer history with him pulls ye back to him. Ah hear now that ye'r spoken for in a different way—that ye'r makin' a vow to yerself—to nae one else until ye ken who ye are and the life ye want to create for yerself. Ah can respect that. Ah can wait for ye to decide."

"But that's just it. I don't want the pressure of you or Ian waiting on me to decide. I want you to go on with your lives, tend to your happiness, and trust what unfolds."

Christ almighty, this woman is exasperating! Angus abruptly stood as Sarah remained curled in the corner of one of his chairs, wearing his sweater. If only it were as simple as she said, that the way to a woman's heart was through cashmere, he'd buy up the whole bloody store.

"Ye'r mighty philosophical since ye put on that cashmere. Shrinkin' it must have activated its latent Tibetan transmission for non-attachment. Let's be practical for a bit and tend to the horses. Ah need to move mah body, to be out into the storm mahself for a wee bit to sort mahself out." Angus walked into his kitchen. "Ah'll feed Jake and take some lamb from the freezer for our dinner tonight."

When Angus left for the kitchen, I stood before the flames. I wanted to extract my habituated patterns of letting everyone else's needs be louder than mine and toss them into the fire to burn. My sensitivity to other people's desires, spoken or unspoken, was sometimes a curse. *It's my own damn fault if I tend to them and ignore myself.* When others voiced a concern, a disappointment, or a hurt, I've felt compelled to try to make it better, but too often, it was at my own expense.

Enough with the fixing! From now on, I'd invoke compassion and pause before I caved to their needs and dismissed my desires as unimportant. Faith isn't just about faith in myself. It's having faith in others to tend to their own needs, bowing to how the Greater Mystery is unfolding in their lives and mine. This year, I planned to make my longings the clear priority and see where they led me, trusting that being in a relationship with myself, inhabiting my longings, would guide me to a place of belonging, be-longing.

---

1. Gerd Ziegler, *Tarot Mirror of the Soul: A Handbook for the Thoth Tarot* (Weiser Books, 2023), 134.

2. Ibid.

3. Ibid, 135.

CHAPTER 21

DATING

I TESTED MY RESOLVE by imagining Ian dating someone else. In theory, it was okay, but theory and reality often bear no resemblance. What about Angus? How would it feel if he were seeing someone else? *Similar.* I wanted them to move on with their lives and, yes, take the pressure off me. If they were happy, could I be happy for them? *Is this what trust and faith feels like in a relationship, when there's no need for control or possession between people, when there's only caring and non-attachment to an outcome? Am I becoming a Buddhist?*

Angus tapped me on my shoulder. "Let's be on our way. Ah give ye pence for ye thoughts?" He tilted his head to the side. "Is that the expression?"

"Close enough. I'll give them freely." We pulled on our coats to brave the outdoors. "I was picturing Ian dating someone other than me and sensing my body's reaction. I even did the same for you."

"Did ye now, and what did ye find?" He walked out the door after me.

"I might be okay with it. If you and Ian were happy, I'd be happy for you." At least, I wanted it to be true.

"Hmph, would ye now? Who are ye fixin' me up with? Ye ken mah type. Ah'd be happiest if ye'd introduce me to yer doppelgänger."

"She's around. I think we all have one."

Angus peered around me. "Bring her on, lass. Ah'd relish the abundance of two of ye to be torn between."

"Maybe with a little grace, we might both see her. But I'm serious. Why not start dating someone, expand your horizons?"

Angus was silent for a few steps as if I'd spoken a foreign language. "Ye'r daft if ye think ah want to date anyone but ye. Before ye came along, ah was quite content with the life ah had. Thank ye very much for disturbin' the whole damn apple cart."

"Well, apparently, your life needed a little disturbance. I prefer to think of myself as good trouble."

"Even mah mum's given up introducin' lasses to me. Kat's been after me for years to try a datin' app. She'd really think ye have magic powers if ah signed up now."

"You mean I don't have magic powers?"

"Ye do over me, Sarah, ye do over me."

"I have a friend back home who works for eHarmony. She attributes their booming popularity to an abundance of harried professionals who obsess over their work because no one else is putting demands on their time. It ensures they don't pursue other interests where they might meet someone. It's not a virtuous cycle. The pace of your life is hardly your problem. Your issue has more to do with distance from civilization."

"Ye'r a cheeky lass. 'Tis another thing to luv about ye. Ye may be surprised to learn that Kat met Roary online."

"Exactly. That's the spirit. It could work for you, too, if you're open to it. You've nothing to lose but your old habits and routines. You might even meet a lovely lass."

He raised an eyebrow—"Cheeky"—and opened the barn door.

The horses were nickering, hungry, and welcoming our company.

They weren't alone on either of those counts. My relief was palpable that Angus and I had navigated this conversation with our budding friendship intact. I had no illusions it would be this easy with Ian. However, this round fortified my convictions to keep my vow to myself before I agreed to make vows to another.

Our attention had shifted from each other to the horses. I mucked stalls, and Angus fed them. We did these tasks while carrying on conversations with Saorsa and Caim. To some, it might have sounded like a one-way conversation, but I thought differently.

Ian felt as if he'd been swimming underwater too long, and his lungs were aching for air as he searched for an exit from a dark cavern. Now, he'd finally surfaced to inhale deeply and float on his back with clear blue skies above. His call with Sarah had reestablished their connection. She sounded genuinely open to him coming and he basked in the feeling. He'd been intentionally vague about his departure date from Iona and had neglected to mention he'd booked her a ticket to accompany him. The image of them having Thanksgiving with their friends was one he clung to. Talking about her return home was a conversation that was best had in person, preferably in bed, after making love, or over a romantic dinner and bottle of wine.

The weather forecast predicted perpetual storms for the next week. *Maybe Sarah will be ready to trade her horses for me when I arrive. Why can't she simply find a stable here at home to ride at?*

When we arrived at Katrine's door, Angus handed me the lamb so he could bring in an armful of peat. The look of raw meat made my stomach queasy. I abandoned it on the counter beside the teapot with my strengthening remedy. Holding my breath, I drank a cool cupful. It left a bitter aftertaste.

I went to the credenza to put on some music, and the album jacket for "Unchained Melody" was on top. How had that been only last night? Tucking the record safely away, I flipped through her collection, and was shocked to see the double album, *Leylines,* from one of my favorite groups, Rising Appalachia.[1] Playing it would bring me closer to home.

Angus approached me. "What have ye found, lass? Ah'v nae heard this before." He opened their album sleeve and read aloud. " 'To this music, we have woven from the earth from the air. May it hold you closely and rock your soul like the steady tide on the wooden boat of this world...' Intriguin'. Ah like their ability to harmonize."

The quote implied their conversation with the elements was a source of their creativity. I pictured the craft that had carried me to Iona's shores only a few days ago. "Their music is my go-to when I want to lift my spirits." We returned to the kitchen.

"Ah'm guessin' this is Maeve's doin'. She loves the music scene in the States. Kat said she was ravin' about a sister duo and gifted her their album."

"Yes, they're sisters." Chopping onions stung my eyes, and they swelled with tears. "Their lyrics bear witness to societal issues, naming what needs our attention without whacking you on the head. They invite a different consideration of the ways our culture has us spellbound, that we'd be wise to question." It reminded me of my conversation with the Hooks.

I sang along with their lyrics as I stirred the onions, coating them with oil, then adjusted the heat to a slow simmer. "Iona feels removed from the culture of consumption that's out of hand in the States. There's so much waste and money spent on superfluous things while people are without homes and hungry. It's hard to witness these behaviors in myself, the abundance of things I have that I don't need while others lack the basic necessities. It's a dilemma I've not reconciled, and it leaves me feeling hollow inside when I consider it. I've been pushing it aside, given I'm not ready to renounce my life and am unclear what actions make any difference."

"'Tis a dilemma for sure, with nae easy answers. Those Tibetan fibers are still workin' ye ah see. What ye speak of is nae unique to the States, though yer approach to healthcare and education certainly widens the gap."

Angus thawed the lamb in a pan of warm water. I hated handling raw meat. It too closely resembled what it was, the muscle of animals. The more I thought about it, the less I wanted to eat it. "How shall we flavor this? I've got garlic but haven't found Katrine's spices. Do you know where they are?"

"Aye, we're in luck. Roary likes to cook, and he leaves his Indian spice blends. Ah'll start some rice with a few sautéd onions."

"Do you often cook for yourself?"

"Well, if ah dinnae, ah would nae eat. Jake's nae much help in the kitchen until ah drop somethin'. Then he's all over it."

"I see your point. How do you spend your evenings?"

"Ah read or listen to music by the fire. Sometimes ah talk with family, friends, or even Jake. He's a fine listener. Sundays, ye already ken, ah eat with Kat. One night a week ah have dinner with mah mum to keep an eye on her, though she dinnae need it."

"How was your visit with her today?"

"Helpful. She wants me to bring ye around for tea. She kens ye'v captured mah heart and wants to check ye out for herself."

"You mean be sure I'm good enough for you. In my experience, no woman is worthy enough for their firstborn son. There's always a special bond with their mum. Maybe that's why so many are confirmed bachelors."

"Nae, she's nae that way. She wants to marry me off and cannae abide by the amount of time ah spend alone. She says 'tis unhealthy. Ah think she's talkin' about herself because she misses mah dah. Ah tell her ah'm rarely alone, surrounded by mah sheep and Jake. That's when she turns violent and cuffs me upside the head if ah'm within reach."

"I think I'm gonna like her." There were moments that I'd wanted to smack Angus's shoulder, but I contained it. I had to contain a lot around him. "When shall we have tea with her? If the rain keeps up, I won't be able to keep my dates with Saorsa and Caim. I'd love to learn more about the remedies she makes if you think she'd talk with me about it."

"She'll talk ye ear off if ye let her. Ah'll have to come to rescue ye."

"I think I can rescue myself."

"That ye can, lass. Ye'v made that perfectly clear. Ah'll phone her up, and she'll probably invite ye for th'morra."

The aroma of simmering onions made the kitchen feel like home. I snitched one of the burned bits and sprinkled cumin seeds in to roast. "Let's brown the lamb first with some garlic. I can chop some."

"Aye, ah'v salted and peppered it. Ah'm about to rub some garam masala on it."

"You know your way around the kitchen. I'd love to try your lamb stew."

"Mah stew never comes out the same way twice. Ah dinnae follow a recipe."

"That's why I can't bake. I'm bad at following recipes. It's too exacting."

"Ye only like makin' rules for others to follow, ah see, while ye live outside the lines."

"I'll admit, there's some truth to that. What about you? Do you like living outside the lines?"

Angus stood beside me, browning the lamb. "A metaphysical conversation 'tis best had on a full stomach by the fire. How about ah distract ye with a glass of wine? Ah brought a bottle of red. It'll go better with the lamb, especially now that we've opted for Indian spice. Do ye like red?"

"I do, especially on cold nights. I don't find scotch pairs as well with dinner."

He smirked and reached for the wine bottle, displaying its label. It reminded me of the stylized Egyptian Eye of Horus. I read "AMON-Ra Shiraz 2010, Barossa Valley, South Australia." I was sure I'd seen that label before in Ian's cellar. *He'd be jealous of me drinking this without him, never mind the company.* Egyptian symbolism fascinated me. I appreciated the tidbits I learned from the Thoth tarot deck. The artist for the images was an Egyptologist, Freida Harris.

Angus poured us both a taste. I watched him raise the glass to the light, smell its bones, swirl, and taste it. "He dinnae disappoint."

"Ah, so red wine is a he?"

"This one is. Amon-Ra 'twas the King of the Upper Egyptian gods, second only to Osiris. Egyptians attributed to him creative powers. He was responsible for all life on earth, in heaven, and in the underworld. Ah thought if ye were willin' to share more of yer journey tonight, 'twas good to invoke him."

"I like how discerning your taste is for tonight's invitation list." Holding the glass to my nose, it smelled of dark cherry fruit and licorice. "Mmm, heavenly." It had a long, juicy finish, so smooth on my tongue and throat. "Tastes heavenly as well. It's like drinking cashmere. More, please."

Angus poured more wine into my glass and then his own. He clinked it on mine. "Sláinte, Sarah."

"Sláinte, Angus."

His eyes penetrated me as we drank. When he pivoted and brought the bottle to the table, I had to pause to recall what we'd been talking about. *Egypt, that was it.*

"I'm intrigued by your knowledge of Egypt. Have you traveled there?" I snitched another onion bit before adding the zucchini, cauli-flower, and chopped kale.

Back at the stove, Angus stirred the lamb. "Nae, only by mah fire at night. Ah mentioned ah read at night—'tis nae all fiction. Ah hope to travel there someday, but nae alone and nae part of a bloody tour group. Ah cannae bide the loud crowds askin' daft questions."

I imagined he had a library tucked away I'd love to peruse. Between Maeve's collection on Celtic spirituality and what promised to be Angus's treasure trove on Egypt, I'd happily read my way through the winter months. My familiarity with the rooms of Angus's home only included the living room and kitchen. Well, plus the bathroom I'd temporarily turned into a phone booth and a dressing room.

My new cashmere sweater felt like a caress across my skin. Talk about dropping into my body. It was so inviting, so sensual, as my hand caressed my opposite arm. "This cashmere is irresistible."

"What else do ye find irresistible?"

His question dangled in the air like bait. I gave myself a moment before replying. "Authenticity and integrity. I admire people who live their life fully, the one only they can lead." I didn't mention my post-card moments, that feeling of "Wish you were here," that arises when I'm living beside myself. "A great example is Jonathon Larson. You've probably never heard of him, but *Tick Tick Boom* is a fabulous movie about his life. He's a struggling artist, about to turn thirty, working in a diner and questioning if he should get a 'real job.' He was an American songwriter and playwright who transformed musical theater with his play *Rent*. Tragically, he died the day before opening night. He was only thirty-five. I wonder if he still heard the thunderous applause from the other side or gleaned its extraordinary impact. *Rent* ran for twelve years on Broadway and won multiple awards."

The next song on the album was "Resilient," one of my favorites.[2] I sang and started dancing to the rhythms as Angus watched. His attention made me feel self-conscious, but I remained determined not to change who I was or how I was moved to act, simply because Angus stood there. The drummer's solo irresistibly made my hips move.

> *…Yeah, I got my crew but truth is what I want*
> *Realigned and on point*
> *Power to the peaceful*
> *Prayers to the waters*
> *Women at the center*
> *All vessels open to give and receive*
> *Let's see the system brought down to its knees*
> *I'm made of thunder*
> *I'm made of lightning*
> *I'm made of dirt (yeah)*
> *Made of the fine things*
> *My father taught me that I'm a speck of dust*
> *And this world was made for me*
> *So let's go and try our luck*
>
> *I got my roots down, down, down, down*
> *Down, down, down, down, down, deep*
> *I got my roots down, down, down, down*
> *Down, down, down, down, down, deep*

I surmised dancing wasn't high on Angus's list of activities, unlike Ian, who loved to dance and play invisible instruments with the musicians as if he were part of the band. Even though my voice didn't carry a tune, I kept singing along with them.

> *…So what are we doing here? What has been done?*
> *What are you gonna do about it when the world comes undone?*

My voice feels tiny and I'm sure so does yours
But put us all together we make a mighty roaaarrrrrr
I am resilient
I trust the movement
I negate the chaos
Uplift the negative
I'll show up at the table, again and again and again
I'll close my mouth and learn to listen

"Someday, I'll show you their music video for this song.[3] It has amazing dancers accompanying the lyrics. Do you ever dance?"

"Ah cannae dance. Secondary school PE class ruined me—sweaty palms, steppin' on toes. Ah'v never enjoyed it like ye do. But watchin' ye now, ah'm beginnin' to feel like ah'm missin' out."

The record had stopped. "It's your turn to choose the music. I'll set the table."

Angus flipped over the record. It was the safest choice, given last night's premature ending. His time before Ian arrived was limited, and he planned to stretch it as much as possible. While he heard Sarah's plan, or more accurately, declaration, he knew that plans changed in an instant. The future was an illusion. All he had was now. The next song surprisingly began with a fiddler. This group was growing on him.

"Angus, do you ever pull tarot?"

"Och aye, ah was the one who introduced it to Maeve. Ah noticed ye have her deck out. Ah felt yer Ace of Swords earlier."

"Sounds like you know it well. Do you need to read about the cards, or can you interpret them on your own?"

"Ah'd say both. Ah like to sit with the symbols first and let them speak to me, the elements, their colors. Ah get the gist, and then ah consult the book. Some days if ah awake unsettled, ah pull in the mornin' and meditate on the suggested statement while ah'm on the land. What did the Ace of Swords have as a suggestion?"

Sarah brought him the book already opened to the page that described it.

He read most of it to himself but spoke the essential guidance, "'Meditate on this statement: The truth which you speak has neither past nor future. It is, and that is all it needs to be.'[4] How did ye interpret that?"

"It's about being in this present moment—now, not being tied to the past nor swept up in the future. It's rather Buddhist in philosophy—be here, now. What about you? What do you make of it?"

"'Tis about the present moment, ah agree. 'Tis a wee bit more than that, the trust part. Ye can trust what ye ken now, unencumbered by the past or future, or in other words, a freedom in now. Ah ken 'tis why ye'r drawn to Saorsa. He's very present and demands it of any rider or anyone near him. He dinnae settle around people who are merely shells. He tends to scare them off."

"I do love that horse. His power is palpable. I don't even have to be riding him, just being near him is enough to feel the rush. He brings me right inside my skin so I can feel myself from the inside more than the outside world pressing in on me. Does that make sense?"

"Ah ken what ye mean."

"Does he have that effect on you too?" Sarah fluffed the rice and turned off the heat.

"Nae. lass. Ah'm already in mah skin as ye say. Workin' yer life on a farm will hone that skill. Ah escape sometimes by the fire into mah head, mah imagination. Speakin' of bein' in mah body, it says dinner's ready."

The aromas of cardamom and cumin tempted me to snitch a piece of lamb from my plate as I walked to the table; the flavors left me wanting more. As Angus served himself, I asked, "What captures your imagination fireside?"

"Lately ah'm wonderin' about yer adventure with Faith. Ah'd like to revisit yer inner landscape if ye'll let me join ye." He sat across from me, and his gaze beckoned for something I couldn't name. "'Tis a wee bit like what ye said about the effect of simply standin' near Saorsa. Ah dinnae need to have had the experience to benefit from it."

He'd deftly dodged my question about him and turned the focus back to me. I glanced at my meal. Ian told me he only wanted to hear about my journey in person, and I longed to share it with someone, to hear myself speak and let the sense-making fall into place. My friends' response to my return was still a wild card. "How about after dinner? It's easier to close my eyes when recalling it." *Will it continue to change and evolve?* I sensed it was a living memory, not the kind that is so easily captured in a picture or on the page. It intrigued me that it wasn't static. Its dynamic nature motivated me to revisit it often instead of tucking it away in a drawer of my psyche.

"Ah can be patient. Contrary to what ye may think of me, ah dinnae always jump the line. Ah'd like to buy a ticket for a front row seat, whenever the show starts. For now, how about ye offer us a blessin', and we enjoy dinner together."

"Patience is still on my list to cultivate." I reached across the table for his hands and felt the electrical charge pass between us as his fingers clasped my palms. "I'm grateful to have returned to Iona and found a place of sanctuary and companionship by the sea. May the power of the Great Mystery continue to have a place in our lives, such that we know grace, the help that comes bidden or unbidden."

"Ah'm grateful to walk alongside ye, neighbor. Mah life's brighter for yer bein' here." He squeezed my hands but waited a few extra moments before he let go.

---

1. Rising Appalachia, Leylines Album.

2. Rising Appalachia, "Resilient," Leylines Album

3. Rising Appalachia, "Resilient (Official Video)," YouTube video, 4:10, May 1, 2018, https://youtu.be/GwAL6aL1yKA?si=5GPaaJ39350Gd0Fx.

4. Gerd Ziegler, *Tarot Mirror of the Soul: A Handbook for the Thoth Tarot* (Weiser Books, 2023), 135

CHAPTER 22

GUIDANCE

A FTER DINNER, WE SAT on the couch angled toward one another from our respective corners, like bookends, a glass of wine in hand, an invisible volume between us.

"Now about that ticket ye promised. Ah ken there's more than one episode to this adventure ye had with Faith. Ah'd like to purchase the unedited version of the whole series, complete with gestures and movements. Ah enjoyed yer dance of opposites by the firelight."

"You're in luck. The unedited version is the only one there is. Maybe this will unlock my writer's block. Where was I? Had I met anyone else on the bridge yet?"

"Nae. Ye were tracin' the infinity symbol like a Qigong movement. It was just ye. Faith was on the other side of the bridge that spanned the river valley."

"I was conjuring the tensions of opposites in my life and finding the centered place in me that could hold both of them simultaneously: masculine and feminine, past and future, fear and trust. Okay, I'll take it from there." *Do I still have the ability to incarnate my feelings, to witness and recognize them? Will remembering mean returning to the same conversation, or will it evolve?* "How about I ease into this and give you a bit of a summary of what I recall?"

"Ah'm all ears."

"Okay, the first aspect of myself that appeared was Curiosity." I recalled her bouncy ponytail, journal, and pen in hand. "She had a lilt in her voice as she asked questions neither I nor Faith could answer, which inadvertently summoned Impatience. I learned Impatience has a way of appearing whenever my expectations are at odds with what is happening in the moment. My conversation with her proved difficult. She repeatedly interrupted me. Not surprisingly, Frustration was immediately on her heels, followed by her parents, Criticism, and Judgment.

"They continuously conspired to convince me I wasn't enough. They told me I wasn't smart enough, productive enough, clear enough—gnawing away at my self-esteem, and hollowing me out. Eventually, I'd had enough of them and their refrain of my inadequacies. When I declared I was enough—not perfect, but enough—ironically, it summoned the final character of my entourage that night: Perfection. At least the illusion of her reminded me it wasn't humanly possible to be perfect and human."

This unedited picture show wasn't exactly putting my best self on display. I chuckled. *Isn't that the point, trying to present myself other than I am at any moment? Those are the thousand tiny ways I betray myself and my ability to live an authentic life.* It was freeing to be so transparent, with Angus as a witness, and stop judging myself. I'd been staring into the fire and turned to see him as he raised his glass to me.

I raised mine in response. "Yes, I'll drink to freedom." *Warts and all.*

Recalling my journey with Faith was easier when I wasn't looking at Angus, so I stared into the fire. "We departed from the bridge and arrived at an octagonal structure, a misty honeycomb that invited sleep. I awoke beside Faith and remained horizontal for what felt like days. It could have been only hours. I lost my grip on time, or better yet—it loosened its hold on me. I drifted in and out of sleep, of dream time. One of the times I woke, there was a tray of prepared fruits: slices of pear, papaya, and pomegranate seeds. Their feminine curves combined with the sheer abundance of crimson seeds were so beautiful I stared at them as if I entered a still life painting. Time slowed. I slowed.

"It was an otherworldly pause to experience the hidden depth of stillness. My attention focused inward. I noticed all the little murmurs and sensations my body offered, often in the language of aches or twinges. Showering this kind of attention on myself was a unique twist on a healing spa. I actually listened to myself for a change." *I need to revisit this spa.* "That's when the weight in my chest revealed itself, or more accurately, I finally paid attention to it." I placed my wine glass on the coffee table and laid both palms on the center of my chest. The weight had mostly lifted. Breathing came more easily.

My left index finger rested on Faith's pendant and touching it reminded me that my journey was real, that my experience wasn't a dream nor a figment of my wild imagination. My thumb felt the soft caress of cashmere, reminding me of Compassion and how being near her was like being gently wrapped in a cashmere shawl. I closed my eyes to summon her presence.

The warmth of my hands on my chest encouraged me to breathe into my heart. My body softened as my shoulders dropped. The heat in the center of my chest spiraled out in ever-widening circles, circles that went beyond my skin to root in the ground and reach toward the sky. My palms gradually lifted off my body, opening outward as my arms stretched wide, with my elbows still bent as if embracing an ancient tree. I heard the line of my blessing. 'May I dwell in the place of infinite capacity, my heart, offering love.' *My heart is the place of infinite capacity. Can I learn to dwell here?*

Compassion told me that her heart lived beyond the borders of her skin, which was why the first contact she made with others was a heart connection. *Maybe I'm not hugging a tree, maybe I'm embracing my own vast heart.* I exhaled and slowly let my hands return to the gesture Forgiveness had taught me, palms curved upward in my lap, cupping an invisible offering.

I opened my eyes and saw Angus had welled up in tears. He placed his right hand on his chest and nodded. I mirrored his gesture and closed my eyes again. I'd left the territory of words behind, appreciating his ability to listen without them.

I watched Grief's hunched posture emerge from the shadows of the curtain. Gravity's force field intensified in her universe. She was laden with loss and unfilled longings. I heard her lament whispered in my ear.

"For years, you have looked to another for the love that will sustain you and missed the love that awaits you within. Only in the presence of this love from within can you find nourishment in what is offered from another. For too long now, you have longed to be seen and heard, acknowledged by others as their equal, yet no amount of their love or encouragement will ever be enough to fill the emptiness you feel within from not loving and acknowledging yourself. You ache from this endless search outside yourself for what, in your heart of hearts, you know can only be found from within. This is your despair. How long will you go on denying what you know to be true?"

I wasn't denying my truth anymore. My choice to 'choose me' this year proved I was no longer seeking outside myself what only I can offer. My fingertip traveled the infinity path of Faith's pendant. *What if this is our communication channel?* When I'm residing in my heart, in touch with Compassion's infinite capacity, it opens me from the center out, like a rose, able to receive guidance. *My heart knows I'm never alone. It's my head that subscribes to the illusion of separation and the inevitable contraction that follows. Disembodied living is what makes me unsafe and reliant on external sources for assurance, acceptance, and discernment.*

Is this what I am to remember? Is this what allows my mustard seed of faith to sprout and grow roots? I smiled inwardly before a slight curve naturally emerged on my lips. *My journey isn't a memory. It isn't over. If I am willing to be open and ask for help, to pause and listen from a still place, their guidance is still here—here for the asking.* I opened my eyes to see Angus watching me intently. I still felt Compassion's presence lingering as I said, "That's enough for tonight."

Angus nodded. "Thank ye, lass. Yer pendant, did Faith give it to ye? When ye touch it, ah feel a wave of comfort wash over me."

"Yes, right before I departed." My index finger returned to tracing it. "Touching it is more powerful than I'd realized. It seems to stop my rational mind from dismissing all the aspects of myself I met on the journey with her. In some mysterious way, it's actually an invitation to engage." I let go of the pendant and stretched my arms out wide, repeating my gesture from earlier. This time, with my eyes open, I noticed how my right hand had come precariously close to Angus. I recoiled and reached for my wine, sipping it as I stared into the fire. "Does Katrine have any of Rumi's books of poetry? I've got one on my mind I'd like to reread."

He reached for his phone. "Which one? Google can find it."

"The one about welcoming every aspect of ourselves as a guest."

"Och aye, 'The Guest House,' that's a fine one." His fingers were typing. "There's an Egyptian translator ah prefer, Dina Al-Mahdy."[1]

He read it out loud:

> *"This human is a guest house.*
> *Every morning, a new guest arrives.*
> *A joy, a grief, a despair, some momentary awareness comes,*
> *as an unexpected visitor.*
> *Welcome and entertain them all!*
> *Even if they're a crowd of sorrows,*
> *who violently sweeps your house empty of its furniture,*
> *Still treat each guest honorably.*
> *They may be clearing you out for some new delight.*

The dark thought, the shame, the malice,
meet them at the door laughing, and invite them in.
Be grateful for whoever comes,
because each has been sent as a mentor from beyond."

I'd invited them all in, and tonight, I'd even invited a witness. By finally welcoming my Grief, she had swept me clean. My guides from beyond had so much to teach me. However, it was time to have the attention off me. "What now, Angus?"

"What are mah choices, lass?"

I heard what he didn't say and ignored it. Maybe I was learning to read his mind after all. "Well, we could pull tarot or talk more about Egypt, or you could tell me about Daphne. Which do you prefer?"

"Ah choose D, none of the above." Angus desired the intimacy that only bodies, not words, could offer. After Sarah had laid bare her inner life to him, his longing for her had only escalated. His gaze moved down her long neck, past her clavicles, craving more skin than her coveted V-neck cashmere revealed. The image of her dancing earlier played on repeat in his mind. He ached to move with his hips pressed against hers, undulating to their own found rhythm.

"Let me reiterate your choices: pulling tarot, talking about Egypt, or sharing your history with Daphne. *Those* are the only offers on the table."

"What if ah have somethin' else to offer? How about ah turn the record over and ask ye to dance?"

"I distinctly recall you said PE classes ruined you for dancing. Besides, the heat between us needs dialing down, not up. If I come any closer to you, I might go up in flames. Remember, we're to be friends, not lovers. It's time to channel this energy somewhere safer."

Everything can change in an instant. Angus groaned as he reached for the tarot deck on the table.

"Excellent, tarot it is. How about one card rather than a full spread."

"Agreed." He shuffled. From his years of pulling tarot, he knew better than to ask a yes/no question—even though he wanted to know if he'd succeed in winning Sarah's heart, he left it open, asking for guidance on how to move beyond friends to lovers. After fanning the cards face-down across the coffee table, Angus chose one, turning over the Knight of Swords; he'd hoped for the Lovers.

It depicted a horse and rider galloping. The Knight's arms stretched forward on either side of the horse's head. His hands held swords, one short and one long, instead of the reins. The energy was full speed ahead, not waiting for an invitation.

"What do you see, Angus?"

He held the card between his thumb and forefinger. "A very determined, well-balanced rider in pursuit of what he wants. He's not hesitating. He's emboldened, chargin' ahead, so to speak. Ah get the sense he kens where he's goin'. This bodes well for me."

"Do you want to share the question you asked?"

"Ah'll wager ye can guess what destination ah have on mah mind."

"Yup, my powers of perception are improving. Shall I read it? You've spoken to most of it, only missing a few points."

He knew she'd been skimming the text as he pondered its meaning. "Enlighten me, lass."

"Okay, there's the propeller on his head. It symbolizes flexible thinking, unhindered by time and space. If your goal is emotionally charged, it will bring on..."

Angus interrupted. "Ye can be sure there's passion involved."

"I was going to say the alignment of body, mind, and spirit, which is also represented by the three flying swallows in the corner of the card.

It seems you're a force to be reckoned with."

"Och aye, lass, ye best keep that in mind. What does the suggestion say?"

Sarah read directly from the book. "Imagine how you will best be able to enjoy your success."[2]

"Well, now we're back to where we started. Ah believe the card is encouragin' me to return to the offer that was nae on the table, at least nae yet." Angus slid from his corner of the couch to hand Sarah the cards, letting go slowly.

My other hand swept the air between us. "Back to your corner. Your determination is admirable, but don't forget the part about flexibility." Shuffling mingled my energy with the cards. I asked for guidance regarding my time on Iona and pulled the Four of Discs, Power. It resembled a fort or an Egyptian temple. I glanced at Angus. "Why are you looking so smug?"

"Shall I read it for ye?"

"Unless you want to interpret it for me?"

"Well, this one is mixed in its meanin'. Only ye can decide which way to interpret it. 'Tis like a fort, with these four alchemical elements in each corner, symbolizin' integrity on all levels of yer bein'. There's nothin' superfluous about it. The fort is strong and could even be thought of as rigid. 'Tis a closed system, with thick visible walls, 'tis solid and dependable. If we apply it to ye, it means ye'r dependable, unshakeable, true to yer principles. Ye have integrity."

Angus paused and peered at me. I felt vindicated for the clear boundaries I'd drawn.

He continued, "However, let me read from the book so ye dinnae think ah'm makin' it up or embellishin' in any way. 'Another possible meanin' is crystallization, holdin' too rigidly to the letter of the law, becomin' a stickler, crusadin' for one's principles. One's guidelines and commandments take on a life of their own—upholdin' the standard seems more important than being vital and human. Natural impulses are suppressed in order not to compromise one's character. Cold, stiff politeness replaces real warmth and friendship.'"[3]

"I'm not cold and stiff!" Despite my protest, I heard the ice queen being described. I thought I'd left her behind years ago.

"Ye do have many rules and boundaries ye'v created around ye. Let me read the indication. 'The meanin' of the card depends on the background of the person who draws it. The card can be an admonishment, indicatin' a need to become more established in one's character and integrity. Or, it could be a challenge to submit one's rules and principles to life and the impulses of the heart.'"[4]

"Hmmm."

"Listen to the question the book offers. It may help ye discern the meanin' better. 'Is yer life, yer behavior, like a rigid fort? Or does yer life, yer behavior need more order, structure, and solidarity?'"[5]

"I'm hardly a rigid fort. If anything, I'd say I need more structure: a place to live, a way to earn a living. It's time for me to get my act together if I want to stay here for more than another week. I've been acting like I'm on vacation, following my momentary impulses." In truth, I'd had six months of following those impulses while I journeyed through my inner landscape. Integration, not vacation, was my task.

"That's certainly one interpretation. Ah might add it looks a wee different from mah corner of the couch. The indication says ye'r meant to study the different aspects of power and yer affirmation is to offer yer power in the service of love."

"Angus, you're still suppressing a smile. What's that about?"

"Let me re-read this one line... 'Or it could be a challenge to submit one's rules and principles to life and the impulses of the heart.'[6]Ah ken that submission and surrender dinnae come easily for ye. Ah'm just sayin' as long as 'tis in service of love, ye'r nae at risk of compromisin' yer principles."

"Okay, point taken. I'll think about it. Hey, on a somewhat related topic, where did you put the green marble heart you found today?"

"'Tis on mah bedside altar. 'Tis too big to carry around in mah pocket. Do ye have yer stone?"

"I do." I produced it as evidence. "Thanks for taking me there this afternoon. I confess I wasn't paying attention to the route. When Ian visits, I'd like to take him there, but I doubt I'd find it again."

"Ah can draw ye a map. If ye walk down the wrong bay, ye can retrace yer steps till ye recognize the cliffs. Ah'll nae be volunteerin' mah services as a tour guide."

"I wouldn't expect you to." The air between us had shifted with my mention of Ian.

Angus stood up. I thought he was going to call it a night, but he returned with the bottle of Amon-Ra and held it above my glass. "Lass, will ye help me finish the bottle?"

"Sure, I imagine it's bad luck to refuse a God. Sláinte, Angus."

He emptied a splash in his own glass. "Sláinte, Sarah"

His gaze held me until I broke away to stare at the safety of the flames.

Angus had retrieved the last of the wine, hoping to eke out more time together. Even when they weren't speaking, her companionship spoke volumes to him. He steered clear of women who weren't at ease with shared silence and filled it with chatter.

His mum advised him to stay open, advice he'd found difficult to follow since returning home and overhearing Sarah and Ian discussing his impending visit. She'd asked him to pack her fox pelt. Why would she own such a thing?

When she'd seen him half naked, only wrapped in his bath towel, he felt the full force of her lust like an electrical current that leapt the length of the stairs between them. Her fleeting kiss on his cheek for his shrunken cashmere turned him into a live wire, sparking. He was so damn attracted to her that it took constant effort to resist the impulses of his body and heart to close the distance between them. It felt unnatural.

The fleeting elation he felt when he'd let himself believe in their future as lovers was decimated by her adamant no. Only her earnest proposal of friendship rescued him. As he gazed over at her profile, backlit by firelight, his fingers wanted to caress every inch of her. Even if her rigid rules handcuffed him, his heart was still his own and his devotion toward Sarah flowed unabated. *Keepin' mah hands to mahself is near impossible. Sarah's right, though. She's wet clay and deserves the time and space to mold her life into the form she chooses.*

As I sipped my wine by the fire, I fleetingly considered the outside world. I hadn't heard or read the news for six months as I journeyed through my inner landscape. The world had carried on without me. Catching up on it could wait. More pressing matters, like where I would sleep after next week, needed resolution. *Will I sleep with Ian when he visits? Can we maintain our friendship if we're not lovers? Is my decision not to decide—to choose myself instead of a lover— too rigid, or precisely the structure I need?*

My habit of fleshing out a plan with more details, or spinning scenarios rather than letting my future unfold, tugged at me. I had no experience tending a garden from seed and the patience that required. *Could I allow my life to emerge and not get ahead of myself?*

Is a friendship with Angus even possible? The force of attraction between us proved impossible to ignore. Resisting it kept me off balance. When swimming in strong currents, I knew better than to attempt swimming against it. Safety entailed swimming diagonally across it. *How do I do that in our budding friendship without landing in his muscular arms?*

He's a stallion. If my attraction to him was only physical, I'd be better at ignoring it, but he meets me at every level—emotionally, mentally, and spiritually. When my body's near him, it has a mind of its own and only wants to be nearer. How do I rein in that hunger, learn to ride it, and redirect the energy? I smiled inwardly.

Tonight, we'd redirected successfully by taking different angles. Mentioning Ian's name helped me tack in the same way I windsurfed—close to the wind, not into it. *I want to keep Ian present, even if he's at a distance, to give our relationship a chance to shape-shift, allowing me to enter into it as the woman I am now, not returning as the woman who left.*

The qualities I'm so attracted to in Angus are what I need to cultivate in myself and owning these projections is the most effective redirect. Naming and acknowledging them is the first step: his powerful groundedness, his gentle kindness, his ability to perceive the unseen and unspoken, and his fluid partnership with the invisible world. He reminded me of Faith, yet in a man's body, which stirred up all sorts of attraction and romantic entanglements. *Angus is no substitute for cultivating my relationship with Faith. My relationship with Faith will lead me home, not astray.*

Reliving aspects of my journey with Faith helped me internalize the messages. Simply sharing it with Angus, without trying to explain it, let me saddle up to it again. It amazed me that the movement I'd experienced as a dance of opposites had new gestures when I returned to it. I'd mistakenly thought of it as a static memory. It wasn't. It was evolving, like me. Revisiting it with Angus as a witness, like in Authentic Movement, required my willingness to be fully seen and to drop the walls

I often hid behind. His ability to listen and understand me even when I wasn't saying or doing anything melted any defenses I tried to erect. *Why is transparency such an aphrodisiac?* Was it because vulnerability invites intimacy? *What if I did surrender to these impulses of my heart? Would it be so wrong when it feels so right?*

I felt Angus's gaze upon me and turned toward him. He'd finished his wine.

"Ah was just goin' over the day with ye. Ah'm grateful to have ye in mah life, Sarah—to be cultivatin' our friendship. 'Tis hard to convey why yer sharin' yer journey with me is such a blessin'. Ah ken that heaviness in mah chest. There's nae accident the sea offered me a heart today."

"Might that heaviness be connected to Daphne? Would you be willing to share your past with me?"

"Aye. 'Tis nae a complicated story. Ah met her. Ah let mahself fall in love with her. Ah thought she loved me, but she decided she could nae be with me. She found mah ability to read her too intimidatin'. She called me an intruder. Ah dinnae see it comin', nor her declaration that she was leavin' me. When she left me without warnin', ah felt dismembered. Today, ye touched on that grief. Yer 'nae' to me was like hearin' her reject me all over again." Angus paused. He crossed his arms to hold his stomach, his shoulders rounded and caved inward.

I wanted to lean over and hold him. Instead, I quietly enfolded him in my heart, reflecting on Rumi's wisdom to welcome the unexpected visitors, even grief.

> *...Even if they're a crowd of sorrows,*
> *who violently sweeps your house empty of its furniture,*
> *Still treat each guest honorably.*
> *They may be clearing you out for some new delight...*[7]

I waited, breathing with him, welcoming his grief. Even though my body remained on the opposite end of the couch, in my heart, I felt like

I'd come alongside him. Surprisingly, I didn't have a compulsion to make him feel better, nor did I feel responsible for his feelings. I accompanied him in his pain without protectively sealing myself off because I trusted his battered heart would mend in its own time. I finished the last of my wine and waited until he found his voice again.

"Sarah, the affection ah feel for ye is more than lust, though ah'll nae deny there's plenty of that. Ye'v awakened a longin' that ah thought ah'd safely locked away, that ah'd promised mahself to never give over to again. Ye'v broken through that resolve despite mah best efforts to wall it off. Ah was startin' to trust it might be possible that ye felt it too. Ah believe ye do. Then ah heard ye say 'nae' to me, and mah whole body went dark. Ah could nae hear another thing. Ah could hardly breathe. Ah was back there with Daphne, hearin' her declare that she was leavin' me."

"I hear you, Angus. Watching you clutch your stomach, my chest clenches. I have to deliberately exhale to release it. I hear how my 'no' is tangled up with the ending of your relationship with Daphne. Thanks for giving me a window into what's moving in you, for trusting me with your pain." I stopped there. I didn't have to mention I'm not Daphne. He'd figure that out in his own time.

The fire was almost embers, and our wine glasses were empty. I looked forward to a conversation about Egypt with him some other time and trusted there'd be more fireside nights with Angus—there was no rush to pack it all in.

Angus reached for my wine glass. "Lass, we're both weary from the day. Ah'll be on mah way. Dinnae get up. Enjoy the last of the fire." He took the empty goblets to the kitchen.

"Thanks for your company today and for sharing your lamb and wine. Both were a delicious pairing." As he came toward me, I placed my palm over my heart. "I'm full of gratitude."

Angus paused behind me and kissed the crown of my head. "Me too lass, sweet dreams."

I remained in my corner of the couch. "Goodnight, Angus." After the door closed, I listened to the hushed crackle of peat that glowed a golden orange. Fire was the one element left out of my odyssey with Faith. *What will it teach me here on Iona?*

The coffee table still held Angus's book of poetry, *Drunk on the Wine of the Beloved*. I opened it randomly and read "From the Large Jug, Drink."[8]

> *"...From the large jug, drink the wine of Unity,*
> *so that from your heart you can wash away the futility of life's grief.*
> *But like this large jug, still keep the heart expansive.*
> *Why would you want to keep the heart captive, like an unopened bottle of*
> *wine?..."*

I stopped. Those lines were enough. It was as if the poem had been listening to our conversation tonight, offering the perfect nightcap to sip from. *Hafiz will be the final voice in my night.* Closing the book, I let the poem's counsel settle, then climbed the stairs to bed.

---

1. Jalal al-Din Rumi, "The Guest House,", translated by Dina Al-Mahdy, Edited by KarimKhater, March 29, 2001, https://dinaalmahdy.com/2001/03/29/the-guest-house-a-poem-by-persian-poet-jalaluddin-rumi-translated-by-dina-al-mahdy/.

2. Gerd Ziegler, *Tarot Mirror of the Soul: A Handbook for the Thoth Tarot* (Weiser Books, 2023), 77.

3. Ibid, 160.

4. Ibid, 161.

5. Ibid.

6. Ibid.

7. Jalal al-Din Rumi, "The Guest House,"translated by Dina Al-Mahdy, Edited by Karim Khater, March 29, 2001, https://dinaalmahdy.com/2001/03/29/the-guest-house-a-poem-by-persian-poet-jalaluddin-rumi-translated-by-dina-al-mahdy/.

8. Shamsuddin Muhammad-i-Hafiz-i-Shiraz, "From the Large Jug, Drink," translated by Thomas Rain, *Drunk on the Wine of the Beloved: 100 Poems of Hafiz* (Boston: Shambhala, 2001), 54.

DRAFT BLESSING VERSION 2

"May the tempo of my life
allow my heart, mind, body, and spirit to move at the same pace,
the pace of embodied presence.
May my breathing and pausing be a reminder to slow down,
ask for guidance, and melt with breath.
May each day unfold with a priority on creative expression,
sensing the deeper currents and stalking the sacred.
May I become patient with uncertainty,
welcoming mystery into my life as my beloved dance partner,
letting go of expectations, even with disappointment,
to honor what is authentic in the moment.
May my conversation with the elements re-source my days,
cultivating courage, faith, and my sense of belonging, be-longing.
May a sense of humor be a source of laughter
for enjoying life more fully.
May I be willing to be lost, to venture into terra incógnita,
letting go of my need to know—my need to figure it out to be safe—
trusting life, even in the darkest moments
believing in renewal.
May I live in the inquiry of what-if, maybe.
May I tend to myself, others, and our environment
from a connection with myself,
offering kindness, compassion, and spacious witnessing.
May my listening be an invitation, an integration.
May I dwell in the place of infinite capacity, my heart, offering LOVE.
May my experience be one of reciprocity with all my relations.
May my presence be enough."

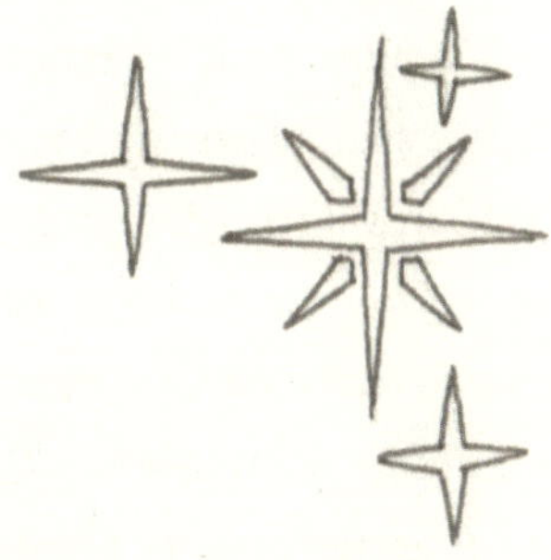

WAVES OF GRATITUDE

A WAVE OF GRATITUDE flows back to the sea for sharing her secrets, her lessons, and for listening to me; beside her or immersed in her, I experience belonging.

Another loving wave flows toward my supportive husband, who lends his strength when I falter, and to our son, who inspired me to follow my longing wholeheartedly through his courageous choices to remain true to himself. My dear family and friends, thank you for understanding my absences, as I've prioritized writing and editing over socializing. While I adore my characters, never doubt I love you more.

Return has involved a flock of beta-readers: A.T. Birmingham Young, Sarita Chawla, Jocelyn Corbett, Kristin Cobble, Andrea Dyer, Anika Fox-Horn, Cary Grey, Christie Lynx, Elise Miller, Catharine Scherer, and Margaux Scholz. Thank you for your time; it's such a precious gift. You've each offered a unique perspective, and your honest feedback helped this story take flight.

Gratitude flows to my assembled team of editors for their thoughtful expertise. Credit for developmental edits flow to Christina Boyd, sensitivity read to Marielle Martin, and copy edits to Dana Lee. Finding all the mistakes is an impossibility, yet A.T. Birmingham Young offers her keen eye to catch another batch in a final read, and I'm so grateful for your capacity for detail.

Another swell of gratitude flows to Connor Ryan's skill in capturing the symbolism and themes of the book with his illustrations. The cover art's inspiration arose from "Currach's Last Wave," sculpted by his mentor, Alexandra Morosco. Read more about the story behind the cover in "Breaking the Frame" in the Re-Source Guide for *Return*, or the Inner-View on my Substack, ENTHRALLING.

A groundswell of gratitude flows to Vivienne Hull for casting the invitation to visit Iona each year and patiently waiting until I knew it was time. Your gracious spirit made that enchanting visit possible. I'll be forever grateful for the chance to see Iona through your compassionate and kind eyes. The light and landscape of Iona wended their way into my inner life, and many years later, they found their way onto the page, becoming the setting for more of the *Rumored Woman Series*.

The *Rumored Woman Series* is finding its way into the world like dandelion seeds blown on the winds. Heartfelt thanks to Sarita, Kristin, Andrea, Alexandra, and Christie, who've gifted copies of *Reflect*, blowing seeds far and wide. One of those seeds blossomed into the gift of a midwife, Jaymie Schoenberg, whose partnership made my Substack, ENTHRALLING, possible with ease and grace. (MorganMagauran.s ubstack.com). Now, anyone can read the first six chapters of each book for free upon release and share it with friends. I think of it as my virtual bookshelf.

Lastly, but in no way least, gratitude flows to *Rumored Woman's* readers, bringing the story to life and perhaps allowing the narrative to mingle and shift the story of their own becoming.

COPYRIGHT ACKNOWLEDGEMENTS

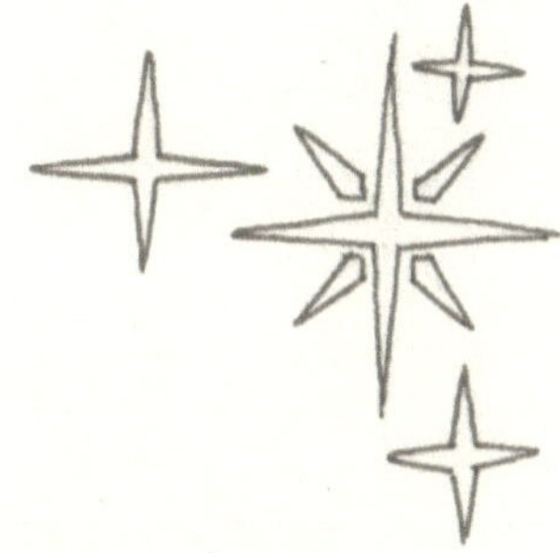

ABOUT THE AUTHOR

MORGAN MAGAURAN WAS BORN and educated on the East Coast of the United States. She now calls home an island in the Pacific Northwest, where she and her husband raised their son.

Readers can purchase the Rumored Woman series and receive discounts at RumoredWoman.com. Subscribers to Magauran's Substack, ENTHRALLING, receive the first six chapters in their inbox upon release. Visit MorganMagauran.substack.com to explore more of the mysterious ties between our inner and outer lives.